Philip Caveney, born in N[illegible] two-year spell at Manchester's Piccadilly Radio, writing and presenting a weekly film review programme. He is a professional writer and freelance journalist, and his previous novels include *Speak No Evil*, *Black Wolf*, *Strip Jack Naked*, *Slayground*, *Skin Flicks* and *Burn Down Easy*. He lives with his wife and young daughter in Heaton Moor.

Also by Philip Caveney

The Sins of Rachel Ellis
Tiger, Tiger
The Tarantula Stone
Speak No Evil
Black Wolf
Strip Jack Naked
Slayground
Skin Flicks
Burn Down Easy

Bad to the Bone

Philip Caveney

Copyright © 1996 Philip Caveney

The right of Philip Caveney to be identified as the Author of
the Work has been asserted by him in accordance with the
Copyright, Designs and Patents Act 1988.

First published in 1996
by HEADLINE BOOK PUBLISHING

First published in paperback in 1997
by HEADLINE BOOK PUBLISHING

A HEADLINE FEATURE paperback

10 9 8 7 6 5 4 3 2 1

All rights reserved. No part of this publication may be
reproduced, stored in a retrieval system, or transmitted,
in any form or by any means without the prior written
permission of the publisher, nor be otherwise circulated
in any form of binding or cover other than that in which
it is published and without a similar condition being
imposed on the subsequent purchaser.

All characters in this publication are fictitious
and any resemblance to real persons, living or dead,
is purely coincidental.

ISBN 0 7472 5456 7

Typeset by Keyboard Services, Luton, Beds

Printed and bound in Great Britain by
Mackays of Chatham PLC, Chatham, Kent

HEADLINE BOOK PUBLISHING
A division of Hodder Headline PLC
338 Euston Road
London NW1 3BH

For Steve, Steve, Chris, Paul, Roy, Gerald, Dave
and all other members, past and present,
of Hieronymus Bosch . . .
the greatest rock n' roll band
that never was.

Prologue

Detective Sergeant Gill walks slowly along the hospital corridor, carrying the acoustic guitar, rather self-consciously, under one arm. It's early evening and the wards resound with the noise of crockery and cutlery being cleared away for the night. The air is thick with the smell of abandoned dinners.

He feels a quiet sense of dread settling over him, the kind of dread that he always experiences when entering such institutions. The young detective has never liked hospitals but at least the oppressive warmth in here gives a welcome respite from the icy winter chill outside. It's stopped snowing now but the weather reporters are muttering darkly about more to come.

He makes his way down a side corridor and comes to a halt at the door of a small, private ward, where a uniformed constable sits reading a paperback crime novel. He glances up at Gill and nods dutifully.

'Anything to report?' asks Gill hopefully.

The constable shakes his head. He looks inquiringly at the guitar under Gill's arm.

'Going to play her a song, are you, sir?'

Gill smiles awkwardly.

'She asked me if I could get her one. It's not much use. I was given it for Christmas when I was a kid and it's been lying around at the back of a wardrobe for years.' He shrugs. 'I suppose it's better than nothing.'

The constable doesn't say anything to this. He returns his attention to his paperback. Gill notices the lurid illustration on the cover, a busty young woman struggling in the grip of a knife-wielding villain. The title of the novel is *Blue Murder*. Gill frowns, opens the door of the ward and steps inside.

Jenny Slade is sitting up in bed today. Her pale face still carries the scratches and bruises of her recent ordeal but she is fully awake and she perks up when she sees Gill and the instrument he is carrying.

'You brought it!' she exclaims. 'Thanks.'

Gill walks over to the bed and hands her the guitar with an apologetic gesture.

'I'm sure it's not what you're used to,' he says. 'It's only a cheap thing, it hasn't been played for years.'

'Doesn't matter. It'll do till I can get my Gretsch back.' She glances at him thoughtfully. 'I suppose it's evidence now, right?'

He nods. 'Be a while before we can remove anything,' he admits. 'But I'm sure you'll get it back at some point.'

She sighs, then cradles the guitar gently in her lap, handling it as though it's some valuable instrument. She strikes a couple of experimental chords and a doubtful expression crosses her face. She reaches her left hand up to the machine heads and does some radical retuning.

Gill settles himself into a metal-framed canvas chair beside the bed and watches her in silence for a few minutes. He is taken once again by a sense of unreality. He's sitting alone in a room with Jenny Slade, for Christ's sake – a bona fide rock legend. Her band, The Deceivers, has always been one of his favourites and back at his flat, amongst his extensive record collection, he has all of their earlier albums. OK, maybe he doesn't have the last couple, but that's mainly because he stopped buying records years ago, when the pressure of work denied him the opportunity to listen to music.

Aside from the bruises, Jenny looks pretty much as he remembers her from television appearances on *Top of the Pops* and *The Chart Show*: a little more petite than he might have expected and a lot frailer, but then, that's hardly surprising after what she's been through. The bobbed black hair is just the same, though, the fringe cut a fraction above her dark brown eyes and she has the same androgynous appeal that he's always admired, the snub nose, lightly freckled cheeks and the wide, sexy mouth that seems slightly out of proportion with the rest of her features.

There's a little part of Gill that longs to ask for her autograph but he realises that this would hardly be an appropriate thing to do in the circumstances. She's clearly been through a terrible ordeal, and, it would seem, she's very lucky to be alive. A lot of other people who've spent time with her lately evidently didn't have that kind of luck. Tucked into his notebook on a torn-off scrap of paper, Gill has twelve names, each one with a question mark after it. He's already tried asking her about these names but Jenny's strange rambling replies have made Gill doubt her sanity.

As he watches, she reaches out to the bedside locker and picks up several scraps of paper on which she has scrawled words with the stub of a pencil. She spreads them out on the bed cover in front of her. Then she lifts the first of them and holds it out towards the foot of the bed, as though showing it to somebody.

'What do you think?' she whispers. 'This for the first verse ... or this one?' She cocks her head slightly to one side, as though listening to a reply. 'Hmm,' she concludes. 'Maybe ...'

'How do you feel now?' asks Gill, hastily. He doesn't like it when she pulls this kind of stuff. It makes him feel strange.

'Better,' she admits, cautiously.

'I was hoping that you might be ready to talk now. We've got a lot of questions, a lot of things that just don't seem to make any sense.'

She nods. 'Yes, I can understand that,' she says.

Gill hasn't got anything resembling sense out of her on his last couple of attempts, mostly because the doctors had her pumped so full of sedatives she could barely stay awake for more than a few minutes at a time. The breakthrough came at lunchtime today, just as he was leaving, when she asked him if he could lay his hands on a guitar.

'We're writing a song,' she'd added mysteriously.

Now Gill looks at her long, elegant fingers moving across the fretboard, describing various chord patterns. She makes the battered old instrument sound as if it cost a thousand pounds. Then her brow furrows and she makes another minor adjustment to one of the strings.

Gill reaches into the pocket of his overcoat and plucks out his notebook.

'If you could just start at the beginning,' he prompts her.

'The beginning?' She looks vaguely startled by the suggestion.

'Yes, if you would, just using your own words. You see, we really need to know exactly what happened out there. We've got people trying to piece it together, but...'

'You'll never do that,' she tells him flatly. She strums another chord sequence and leans back her head, as though trying to remember something. 'Let me see now, where to start, where to start...' She cocks her head to one side and goes though the elaborate pantomime of listening to another voice, and Gill can't help it, he finds himself looking in that direction, almost expecting to see somebody standing there at the foot of the bed. 'That far back?' murmurs Jenny, doubtfully. 'Well, yeah, I suppose it *was*. We'd have to start there, wouldn't we?' She looks back at Gill sharply. 'We'll have to go back around three months, mind.'

Gill smiles. 'OK, I guess I can handle that.'

She thinks for a moment, then seems to come to a decision. She hits a major chord with a theatrical flourish and leans forward to speak into an imaginary microphone.

'Ladies and gentlemen!' she drawls in a convincing American accent. 'Welcome to the Seattle Astrodome! Would you put your hands together please, as we present, live on stage, for their first visit in three years, England's number one rock n' roll band . . . The Deceivers!'

PART ONE

Hell is full of musical amateurs:
Music is the brandy of the damned.

George Bernard Shaw
Man and Superman

Chapter One

Jenny Slade and the other members of The Deceivers are sprawled out in the underground dressing room below the massive football stadium. They are on the last leg of their American tour and it seems as if they've been away from home for ever.

Seattle is just another huge city that they won't get to see. The support band have long since quit the stage and the roadies have finished re-setting the drum and keyboard rigs. Even down here in this graffiti-scrawled bunker, Jenny can sense the air of expectation up there in the stadium as the impatient crowd, fuelled on alcohol and cannabis and Quaaludes, prepare themselves to rock out one more time with their favourite British import. Already they are clapping their hands, stamping their feet and chanting the two words like an incantation, louder and louder, as they try to coax their heroes up on to the stage.

'Jen-ny, Jen-ny, Jen-ny!' Down here the sound is like the stirring of an unseen ocean.

It's Jenny's thirty-second birthday and a cake in the shape of a huge guitar adorns the refreshment table. It lies there festooned with melting candles, besieged on all sides by the other junk specified in The Deceivers' contract: bottles of Mexican tequila, Irish whiskey, English beer, French mineral water; an elaborate cold buffet including a special spread for the keyboard player who's a vegetarian; various throat medicines, tablets, ointments and preparations; newspapers, magazines, crossword puzzles; a Sega Megadrive and a VDU with a selection of computer games; the top ten video films and a widescreen colour television; you name it.

Most probably none of this stuff will be touched, but over the years an occasion has arisen where somebody actually wanted one of these things and somehow it got added to the list. Now The Deceivers are absolutely forbidden by their management to even enter a dressing room unless all these items are present.

Tonight all Jenny wants is to reclaim a few years of her life. She's feeling her age and just a little bit dazed. It seems inconceivable to her that she's still a member of The Deceivers, that she's still gigging and selling records and it's what, fourteen years since they first got together? It's gone so quickly. It seems like only a couple of years ago they were doing their first gigs, playing greasy little shit-holes around their home town of Manchester, being spat at or canned off or, even worse, ignored.

How has it ever come to this? The sheer brutish scale of their tours. When they first started, everything, themselves included, packed neatly into the back of a Transit van. Now it requires three articulated lorries to carry their sound and light equipment alone. A legion of roadies and gofers and lighting technicians travel ahead of them setting up the equipment for the next gig. And for The Deceivers, life has receded into an endless grey blur of Holiday Inns, interspersed with long periods of boredom as the tour bus drives along featureless grey highways to barely glimpsed cities in the American heartland – and all this so that for an hour or so, Jenny and the others can explode like fireworks on stage, grinding out *the product*: a carefully planned package of established hits liberally peppered with material from the latest album, *Red Tape*.

OK, so the bigger venues haven't been quite full this tour, but the reviews have been good. Not ecstatic but solid, respectable. As always they've likened Jenny's voice to that of Chrissie Hynde, a problem that's plagued her all her professional life. It bugs her. Maybe their voices *are* a bit similar, but she can't help that, can she?

Jenny looks across the dressing room at Scott Griffin. He's slumped in a battered armchair, his fingers strumming nervously on the strings of his battered Fender Jaguar, but he looks calm, detached, his pale blue eyes staring thoughtfully up at the low ceiling where a dark stain resembles the map of India. His trademark shoulder-length blond hair is tied back with a red bandanna and he sports a silver skull and crossbones through his right earlobe.

The other guys in the band are OK, but with Scott it's special, because he and Jenny are the last members from the original lineup. Jenny finds herself ticking the missing faces off in her head, a familiar pastime. So many of them over the years, but the names and the faces stay fresh in her mind.

It has always been drummers and keyboard players she's had trouble with but at least the lead guitarist's position has remained reassuringly filled since day one. Scott Griffin is more than just a good guitar player: he's also Jenny's songwriting partner. All of the band's biggest hits have been co-written by him. Over the years, he and Jenny have forged a real partnership: he knows exactly what embellishments to place against the sparse rhythms she hammers out of her Gretsch semi-acoustic. In the writing process he knows just when to push her and just when to let her simmer, and he's strong enough to stand his ground and tell her when she's made a balls-up of something, when it's time to dump a song that isn't working and go back to the drawing board.

And it isn't like they're lovers or anything, though there was one time in a hotel room in Germany, both of them loaded after an impromptu gig at a club in Hamburg, when the two of them came dangerously close to getting it on. At the last minute, they both pulled away from it, sensing that it could only damage their professional relationship.

Looking at Scott now, Jenny can't help but wonder if they did the right thing. He's one of the good guys and the two of them have so much in common – and there sure as hell isn't anybody else in her life right now. The problem she has with men is that they approach her on their hands and knees as they would approach some deity – 'Hey, aren't you Jenny Slade from The Deceivers?' And the moment they say *that* she knows that it's pointless to take it any further. To them she's some kind of rock icon, not a real person with real needs and real desires.

Scott at least has no illusions about her. He's seen her hunched over the toilet, spewing her guts up after downing one too many tequilas. He's seen her first thing in the morning before she's had a chance to put on her 'face'. He's seen her drunk and he's seen her angry and he's seen her naked, which, Jenny knows only too well, is not the dream of perfection that so many young male rock fans fantasise about. Major flirtations with cocaine and alcohol have taken their toll on Jenny's body over the years and though she's clean now and doing her best to keep in regular exercise, she will never again be the lithe, leggy creature she was when she started in the business.

Scott has changed too, Jenny thinks. He's lost the happy-go-lucky character he used to have and has become morose, inward looking, self destructive: he's also started using heroin in a major way. He's always had a weakness for narcotics, but in the past he's kept it down to smoking, snorting or dropping pills. At the beginning of this tour he let the drummer, Chris, talk him into mainlining heroin and Jenny hates to see that, she went through the same thing some five years back and she knows the misery he's storing up for himself. But she can't say anything about it, just as Scott never said anything to her at the time. It's like an unwritten rule they have between them.

Mike Watton, the road manager, ducks his head into the room.

'Ten minutes,' he says.

Everybody goes into the little rituals they always do before heading for the stage. Chris Spencer, the current drummer, starts going through some quasi-Jackie Chan routine, whirling the drumsticks around his head like they're a set of nunchakus. Steve Lampton, the bass player, goes off quietly in the corner and has a cigarette. Adrian Langan, the keyboard player, sits cross-legged on the floor and starts intoning some weird Buddhist chant he always does, and Scott slips away into the toilet where his gear is stashed.

Jenny thinks about asking him to give it a miss tonight. It's on the tip of her tongue to say something like, 'Hey, Scott, let's do it straight like we used to.' But for some reason she thinks better of it. Instead she does some simple voice exercises that her vocal coach taught her, making the sounds from deep in her chest and letting them swell and rise in volume as they emerge from her open mouth. It suddenly strikes her that anybody entering the room is going to think they've inadvertently wandered into a madhouse.

Mike reappears, though he only seems to have been gone seconds.

'OK, everybody, it's time.'

Jenny feels the familiar fluttering sensation in her gut.

Fourteen years in the business and it's never gone away. Maybe that's a good thing. The day she loses it she'll figure it's time to throw in the towel. She stands up, straps on her guitar, then shakes her arms and fingers, trying to dissipate the tension that's gathering there.

The toilet door opens and Scott comes out, a beatific grin on his face. His eyes have a vacant look, the pupils shrunk down to two tiny dots. He gazes around the room for a moment as though he's not sure where he is. Then he picks up his guitar from the armchair and slings it around his neck.

'You OK?' Jenny asks him.

He nods. 'Let's kick ass,' he says.

They follow Mike out of the room and up the stairs. The sound of the crowd rises in volume as they reach the top and then they angle left, through a safety door and they find themselves at the edge of the stage. Night is falling now and the lights are on, flooding the playing area in a lurid red glow. The sound of the crowd rolls around them like restless thunder.

They have a new way of starting on this tour. No cheesy introduction, no fanfare, no pomp and circumstance. Chris just strolls out to the drum podium and takes his seat, grinning to acknowledge the cheers of the crowd. He launches straight into a chunky four-four rhythm on snare and high hat, the beat of the amplified bass drum so solid that Jenny can feel it thudding in her chest like a fist. Now Steve shambles out, gives a shy smile as a roar of approval goes up. He plugs in his custom-made Rickenbacker and drops a simple walking bass line on to the rhythm. Even the slowest-witted fans out there recognise the intro to *Love's Like a Hunger*.

There are whoops and whistles of delight from the crowd for what must be The Deceivers' best-known song, a top ten hit on both sides of the Atlantic and across much of Europe and the

Far East. Lifted from the band's third album, it's the song that made Jenny's career, bringing her and Scott millions in revenue and catapulting the band headlong into the rock first division. Ironically, Jenny's spent the interval since its release trying to pen another song that's as successful, but though she's had other substantial hits, none of them have quite matched the success of this simple, straight-ahead rocker with its no-nonsense lyric.

Now Adrian trots out to his keyboards and starts laying down brooding slabs of sound, one hand on the Yamaha synthesizer, the other stabbing out a restless sequence on his Fender Rhodes. His skinny frame is almost dwarfed by the banks of different keyboards stacked up on three sides of him.

It's Scott's turn to go out there but he hesitates and lifts one hand to his forehead, as though he's experiencing some kind of discomfort. Jenny looks at him nervously. She can see a thin sheen of sweat on his face.

'Are you all right?' she mouths at him, over the blast of the music.

He grins, nods, strolls out to his familiar spot at the backing microphone on stage left. A huge roar goes up from the crowd and he acknowledges it with a wave of his hand. He stoops, plugs his guitar into the pedal unit and starts the introductory riff, using the flanger to keep the guitar fuzzed and just on the edge of feedback. He starts to strut around the stage, nodding his head to the beat, then he turns to look expectantly at Jenny. It's her turn.

This is the moment she hates most, that short walk to the microphone, as the follow-spot bathes her in a circular pool of white light. She's always afraid she'll trip, fall flat on her face or do something equally stupid. The other fear that constantly nags at her is that she'll get out there and forget the words of the song. It hasn't happened to her yet but the fear never goes away. She takes a deep breath and launches herself out on to the stage.

The light clicks on her and she feels like an unfortunate bug caught in the glare of the sun. The roars of the crowd envelop her and, looking out over the footlights, she can discern only a blur of colour and movement stretching away as far as she can see. She makes it to her amplifier without further mishap, plugs in and begins the easy chopping rhythm on the Gretsch, the penultimate piece in the three-chord jigsaw puzzle that is *Love's Like a Hunger*. Now all that remains are the lyrics. Jenny leans in to the microphone, touching her lips to the soft foam pop sock. Closing her eyes, she begins to sing.

'Love's like a hunger.
It tears you up inside.
It creeps in like a burglar
and robs you of your pride.
You try to run away from it
but you can never hide.
Love's got you,
Love's got you,
'cos love's like a hunger.'

Such simple words. The song took maybe fifteen minutes to write and can hardly be described as poetry: yet it has persuaded millions of people to part with their hard-earned cash and that's all that matters in this game. And the song has become something of an anthem for the band. As she sings the lyrics Jenny is gleefully aware of thousands of voices singing them right back to her.

Suddenly everything is all right. The nerves are gone, her voice is in tune and she's feeling terrific. The gig's going to be a good one, she can relax and enjoy herself and just for a moment, remember why she wanted to do this stuff in the first place. It's that buzz you get, that weird chemistry between band and audience where some kind of adrenalin-fuelled euphoria is created and for a short time it's better than any drug you can name, it's better than money, it's better than sex.

The band slide into the second verse and the weeks spent on the road have really paid off, they are locked together as tightly as a series of well-oiled cogs. Jenny's confidence seems to spread to the others and the song just takes off and soars up into the night.

And then, just as suddenly, Jenny senses that something is wrong. She feels rather than hears that Scott's guitar is sliding out of sync with the rest of the band. The riff he's playing is slowing down, speeding up, slowing down again. She glances across at him and she sees that he's weaving unsteadily on his feet, like the rush from the heroin has only just hit him. He's got that slightly dazed expression on his face again, he's glancing around the stage as though he's just woken up and found himself playing in front of thousands of strangers. He seems to realise that something is wrong and shakes his head, as though he's trying to shrug off a powerful sleepiness. His guitar playing settles again and Jenny tells herself that the crowd probably didn't even notice. She gets through the second verse without further mishap and goes into the chorus.

'So come on feed me,
I'm hungry for love
And I said feed me
I'm hungry for love.'

The chorus is even more basic than the verses but with thirty thousand voices roaring it straight back at her it seems to transcend its simplicity and become a thing of rare beauty.

Jenny steps back from the microphone as the follow-spot flicks across to Scott for his eight bar solo and...

She feels a jolt of horror inside because now something really bad is happening. Scott looks like he's in pain. His thin face, chalk-white in the glare of the spot, is contorted into a grimace of agony, as though a knife has just been plunged into his guts. His back is arching and he's still trying to play but what's coming out is a series of protracted metallic screams as his guitar volume slips over the edge into teeth-grinding feedback. Jenny stops playing but the rest of the band lumber on, oblivious to the fact that something is amiss. As Jenny watches, rooted to the spot in terror, Scott's body gives a convulsive shudder. The colour drains from his face, his eyelids flicker and he falls backwards on to the stage, his shoulder blades raising a cloud of dust from the floorboards and...

Someone is screaming, someone in Jenny's head, screaming Scott's name over and over, as Scott's body begins to jerk and flop like a frenzied marionette, his hands on the strings producing a macabre musical accompaniment to his movements and his eyes ... his eyes are bulging out of his skull as though they are about to burst and...

Only now are the other members of The Deceivers realising what is happening. They stop playing one by one and stand there, open-mouthed in shock as...

Jenny moves to the microphone and hears her own voice, shrill with terror, echoing out over the heads of the abruptly silent crowd.

'Medic! For Christ's sake, get a medic up here!'

Scott's spine is arching up from the floor now, his head is snapped back and his mouth is wide open, gasping for air, fighting for breath. Jenny flings her guitar aside, oblivious to the amplified crash it makes as it hits the boards, and she runs over to Scott, flings herself down on her knees, tries to get the guitar away from him, but his hands are clasping it so tightly, she cannot shift it and Scott's whole body is shaking uncontrollably now, he's dying, she can see he's dying and there's nothing she can do about it. His pale blue eyes are staring up towards the lighting rig above his head and he gives a last ragged gasp. Then his body relaxes, sinks slowly down on to the stage and lies still.

Desperately, Jenny throws herself on to him and she clamps her mouth on his, tries to breathe life back into his lungs, using the simple technique she learned years ago when she had a summer job at the biscuit factory, before she was Jenny Slade, rock star: when she and Scott were real people and they used to meet up in the lunch breaks and talk about the band they'd form one day, when they'd earned enough money to pay for their guitars...

Then the medics are pulling Jenny away, moving in with their defibrillators and their oxygen and their various other instruments of resuscitation, but Jenny knows that they will be useless, Scott's heart has stopped as effectively as if he had been hit by a train. He's dead. Scott Griffin is dead.

A numbness spreads through her like she's been spiked with Novocain. She stumbles into Steve who puts his big arms around her, holds her close while the medics go through their frantic routine. They've got Scott's guitar away from him and torn his shirt open, they keep zapping him with the defibrillator but his body just jolts lifelessly and on the portable VDU they've set up, he continues to flatline...

Tears well in Jenny's eyes and she turns to look out towards the crowd, who are still standing there in shocked silence. The giant video screen at the back of the stage is relaying the tragedy to everyone in the stadium, so that even the most stoned members of the audience have stopped their catcalling and whistling. Apart from the hum of the generators and the last fading tones of Jenny's dropped guitar, no sound is heard. Jenny has never experienced this from a crowd before: she's heard them applauding and singing and cheering and heckling. But never this eerie silence.

Now the medics are shaking their heads. One of them takes off his jacket and drapes it over Scott's face. Jenny feels the sobs coming then, wrenching themselves from deep inside her with such force that they double her over. Steve hugs her close and guides her off the stage into the wings and she feels his body shuddering and realises that he is crying too.

Jenny realises it's over. The gig is over, the tour is over, and almost certainly The Deceivers are finished too. They've come back from the edge several times in the past but this blow feels too powerful. This one has hurt her to her very core and she feels sure, as she stumbles down the steps to the dressing room, that nothing . . . nothing will ever feel right again.

When she enters the dressing room, the candles on her cake are still burning brightly.

Chapter Two

She was running through a forest.

It was almost pitch dark and the ground was treacherous with a deep fall of snow, but she had to keep moving because she was being pursued by something that she couldn't see. In the blackness behind her, she could only hear the awful, grunting, slobbering sounds it was making as it loped after her on silent feet. She kept thinking that the forest would end soon, that she would emerge on to a road or into a clearing: but the ranks of trees seemed to stretch away into infinity and the beast was so close on her heels, she could feel its warm breath gusting on to her back as she ran and ran into the endless night...

Jenny woke in the grey surroundings of her parents' spare bedroom: the same room in which she had slept when she was a child. She lay on her side and allowed her breathing to settle back to its more usual rhythm. The dream was familiar to her now; she'd been having it on and off for the last three months, ever since Scott's funeral. She turned on to her back and gazed up at the ceiling, wondering why the hell she was still here.

After discharging herself from the nursing home where she'd spent a month recovering from what was politely referred to as a 'nervous breakdown', she'd headed back to her folks in Manchester. She'd told them it was an attempt to avoid the reporters and photographers but, in truth, Scott's death was already old news and they'd long since stopped pestering her.

Now it was mid January and yet here she still was, holed up in her old bedroom with her 70s pin-ups, her record collection and a battered one-armed teddy bear called Johnny Rotten. She was still reluctant to return to her big, empty flat in London, even though living here was slowly killing her.

She had thought that coming back to Manchester would be a good move. She could re-visit her old haunts and look up all the friends she had lost touch with: but when it came right down to it she just didn't feel that she belonged here any more. Many of her old hang-outs had been demolished or changed out of all recognition and when she located the few venues that were still the same, it was hard to remember what the appeal had been in the first place. She managed to contact a couple of her former school friends, both of them married with kids now, and arranged to meet them at a local pub. The first thing they'd done when she walked in was to ask for her autograph.

'Not for us you understand, for our kids, they'll kill us if we go back without them!' Then they'd sat there all night with their mouths open, staring at Jenny like she was some kind of freak. She'd had no inclination to repeat the experience.

A problem closer to home was her total inability to talk to her parents. They'd been kind when she'd first showed up, making sympathetic noises about Scott, whom they'd met many times in the early days of The Deceivers' existence. But once that was out of the way it was business as usual and Jenny remembered why she'd been so keen to get away from them in the first place.

Her father wasn't so bad. He seemed to spend his life in a kind of blank smiling catatonia, seated in front of a television set which was invariably showing a nature documentary, featuring Dad's favourite TV personality, David Attenborough.

Jenny's mother was more difficult to deal with. She had always seemed to consider it her God-given right to criticise her daughter at every opportunity, and once a decent interval had elapsed she went back to it with well-practised ease. After just a few weeks Jenny was ready to climb the walls with frustration and really, that was the point when she should have upped sticks and gone back to London. But still she resisted. Why?

The answer that came back was unexpected. She didn't want to go back to London because she was *scared*. Scott had always been there for her. If she was feeling lonely she only had to pick up the phone and he was knocking at her door, bringing his lively wit, his guitar and maybe a couple of choice vinyls from his superb record collection. They would sit for hours at a time, chatting, fooling around, swapping stories. Now if she rang his flat at three o'clock in the morning, the phone would just make that weird 'number unobtainable' sound. That thought scared her shitless.

The clock on the bedside table told her that it was after ten a.m. and she thought wistfully about going back to sleep until midday, but knew that her mother would already be tut-tutting about the lateness of the hour. With a sigh of resignation, she threw back the duvet and got out of bed, then padded to the bathroom and showered herself awake. Back in the bedroom, she dressed in jeans and sweatshirt and drew back the curtain a little to peer down at the front garden.

A light drizzle was falling but despite this a straggle of fans, some twenty in all, were waiting dispiritedly outside the garden fence, hoping to catch a glimpse of Jenny or maybe even to blag an autograph. Jenny had thought that the band had finished with all that stuff long ago, but Scott's death seemed to have lured a new batch out of the woodwork, younger than you might have expected but just as obsessive as their predecessors. Jenny recognised several of the morose faces as regulars. She didn't know how they had first found out she was here but it was a rare day indeed when nobody turned up. Her mother had started taking out cups of tea to them, a habit that Jenny had tried to discourage. Let it be known that there were free refreshments in the offing and there'd be even more of them hanging around.

Jenny sighed and let the curtains fall back into place. Mother would have preferred her to open them but then Jenny might get noticed and frankly, she wasn't in the mood to deal with her public today. She wasn't in the mood to do much of anything. She felt lately as if there was a big empty space inside her, sapping her of the will to motivate herself. Maybe she'd retire from the business. She had money in the bank and she ought to see the rest of the world from somewhere other than a tour bus, before she died.

She went downstairs and found her mother in the kitchen (where else?) doing some baking. Her mother was inordinately proud of her scones and rock cakes and made them every few days. Jenny never had the heart to tell her that they tasted of absolutely nothing.

'Good *afternoon*,' said Mother, glancing pointedly at the kitchen clock. 'Nice of you to join us. What can I get you for breakfast?'

Jenny shook her head.

'Nothing, thanks. I'm not hungry.' From the lounge she could hear the sounds of the television set. A familiar voice was speaking, the hushed tones dripping with reverence.

'Night time – and the family of badgers sets out on its nocturnal perambulations. Life can be hard when you have to forage for food, but the youngest members of the clan still find time for a little rough and tumble . . .' Jenny smiled to herself.

Dad was worshipping at the shrine of Saint David again. His extensive collection of videos made it possible for him to obtain a fix at any hour of the day or night.

Mother, meanwhile, was not going to give in so easily.

'You must eat something, dear. You'll waste away.'

Jenny frowned, slapped the palm of one hand regretfully against her rump.

'I doubt that, Mother. I'll just have a cup of coffee.'

She slumped down at the kitchen table while Mother busied herself with the kettle.

'Some of your young friends are waiting for you outside.'

Jenny gritted her teeth. Every morning, the same remark. They were never fans or punters or people. They were 'young friends'. Scott used to have his own name for them, Jenny remembered. Trolls. She had no idea why he called them that.

'Let them wait,' she replied grouchily. 'I'm not in the mood for it this morning.'

'Not in the mood for it! That's very nice, isn't it! Those poor youngsters coming all that way to see you ... and in the rain, too! They're the ones who put you where you are today, young lady. I think you at least owe them an autograph, it wouldn't take five minutes.'

'After I've had my coffee,' growled Jenny, obstinately.

There was a brief silence, during which they could hear the television playing *The Blue Danube Waltz*. No doubt it was being used to accompany some mawkish sequence featuring a dancing dormouse.

'Heard you bashing away on your guitar last night,' observed Mother ruefully. 'Kept me awake for ages, it did.'

'Sorry. I'm trying to write another song.'

Her song folder now had two new additions and she was trying for a third. An average of one a month. When she was writing with Scott, she'd rarely spent more than a couple of hours on a song. These had been dragged kicking and screaming out of her head and she had absolutely no idea if they were any good. The latest one was about Scott. It seemed fair enough. His death had been the biggest event in her life for years – but she didn't want the result to be some sentimental dirge. She was trying for an uptempo rocker, the kind of thing that he would have relished playing himself. The working title was *Live Fast, Die Young*, something that Scott had always been fond of saying, though in a self-deprecating way. He would have been as surprised as anyone to discover that the joking prophecy was self-fulfilling.

Mother set down a mug of coffee in front of her and Jenny sipped at it without enthusiasm.

'And why you have to write your songs at three o'clock in the morning is quite beyond me,' continued Mother. 'I mean, you have the whole day to write. You could go out to the garden shed, where you wouldn't disturb anyone. That's where you used to practise in the old days, isn't it?'

Jenny smiled. She had a brief mental image of her and Scott, with a couple of cheap acoustic guitars, sitting amidst all the junk in the shed, feverishly trying to compose their first song. They were what, fifteen, sixteen years old? The formation of The Deceivers was still a good year away. They had a couple of school exercise books and they were scribbling down lyrics as they occurred, both of them chipping in ideas. That first song was called *Don't Worry, Baby*. It consisted of two chords, mainly because that's all they'd yet mastered from the ancient guitar tutor that Jenny had found in the loft. *Bert Weedon's Play In A Day*. Christ, whatever happened to that? Looking back over fifteen years, Jenny was surprised to discover that she could still remember the lyrics of that first effort perfectly.

She wondered whether she should try Mother's suggestion, get out to the old shed and attempt to seek inspiration from the past – but instantly, she dismissed the idea. It would feel wrong to do that. It would feel somehow like she was pissing on Scott's grave. But she could hardly tell her mother that.

'The ideas only seem to come late at night,' she said lamely.

'Hmm. After you've imbibed enough alcohol, I suppose. I found another empty bottle of that tequila stuff in the bin this morning.' Mother sniffed disdainfully as though somebody was actually holding the open bottle beneath her nose. 'It smells like paraffin.'

Jenny winced. Why did she always feel like a teenager whenever she stayed at her parents? She had actually crept out of the house in the early hours of the morning to tuck that bottle into the bin, knowing that Mother would disapprove. But she hadn't wanted to confirm what her mother so obviously suspected: that Jenny's 'nervous breakdown' had actually been due to a combination of exhaustion and alcohol abuse. In fact, she'd done so much drinking in the weeks following Scott's death that she'd started suffering from delirium tremens, experiencing a series of hideous visions featuring cats, rats, snakes and spiders.

She'd left the home telling herself that she'd never touch another drop but her resolve had lasted only a couple of weeks: now her intake was steadily creeping up again. Still, she told herself, that was nobody's business but her own.

'I'm thirty-two years old,' she reminded her mother.

'Yes, then maybe it's time you started acting like it. It's been one thing after another with you, hasn't it? You've got what's called an addictive personality.'

'What nonsense!'

'Nonsense, is it? I don't think so, lady! It started with cigarettes, when you were still at school. Twenty a day you were smoking, it's a wonder you've any kind of a voice left. Then there was that awful business with the drugs, it was all over the newspapers. I couldn't go out without one of the neighbours making some comment. And now it's drink. Have you any idea how many bottles of that stuff you've got through since you came to us?'

Jenny clasped her hands and put them in her lap, overriding the impulse to snatch up her coffee and dash it into her mother's disapproving face.

'I've been through a hard time,' Jenny reasoned. 'I need a couple of shots to get me through.'

'A hard time! You don't know the meaning of the word. Look at you, you only have to snap your fingers and you've got a limousine waiting to take you anywhere you want to go.' Mother snatched up a dishcloth and started frantically mopping down the work tops. 'When George and I were first married, we had nothing. No hot water, let alone a washing machine. And it's still a struggle to meet the bills...'

'Mother, you know perfectly well it doesn't have to be,' said Jenny wearily. 'When the third album took off I phoned you and told you to choose yourselves a new house, anywhere you liked, price no object. But you wouldn't leave this place.'

Mother sniffed and flicked her duster.

'We've always paid our own way. And this house might not be much, but it's good enough for you to come running to whenever you're in some kind of trouble.'

'I'm not in trouble! I'm sad, that's all, surely you can understand that? I was very close to Scott, I... suppose I loved him in many ways and now I just feel kind of *lost*. And the last thing I need is you nagging at me to cut down on my drinking.'

Mother made a face. She picked up a spray gun on the worktop and transferred her attention to the cooker hob.

'Now look, Jennifer, I don't like to criticise...'

'Oh yes you do,' muttered Jenny, under her breath.

'...but don't you think you've let this go on long enough?

Of course it was tragic what happened to Scott – though by all accounts the poor boy did bring it on himself…'

'Oh, so that's less tragic, is it?'

'No, dear, of course not. But moping around the place like this, feeling sorry for yourself: what good is that going to do? I'm sure Scott wouldn't have wanted to see you waste your life. Isn't it time you pulled your socks up and got back in the swim?'

Jenny felt a wave of irritation go through her. It was fuelled not so much by anger at her mother's insensitivity but rather by the suspicion that she was probably right. Jenny got up from the table and went to the front door, grabbing a waxed jacket from the hall closet on the way.

'Where are you going?' Mother called after her.

'To talk to my "young friends",' growled Jenny. 'Perhaps then you'll get off my fucking back!'

She stepped out into the rain and slammed the front door before Mother could get another word in. Then she tramped across the lawn to where the fans were still waiting patiently. As she neared the fence, they all started talking at once, pushing sodden autograph books and pens into her hands.

'Jenny, Jenny, I really loved the new album!'

'Er … could you write, to Billy with *love*, please?'

'Wow, like… I can't believe this, you know? It's like… it's you, right? You're really you!'

'Jenny, I'm sorry about Scott. Are you going to get a replacement or carry on without him?'

A damned good question that last one – and one that Jenny couldn't answer.

She scribbled her name on pieces of paper and mumbled monosyllabic replies to a few of the less difficult questions. She was about to make her excuses and head back to the house when she noticed one young man standing slightly apart from the others. He had a thin, pale face that smiled serenely at her from beneath the hood of a khaki duffle coat. There was something about the smile she didn't like: and something about the youth's pale eyes, too big in that skinny face. They seemed to be surveying her with an almost predatory interest. The youth's smile broadened into a grin that displayed rows of overcrowded teeth, discoloured by too much nicotine.

'I talked to Scott Griffin last night,' he announced. 'He isn't happy. He wants to speak to you.'

Jenny looked at the youth and thought about telling him to get out of her face, but she felt a coldness settle in her stomach, a genuine sense of dread.

'Scott's dead,' she told him, and felt stupid saying it. She knew perfectly well that the youth wasn't suggesting otherwise.

'His spirit can't find rest, Jenny. Scott wants you to get in touch with him. I told him I'd try to help.'

'Oh yeah?' Jenny felt a sudden rush of anger. 'That's nice of you. And how much is that going to cost me, eh?'

'Just my usual fee for a consultation.' The youth continued to grin at her as though he was enjoying some private joke. 'I've contacted lots of people on the other side. Rock stars are my speciality. I've talked to Bolan, Freddie Mercury, Jimi Hendrix...'

'You mean you *think* you have. Frankly, I don't believe in any of that supernatural bullshit, OK? Far as I'm concerned, the dead are dead. End of story.'

The youth laughed. 'But you don't really believe that,' he said, and he seemed to speak with absolute conviction.

'What are you talking about?' snapped Jenny. 'How would you know what I believe? You don't know anything about me.'

'Yes I do. What about that song on the second album?'

'Which song?'

'*Frightened of the Night*?'

She stared at him.

'What about it? It's just a song.'

'No. It's more than that.' The youth shook his head and the hood slid back to reveal a cleanly shaven skull. 'It's about how you really want to believe in the supernatural but are too scared to admit it.' He began to quote the lyrics at her, speaking them as though reciting a Shakespearian sonnet. He was staring into her eyes the whole time, the awful grin still on his mouth.

> 'We came to a river,
> the banks were yawning wide,
> I stayed on the left bank,
> you crossed to the other side.
> Sometimes in the darkness,
> I hear you calling out to me,
> I want to cross over
> to where I can be free.
> But I cannot come to join you,
> to step into the light –
> I'm stranded in the darkness,
> I'm frightened of the night.'

The youth's grin subsided back into a knowing smile.

'That's not what the song's about,' Jenny told him. 'That may be your interpretation of it, but...'

'A pretty accurate one, I'd say.' The youth glanced around at the other fans for support, but they didn't seem to know how to take him. They were just average kids and he was a little too weird for comfort.

Anyway, he was way off beam. The song was actually about a disastrous backpacking holiday in the Lake District with a former boyfriend, a pretty but dumb slab of beefcake who Jenny had briefly had the cat scratch fever for. Out for a hike one afternoon, the two of them had encountered a river, the banks swollen by flooding. Jenny's macho companion had waded across it but Jenny, smaller of stature, had been too worried about being washed away. There'd been a terrible argument, the two of them shouting insults back and forth across the river: it had resulted in the boyfriend storming off, leaving Jenny stranded alone with a flimsy pup tent for shelter and a tin of beans for her supper. Needless to say she hadn't seen the boyfriend again, but afterwards she'd vented her anger by writing the experience down and setting it to music. She thought briefly about explaining this to the kid but in the end, she didn't have the patience.

'Just take it from me,' she said quietly. 'You're talking through your arse.'

For the first time the youth's smile slipped right off his face. There were some sniggers from the other fans and his cheeks reddened.

'Well listen, that may be true and it may not, but it doesn't really matter. Scott still wants to talk to you. He's going through a really bad time and he says only you can help him to find rest.'

'Is that so? Well, you tell him . . .'

She was interrupted by the sound of her mother's voice calling from the front doorway.

'Jenny. Phone call for you, dear. It's Mr Lezard.'

Josh Lezard. Her longtime manager. As in, long time, no see.

'. . . tell Scott to get in touch,' she concluded, flippantly. She turned away and walked back across the wet lawn to the house, pausing at the door to wipe her feet. Something made her glance back. The other fans were trudging away through the falling rain but the youth was just standing there, watching her intently. That creepy smile was on his face again.

'Fucking weirdo,' she muttered. She went inside, slamming the door behind her.

Chapter Three

It was good to hear Josh Lezard's voice again. His familiar New York drawl, softened by his twenty years of residence in London, came down the line as clear as a bell. He could have been phoning from the next room.

'Hey there, lady, you ready to talk yet?' Josh had phoned a couple of times since Scott's death but on both occasions, Jenny hadn't felt up to speaking with him. Now she thought, it was time that she at least made an effort.

'Hello, Josh, how's business?'

'Business is booming, Jenny, but I've missed you phoning me up every time there's something in the contract you don't understand. How are you bearing up?

'Tell you the truth, I've felt better. But you know, I suppose I'm healing. Hey, guess what, I was just talking to some sick fuck who said he spoke with Scott the other day. Great, huh?'

'Oh Jesus. There are some real assholes out there.' There was a pause. Lezard seemed to be considering whether he should continue. 'Listen, I know it's only been a few months but there are things we need to talk about, kiddo. I was wondering if I could come up and see you.'

'What? You mean, *here*? You'd actually leave London and drive 'oop North?' Must be really important, Josh, whatever it is. Don't you know we still eat our babies in Manchester?'

He chuckled.

'I guess I'll have to risk it. Look, tell you what, I could leave this afternoon before the rush starts. It'd give the BMW a good run and I could be there by early evening. Meet you for dinner.'

'A drink sounds better. I haven't much of an appetite lately.'

'You're drinking again?' She heard the apprehension in his voice but it was hard to feel resentful. After all, Lezard had had the unenviable task of putting her into the nursing home, and he had been present when she'd had an attack of the DTs, when she'd been convinced that multi-coloured snakes were crawling all over her bed. She'd just about screamed the place down.

Jenny glanced along the hall. Mother was quite obviously listening in. She was pretending to be cleaning the hob, even though it was shining from her earlier assault on it. Jenny lowered her voice to a whisper.

'Relax, Josh. Just a little social drinking, that's all. Nothing I can't handle.' Then she spoke louder. 'Actually, Mother was just telling me I should get out more. How did she put it? Get into the swim. I guess you could come to my local in the village. It's not exactly the Groucho Club but they know how to do a tequila slammer. Get there for seven o'clock and they're half price.'

'That sounds like an offer I can't refuse.' A pause and then a note of concern crept into his voice. 'I hope you've not been overdoing it, Jenny.'

'Will you give me a break? I'm a big girl now. Nearly an adult. They won't even let me into the pictures for half price.'

Lezard laughed. 'OK, seven o'clock then. I'll check in to a hotel for the night and travel back tomorrow morning. Just give me some directions for this pub and I'll transfer them to my pen pad. Unless you want me to pick you up from your parents?'

'Christ, no!' Jenny couldn't bear the thought of Mother peering speculatively at Lezard as though he was some prospective suitor. Mind you, it would be no great hardship. He was a handsome bastard who looked a good ten years younger than his actual age of forty-five. 'I'll meet you in the pub. Leave your car at the hotel and hop a cab.'

'How will you get there?'

'Hey, all I have to do is snap my fingers and there's a limousine waiting at the door.'

Lezard seemed puzzled by the remark.

'You're in a strange mood,' he observed.

'It's been a strange day,' she said. 'No, don't worry, I'll walk. It's just around the corner. Me and Scott used to do our drinking there in the old days.'

'Maybe you'd rather go somewhere else?'

'Uh uh. No, the Red Lion is fine. Besides, I can't spend my life avoiding places he used to go, can I?' She couldn't help wondering what all the urgency was about. Like most people who lived in the capital Lezard had an ingrained reluctance about venturing north of Watford Gap.

'See you tonight,' he concluded. 'Hey! Better wear a carnation in your lapel, so I'll know you.'

'You'll know me all right,' she assured him. She glanced towards the kitchen and raised her voice a little. 'Just look for a pathetic drunk clutching an empty tequila bottle.' She hung up and strolled back into the kitchen. Mother eyed her disapprovingly.

'This place not good enough for Mr Lezard, then?'

Jenny shrugged, took off her wax jacket.

'You said yourself I should get out more.'

'Yes, but the Red Lion? It's a bit seedy, isn't it? Couldn't you take him to a nice wine bar in town? We don't want to give him a bad impression of Manchester, do we?'

'I love the "we". Thinking of tagging along, were you?'

Mother sniffed, made a few flourishes with her cloth.

'I must say he sounds charming. They are always so well mannered, the Americans, aren't they?'

Jenny looked at her sharply.

'You obviously never played Kansas City,' she said. 'One time we played there a guy greeted me by pressing his naked arse against the window of my limousine. He'd had my name tattooed across his buttocks.'

Mother grimaced. 'I don't know why you feel it necessary to tell me things like that, Jenny. I sometimes think you just like to upset me.'

Jenny considered the comment and decided that Mother was probably right: but she didn't own up to it.

'Mother, you know I wouldn't upset you for the world.'

'Perhaps you might decide to bring Mr Lezard back here for coffee afterwards? I'd like to meet him.'

'Perhaps,' said Jenny, but knew that she wouldn't. She didn't want Lezard to see this side of her, her roots, the place she came from. It would be like standing naked in front of him.

Jenny folded the wax jacket over a chair but Mother tutted and pointed down the hall.

'The cupboard please. I've only just finished tidying up.'

Jenny sighed but trudged back into the hall and hung the jacket on a hook. Then on impulse, she went to the front door and pressed her face against the stained glass panel in the centre of it, checking to see if the weirdo was still out there. As far as she could tell, everyone had gone...

Suddenly, a grinning, multi-coloured face loomed at her from the other side of the glass: she stepped back with an oath, her heart jumping in her chest. A couple of seconds later, several envelopes dropped through the letter box on to the door mat.

'What's the matter with you?' she heard her mother say. 'It's only the second post!'

Jenny laughed nervously and stooped to collect the letters. Now she heard the postman's tuneless whistle and his big feet crunching along the gravel path.

Get a grip on yourself! Her heart was pounding, she felt really spooked. For a moment there she had thought – what? That the weirdo had come after her? For Christ's sake.

She carried the letters back to the kitchen and was surprised to see that one of them was addressed to her. So far as she was aware, only a very few trusted people had a note of this address. The envelope was postmarked Romford, London, and the name and address had been printed in bold, black felt tip pen. She noted that her name had been incorrectly spelled, but whether by accident or on purpose, she wasn't sure. JENNY SLAYED, it read. She handed Mother the other letters and went to sit at the table. She tore open the envelope and withdrew one small sheet of plain white paper. A short 'poem' was printed on it in a large childish hand.

SCOTT THE ROCKER'S DEAD AND GONE
HIS GROOVIN' DAYS ARE OVER
THE DRUGS HE HIT WERE CUT WITH SHIT
AND NOW HE'S 'NEATH THE CLOVER
BUT JENNY SLAYED SHOULD BE AFRAID
THE DECEIVERS ALL SHOULD KNOW
THOUGH SCOTT DIED FAST – HE AIN'T THE LAST
ONE DOWN . . . AND FOUR TO GO!

The nasty little missive was signed 'Hoochie Coochie Man'.

Jenny felt a stab of revulsion. She'd had hate letters before but few of them had been quite as nasty as this one. Like Lezard had just said, there were some really sick people out there. What particularly worried her was the fact that someone had managed to trace her to this address. She folded the letter, put it back into its envelope and slipped it into her pocket. She'd show it to Josh Lezard when she met him later on.

Mother was flicking glumly through her own post, a drab collection of bills and circulars.

'Who was your letter from, dear?' she inquired.

Jenny forced a smile. 'Fan mail,' she said.

She got up from the table and went into the lounge to watch David Attenborough with her father. Settling herself on the sofa beside him she was surprised to see that the green fields of Buckinghamshire had been replaced by the dry plains of the Serengeti. A pride of lions was in the process of dragging a bawling young wildebeest to the ground. It struggled desperately but was no match for the powerful jaws and claws of the hungry predators.

As Jenny watched in numbed silence, they proceeded to eat it alive.

Chapter Four

When Jenny got to the Red Lion, at about seven fifteen, Lezard was already seated in a little alcove, away from the other drinkers. He was sipping an Evian water. Typical American, she thought, obsessed with good health and exercise. Well, stuff it, tonight he could take a break from all that.

She went straight to the bar and ordered a couple of tequila slammers, aware as she did so that the conversation in the big old-fashioned pub had stopped abruptly and that the other drinkers were all watching her with open curiosity. She hated this aspect of celebrity and though she was well used to being stared at she had never really felt comfortable with it.

'You're that Jenny Slade,' said the barman, as though she hadn't been aware of it.

'That's me,' she said.

'I'm a real fan. I'm not just saying that now, for my money you're the best in the business.'

'That's nice.' Jenny looked at him and immediately didn't believe a word of it. He was a big, bearded individual, his swollen beergut barely contained behind a T-shirt that bore the legend 'Save a child – kill a social worker'. She seriously doubted that he'd ever heard a Deceivers album in his life.

'Hey, I loved that last one you did. What was it called now?' He did an elaborate pantomime of trying to remember something that was just at the back of his mind. 'Something like...'

'*You Turn Me On*,' said Jenny dutifully.

The barman fluttered his eyelashes playfully.

'Thanks very much. But what was the song called?' Jenny felt like groaning.

'No, but seriously,' she muttered, under her breath.

'No, but seriously,' he said. 'Great song.' He hummed a few bars of something that sounded suspiciously like a Status Quo number and waggled his backside to the rhythm. 'You were on the telly must have been ... oh, a couple of weeks back. You were wearing this bright pink jacket...'

'Yeah, that was me,' said Jenny quickly. She had been convinced from the start that the jacket was a big mistake but the video director had insisted on it. '*The Chart Show*. And it was over three months ago.'

The barman scratched his black curly hair.

'Christ. *That* long? What you been doing since then? Having a rest are you? That's what you showbiz types call it, right. A rest. Smoking some of that wacky baccy, I shouldn't wonder, going to parties with Mick and Jerry!'

'Look, I'm not being funny, but...'

''Ere, wait till I tell my missus you were in. She's off down the bingo tonight. Maybe you could sign a beermat for her? She could put it with her collection. She's got Des O'Connor and Peters and Lee!' The big man tilted back his head and laughed gleefully, as though he'd just cracked the world's funniest joke. Jenny experienced a powerful urge to grab a bottle off the bar and smash it over his head. In the end, she managed to get her drinks and pay for them but only by being monosyllabic to the point of rudeness. As she walked away she knew exactly what the barman would be telling his punters for weeks to come.

''Ere, we had that Jenny Slade in the other night. Surly, stuck-up cow she was. Got dead snotty when I tried chatting to her! I mean, these people, they get a record in the hit parade and they think they're bleedin' royalty!'

Jenny slipped into the booth beside Lezard with a sigh of relief. She slid one of the glasses of tequila in front of him and he looked at it doubtfully.

'What are we celebrating?' he asked her.

'Me getting away from that arsehole at the bar. A big fan of mine who seems to think I wrote *Rockin' All Over the World.*'

Lezard winced.

'That would go down well,' he said drily. 'Still, at least he recognised you.' He lifted his glass in a toast. '*Salud*!' he said.

They put their hands over the tops of the glasses and brought them down hard on to the table top. The lemonade and tequila mixture effervesced and they gulped down the contents in one swallow.

Jenny set down her empty glass and smacked her lips.

'I'll let you get the next round,' she told him.

'Sure.' Lezard raised an arm and gestured to the bearded barman. 'Two more over here, pal, whenever you're ready.'

Jenny laughed.

'Now why didn't I think of that?' she said. 'That's why you're the manager and I'm just the guitar player.' She reached into her handbag and found a packet of cigarettes. She extracted one and lit up. Lezard raised his eyebrows.

'Back on those things? I thought you'd kicked it for good.'

Jenny shrugged.

'So did I. But what can I tell you? I'm only smoking a couple a day.'

'A couple of cigarettes ... or a couple of packs?'

She looked at him and saw that he had a 'holier than thou' expression on his face. 'Oh for fuck's sake, Josh, don't give me a hard time! Anyway, what was so important you had to drive all the way up here to see me?'

'Well, a few things, Jenny. First up, it was to give you the good news about *Red Tape* ...'

'It's still doing good business?'

'Better than good. It's officially gone platinum.'

Jenny inhaled on her cigarette. Three months ago this news would have had her dancing for joy: now she just felt slightly sickened by it. *Red Tape* had been clocking up only moderate sales before Scott's death and the songs had been as good then as they were now.

'Christ, Josh, that's sick.'

'I suppose so. But it's no surprise, Jenny, it happens every time. In this business, a death is one of the best things that can happen to a band.'

'Yeah, well it certainly wasn't the best thing that ever happened to Scott.'

'Sure, I didn't mean—'

Lezard broke off as the barman brought over a tray of drinks. He set down the new ones and collected the empties. He was looking at Lezard with interest.

'You a musician, then?' he asked.

'No.' Lezard dropped a ten-pound note on to the tray. 'Keep the change. Now if you'll excuse us, we're having a private conversation.'

'Sorry, I'm sure.' The barman retreated with an aggrieved expression on his fat face.

Lezard hunched forward over the table and lowered his voice as though afraid of being overheard.

'I've had calls from the guys in the band over the last few

days. They're anxious to consolidate this success. As you know, the last tour was aborted halfway through, and we stood to lose a lot of money. Now we figure we can reschedule the tour dates for a couple of months' time, and play to sell-out audiences across the world off the back of the *Red Tape* album. Also Gem Records want to rush-release a new single. They're thinking about *Diamonds and Dust* ... and the band will be needed for promotional appearances so...'

Jenny stared at him.

'Whoah! Hold it, Trigger! What's the big rush on this? We aren't exactly on Skid Row, are we?'

'Well, *you* may not be: but don't forget, it was you and Scott that made the big bucks, you were the ones with the publishing deal. The other guys are on a wage.'

'A pretty bloody lucrative one,' retorted Jenny. 'Not bad considering all they ever do is turn up and play.'

'Well, nobody's denying that. But as you know, Chris has several expensive habits to support, Steve's just bought himself a mansion in Buckinghamshire and Adrian phoned me the other day, in a sweat about needing cash for some new project...'

'Jesus. Whatever happened to rock n' roll?' Jenny slammed her glass and gulped down the foaming contents. She gasped, smacked her lips. 'Anyway, aren't we overlooking one tiny little detail? We don't have a lead guitarist.'

Lezard looked wary.

'Er... well, that was the other thing. The guys have found a replacement and they'd like you to attend an audition, to see what you think of him.'

'They *what*?' Jenny was stunned by this information. 'What do you mean, *they've* found a replacement? What gives them the right to do that?'

'Calm down, Jenny, just hear me out. Of course, it's subject to your approval. They just thought that feeling as you did, you wouldn't be up to attending a whole bunch of auditions. So Adrian and Steve handled all that and sifted the wheat from the chaff. The guy they have in mind is Robbie Porter...'

'Who the fuck is Robbie Porter? I've never heard of him. Who's he played with?'

'Nobody much. Actually, he's only in his twenties, but he plays like a dream. He's a big fan of The Deceivers and he's got Scott's style down to a T. Here.' He pulled an audio tape from his breast pocket and pushed it across the table to her. 'Have a listen to this when you get home. It's a demo they put together with Robbie playing on some old Deceivers' tracks...'

'Hey, now just wait a fuckin' minute!' Jenny was beginning to feel irritated by the way this was being handled. 'Is it my imagination or do I get the impression that a whole skipload of shit has been going down behind my back? New tour, new guitarist, demo recordings... as a founder member I was under the impression that stuff like that needed my approval.'

'That's true, Jenny, but everyone knew that you weren't feeling up to very much. Let's face it, the last couple of times I called, you didn't even want to talk to me. So, we were just, you know, trying to take the reins a little...'

'*We*? What's all this "we" stuff? It sounds like you're on their side.'

Lezard laughed dismissively.

'Now you're just being paranoid. If for any reason you don't like Porter, then you have the power of veto: but I should add that Adrian and Steve think he'll fit in very well.'

'Yeah? And what do you think, Josh?'

'I'm just the manager, that's not something I feel qualified to make a judgement on.'

'Well, thank God for that.' Jenny motioned to the barman to bring more drinks. 'I was beginning to think there was some kind of conspiracy going on. As for touring again . . . well, I just don't know if I'm up to it yet.'

'I understand that perfectly. That's why I have a suggestion to make. A friend of mine, Gareth Reed, has just opened a new studio and rehearsal space in Wales.'

'Gareth Reed. I know that name. Didn't he produce the last album by The Serial Messiahs?'

'Yes, he did. Good sound on that and they've lifted three singles, all of them top five. Anyhow, he's got this fantastic new place. Well, I say "new" because it's only been open a matter of days but it's actually very old, a converted monastery. Beautiful old building but inside, it's state-of-the-art digital gear. He's got living accommodation there too, and the place is very remote, so there'd be no distractions. What I thought we might do is just book the rehearsal space for a couple of weeks, with an option to use the recording facilities if any new material occurs. You could see what you think about Robbie Porter and I could be there to discuss the business side of it with you all.'

Jenny frowned.

'I don't know,' she muttered. 'I'm not mad about the country, I always fall in some cow shit. What's so great about this place, anyway?'

'Jenny, you'd have to see it. It's just the most extraordinary set up. I went to take a look at it last week and I was blown away. I also happen to think that Gareth might be a good choice to produce the new album.'

'If there ever is one.'

'Sure there will be! And you said yourself you like his work.'

'I said I liked what he did for The Serial Messiahs. That doesn't mean he'd be right for us. Still . . . he couldn't be worse than the last guy.'

'John Morse? He seemed nice enough.'

'Yeah, but he was wrong for us. I kind of let Adrian talk me into having him on board but I didn't like the sound he gave us.' She frowned. 'Anyway, maybe you should save your money on the studio. I've only written a couple of things since Scott died and I'm not at all sure about them.'

'You get out in those mountains and forests and you'll soon feel inspired, kiddo! I happen to think that solitude would be really good for you right now, give you a chance to get your head together. Anyway, at least tell me you'll think about it.'

'Yeah, sure, I'll think about it.' Jenny glanced impatiently in the direction of the bar. The first couple of tequilas had begun to kick in and she was starting to feel like letting loose. She saw that the barman was making his way over with more drinks. 'For tonight though, we're going to forget all about the bloody band and we're going to have some fun. Remember fun, Lezard? It's about time we had some.'

Lezard looked doubtful.

'Oh, I don't know about that. I've got a heavy meeting tomorrow afternoon . . . and it's a long drive back to London.'

'Pah!' Jenny waved a hand dismissively at him. 'Josh, for once in your life, loosen up and enjoy yourself. We'll have a few more drinks here, then we'll hop a taxi into town. I'll show you what the Manchester clubs are like.' She frowned. 'If I can still remember where any of them are.'

The barman arrived with his latest consignment and Jenny thrust a fifty-pound note at him.

'Just keep 'em coming,' she told him.

Lezard looked worried.

'I'm really not sure about this,' he muttered.

'Shut up and drink.' She thrust a glass into his hand. 'Trust me, Josh. What have you got to lose? Don't worry, I'm not going to seduce you or anything.'

He shot her a look.

'That's a pity,' he said, and she couldn't tell if he was joking or not. She lifted her own glass.

'Well, we've grieved for Scott,' she said. 'We've missed him, some of us have prayed for him. Now it's time to see him off the way he would have wanted. *Salud*!'

They clinked glasses, slammed them down and drank.

The night began in earnest.

Chapter Five

'What the fuck are these?' muttered Lezard, peering at the sheet of white paper in the uncertain light. 'Song lyrics?'

'No, Josh. I just told you, they came in the post.' Jenny was obliged to shout over the racket blasting from the stage.

They were sitting in the crowded interior of the Night and Day Café on Oldham Street, currently considered one of the city's trendiest venues. They were both feeling pretty well oiled by this point and had been enjoying themselves immensely until a jazz/fusion quartet had taken the tiny stage and started pumping out a stream of rambling improvisations at ear-splitting volume. Jenny figured she must be losing touch with what was happening in the music business. For the first ten minutes or so, she'd thought the band was just tuning up. Then they'd stopped abruptly and the painfully hip audience had broken into wild applause.

'Josh, is it that I'm getting old, or is this the biggest bunch of crap ever?' she yelled into Lezard's ear.

'Yes, you *are* getting old,' he bellowed back. 'And yes, it is a bunch of crap. But these people seem to be into it.' He gestured around at the nodding heads and blissed-out expressions. A lot of people were smoking draw, which might have accounted for the apparent euphoria, but Jenny couldn't help thinking about the old story of the Emperor's New Clothes. For her, the acid test about any music was essentially simple: could you dance to it, could you sing along to it, could you fuck to it? A song that satisfied all these criteria was a rare creature indeed and she liked to think that two or three of her own compositions just about qualified. But what she was listening to now was the aural equivalent of watching a basketful of seal pups being clubbed to death with a baseball bat. Looking around, she felt sorry for the kids in here. It must have been awful having to pretend that they enjoyed music like this.

'It's a stance, Josh,' she yelled. 'It's like saying, hey, I dig this music, I understand it – so I'm superior to you. Then everyone else has to pretend they understand it too. Nobody wants to get left out, so you end up with hundreds of people listening to music they don't really enjoy.'

'Yeah, I get the general idea, Jenny, but in this business there's one criteria you can never forget. Give the audience what they want. Now, about this poem. You got any idea who could have sent it to you?'

'That's the weird thing. It came to my parents' address. As far as I'm aware, there's only a few people who—' Jenny broke off as the bass guitarist stepped across to the mic and started bellowing semi-incomprehensible lyrics into it. These too appeared to be improvised and consisted of a rambling rap-monologue that addressed itself to all manner of subjects. Jenny could only make out the occasional word but some of the ones she identified were 'abortion', 'health service', 'America' and 'orifice'. When she heard the words 'rain forest', she figured it was time to leave.

'For fuck's sake, Josh, let's go somewhere else, huh?'

Lezard nodded eagerly. They finished their drinks, got up from the table and pushed their way through the crowds to the exit. It was cold outside. They got on to the street and stood for a moment in the doorway, their breath clouding on the chill air, uncertain of which way to head. Lezard was still holding the sheet of paper with the poem on it.

'Jenny, I don't like this. It strikes me as distinctly creepy. This bit at the end, it sounds like a threat.'

'Oh, don't worry, Josh. It's just some sick jerk-off with a problem. You get stuff like that from time to time, it's no big deal.'

'Yes, but—'

'Jenny? Jenny, is that you?'

Jenny glanced up in surprise to see that a man had just stepped into the doorway from the street. He was a thin, wizened individual in loose-fitting Gangsta-style clothes. His hair was cut in a popular Manchester fashion, cropped to a stubble on his skull save for a tiny black cow-lick hanging over his forehead. He also sported a goatee beard and, Jenny noticed, he had a mobile phone clutched in one hand. It took her a few moments to recognise him.

'Des!' she exclaimed. 'Des McGuire.'

McGuire had been the original drummer for The Deceivers, way back when they were just starting out. He'd only been with them a matter of months, before his aggressive personality and his inability to make it to a rehearsal on time had caused him to be dumped in favour of Peter Harvey, who'd remained with the band for the first two albums. Now Des stood there, thinner and more grizzled than she remembered him. He gave her a cheesy grin, showing sharp white teeth flecked with gold fillings.

'Hey, how's it going, Jenny? What are you doing back in Manchester, slumming?'

Jenny smiled inanely. This kind of thing was always difficult and she wasn't helped by the fact that she had never really got on with McGuire in the first place.

'I, er ... was just home visiting my parents and stuff. I needed some time after what happened to Scott. I guess you heard about that?'

'Couldn't miss it. It was all over the papers like a rash. Bad news sells, Jenny. It always did.' McGuire was looking at Lezard now, his eyebrows raised inquiringly.

'Oh, this is the band's manager, Josh Lezard. I was just showing him the sights. Josh, this is Des McGuire, he was our first drummer.'

'Pleased to meet you, Des.' The two men shook hands. 'You were before my time, I'm afraid. I didn't handle the band until just before the third album.'

'*Blood Heat*?' McGuire winked. 'Well you came in at the right time, didn't you? That was the big one. You know I was just saying the other day, you look through the record collections of people of a certain age and there's two records you're sure to find. *Parallel Lines* by Blondie ... and *Blood Heat* by The Deceivers. Must have made a few bob out of that one, eh, Jenny?'

Jenny shrugged.

'Yeah, we did all right.'

McGuire glanced at Lezard.

'Me, I never made a penny out of the band. We didn't even have a manager in those days. Truth is, we didn't have a bloody prayer!' He laughed nervously. 'I never really got on with the others, so they dumped me.'

'Oh now, Des, it wasn't quite like that,' protested Jenny, though in her heart, she knew that was pretty much what happened.

'Sure it was! Tough old business, the music scene. Looking back, I should have tried a bit harder. When you got the recording deal a few months later, I felt like kicking myself.'

'It was more than a *year* later,' Jenny reminded him. 'And there was a lot of hard gigging before we got to that position.'

'Yeah, well, whatever. I was dumped and you got a shot at the big time. That's the way it goes, huh?'

'Are you ... still in the business?' ventured Lezard warily.

'Nah. I couldn't cut it. Had to sell the drums when I got into cash flow problems.' He lifted a hand to stroke his beard and Jenny noticed the profusion of gold and diamond rings that glittered on his fingers. *No cash flow problems now*, she thought. She glanced at the mobile phone in his other hand and immediately put it together. He was dealing. He'd been on his way into the club to tout for trade.

'Well, listen, Des, we've got to be going now—'

'No, hold on a minute!' McGuire flung out a hand to grab Jenny's shoulder, stopping her in her tracks. He leaned closer to speak confidentially. 'Listen, Jenny, if you want anything special while you're staying here, you just get in touch with me, OK.' He handed her a plain white card with a mobile phone number printed on it – no name or address, just the number. 'I can get anything you want and seeing as it's for an old friend, I'll personally ensure that it's top grade.'

Jenny studied him with undisguised contempt. 'I'm clean now,' she told him.

'Yeah?' McGuire grinned, wolfishly. 'And I'm Princess Grace of Monaco.'

Jenny felt irritated by his attitude. She hadn't even seen the little shit for years, how dare he make such an assumption about her?

'Look,' she said, 'don't come touting your wares to me, dick head! I'm not interested. Scott died and I—'

McGuire made a dismissive gesture with his right hand and the rings glittered in the neon light from over the doorway.

'He knew the score,' he said. 'Everybody who goes down

that road knows it. You get a bad break and that's the end of the story. But hey, he enjoyed himself up till then, didn't he?'

Now Jenny's irritation was quickly giving way to anger.

'Enjoyed himself? On heroin? Who the fuck are you trying to kid? I've been there, Des, and I know how much fun it is. Oh yeah, it's a hoot being so fucked up that you can't even function on the most basic level.' She took a step closer to him. 'But you know what really pisses me off? The way dealers like you make out that everything's hunky dory, that you're just providing a service. Scott died because the heroin he bought had been stepped on with toilet cleaner.'

McGuire made a face.

'That happens,' he said. 'But I hope you don't think...'

'Oh, spare me the excuses!' Jenny told him. 'What do you cut your shit with, huh? Baking soda? Talc? Or are you going to tell me that you leave it just the way it is when you get it. When it's already been stepped on by some motherfucker back in Colombia.'

'Jenny, calm down,' Lezard advised her. People were moving in and out of the doors of the club and many were pausing gleefully to observe the scene. Whenever the door was open, Jenny and McGuire were obliged to shout over the blare of the music. 'Let's not make a scene, OK?'

But McGuire too was getting angry.

'Listen, woman, don't you preach to me. From what I've read about you in the press, you've put enough junk away over the years to trip a herd of elephants.'

'That may be true, Des, but it's not something I'm proud of: and one of the worst parts was dealing with slimeballs like you.'

'Hey, fuck you! At least you had a choice. You swanned off to London and made millions with the band. What did I have? I got kicked out. I got shat on from a great height. And as for

Scott Griffin, what do I owe that motherfucker? He's the one that dumped me from the band. Maybe the son of a bitch had it coming to him.'

'Listen, you two,' pleaded Lezard. 'This is getting out of hand. Now why don't we—'

'Keep out of this, Josh,' said Jenny. She turned back to Des. 'What are you talking about, Scott dumped you? We *all* dumped you. It was a democratic decision. You were a lazy good-for-nothing who couldn't even get out of bed to attend a rehearsal. And you let us down at a very important gig. So we all got together and we took a vote...'

'Yeah, but Griffin was the prime mover in the band, he made those kind of decisions: and funnily enough, *he* was the one who came round to my place and gave me the news. "Hey, kid, the band's had a meeting and we've decided you ain't cutting it." Standing there in my mother's house like he was somebody special...'

'He *was* somebody special!' cried Jenny, and was aware of hot tears welling up in her eyes.

'Yeah, and who was I? Some piece of shit under his shoe? Christ, we'd hardly begun, he probably didn't know more than three chords and he was telling me that I couldn't cut it as a drummer. I was as much of a musician as he was!'

'It's not about that, you arsehole! It's never been about that. Scott Griffin had something that you never had – and that's why he stayed with the band and made records and got famous.'

'Yeah? And what's that?'

'Commitment,' said Jenny. 'He saw something he wanted and he had the guts to go after it. You never cared for hard work, Des. You wanted the success but you wanted it on a plate. That's the difference.'

McGuire laughed bitterly. 'Oh yeah, let's all hear it for Saint

Scott! Don't forget, baby, despite being so godlike and generally wonderful, Griffin still managed to fuck up his brilliant career, big time.'

'Not on his own,' growled Jenny. 'He had help from scum like you.' And before McGuire could come back with a reply, she swung back her fist and punched him in the jaw. Taken by surprise, he lost his footing and fell backwards into the doorway, striking his head against the metal shutters as he went down. The mobile phone clattered across the pavement and was pounced on by a passing kid, who snatched it up gleefully and took off along the street. A small crowd that had been watching the confrontation burst into spontaneous applause.

McGuire sat there, dazed and blinking. He opened his mouth to speak but only a groan emerged. Lezard grabbed Jenny's arm and pulled her bodily out of the doorway and along the street. From behind them, they heard a voice in the crowd saying, 'Hey, wasn't that Jenny Slade?'

'Oh, perfect,' muttered Lezard. He turned up the collar of his jacket and kept walking. 'What the hell got into you?' he hissed.

'I couldn't help it. Smug bastard, talking about Scott like that . . . and making out there was some big conspiracy against him. Christ, that kind of thing happens in every band. It's just the breaks.' She fumbled in the pocket of her leather jacket and pulled out her cigarettes. 'I never liked that guy,' she said. 'None of us did. We only took him on because he had a decent drum kit, but then we found out he was just borrowing it from a friend.' She lit her cigarette and puffed out a cloud of smoke. The knuckles of her right hand felt sore where they'd connected with McGuire's jawbone.

'Hmm.' Lezard put a hand into his pocket and pulled out the crumpled sheet of paper with the poem on it. 'I was just thinking. Does McGuire know your parents' address?'

She frowned.

'Yeah, I guess he would. We used to rehearse in the garden shed in the early days. But he seemed really surprised to see me just now.'

'Could have been an act. I seem to remember that a couple of the national papers carried stories about how you'd headed back to Manchester after Scott's death. It wouldn't take a mastermind to put two and two together, would it?'

'But the postmark was London.'

Lezard shrugged.

'That's easily done. Only takes a couple of hours to drive down there and pop it in a postbox.'

'It could have been you,' Jenny pointed out. 'You live there already, *and* you knew the address.'

Lezard looked at her.

'Nice,' he said. 'That's why I've always enjoyed being your manager. We've established such trust between us.'

Jenny laughed. She could feel the tension going out of her now. Hitting McGuire had felt pretty good. If it had been anybody else she'd be worrying now about potential litigation, McGuire trying to screw her for a big cash pay out: but a man who was an active drug dealer was hardly likely to go to the cops with a complaint against her. And few men would want to admit that they'd been punched out by a woman.

'So you're saying that the poem could be from an ex-member of the band: somebody with a grudge?'

'Well, it's only a suggestion. McGuire did seem pretty eaten up over what happened to him.'

'He's only one of many. I can think of four or five other people who got the elbow before we made it to the third album: before we really took off.'

'You were a pretty ruthless bunch, back then, weren't you?' observed Lezard, drily. He glanced back up the street but there seemed to be no sign of pursuit. He frowned, studied his wrist watch. 'Eleven fifteen,' he said. 'Maybe I should think about heading back to the hotel.'

'No way, Josh! I told you, this is clubbing night. We'll head down to the Hacienda, show all those spotty little ravers how it should be done.'

'The Hacienda?' Lezard looked doubtful. 'Think they'll give me a discount if I show them my bus pass?'

'Hey, none of that ageist crap. Come on.' She linked arms with him and pulled him along the street with her. 'By rights, they should let us in free. After all, I'm a major rock star and you're one of the hottest managers in the business.'

'Jenny, I'm not sure about this . . .'

'Relax, Josh. We'll have a few drinks and shake some action on the dance floor. What could be wrong with that?'

'Depends how many ex-members of The Deceivers we bump into,' said Lezard gloomily, but after a half-hearted attempt to resist, he gave in and allowed Jenny to pull him along the street towards the lights of Piccadilly.

Chapter Six

Jenny and Lezard left the Hacienda at about three a.m. They were both pretty drunk and Lezard's suit looked as if it had been put through a cycle in a washing machine, but the rest of the night had been relatively uneventful.

The club had been pretty much as Jenny remembered it, crammed full of doomy poseurs in black clothing, who all seemed intent on being hipper than the person standing next to them. Only the haircuts had changed. The music at least had been an eclectic mixture of the old, the new and the downright obscure. The resident DJ clearly had an obsession with Salsa and Jungle but there were enough familiar tracks mixed in to keep Jenny happy and she even managed to drag Lezard out on to the floor for a couple of old Rolling Stones numbers. Like most Americans, he was a terrible dancer.

Afterwards, she walked him back to the Midland Hotel. They stood for a moment in front of the imposing entrance.

'Thanks for an action-packed evening,' he told her. 'Care to come up to my room for a night cap?' He waggled his eyebrows suggestively at her and she laughed.

'I'd love to,' she admitted. 'But something tells me that wouldn't be a good idea.'

He looked disappointed.

'Aww, what's the problem?' he asked her.

She leaned closer.

'Confucius say, rock singer who fuck with manager is walkover when it comes to renewing contract.'

'Oh you, you're *so* practical.' He made an attempt to take hold of her shoulders and kiss her, but she evaded him easily and pecked him dutifully on the cheek.

'Time I was in bed,' she said, flagging down a passing taxi.

'My sentiments exactly,' sighed Lezard. He watched glumly as Jenny climbed into the cab. She opened the window and leaned out to blow a kiss to him as she drove away. 'Coward!' he yelled after her, and she threw him a last wave before settling down for the short journey out of town, noticing as she did so the way the driver was studying her in the rear view mirror. He'd recognised her from somewhere and was working himself up to asking who she was, but sitting there half cut with her head spinning, she wasn't entirely sure of that herself.

Back at her parents' house she felt like a guilty teenager, creeping home after some illicit date. She let herself in to the darkened house, cringing every time she stumbled into something. Happily, her parents must have been sleeping soundly. She made it into the kitchen and turned on the light, then saw to her surprise that the table was set for four people. Mother had put out the best china and there were biscuits and pieces of cake under a cover of cling film. Jenny remembered saying that she might bring Lezard back for coffee and she winced, anticipating the nagging she'd get over this in the morning.

She sighed, went to the sink and forced down a couple of glasses of water in a desperate attempt to head off the awful hangover she was going to have come tomorrow. Then she stumbled upstairs to her room. In the darkness, she flung off her clothes and collapsed on to the bed. She fell quickly into a deep sleep.

She woke again after what seemed a very short period of time but it must have been a couple of hours, because daylight was filtering in through a gap in the curtains, filling the room with a watery light. She lay there for a moment, trying to identify what had woken her – then she realised. The door to her room had opened, the old lock making a pronounced clicking sound. She expected her mother, prowling vengefully into the room in her bathrobe, demanding to know where her daughter had been till all hours.

But it wasn't Mother who came into the room. It was Scott Griffin.

He looked terrible. His thin face was haggard and wasted, the flesh stretched tight over the skull beneath. His skin had the colour and texture of candlewax. His long blond hair, tied back with the trademark red bandanna, looked lank and greasy: and his pale blue eyes seemed to look right through her. Jenny felt a cold jolt of fear lancing into her chest even as she strove to convince herself that there was nothing to be afraid of.

It's a dream, that's all. Scott is dead, this can't be happening.

Scott walked to the corner of the room and began to remove his clothes, taking them off one at a time and draping them over the chair. Jenny lay there with the covers pulled up to her chin, trembling with fright. Scott's lean back looked a blotchy greenish-grey colour and she could see quite clearly the track marks along his arms, the bluish-grey discolorations where he'd pumped the poison into his veins. When he was finally naked he turned and began to walk towards the bed.

'I'm cold,' he said. 'I'm so cold.'

'No, Scott,' she whispered. 'Don't . . .'

But he was already pulling the covers aside and though she tried desperately to hang on to them, his strength seemed extraordinary. The cotton fabric slipped through her hand, the friction burning the flesh of her palm. Oddly, it was this tiny detail that frightened her most.

That's too real to be a dream!

But she couldn't think about that because Scott was crawling under the sheets now and his wasted arms were enclosing her, wrapping around her waist like two chilly tentacles. His face brushed against hers and she felt the touch of his bloodless lips against her ear.

'I'm cold,' he said again. 'Warm me, Jenny. Warm me.'

She struggled desperately, hardly able to draw breath. His grip was so tight, it was squeezing all the air from her lungs and she opened her mouth to scream but, at first, all that emerged was a long exhalation of tortured breath.

'No,' she gasped. 'No, Scott, please! Please, let me go!'

'Jenny. I'm cold. Cold.'

His breath was clouding even as he spoke, enveloping her and transmitting a terrible chill to her own body. Then, with a wave of disgust, she felt him throw one skinny leg over her and she became aware of the hardness between his legs and that too was as cold as death, even as it lengthened, grew harder.

'Scott, no, I beg you, don't do this!'

The arms gripping her like a vice and the breath, clouding, clouding as his cold, dry tongue emerged from between black lips, flicking at her like a snake, then plunging into her mouth, and thrusting inside.

She gagged, choked, tried to pull away from him but there was no escape, he was stronger than he ever had been in life. And now inexorably, irresistibly, she felt the hard thing entering her, pushing its way up between her thighs: it was like being pierced by a long sharp shaft of ice.

After he had dressed himself and left the room, Jenny lay there waiting for the dream to end: waiting for the moment when she would wake up screaming. That's what always happened, wasn't it? You saw it in a film or read it in a book and you woke up screaming...

It didn't happen. She was just lying there in the bed and gazing fearfully around. She saw that every detail of the room corresponded with normality. She looked at the palm of her hand where the sheet had given her a friction burn. The skin was red but she could have done that herself, in her sleep. She was sure now that she was awake. Gingerly she pulled back the sheet and looked at her naked body, searching herself for physical evidence of an assault. She saw no scratches or bruises, despite the apparent power of the attack, but she still felt the lingering coldness inside where he had entered her. She put two fingers into her vagina and let out a slow sigh of relief when she found no evidence of any ejaculate.

She got out of bed and she was trembling now, telling herself over and over that yes, it was a dream, of course it was a dream, there could be no other explanation – unless it was some vivid hallucination, a return to the awful *delerium tremens* she had suffered before. Those waking nightmares had been bad enough but they had not been one bit as frightening as the ordeal she had just experienced. She grabbed her jeans off the back of a chair and searched through her pockets for a scrap of paper. Some time during the previous night she had scribbled down a note of Lezard's hotel phone number. She dialled the number and asked to be put through to his room. The desk clerk enquired politely if she realised what time it was and she nearly bit his head off.

'Just put me through, it's a fucking emergency, all right?'

'Very well, madam.'

The phone rang in what sounded like a distant part of the world. It went on ringing for ages before it was finally answered by a kind of strangled groan.

'Uhhh . . . h'lo?'

'Josh, it's Jenny. Listen, you've got to—'

'Jenny?' A long, weary sigh. 'Fuck's sake, you any idea what time it is? It's four o'clock in the morning.'

'Listen, Josh, the most horrible thing just happened. I'm so scared. I . . .' She started to sob and Lezard seemed to come abruptly wide awake.

'What is it, kid? What happened?'

'Josh, I just had a visitor. He came into my room and he . . .'

'Christ, Jenny, that creep from last night? Did he hurt you? Look, put down the phone and I'll get the police straight round there.'

'No, Josh, no. It wasn't McGuire. It . . . it was . . .'

'Who, Jenny?'

'It was . . .'

A silence. Jenny imagined what Lezard would think when she told him. She could picture the look on his face. Eyes crossed, one index finger drilling into the side of his skull. Jenny Slade had finally flipped her wig. All those years of drug abuse had taken their toll, after all.

'Jenny, for God's sake, tell me!'

'Uh . . . it . . . it was a dream, Josh. I've just been having a bad dream. I . . . I panicked, I guess.'

'A dream? But I thought you said . . .'

'No. I was confused. I had too much to drink last night and I can't handle it like I used to. I had a bad dream, that's all.'

'Look, you want me to come over there?'

'No. No, I'll be all right. It just . . . for a moment there, it seemed so real. I . . . I'm sorry for waking you.'

'Don't be silly, that's all right. You sure you'll be OK now? You sound kind of freaked.'

'I was for a minute.' Jenny forced an unconvincing laugh. 'I'll have to lay off the firewater for a while, huh? Listen, Josh.

While you're on. That place you talked about. You know, the studio in Wales? Maybe you should go ahead and fix it up. I'll go crazy if I stay here much longer.'

'That's great news, Jenny. You're sure you're ready?'

'Ready as I'll ever be.'

'Well, it's like I told you, the place has only been open a matter of days. I figure I could have everything ready to go by the end of next week.'

'That soon?'

'Er... well, tell you the truth, I kind of provisionally booked it anyway. I figured that with my natural charm and enthusiasm, I'd be able to talk you round. But listen, if that's too soon...'

Jenny shook her head.

'No. The sooner the better, I think. Get myself into gear again. Sort out all these crazy things in my head...'

'Jenny, you *sure* you're all right?'

'Yeah, I'm fine, Josh. Ring me when you've got all the details. I'll talk to you soon.' She put down the receiver and sat there on the bed, her arms wrapped around herself. She still felt cold. She lay down again and pulled the covers over her.

'A dream,' she murmured. 'Has to be.' She had simply failed to notice the point when she had woken up. She'd heard of that happening before. She'd read about it somewhere. Hadn't she?

She closed her eyes and tried to make her mind go blank. But the fear had rooted itself deep inside her and it wouldn't go away.

She didn't get any more sleep that morning.

Jenny stops talking for a moment. She sits there on the bed, the acoustic guitar still cradled on her lap. She is staring into space as though she has just remembered something.

Sergeant Gill sits watching her, his pen poised above a half completed page of his notebook. Glancing down, he is surprised to discover that he has already filled several pages with his small, neat handwriting.

'So you . . . decided to go?' he prompts her.

'Hmm?' She looks up at him with an expression of surprise, as though she has forgotten that he is there. Confusion flickers momentarily across her face.

'To the studio,' he prompts her. He leafs back a page to check his notes. 'The Grange.'

'Yes.' She shrugs. 'Lezard suggested it and . . . it seemed like a chance to get away from all the things that were crowding in on me. The bad dreams. I . . .' She glances suddenly to one side, as though a third person has spoken. 'Yes,' she says. 'Of *course* I'll tell him. But I haven't got to that bit, yet . . .'

Her manner is so convincing that the detective feels compelled, once again, to look in the direction she is indicating. He knows it's ridiculous, but part of him half expects to see . . . what? Something pale and shimmering, floating like a spectre in the corner of the room? Some wizened, troll-like creature crouched on the bed covers? He jerks his head around as Jenny strikes a chord on the guitar.

'So off I went,' she tells him. 'A relatively short trip for me, only a couple of hours' drive from Manchester.'

'And you were headed for mid Wales?'

'Yes,' she told him.

'And this would have been, what . . . four days ago?'

She blinks, stares at him.

'No, that can't be right, can it? Four days. It seems much longer . . .'

She cocks her head to one side, as though listening to a tiny voice in her ear. 'Four days,' she agrees. 'But then, I suppose a lot can happen in four days.'

PART TWO

In sweet music is such art
Killing care and grief of heart
Fall asleep, or hearing die.

William Shakespeare
Henry VIII

Chapter Seven

Jenny was lost. She acknowledged the fact not with apprehension but with a sense of inevitability. The roughly scrawled map that Lezard had sent her lay on the passenger seat of her vintage Aston Martin DB5, but it was a sketch at best and gave no real indication of distance. Furthermore, Jenny had always been cursed with a poor sense of direction.

She was driving south-west along a winding ribbon of tarmac, heading into the Brecon Beacons, and it was a good twenty minutes since she had seen any kind of signpost. On either side of her, thick ranks of forest crowded the road. It would doubtless have looked lush and picturesque in the summer months but now in the grip of winter, the denuded branches suggested nothing so much as legions of wizened limbs reaching helplessly for the grey sky.

It was cold too and Jenny was obliged to keep the car's ancient heater on full blast, despite the thick sheepskin flying jacket she was wearing. She began to wonder about the wisdom of shutting herself away in some draughty old monastery for the next two weeks. Her days of roughing it on the road were well behind her and success had taught her to enjoy her comforts. She thought about The Deceivers' first few tours, the way they'd all bunked down in the back of the Transit van, bundled into sleeping bags amidst the amps and speakers, often unable to wash or change their clothes for days at a stretch. Christ, she'd hate to go back to that now.

She saw a flash of red against the dark background of tree trunks up on her left and realised it was an ancient tin sign that said simply: PETROL. A few moments later, she discerned the garage itself and she instinctively braked, slowing down to pull into the tiny asphalt forecourt. She was getting low on petrol and she could take the opportunity to ask directions.

It wasn't much of a garage. There were just two rusting pumps, neither of them self service by the look of it: and an open-fronted breeze block building, the entrance to which was heaped with oily metal detritus. Next to this, a small clapboard lean-to completed the establishment. There was a window set into this but it was so dirty, Jenny couldn't tell if there was anyone inside.

However, a hand-written sign on the door read 'Open'. She waited in the car for a few moments to see if anyone would come out, but nobody did. Growing impatient, she climbed out of the car, hunching her jacket tighter around her in a vain attempt to ward off the cold. She crossed the forecourt and, opening the door of the lean-to, she stepped inside.

There were three men sitting on wooden chairs which were arranged around a small cast iron wood stove. Jenny had timed her arrival to coincide with the punchline of what was clearly a pretty filthy joke.

'... and there I was, back in Omar Sharif's moustache!'

They were big men, all of them, and they threw back their heads to bellow with laughter. Then the man who had told the joke noticed the new arrival. He stopped laughing abruptly, like somebody had pulled a plug. His companions trailed off too. They turned their heads to look at Jenny. It wasn't so much a look as an open-mouthed stare.

She was reminded of a scene from a B-movie western, the

one where the stranger steps in through the swing doors of the local saloon. She kept expecting the men to become self-conscious and look away but they didn't. They simply stared, examining her as they might examine some inanimate object they'd found, their eyes moving slowly from her feet to her head and lingering intimately on all points in between. After a few moments, she felt prompted to say something in order to break the awful silence.

'Any chance of some petrol?' she asked, and she was annoyed by the apologetic tone in her own voice. What did she have to apologise for? *They* were the ones who were being rude.

The joker seemed to come out of some kind of trance. He gave her an oily smile. He was a ruddy-complexioned man with big jowls and a bulbous red nose. He had small, suspicious eyes and he was dressed in what looked liked American army combat fatigues. The effect was completed by a peaked canvas camouflage cap with thick woolly earmuffs that hung down on either side of his fat head. When he spoke it was with a broad, mid Wales accent.

'Well now, look what the wind's blown in! Lost your way, have you, luvvy?'

'As a matter of fact I have,' said Jenny. She closed the door behind her and approached the counter, aware of the ancient floorboards creaking under her boots. 'But I also need a tank of petrol.'

'We've got none of your *green* petrol!' said one of the other men. He wasn't as fat as the joker, but he was very tall and solidly built. He had wiry red hair that stuck up in tufts and, Jenny noticed, only a small number of teeth left in his mouth.

'That's OK, my car doesn't use it.'

There was another uncomfortable silence. Then the joker spoke.

'Go on then, Ivor,' he said. 'Give her what she wants.'

'Eh?' Ivor stared at him uncertainly.

'The *petrol*, you idiot!'

'Oh, right. Fill it up, is it?'

Jenny nodded and Ivor got up out of his chair. He moved past Jenny to the door, walking with the lumbering gait of a bear. As he went out, a fierce gust of wind blew in over one prodigious shoulder, blowing a sheaf of bills off the counter top.

'And shut the bloody door, you barn dweller!' roared the joker. Ivor turned back and did as he was told. The joker gave Jenny a knowing look. 'Can't get the staff these days, can you?' he said, with a wink. He rubbed his plump hands together in an elaborate pantomime of coldness. 'Brass monkey weather. There's a real cold snap on the way, I reckon. Here, come on, love, don't be shy. There's room for a little one.'

He indicated the empty chair by the stove and the third man moved his seat obligingly aside as if to give her more room. He was older than the other two, dark haired with a thin bootlace moustache. He gave Jenny what was probably intended as a Jack-the-lad grin but the effect was somewhat marred by a dewdrop of bright green snot that hung suspended from his nose.

Reluctantly, Jenny moved closer to the stove, extending her hands to absorb some of the meagre warmth.

'Why not take the weight off?' asked the joker, nodding at the vacant chair.

'Thanks, I'd rather stand. I've been driving for hours, I need to stretch my legs.'

'Suit yourself,' he said. 'Come a long way, 'ave you?'

'From Manchester.'

'Well, you've come to the right place, anyway! I'm Cadfan Morris, the owner of this delightful establishment. And this y'ure is Hugh, my partner. Now, what can we do to help you, my love?'

Jenny thought about pointing out that she wasn't his 'love' but decided not to pursue it. Irritate him and he might send her in the wrong direction entirely.

'I'm looking for a place called The Grange,' she told him. 'It's a recording studio...'

'A bloody recording studio!' roared Cadfan. He grinned at Hugh triumphantly. 'See, I said it wasn't an old folks home they was building! That's a fiver you owe me, boy.'

Hugh made a face.

'Bugger off! You didn't say it was a recording studio, neither! A hotel, you said. For rich tourists.' Hugh spat on to the lid of the stove and the gob of saliva danced and sizzled briefly before evaporating. Jenny had to mask an expression of disgust.

'Well it will be, in a way, won't it? I mean, they'll have living accommodation, won't they? Recording artistes are not going to commute back and forth every bloody day, to the arse end of nowhere.' Cadfan looked at Jenny. 'I'm right aren't I, love? There's accommodation?'

'Er ... well, I hope so. Or I'm going to be sleeping rough tonight.'

Cadfan leered unpleasantly.

'Oh, no need for that, girl. We'll find you a bed, won't we, Hugh? Never ones to let a lady stand when she can *lie down.*' He waggled his eyebrows suggestively, as though expecting her to laugh, but Jenny wasn't going to give him the satisfaction.

'You know where it is then?' she said.

'Oh aye, we pass by it when we go hunting, don't we, Hugh?' Cadfan waved a hand at some moth-eaten trophies fixed to the wall behind him, a couple of stags' heads that had been so amateurishly stuffed, they looked like outlandish cuddly toys. 'Been building work going on there for the best part of a year. Somebody must be sinking a lot of money into that old place.'

Jenny shrugged.

'I wouldn't know about that,' she said. 'I just need to—'

'You a whatsit, then? A pop star? I thought to myself when you came in, there was something familiar about your face. Said to myself, I've seen her mug before and not on a wanted poster!' He laughed at his own poor joke. 'Should I be asking you for an autograph or something?'

Jenny shook her head. She didn't want to get into this routine again.

'No, I'm just a . . . a technician. I work on the other side of the glass.'

Cadfan looked unconvinced.

'No, I reckon I've seen you on the box. *Top of the Pops*, isn't it? What do you say, Hugh?'

Hugh nodded.

'I shouldn't be at all surprised, Cadfan. Pity my lad Dafydd isn't y'ure, *he'd* be able to tell you. He knows all them pop stars, does Dafydd.'

'Look, about these directions,' Jenny prompted them. 'I'm kind of in a hurry.'

The door opened and Ivor shambled back in. He had a look of absolute amazement on his face.

'A bloody Aston Martin!' he announced to the room at large. 'There's lovely, it is. Barely a mark on it, but it's the genuine article. Must have cost a bloody fortune.'

Cadfan gave Jenny a knowing smirk.

'Pays well being a technician, does it?'

'Yeah, not bad.'

'Come off it, you're a pop star. I've *seen* you, girl, and I've a good memory for faces. Going to sing us a little song before you go, are you?' He laughed and glanced at Hugh. 'What do you reckon, Hugh? Think she should make her sing for her supper?'

Hugh grinned and wiped his snotty nose on his sleeve.

'Aye, I reckon we could do with a bit of entertainment, Cadfan. Gets a bit quiet round here in the winter.'

Jenny was getting tired of this. She pulled out her wallet.

'How much?' she asked Ivor.

He stared at her. 'Uh?' he grunted.

'For the petrol?'

He shrugged. 'Call it a tenner.'

'Thanks.' She handed Cadfan the money and turned to go, but he reached out and grabbed her sleeve.

'Hold on, darling, what about your directions?' he said.

She snatched her hand away.

'Forget it. I'll ask somewhere else.'

'Somewhere else?' This seemed to amuse him. 'There *isn't* anywhere else! Very lonely part of the world this.'

'I'll find it,' she told him, turning towards the door.

'Hey now, hang about a bit! What's your hurry? I mean, it's not every day we get a celebrity in y'ure. A chance to mingle with the stars.' Cadfan must have made some small gesture behind her back because Jenny saw that Ivor was moving his considerable bulk in front of the door. She felt a sinking sensation in the pit of her stomach but told herself to stay calm.

'Look,' she said, turning back. 'I have an appointment and I'm going to be late.'

Cadfan grinned, a horrible, sleazy grin.

'You want to learn to slow down a bit, love. You're not in the city now. We do things different out y'ure. We take a bit more time to get to know people, see?'

'Yes, well it just so happens that I don't particularly *want* to get to know you, so if you'd tell laughing boy there to get out of my way...'

'Here, here, that's not nice, now is it? Decidedly rude, I'd say. What do you think, Hugh?'

'Very rude,' said Hugh. 'Now you mention it.'

'I mean, I could point out that you're all by yourself in the middle of nowhere with three men. If they were to take it into their heads that they didn't like your tone, well, I wouldn't like to say what the consequences might be...'

Jenny took a deep breath.

'And I might just point out that I'm an expert Thai kick boxer: and that I could hammer six kinds of shit out of three fat bastards like you with one hand tied behind my back.'

It was a hopeless exaggeration: she'd had maybe a dozen lessons in her entire life – but it was delivered in a calm, even tone that she hoped would convince them that she knew what she was talking about.

There was a long silence. Cadfan sat there staring at her as though weighing up what she had said, his little eyes narrowed down to suspicious slits. Jenny became aware of the ticking of an ancient clock that hung above the door. Outside, the wind gusted, rattling the glass in the window. She was aware of the apprehension mounting within her and told herself that whatever happened, she mustn't panic. Finally, Cadfan spoke.

'Carry on down the road for another two miles,' he said. 'You'll come to a place where the road forks to the right. Follow that fork through the forest for another two miles and you'll come to a steep hill. When you get to the top, the Grange is straight ahead of you.'

Jenny took a deep breath.

'Thank you,' she said. She turned slowly away and moved towards the door. Ivor stood there uncertainly for a moment, looking at her. Then as she drew close, he muttered something under his breath and stepped aside. Jenny opened the door and a chill wind swept into the room.

'We'll have to drop by for a visit,' Cadfan shouted after her. 'Perhaps we'll get you to sing a song for us, yet.'

Jenny glanced over her shoulder. He was sitting there, grinning at her, from under his hunting trophies. She went out slamming the door behind her and hurried across to her car, half expecting them to follow her outside. But thankfully, they didn't.

Secure in the cramped interior of the Aston Martin she started up the engine and accelerated out of the forecourt with a screech of rubber. In the driving mirror, the garage dwindled quickly to a speck and was lost beneath the horizon.

'A welcome in the hillside,' muttered Jenny. 'Jesus.'

She sped on, into the heart of the forest.

Chapter Eight

After she took the right fork, the road narrowed as it cut deeper into forest. The trees that flanked the road on either side seemed to be crowding in on her and in places their skeletal branches interlaced overhead to form a canopy. Jenny reflected that in summer, when the trees were thick with foliage, very little sunlight would filter through.

After motoring for what seemed an age, the road inclined abruptly upwards for several hundred yards, the gradient steep enough to make the engine labour: but then the car crested the rise and Jenny got her first look at The Grange. It lay directly ahead of her.

The first word that sprang to mind was 'forbidding' – it was an ancient three-storey pile of weathered grey stone occupying an area that seemed to have been hacked out of the surrounding woods. To Jenny's untutored eye the place looked more like a castle than a monastery. The walls were high and sheer like a fortress and at each corner stood a tall slate-roofed turret with vertical slits for windows.

As she drew closer, Jenny noted the elaborately carved gargoyles above the stone arch of the massive entrance gates. They gazed balefully down at her as she drove beneath the arch into the cobbled courtyard beyond. She noticed Lezard's second car, a Mitsubishi Shogun, parked alongside a muddy looking Landrover Discovery, and she sounded her horn to announce her presence. Then, climbing out of the car, she reached into the boot to collect her guitar case and her luggage.

A door at the top of a short flight of stone steps opened and Lezard emerged, closely followed by another, younger man. Lezard grinned and waved at Jenny, then he and his companion descended the steps and came across the courtyard to greet her. Jenny took the opportunity to check out Lezard's companion, whom she assumed must be Gareth Reed.

He was in his early thirties, she judged, and for once, handsome Josh Lezard had some serious competition. Reed was lean and rangy with the kind of looks that used to be termed Saturnine. He had black, shoulder-length hair and thick arched eyebrows that almost but not quite met over the bridge of his sharp nose. He was dressed casually in old blue jeans and a biker's jacket and as he drew closer, he volunteered a grin, revealing two rows of even white teeth.

Jenny felt a stab of apprehension. Reed was exactly the kind of man she tended to fall for, right down to the studs on his Nickleson leather jacket: and that didn't bode well for any kind of professional relationship they might have. Her last producer had been reassuringly unattractive, a tubby, balding little guy with a wife he adored and two kids he worshipped. OK, so the resulting album had been a disappointment but at least Jenny had felt she could speak her mind to him. Which she had, at considerable volume, several times during the tortuous sessions that resulted in *Red Tape*. But how were you supposed to bellow at something that looked like your darkest fantasy come to life?

'Jenny, you made good time!' Lezard bustled up and gave her his usual peck-on-the-cheek greeting. 'Believe it or not, you're the first one here.'

'Don't look so surprised,' she told him. 'I'm famous for my punctuality.'

'Yeah, like Pavarotti is famous for his exercise video!' Lezard grinned mischievously. 'Jenny, I'd like to introduce Gareth Reed, the owner of The Grange. Gareth, this is Jenny Slade.'

Reed stepped forward and flashed her another of his movie star smiles. 'It's a real pleasure, Miss Slade, I've been looking forward to meeting you.' He reached out and took her hand in his. Jenny had expected the standard businesslike shake but no, he lifted the hand to his mouth and gently brushed the back of it with his lips.

Creep, thought Jenny automatically: but annoyingly, she couldn't help feeling impressed, not so much by the gesture itself, but by the way he carried it off without a trace of self consciousness. *Smooth bastard*, she ventured, but that didn't feel right either.

'I hope you had no trouble finding your way here,' he said: and now Jenny noted the rich resonance of his voice, which was more Anthony Hopkins than Richard Burton, only the faintest evidence of a Welsh accent way back in the mix.

'Well, I've already had a close encounter with the natives,' she told him. 'I ran into three retards back up the way. Unfortunately, I wasn't in my car at the time.'

Reed looked concerned.

'Retards?' he murmured.

'Yeah, they have this little garage a couple of miles back up the road?'

'Ah, yes. That would be Cadfan Morris and his cronies. I'm afraid they have a certain reputation around here, Miss Slade. I hope they didn't bother you unduly.'

'Nothing I couldn't handle. And at least they gave me some

directions. This place really is off the beaten track, isn't it?' She glanced at Lezard. 'I know you said it was remote but . . .'

'It's great once you get used to it,' Lezard assured her. 'Takes a couple of days to adjust, is all.'

Jenny was unconvinced.

'I don't know, Josh, I go a little weird in the countryside. I start itching for clubs and cinemas . . . you know, all the things you never get around to when you actually *live* in the city.' She glanced warily at Gareth Reed. 'What do you do for entertainment around here?' she asked him.

He smiled.

'We make our own,' he said. 'We read, walk, sleep. If we feel like living dangerously there's a little pub in the next village where they play a demon game of dominoes.'

'The next village? Where's that?'

'About six miles south.'

'Jesus. I don't know if I'll be able to handle this. I'm not used to being so . . . isolated.'

Reed leaned over and picked up one of Jenny's suitcases.

'I look on that as a plus point, Miss Slade. When it comes to the creative process, solitude can be a very useful quality.'

'Yeah, but there's solitude and there's solitude. Hey and look, call me Jenny, OK? Only my bank manager calls me Miss Slade.'

'Yes, of course. Jenny. Maybe you'd like to see your room first. Then if you want, I'll give you a quick tour of the facilities before lunch.'

Jenny sighed.

'Lead on, Macduff,' she said. She reached for her other case but Lezard got to it before her and she felt vaguely irritated. Since Scott's death people had a tendency to treat her like an invalid. At least neither of them had tried to commandeer her guitar. She picked it up and the two men turned and headed back across the courtyard. There was nothing to do but follow them. They climbed the steps and went in through what must have been one of several back entrances. This one led into a large kitchen with a stone-flagged floor. There was a scrubbed pine table and the walls were lined with old pine shelves and cupboards.

They passed through an adjoining doorway into a formal dining room, with a long oak table big enough to accommodate perhaps ten diners. A young woman was setting out plates and dishes in there and she glanced up and smiled as they entered.

'Jenny, this is Cassie Morgan,' announced Reed. 'She's the cook and housekeeper at The Grange.'

Cassie was in her early twenties, Jenny thought, a tall, slim girl with shoulder-length straight hair that had been dyed with henna to a vibrant purplish red. She wore standard New Age hippy clothes: a sloppy cable jumper over a long Indian print skirt and a pair of Jesus sandals. Her slim wrists were festooned with bracelets, she had large metal hoops through her ears and a ruby stud through one nostril. Despite all the paraphernalia, she managed to look good enough to eat and Jenny couldn't help envying her two things – her youth and her tall, willowy figure.

'Hello, Cassie,' she said.

'Wow!' Cassie seemed somewhat in awe of Jenny. 'It's really great to meet you. I am a major fan of your band, I really mean that. I've got every album you ever made.'

'That's nice,' said Jenny.

'I bought your first one when I was just a little girl.'

Jenny gave her a sharp look.

'Now you're spoiling it.'

Cassie put a hand up to her mouth.

'Oh, I'm sorry, I didn't mean . . .'

'Relax, I was kidding.'

But Cassie's face had coloured a deep red, as though she had committed some unforgivable error.

'Gosh, I hope you don't think I ... I mean, I'm not one of those who believe that people over thirty can't be cool...'

'That makes two of us,' Jenny assured her. 'So how does a wild young thing like you find life out here in the middle of nowhere?'

'Oh, it's great, really! At first I thought I'd hate it, but the vibes in this place are really terrific, you know? And listen, if there's anything you want, you just be sure and holler for me or Idris, OK?'

'Idris is Cassie's husband,' explained Reed, before Jenny could ask. 'He's also my engineer and sound man. He and Cassie have their own quarters in the building, so they're on call whenever you need them.' He glanced at Cassie inquiringly. 'Where *is* Idris, by the way? I haven't seen him this morning.'

Cassie waved her hands in a gesture of helplessness.

'Oh, er ... he said something about going into the forest to check on his traps. You know Idris. I expect he'll be back soon.'

Reed didn't say anything but the silence had an edge to it, and Jenny could almost imagine him saying, *Yes, I know Idris all right.*

'Cassie is a terrific cook,' announced Lezard, as though trying to fill an uncomfortable silence. 'You should taste her game pie, Jenny, all made with local produce. Idris traps 'em and Cassie cooks 'em. They're quite a team.'

'Oh, it's nothing!' Cassie waved a hand dismissively but beamed with evident pleasure at the compliment. 'But seriously, if there's anything special you like, you only have to ask.'

'Well, I'm not a great eater,' Jenny told her. 'I just tend to pick at whatever comes to hand. Our keyboard player's the awkward sod when it comes to eating.'

'Oh yes, Mr Lezard warned me about that. I'll be preparing some vegan alternatives for him. Actually, I'm a vegetarian myself, so it's no hardship.'

Jenny raised her eyebrows.

'And you cook *game pie*?' she said.

Cassie shrugged.

'Idris is a real carnivore,' she explained. 'He wouldn't eat anything that didn't have blood in it.' She made a gesture with her arms that said 'what can I do?', then with a smile, she went back to setting the table. Reed led the way through the dining room into a long, stone-flagged hallway. Off to their left, an ornate wooden staircase swept in a curve up to the first floor.

'Pretty impressive,' observed Jenny.

'The staircase is sixteenth century,' Reed told her, as he led her up the steps. 'The building however dates back to the early fourteen hundreds. It was built by an order of monks who were seeking a retreat from the world.'

'I'd say they found what they were looking for,' said Jenny. 'The fourteen hundreds. I hope the heating system is more recent. Feels like there's cold weather on the way.'

Reed grinned.

'Don't worry, we had a new central heating system installed just a couple of months back. And though we've preserved the original look of the building throughout, we've used modern insulation techniques wherever possible. This place is as snug as you could reasonably ask.'

'Must have cost you a fortune,' said Jenny. 'My friends at the garage were speculating how much you forked out to get the property back into shape. They figured we were talking an arm and a leg.'

Reed grinned, shook his head.

'No, it's worse than that. We're talking two arms, two legs and most of the torso,' he said. 'But I'm sure we'll see a return on our investment in the long run: especially when news gets around that The Deceivers have recorded here.'

'I hope you haven't overestimated our credibility,' Jenny warned him.

'Our credibility has never been higher,' Lezard assured her. 'We've got a platinum album.'

'And a dead lead guitarist. Cynics would point out that these two events are not unconnected.'

Reed looked distinctly uncomfortable at this comment.

'Jenny, I just want to say how sorry I was to hear about Scott Griffin. For my money, he was one of the best guitarists in the business and I'd have been honoured to work with him.'

'Yeah? Our last producer made similar remarks just before we started on the *Red Tape* album. After two weeks in Scott's company, he was about ready to make him *eat* his guitar. Scott could be . . . abrasive . . .'

Reed gave her a strange look.

'So can I,' he assured her.

They had reached the first floor now and Reed led the way along the landing. He indicated a series of doors on their right.

'The guest rooms,' he said. 'We have six on this floor and another six up on the second. And don't worry, Josh warned me to put you and Mr Spencer as far away from each other as possible.'

'Good. It's not that I don't love him or anything, and he's a shit-hot drummer; but he's also the noisiest, most out-of-control sonofabitch that ever walked the face of the planet.' She gave Reed a meaningful look. 'You have been warned.'

'You're next to me, Jenny,' said Lezard. 'I tried to talk Gareth into letting us have connecting rooms but he wouldn't hear of it. Must have thought my intentions were dishonourable or something. But if you need any company in the night, I'll be right next door.' The two men exchanged glances and laughed, as though sharing some private joke: and Jenny got the distinct impression that they were close in some way that went beyond mere acquaintance.

'One of these days, Lezard, I'm going to respond to your come-on line: and you'll probably run screaming into the night.'

'Don't count on it,' he warned her. 'Now, if you'll excuse me, I have some paperwork to sort out before lunch. I'll leave you in Gareth's very capable hands.' Lezard handed Jenny her case and opened the door to his room. Jenny caught a glimpse of a palatial suite inside. 'See you at one thirty,' he said.

'Yeah, catch you later.'

Lezard went into his room, closing the door behind him and Reed led Jenny on to the next door.

'We don't actually *have* any connecting rooms,' he told her apologetically.

'Oh, don't take any notice of Lezard. He was just kidding around. There's nothing between us aside from business.'

'Really?' Jenny couldn't be sure but she thought Reed seemed pleased at this news. 'Anyhow, I'm sure you'll like this suite,' he said. He opened the door and stepped respectfully back to let Jenny enter. She went inside and stood looking around for a moment. The large main room consisted of a bedroom/lounge combination, decorated in soft earth tones. There was an antique iron bed frame, the mattress covered by what looked like Indian cotton throws and off to one side, a sofa and an armchair covered in a textured caramel fabric. Through an open doorway, she could see a good-sized bathroom, the walls covered in bottle green, glazed terracotta tiles.

Jenny let out an appreciative whistle.

'Hey, this is nicer than home,' she said. 'Christ, I hope you didn't give Chris a room like this! He's better on surfaces that can be hosed down afterwards.' She threw her guitar case on to the bed and walked to the leaded window. Looking out, she could see the gardens at the front of the house. In the bare trees that flanked the drive, she saw what looked like a series of black rags fluttering from the branches. Then she realised that they were birds, beating their big wings and squabbling with each other. She unlatched the window and could hear the sound of them, cawing and shrieking.

Reed came over to stand beside her.

'Bloody things,' he muttered. 'Can't seem to get rid of them. Idris goes out with the shotgun every few days and blasts a dozen or so, but they just come back again as soon as he turns his back.'

Jenny sighed.

'Crows have as much right to be here as anyone,' she said.

'Rooks,' he corrected her. 'You see they have a little smudge of white around the beak.'

Jenny looked at him, vaguely irritated by his remark.

'Let me explain how this works,' she said. 'I'm the famous rock star, you're the would-be producer of my next album. You're supposed to agree with everything I say.'

He laughed delightedly, and Jenny felt a powerful rush of attraction to him. She told herself not to be stupid.

'That may be so, but they're still rooks.' Reed studied her for a moment, his dark eyes flashing with mockery. 'So what do you say? You want to check out the studio?'

Jenny sighed, shrugged.

'Why not?' she said. 'I guess it can't harm to take a look, can it?'

She closed the window, blocking out the cawing, squabbling

sound of the rooks. As she glanced out a whole flock of them took off from the trees and rose in an ominous black cloud against the gunmetal grey sky.

Turning, Jenny followed Gareth Reed out of the room and back downstairs to the studio.

Chapter Nine

It was state-of-the-art all right. Accessed by a doorway and an equipment lift located under the staircase, the studio space had been created in what had previously been the building's crypt. The result looked like the console of a spaceship that had suddenly materialised in the vault of a cathedral.

There was a good-sized control room housing a 36/24 track Teac mixing desk, backed up by all the attendant paraphernalia that modern recording demanded – digital mastering, midi automation, Tascam MSR, Dolby . . . you name it, The Grange studio had it.

On the other side of a glass screen, there was 250 square feet of air-conditioned studio floor and three isolation booths. The music equipment was of the very best pedigree – Fender and Orange amplifiers, ARP and Yamaha keyboards, Shure and Beyer microphones.

Jenny sat down in the producer's chair and put her feet up on the console. Reed settled into the engineer's chair beside her. They sat in silence for a few minutes, gazing through the screen at the midnight blue Tama drum kit that was set up in the centre of the studio floor: even Chris Spencer couldn't complain about that, it matched his own kit right down to the Avedis Zyldjan cymbals.

Jenny reflected that she really ought to be itching to get in there and try out all that technology: but on the contrary, she felt anxious, apprehensive at the very idea of plugging in her guitar and stepping up to that microphone to sing. Reed seemed to sense her mood. He glanced at her quizzically.

'Josh tells me you've written some new material,' he said.

'Couple of songs,' said Jenny dismissively. 'But I'm not sure about them. I guess you know I've always co-written with Scott?'

He nodded. 'It's difficult when you lose a songwriting partner,' he said. 'That's a bereavement all in itself. It's obviously going to take some time. If it would help, you could always try them out on me first.' He indicated an Ovation twelve string acoustic propped on a stand in the corner of the control room.

'You have to be kidding,' she told him. 'I'd just feel stupid, doing that. Like I was on trial or something. No, I guess I'll wait until the time is right. Anyway, forget about new material, the first thing I need to do is see if I can still play the *old* songs.'

Reed frowned.

'You really feel that insecure?'

'I feel like I'm eighteen again and attending my first audition. I know it's crazy: but without Scott here, I just feel . . . bogus, somehow. Like I'm some kind of imposter.' She swung her legs off the desk and got up out of the chair. Suddenly she couldn't stand to be down there a moment longer.

'Let's look at the rest of the house,' she suggested.

'OK.' Reed got up from his seat and followed her up the flight of stone steps that led back to the hallway. They emerged from under the staircase and stood there uncertainly for a moment.

'Now,' said Reed, 'where shall we start? Well, there's a communal lounge down this way.' They strolled across the stone flags to the end of the hall and went into a large room at the front of the house. There were two long sofas and several arm chairs placed around the interior and the flags had been carpeted with a rich charcoal berber, to give it a warmer feel.

Between two leaded windows, a huge stone fireplace dominated the room, and a log fire was blazing cheerfully in the hearth. Above the arch of the fire hung a large portrait. It depicted a severe-looking middle-aged man with the abundant beard and side whiskers of the Victorian era. He had a disagreeable sneer on his face and there was something malevolent about his fierce brown eyes.

'The room's great,' said Jenny. 'But I can't say I like your taste in art much. That guy's face could strip paint.'

Reed chuckled.

'Yes, he's not exactly Mel Gibson, is he? But I couldn't bring myself to leave him down in the crypt, where I found him. That's Obediah Wadleigh, the Grange's most famous resident.'

'Yeah? What was so great about him?' Jenny moved closer to the fire, staring up at the painting.

'Well, let me see. Where do I start? He first came to public attention in his home town of Hereford, when he set up house with his family.'

'What's so odd about that?'

'It wasn't a family in the conventional sense of the word. He never married. I suppose "followers" would be closer to it.' Reed was gazing up at the portrait now in apparent admiration. 'Wadleigh had incredible charisma. He was like a Victorian prototype of David Koresh, with a dash of Aleister Crowley thrown in for good measure. He attracted a large band of followers, many of them respectable middle-class women who seemed to find him sexually irresistible...'

'What, *him*?' Jenny shook her head. 'Can't see it myself. Maybe the artist got him on a bad day.'

'Could be. At any rate, Wadleigh had the bright idea of starting his own religion. A lot of his detractors suggested that it was just a way to part gullible people from their money and to indulge in sexual orgies. Needless to say, the sect soon outstayed their welcome in Hereford: so he purchased The Grange in 1894, selected twelve of his most dedicated followers and set up shop.'

Jenny smiled. Reed had taken on the demeanour of a college professor discussing a much loved topic. He'd obviously studied the history of The Grange in some detail.

'Why twelve?' she asked.

'Nobody really knows. Some people thought it might have been in mockery of Christ's twelve disciples. Wadleigh's religion made a lot of room for The Cosmic Joker. You're familiar with that?'

'Can't say I am. Sounds like the name of a band.'

'It's the theory that God exists purely to play horrible practical jokes on mankind. Wadleigh himself was noted for his bizarre sense of humour.'

'Yeah, he looks like a regular court jester. So the twelve of them . . . no wait, the *thirteen* of them, settled down here in a kind of commune, right?'

'A *coven* would perhaps be a more accurate term. But yes, essentially, that was the idea. Of course, other followers were permitted to visit but only the thirteen were allowed to stay on a permanent basis. They all settled down here . . .'

'And lived happily ever after, shagging like rabbits?'

'Yes. Well, for a couple of years, anyway. Then one night in 1896 . . .'

Jenny smiled.

'One dark and stormy night, no doubt?'

Reed shrugged.

'It was, as it happens. Heavy snow, high winds . . . the worst

January on record for something like a hundred years. The Thirteen were cooped up in the house, unable to step outside. And something bad happened.'

'Now why am I not surprised to hear that?' muttered Jenny. It had occurred to her that Reed was trying one of the oldest tricks in the book. He was attempting to put the frighteners on her, perhaps in the belief that a spooked woman would be that much easier to entice into bed. She could have saved him the trouble.

Reed didn't seem to notice her remark. He moved to the fireplace and picking up a long poker, he stirred the logs, sending bright flurries of sparks up the chimney. 'You want the official version?' he asked her. 'Or what really happened?'

'There's a difference?' asked Jenny.

'There certainly is. The authorities were nervous of the truth getting out, so they concocted some half-arsed story about the entire commune wandering off into the blizzard and freezing to death. What actually happened was rather more disturbing.'

'Oh, goody,' murmured Jenny, 'let's have that version!'

Reed studied her for a moment before continuing.

'Two days later, when the storm had abated, a visitor couldn't get an answer to her knock. She found an unlocked door, entered and discovered all twelve followers lying dead in various places all over the house. Her first impulse was to run out of there screaming but she was concerned for Obediah and somehow managed to conquer her fear. She went up to Wadleigh's room and found his body too. His throat had been cut. The first impression was that they'd had some kind of ritual suicide pact. But...'

'What a charming story,' interrupted Jenny. She moved across to one of the windows and stared out. 'But frankly, I don't believe a word of it.'

Reed stopped poking the fire and looked up at her in surprise.

'Why not?' he asked her.

'Oh, come on, I know it's customary to try and scare the pants off visitors who come to stay in creepy old houses, but I think you could have made it a bit more believable.'

Reed shrugged.

'Whether you believe me or not is immaterial. It happens to be true. I have several books on the subject if you'd like to verify the facts. I got quite interested in it when I bought this place. One of the things that attracted me to it, actually.'

'Oh right, and I suppose the next thing you'll tell me is that the house is haunted by Obediah's ghost.'

'I wasn't going to tell you anything of the sort, since it doesn't happen to be the case. However, an apparition of a monk has occasionally been seen in the grounds...'

'Give me a break!' Jenny laughed bitterly. She stared out of the window at the rooks flapping in the branches of the trees.

'What's the problem?' Reed seemed amused by her reaction, rather than offended.

'I just don't buy all that supernatural shtick, that's all. It's bollocks.'

'Well, that's your opinion...'

'It's all this New Age nonsense that I blame. I bet Cassie goes for those stories of yours, doesn't she?'

'She does as a matter of fact. But I don't see...'

'People seem to want to believe in the most ridiculous things these days – ghosts, alien abductions, crop circles... you name it.'

'Yes, but there's nothing supernatural about the Wadleigh case. It's documented fact. And as for alien abductions and crop circles, there's plenty of evidence to suggest...'

'Please! Give me a break. You know, I was talking to some

arsehole the other day who was trying to tell me that Scott Griffin wanted to contact me.'

Reed frowned.

'And that seems unbelievable to you?'

'Of course it does,' said Jenny, scornfully. 'Dead is dead. There's nothing afterwards, no heaven, no hell, no limbo. So you may as well make the most of it while you've got the chance.' She glanced challengingly at Reed. 'I suppose you'll try and tell me different.'

He shook his head.

'I wouldn't presume to. But I think you're protesting too loudly. I think part of you suspects that there's something in what this person said . . . and the idea of it scares you.'

Jenny smirked.

'Nonsense! He was just some little toerag on the make. I get hundreds of them.'

Reed put down the poker and moved over to stand beside her at the window.

'I wouldn't dream of trying to argue the point,' he said. 'But I will say this. You and Scott obviously had a very close relationship. It doesn't seem unreasonable to me that he should be reluctant to end the partnership, just because something as irrelevant as death got in the way.'

Jenny was about to offer a scathing reply when she noticed a yellow Morgan roadster motoring sedately up the drive and she recognised it as belonging to the band's bass player, Steve Lampton.

'Well, one of them's here at any rate,' she said, grateful for the chance to change the subject. But then she saw a second car cresting the hill behind the Morgan, a bright red Pontiac Firebird TransAm. It came hammering along in pursuit, weaving erratically from side to side and as it swung out to overtake the Morgan, it suddenly veered off the gravel completely and out on to the lawn, the wheels cutting deep ruts into the rain-soft turf. It slewed around in a series of manic circles as though it was actually in a circus ring. Jenny didn't recognise the woman in the passenger seat but the wild-haired figure crouched malevolently over the steering wheel was all too familiar.

'Oh boy,' she said. 'Somebody's been at the cooking sherry, I think.'

Reed was staring over Jenny's shoulder, his mouth open in an 'O' of indignation. The Pontiac performed a rear end skid, flinging out twin trails of mud, before straightening and heading back onto the drive towards the main entrance, narrowly avoiding a collision with the Morgan. Jenny saw Steve's fist come out of the window, one finger raised to the other driver in the time-honoured gesture. As the two cars moved by the window, Jenny could hear quite clearly the sonic roar of the Pontiac's stereo system.

'Who the fuck is that maniac?' cried Reed. 'He's ruined my lawn!'

Jenny smiled.

'That's our drummer,' she said brightly. 'The more considerate driver is our bass player. Tell you what, why don't you come out and meet them? That's if Obediah has no objections.'

She glanced up at the scowling portrait above the fireplace and laughed dismissively. Then she followed Reed out of the room and through the house to the back courtyard.

Chapter Ten

Descending the stone steps to the courtyard, Jenny saw that Steve Lampton had parked up the Morgan and had managed to manoeuvre his massive frame out of its cramped interior. He was standing there, hands on his hips, staring disdainfully at Chris Spencer's Pontiac which was now careering madly around the cobbled yard in a series of erratic circles.

Steve glanced up as Jenny and Reed approached and his bearded face broke into a welcoming smile. He crossed to the foot of the staircase and gave her a fond hug. It was only because she was several steps higher that she wasn't obliged to stand on tip toe in order to peck him on the cheek. Steve's six foot four height and solid physique had long ago earned him the nickname of 'The Bear'.

Jenny had always had a lot of time for Steve Lampton. The most stable member of The Deceivers, he was also the only one of the current lineup who had ever succumbed to matrimony. Devoted to his wife Peg and their two young daughters, Steve had always seemed to Jenny to be the one reliable rock in an ocean of madness: and just as his simple, metronomic bass lines provided a firm foundation on which the rest of the band could hang their melodies, so it was always to Steve that Jenny looked for her equilibrium in times of uncertainty.

She knew that the other members of the band thought of him as boring and predictable: and his steadfast refusal to participate in the rock n' roll lifestyle inevitably made him the butt of many of their jokes ... but Jenny actually admired the way he was able to detach himself from the craziness all around him. Furthermore, he never seemed to condemn those who *did* choose to wallow in excess, but simply accepted their behaviour in the same quiet, good-natured way that he accepted everything else in his life. Jenny often wondered if Steve Lampton had any dark and awful secrets. If he did, he had managed to conceal them well.

He was dressed today in typical Steve fashion, choosing his clothes for comfort rather than to make some kind of statement. He wore a padded denim jacket, blue jeans and light tan Timberlands. His long brown hair was gathered into a ponytail and a Deceivers black baseball cap disguised the fact that he was receding on top. A casual observer would never have pegged him as a wealthy rock star, but they'd probably have figured out that he was a musician.

'How you doing, big feller?' said Jenny.

'I'm OK. It's good to see you at last.' He stepped back from the embrace and beamed at her amiably. 'Been a while, Jenny. I was beginning to get worried. Thought maybe you were planning to call it a day, something silly like that.'

Jenny sighed. 'Don't think I haven't considered it. Without Scott...'

She didn't finish the sentence but there was no need to. Steve nodded.

'Yeah, I know,' he said. 'I felt the same way for a while. Like I never wanted to set foot on a stage again. Now I'm fairly itching to get back to it. How about you?'

'Still haven't made my mind up one way or the other. I guess we'll just have to see how it goes.'

Steve glanced in the direction of the Pontiac. 'Well, at least Chris is on his usual form. You must have missed *him*.'

Jenny chuckled.

'Yeah, like you'd miss a toothache.' She turned back and introduced Steve to Gareth Reed.

'Nice to meet you.' Steve held out a huge hand to shake. The tips of the fingers and thumb were calloused like the hand of a bricklayer, a result of his preferred 'finger-picking' style of bass playing. He'd never used a plectrum in his life.

'Quite some place you have here,' he observed. 'Lezard told me you restored it from a ruin.'

'That's right ... unfortunately your drummer seems intent on demolishing it.' Reed was staring edgily at the Pontiac which, despite being enclosed in the courtyard, had not noticeably diminished its speed. From the open windows, the stereo was blasting out what sounded suspiciously like Motorhead's *The Ace of Spades*.

'Let me tell you something about Chris,' said Steve, with a grin. 'A lot of people think he's an irresponsible, drug-crazed, mind-fuck.' He paused for effect. 'They are all absolutely right.'

Reed made an attempt to laugh it off.

'I suppose it's just high spirits,' he said.

As it made a turn, the car's front right bumper narrowly avoided hitting an expensive-looking stone balustrade and Reed was unable to suppress a wince.

'Relax,' Steve advised him. 'There's nothing you can do. He'll run out of petrol, he'll run into something or he'll get bored.' A hub cap span off the Pontiac and went flying across the courtyard like a discus. It pinged off a wall, narrowly missing a leaded window. Steve frowned.

'I hope he stays away from my motor,' he muttered. 'I just had it resprayed.'

Steve sounded only slightly worried at the possibility of his beloved Morgan being damaged – his years spent on the road with Chris Spencer had evidently taught him not to hold his personal property in too high esteem.

'How are Peg and the kids?' ventured Jenny.

'They're great. They send their love. More to the point, how are you?'

'Better,' she told him: but was aware even as she said it that her voice lacked conviction. 'I think I'm finally starting to – Jesus, watch out!'

All three of them retreated a short distance up the steps as the Pontiac zoomed past them and back out through the archway again, seeking the less confining reaches of the front drive.

'Let's leave him to it and go inside,' suggested Jenny. 'I expect he'll find his way in when he's finished.'

'OK,' said Reed uneasily. From the look on his face, it was evident that he half expected Chris to gain entry to the house by driving the Pontiac through one of the windows.

'Try not to worry,' Jenny advised him, as they climbed the steps. 'People like Chris are the reason why they invented insurance.'

Reed led them back through the house to the front lounge, where they had a grandstand view of the Pontiac tearing up the lawns. Reed stood at the window, watching anxiously, while Steve and Jenny settled themselves on one of the sofas. They both lit cigarettes and chatted amiably.

'I hear you and Peg have moved into a big new house,' said Jenny.

'Uh ... yeah, big is definitely the word I'd use,' agreed Steve. 'Big and expensive. You'll have to come down and visit some time. You've spent too long hiding yourself away from the world. I heard you'd gone back to Manchester.'

'That's right. Figured I'd look up some of my roots. Chasing after my youth, I guess. But it didn't work out too well. I bumped into Des McGuire one night.'

'Oh, yeah, I remember him. The band's original drummer, wasn't he? Turned up at some gig we did in Manchester a couple of years back . . . the Apollo?'

'Yeah, that's right. Anyway, he's still his charming self. Which means he has all the charm of a snake with haemorrhoids. These days he seems to be dealing for a living.'

'Drummers,' muttered Steve. 'They're always a problem.' He glanced over at Reed. 'How's Damon Hill doing out there?'

'He's getting awfully close to one of the trees,' said Reed apprehensively.

Steve grinned.

'Just be thankful you don't have a swimming pool,' he said.

Reed looked at him quizzically.

'It's Chris's speciality,' explained Jenny. 'Driving cars into swimming pools. It was funny the first time, because it was at an awards ceremony in LA and everyone else was on their best behaviour. Now he seems to feel it's expected of him. It just becomes tedious.'

'He nearly drowned last time,' Steve reminded her. 'That made it a bit more interesting.'

'Oh yeah, I forgot. Who's the girl with him?'

Steve shrugged his broad shoulders.

'Probably some hitch hiker he picked up along the way and refused to let out. You know Chris.'

'Yeah,' said Jenny, regretfully. 'I know Chris.'

'Lezard tells me you've written some new songs,' ventured Steve.

Jenny frowned.

'I've written *something*,' she admitted. 'Whether they qualify as songs is another matter.'

Steve stroked his beard thoughtfully. 'I'm looking forward to hearing them,' he said.

'Well, I hope you're not disappointed. Scott just seemed to have this knack of ... bringing something out in me. And I could always tell from his expression if we had a good product. Now the only person to bounce ideas off is myself. I need to—'

She broke off, wincing at the sound of a sudden loud crash from outside. Glancing up, Jenny saw that Chris had somehow managed to run the Pontiac head on into one of the massive oak trees that flanked the drive. Steam boiled from under the car's crumpled hood and a great cloud of rooks flapped up into the sky, cawing loudly.

'Oh, Jesus,' said Reed. 'He's killed himself!'

He hurried out of the room and Jenny and Steve heard him throw open the front door. Then he was back again a moment later.

'The nearest phone is in the hall,' he shouted to them. 'Jenny, perhaps you'd be good enough to call for...' He hesitated, clearly puzzled by the fact that they seemed to be in no particular hurry to get up off the sofa.

'A tree surgeon?' ventured Jenny brightly: and Steve laughed.

Reed stared at her, astonished by her apparent indifference. 'But the ... crash ... aren't you ... worried?'

Jenny gazed at him for a moment, then laughed scornfully.

'Oh, *he'll* be all right, he's bloody indestructible, our Christopher.' She glanced at Steve. 'Remember that Porsche he wrote off in Detroit? Jesus, how anyone walked out of that is beyond me. Thing looked like a squashed tin can, it took the firemen three hours to cut him out of it.'

'Yeah and he's lying there, talking ten to the dozen and trying to get somebody to light his cigarette,' added Steve. 'There was petrol everywhere, rescue workers were shitting themselves. And after all that the jammy bugger walked out without a scratch.'

'But there's nobody moving out there,' said Reed. 'I really think ... I think we should...' He scuttled out of the room again and they heard his feet crunching on the gravel outside.

Jenny and Steve sighed and exchanged glances.

'I suppose we'd better go and have a look,' said Steve.

'Yeah, right,' agreed Jenny. 'That tree could be seriously damaged.'

Reluctantly, they stubbed out their cigarettes, got to their feet and strolled out to the front garden to see what was happening.

Chapter Eleven

When they caught up with Reed, he was standing a short distance from the car, watching in mute disbelief as Chris Spencer staggered out from behind the wheel. The only evidence of any damage was a discreet smear of blood on his forehead but Jenny knew it couldn't be all that serious, because he'd managed to retain his grip on the bottle of vodka he was holding. Reaching up his free hand to grab the door of the car, he clawed himself upright and stumbled around the vehicle to greet the others.

Chris always put Jenny in mind of some kind of deranged bird, a stork or a crane, maybe. He was tall and stick thin and his dominant feature was the great hooked beak of a nose that seemed to protrude from between two curtains of shaggy black hair. He always wore mirrored shades, indoors or outdoors, presumably in order to conceal the bloodshot pinpricks that were his eyes. He was dressed in a shapeless leopard skin print jacket that looked as if it had been slept in, tight black jeans and a pair of truly hideous snakeskin boots that only served to emphasise his huge, clumsy feet. He grinned, revealing large, nicotine-stained teeth. In one incisor, a tiny diamond sparkled ostentatiously.

'Greetings earthlings. Take me to your larder!' He threw back his head and cackled gleefully. Then he jerked a thumb over his shoulder at the car. 'Had a bit of trouble during re-entry,' he concluded. 'Some idiot planted a tree in me way. Cheers.' He raised the vodka, drained the last of the contents and flung the empty bottle over his shoulder. Then he walked across the grass to the path, fumbling a pack of Marlboros from his pocket as he did so. He lit up and puffed a thick cloud of smoke before speaking again.

'All right, Jenny, you frightful old scrubber. You're looking as rough as the proverbial bear's arse!'

'Thanks. You look like a piece of shit, yourself.' The insulting banter had become a tradition between them. It would have been unthinkable to have dispensed with it.

Chris looked Steve slowly up and down and curled his top lip into a sneer that would have made Elvis envious.

'Steve, you fat bastard! I thought I told you to go on a diet?'

'Yeah, and I told *you* to go on the wagon.'

'I did. Worst fackin' day of my entire life. Lucky I had a stash, or I wouldn't have hung on that long.' He paused, blew out smoke and turned to study the one unfamiliar face in silence for a few moments, as though considering how best to insult him. After lengthy deliberation he simply asked, 'Who's the gimp?'

'This is Gareth Reed,' said Jenny, trying not to smile at Reed's outraged expression. 'He owns the studio. And before you insult him further, it's only fair to warn you that he may also be producing our next album.'

'Yeah?' Chris cocked his head to one side, a habitual gesture. 'I like snare, Gareth, all right?' Chris thumped an imaginary drum with his left hand and waved his cigarette over an equally imaginary ride cymbal. 'I mean, *lots* of snare.'

Reed nodded.

'I get the general idea,' he said cooly. Jenny sensed his instant dislike of the drummer, but there was nothing unusual in that. Most people disliked Chris on first meeting. It was only when you'd had a chance to get to know him that you had to admit a grudging admiration for the way he survived against all odds.

Though Jenny constantly made disparaging remarks about Chris, the truth was that she enjoyed being in his company. She loved the sheer unpredictability of it. Chris was an agent of chaos, an arrested adolescent who saw the world as a gigantic rumpus room for him to run wild in. Yes, he could be a pain in the arse most of the time, but then, so could lots of people, in much quieter, more devious ways. Chris made no compromises. He did what he wanted, when he wanted and never gave a thought to the consequences.

Over the years, Jenny had seen him shovel enough drink and drugs into his system to finish off the population of a small country: but somehow, he always came out of it in one piece, slightly dazed and profoundly unrepentant. Despite his frail appearance, he had the constitution of a bull ox. Years ago, when he'd first joined the band, Jenny had assumed that if any member of The Deceivers would eventually succumb to death by drugs, Chris, not Scott, would be the most likely casualty.

'So what's new?' Chris demanded. 'Where's that mincing pouf, Langan?'

'Not here yet,' Steve told him.

'Typical. I drove like a fackin' maniac to get here.'

'That's how you always drive,' said Jenny.

He didn't contradict her.

'So who else are we waiting for? Lezard?'

'He's already here. So it's just Adrian, Mike Watton and . . .' She glanced sharply at Steve. 'The new kid.'

Steve frowned, glanced away. There was an uncomfortable silence, broken only by the distant cawing of rooks.

'Yeah, I hear "kid" is the operative word,' said Chris. 'From what Steve's told me, he's barely out of short trousers. By all accounts, Adey picked him up off the meat rack in Piccadilly.'

Jenny winced at that one. Adrian Langan had never made any secret of his sexual preferences, but Chris always seemed to take a particular delight in taunting him about it. Lezard had certainly given her no indication that the new guitarist was one of Adrian's 'conquests'. She glanced sharply at Steve.

'That true?' she asked him.

Steve looked uncomfortable.

'I don't see that it matters,' he retorted. 'The kid can play, so...'

'The point I'm making is that Adrian isn't going to be entirely objective about Porter's ability, is he? And you know Adrian, once he decides on something, a stick of dynamite won't deter him. I'd like to be able to have the option of saying "no", that's all.'

'Well, you listened to the tape we made, didn't you? I asked Lezard to pass on a copy.'

Jenny shrugged.

'I mislaid it,' she lied.

Steve frowned, glanced at Chris.

'I don't suppose you...?'

Chris held up his hands in a helpless gesture.

'I never even *saw* my copy,' he said. 'I had a friend staying with me and I think he may have taped over it, by mistake.'

'Great,' muttered Steve. 'Perfect. Why did we bother?'

Chris changed the subject promptly.

'I don't know about you,' he said, 'but I could murder a drink.'

'You surprise me,' said Steve.

'Well, the table *is* all set for lunch,' announced Reed. He glanced at his watch. 'It's well past the appointed time, so I suppose we could go in and start without the others.'

'Sounds good to me, squire.' Chris gazed up at the ancient edifice of the old monastery. 'I trust there'll be flagons of ale served by lusty, buxom wenches? Hey, I can be the court jester! I'll be good at that. I know that old routine, you know, the flagon with the dragon and the chalice from the palace . . .' He had started to walk towards the building but Jenny placed a restraining hand on his shoulder.

'Hang on,' she said. 'Aren't you forgetting something?'

Chris gave her a blank look.

'Like what?' he muttered.

'Like, aren't you going to introduce us to your passenger? That is, if the poor kid hasn't bashed her brains out against the windscreen.'

'Fack, I forgot about her!'

Chris did an elaborate pantomime of dismay. He wheeled around and ran back to the car, flinging open the passenger door to reveal the girl slumped back in her seat. Her eyes were closed but whether she was asleep, unconscious or inebriated, it was hard to say.

'Emma, wake up, we're here!' he yelled. He shook her roughly by the shoulder and she sat up, blinking around at the unfamiliar location. She was maybe sixteen, seventeen years old, Jenny thought, a punky-looking waif with Afro plaits and severe makeup that made her look like she'd been punched repeatedly around the eyes. She wore a T-shirt with the word 'Slag' emblazoned upon it in shocking pink: a black micro skirt and fishnet stockings, the feet of which were tucked into Doc Martens high lace ups. Judging by the size of her pupils, which resembled two drops of black tar, she was very stoned: more disturbingly, Jenny thought that there was something naggingly familiar about her.

'Come on, darlin',' Chris prompted her. 'Get your shit together. We've arrived!'

The girl covered a yawn with one hand, the fingernails painted black. Then she put a skinny leg out onto terra firma and pulled herself unsteadily out of the car.

'Jesus,' she said. 'I dreamed we had a crash.' Her stoned gaze wandered across to Jenny and her mouth rearranged itself into an unpleasant sneer. 'Jenny Slade!' she observed. 'In the flesh and larger than life. This is a real pleasure.'

'Do I know you?' asked Jenny, suspiciously.

'Jenny, I'd like to introduce Emma Savage,' Chris announced. 'My fiancée.'

'Your . . . ?' Jenny was stunned, not so much by the news that Chris was engaged – he got engaged on a regular basis but the liaisons rarely lasted past a couple of days – but because she had just realised why the girl's face had seemed so familiar. She normally saw it scowling at her in black and white from the header of the weekly lifestyle column she wrote. 'For God's sake, Chris, what the hell is *she* doing here?'

Emma Savage was a journalist of sorts. At the tender age of fourteen she'd started her career writing for a fanzine called *Flesh Wounds*, an irregular journal devoted to filth, depravity and scurrilous rumour. The fanzine had survived for less than a year but Emma had quickly been snapped up by one of the quality Sunday papers and touted as 'the voice of the blank generation'. Now she wrote a weekly column where she held forth about music, cinema, videos and fashion, employing a smug, bitchy, precocious tone that attempted (and generally succeeded) in getting up as many noses as was humanly possible.

One of her habitual targets was the aging rock star: in Emma Savage's oft-voiced opinion, any musician over the age of twenty-five had a moral obligation to pack it in and make way for new talent.

But what had really bugged Jenny was a recent article about 'celebrity deaths', which included a claim that Scott Griffin's demise had been 'a pathetic attempt to score some much needed street-cred'. It was a flip, sneering remark made by somebody who was herself obsessed with her own ice cool image but Jenny had been unable to laugh it off. With the originator of the remark standing right in front of her, she was even less inclined to be forgiving. Indeed, it occurred to her that a punch in the teeth might be the most satisfying way of demonstrating her feelings on the matter. Meanwhile, Chris was staring at Jenny open mouthed, as though he couldn't understand why she should be anything less than welcoming to his latest girlfriend.

'Is there a problem?' he asked.

'A slight one. Your young friend there just happens to be a sleazy little hack who slags off bands like The Deceivers for a living.'

Chris looked affronted.

'I know that,' he said. 'But she's not here in a ... whatsit, professional capacity, are you, Em?'

'Of course not.' Emma smiled with exaggerated sweetness. 'I'm on vacation, aren't I? I just wanted to spend a bit of time with Chris.' She slipped an arm around the drummer's waist as though trying to emphasise the point.

'Oh right, so it's love, is it?' Jenny smirked. 'Pull the other one! I suppose the prospect of sitting in on one of our recording sessions was never even a consideration?' She turned to face Chris. 'She's trying it on, you pillock. Get rid of her.'

'Hey now, just a minute.' Chris was rapidly becoming indignant. 'I told you, we're practically engaged.'

'Since when?'

'Since the other night. Since we met at . . . a concert . . . in . . .' He looked confused and Jenny knew that he couldn't actually remember the details. Short term memory loss was an inevitable consequence of ingesting so many dangerous chemicals. 'Anyway, when I told her I was coming up here, Emma said she'd like to come along, just to, you know, hang out with the band and stuff.'

'And you honestly think she wouldn't mention it in her column?' cried Jenny. 'Get real, Chris! She just saw an opportunity to dish some dirt. Or did you think she was after you for your sex appeal?'

'Probably saw him as a father figure,' said Steve, grinning.

'You cheeky facker!' protested Chris. 'I can still give these youngsters a run for their money. Just because you're past it, there's no need to point the finger at me.'

Emma, meanwhile, was defiantly standing her ground, glaring at Jenny the whole time.

'I know what you're angry about,' Emma said. Her voice was slurred, probably from a mixture of alcohol and Quaaludes, judging by the sound. It resembled a tape recorder that was gradually running out of power. 'It's that comment I made about Scott Griffin, right? But fuck, that was just a flip remark. It didn't mean anything.'

'Your whole career doesn't mean anything,' Jenny told her. 'That's hardly the point. What infuriates me is when a jumped-up little no-talent like you has the nerve to insult the memory of a gifted musician like Scott.'

Steve took an exaggerated intake of breath. He glanced at Reed and grinned.

'Only here five minutes and things are hotting up already!' he observed. 'Next thing you know they'll be scratching each other's eyes out.'

'Err ... yes, look maybe we should go inside for some lunch?' suggested Reed, sensing a potential bloodbath.

'Suits me,' said Jenny. 'But *she* stays out here.'

'No way!' protested Emma. 'I'm with Chris. We're *engaged.*'

'Sure, until he wakes up tomorrow and can't remember who you are! Besides, I thought you didn't have a lot of time for aging rock stars. Sleeping with one is a bit of a double standard, don't you think? Especially one as fucked up as Chris.'

'Now that was unkind,' said Chris. He looked at Steve for support. 'Wasn't that unkind?'

Steve stroked his beard.

'Yeah, but you must admit, there was a certain amount of truth in it.'

Chris bridled. He drew his skinny body up to his full height and crossed his arms over his chest.

'Listen, if she don't stay, *I* don't stay,' he announced. 'I thought this band was a democracy, not the fackin' Jenny Slade show.'

'Maybe we should let her in,' reasoned Steve. 'And what the hell, let her write whatever she wants. Could be good publicity.'

'Oh, I can imagine! Listen, Steve, to her we're dinosaurs that should have become extinct years ago. She'll do the literary equivalent of a Jack the Ripper murder on us.'

'I already told you,' said Emma. 'I'm just here to hang out. I've got no axe to grind and I've got absolutely no intention of mentioning it in my column. Honest.'

Jenny took a step closer to the girl and prodded her sparrow chest with an index finger.

'That had better be true, kid. Because if I detect one sniff of you writing anything about what happens here, I'll have a major law suit slapped on you, pronto. I'll personally fix it so you won't be able to sharpen a fucking pencil without paying a fine. Do I make myself clear?'

'Perfectly,' said Emma, through gritted teeth.

'Good. Just so we understand each other.' She stepped back from Emma and looked at the circle of anxious faces in front of her. She was starting to feel a little bit more like her old self, she thought. Maybe it wasn't going to be so bad after all. 'Well then,' she concluded. 'We'll go in and have that lunch, shall we? And while we're eating, Steve can tell us all about The Deceivers' wonderful new guitarist.'

Steve's normally jovial face became a mask of apprehension. Chris grinned and slapped him on the back, doubtless grateful that the heat had been transferred to somebody else.

'There you go, Stevie boy,' he chortled. 'Better make it good!'

'This way,' said Gareth Reed, uneasily, and he led them back along the drive and in through the front door of the house.

A loud cawing noise made Jenny glance back over her shoulder. Up in the oak tree, above the steaming wreckage of the Pontiac, the rooks were congregating again, coming back to stake their claim in the naked branches.

Chapter Twelve

In the dining room, Cassie had laid out a sumptuous cold buffet on the huge oak table. Bottles of red and white wine were already open and, nearby, a well-stocked bar was available for those who liked something harder to accompany the meal.

Gareth Reed took a seat at the head of the long table. Jenny and Steve settled themselves to his left and Chris and Emma slid on to a couple of high-backed chairs to his right.

'Fack me,' said Chris, grinning. 'Looks like the second sitting for the Last Supper!'

Josh Lezard appeared in the doorway. He'd changed into a pair of jeans and a sweatshirt and Jenny felt a dull stab of surprise. In all the years she'd known him, she'd never seen him wear anything other than his trademark Armani suits. He took the vacant seat next to Steve and greeted him and Chris.

'I thought I heard you arriving,' he told Chris, drily. Chris grinned and introduced him to Emma Savage.

'*The* Emma Savage?' asked Lezard – and Emma looked very pleased with herself.

'The one and only,' she said.

'This is an honour,' said Lezard, reaching across the table to shake her hand.

'Stop crawling,' Jenny told him tartly. 'It's not an honour, it's a bloody imposition and she's been warned to behave herself while she's here.'

'Ah . . . yes, right.' Lezard made a valiant attempt to change the subject. 'The food looks delicious,' he observed, rubbing his hands together in a show of appreciation: but there was no disguising the hostile atmosphere around the table.

'Well, please, make a start,' suggested Reed, anxious to mellow everybody out. 'Cassie, perhaps you'd like to do the honours.'

Cassie picked up a couple of bottles of wine and went dutifully around the table charging up the glasses. Steve began to fill his plate from the selection of cold meats, cheeses and salads on offer but Jenny just picked halfheartedly at whatever was within reach, while Chris and Emma ignored the food completely.

'I try to avoid eating,' Chris told Reed, with a sly wink. 'I find it interferes with me drinking. Still, cheers.' He raised a glass of chardonnay and drained it in a single swallow. Then he waggled the empty glass meaningfully at Cassie. She moved obediently back around the table and topped him up again. 'I can see we're going to get on famously,' said Chris, putting his head on one side and studying her intently. 'I like a woman that's generous with the drinks.'

Cassie blushed but smiled with evident pleasure.

'Must be your dream date,' said Jenny. 'Refills your glass at the drop of a hat.' She noted the glowering look that Emma directed across the table at her and she awarded herself a Brownie point. Winding up Emma Savage was clearly going to be one of the few pleasures of her stay at The Grange.

'Well, here's to a successful partnership,' said Reed with exaggerated cheerfulness. He raised a glass of mineral water in a toast.

'Jumping the gun a bit, aren't we?' muttered Steve, through

a mouthful of wholemeal bread and pâté. 'We haven't exactly decided if we're using you yet.'

Reed looked crestfallen.

'Oh no, I was just referring to our session *here*. A new album is another matter entirely.'

'Too right it is,' agreed Chris. 'And I don't much like the idea of working with a producer who proposes toasts in fackin' Perrier Water.' He motioned to Cassie. 'Pour him a glass of alcohol, for Christ's sake!'

'No, really,' protested Reed. 'I never drink in the daytime. It doesn't agree with me.'

'Bugger that, squire. We'll have you on a bottle of vodka and forty fags a day by the time we've finished with you. Give him a glass of white, darlin', it'll match his complexion.'

Cassie poured the wine and Reed looked helplessly along the table at Lezard. The American simply shrugged his shoulders.

'I *did* warn you about this, Gareth. Working with The Deceivers can be detrimental to your health.' He reached up a hand to pat his head of prematurely grey hair. 'When I started with them, this was jet black.'

'Bollocks!' said Jenny. 'It was just the shock of having to pay out that first big royalty cheque for *Blood Heat*. Changed colour overnight.'

Everyone laughed at this remark and the ice in the room seemed to thaw a little. Jenny studied Reed for a moment, a glint of mockery in her eyes.

'We'll have to see what changes we can make to you,' she observed. 'A couple of lines wouldn't go amiss on that baby face of yours. Give it a bit more character.'

Reed smiled and took a tentative sip of his wine.

'I'm older than I look,' he assured her. 'What you see here is just the result of good clean living. Early nights, a healthy diet and no drugs or cigarettes.' He glanced ruefully at his glass. 'And hardly any alcohol.'

'Jesus,' muttered Emma. 'Who are you, Julie Andrews's love child?' She waggled her empty glass at Cassie, clearly irritated that she wasn't getting the same prompt service that Chris had received. 'Hey, Jennifer Juniper! Who do you have to go down on around here to get another drink?'

'Oh, sorry, I didn't notice...' Cassie topped up Emma's glass but Jenny didn't much like the way Emma had spoken to the girl.

'Hey, Cassie, why don't we dispense with the servant/master routine?' she said. 'We're all adult enough to help ourselves to whatever we need. In fact, why don't you sit down and join us?'

'Oh, er... I don't know.' Cassie glanced uneasily at Reed as though seeking his permission, but he just shrugged non-commitally. 'Maybe later,' she concluded. 'I've got the sweets and coffee to attend to.' She put down the bottles and went through to the kitchen.

'Well, you sure got that one well trained,' sneered Emma, and for once, Jenny found herself in agreement. Cassie seemed somehow to be a throwback to less liberated times when a woman's main ambition was to stand in the background and serve the menfolk. It was a role that didn't fit with her New Age image one little bit.

'I don't take any responsibility for Cassie,' said Reed dismissively. 'You'd best talk to Idris about that.'

Chris grinned inanely.

'Me, I'm all in favour of women doing what they're told.'

'So it would seem,' said Jenny coldly. 'I take it you were in on the recruitment of our new lead guitarist, behind my back?'

Chris looked dismayed.

'I didn't know anything about it,' he told her. 'Honest,

Jenny, that was Adrian and Steve. You know they never tell me anything. I didn't even know about our last tour until three days before it started!'

Lezard frowned.

'Oh, come on, Jenny, we already discussed this. And I explained to you that...'

'Yes, I know, I was in too much of a state to be bothered with a tiny detail like that. And naturally, I have the power of veto.'

'Absolutely. So I don't see the problem.'

'I'll tell you the problem, Josh. For one thing, I get the distinct feeling that his joining The Deceivers is already a foregone conclusion. And if Adrian really is...' She caught herself at the last moment, reminding herself that Emma Savage was likely to repeat anything she heard here through the mouthpiece of her weekly column. Adrian was no closet homosexual but he might not want the entire country to read about his proclivities over their Rice Crispies and toast. 'If Adrian's already *keen* on the kid, it's going to be pretty damned difficult to give him the brush off, isn't it?'

'Why would you want to?' muttered Steve. 'He's a bloody good guitarist.'

'It doesn't matter if he's Eric Clapton, Jimi Hendrix and B.B. King all rolled into one. I just might not get on with him.'

'Hard to imagine that,' said Emma caustically. 'Maybe it's his *age* that worries you, Jenny. After all, he's only twenty-five and he's a good-looking boy. I can appreciate it might make you feel threatened.'

'What do you know about it?' snapped Jenny, irritably. She fixed Chris with an accusing glare but he just spread his hands in a gesture of helplessness.

'Didn't know it was supposed to be a big secret,' he muttered. 'Anyway, Em already knew him.'

'Oh yes?' Jenny scowled across the table and Emma simpered, enjoying having the upper hand for the moment. She flicked a strand of hair out of her kohl-lined eyes.

'Yeah, from when he played lead guitar with The Coprophiliacs. They had that single, you know, *Gob Shite*? It didn't do anything despite the record company doing big time payola on it. Anyway, Robbie was all wrong for that group. He was too good looking and he could play his instrument.' She took a swallow of wine, leaving two red smudges at the corners of her mouth. 'To be honest, I'm not convinced that musicians have any place in rock music, these days.' It was a typical Emma Savage comment and could have been lifted straight from one of her columns: probably *had* been, Jenny thought. It was obviously designed to infuriate her companions but Jenny was determined not to lose her cool over it.

'You may as well fuck off home, then,' she said calmly. 'It's going to be hell for you here. All those annoying chords and riffs and melodies.'

Emma sniggered.

'I'll look on it as an education,' she said.

In the ensuing silence, they all heard the sound of a car engine outside, the smooth mellow purr of a vintage Rolls-Royce Silver Cloud.

'That'll be Adey's Skoda,' said Chris, and he collapsed over the table, laughing. For some reason, he had always found Adrian Langan's choice of transport an absolute hoot.

'I'll go and meet them,' said Lezard. He glanced warily at Jenny. 'I believe Adrian and Robbie were travelling down together. At least give the guy a chance, huh?'

Jenny rolled her eyes at the ceiling but said nothing. She reached for her cigarettes and lit one up as Lezard went out of the door. Steve pushed his empty plate away and wiped his mouth on a serviette.

'Look, Jenny, I just thought it was for the best, really. Adrian was raving about the kid and the demos he made were great. But I didn't mean...'

'Forget it.' Jenny lifted a hand to silence him. 'It was an unusual situation and I guess unusual measures were called for. But if I don't like him, I'm leaving it to you and Adrian to give him the boot, OK?'

'Gee thanks.' Steve glanced down the table at Gareth Reed. 'She's all heart, this one. You'd better pray she gets on with you or it could be two sackings before the day's out.'

Reed smiled serenely.

'Oh, I'm a great believer in destiny, Steve. The first time I heard *Love's Like a Hunger*, I knew Jenny and I were going to work together one day. Whether it happens now or later doesn't really matter.'

'Maybe you should go back to the Perrier Water,' muttered Chris. 'You're starting to sound like Mystic Meg on a bad day.'

Reed laughed.

'You can make fun of it, by all means. But I know what I know. Jenny is a special talent and she just needs the right producer to bring out the best in her. That happens to be me.'

Now it was Emma's turn to laugh.

'Excuse *me*! That's pretty big talk for a guy who's produced, what ... *three* records.'

'Three *platinum* records,' Reed corrected her. 'Not that the figures matter, that's just a side issue. To me, it's more important that each of those records captured the respective band's essence to the maximum. I won't compromise the integrity of any musicians I work with.'

'Sounds like somebody's making a pitch,' observed Steve coolly.

'Big time,' agreed Jenny: but once again, she found herself impressed by Gareth Reed's apparent sincerity, by the way he wasn't afraid to blow his own trumpet. He was sitting there now, his hands caressing the bowl of his wine glass and he was gazing at her with those sexy, brown eyes, giving her a tingle in a place where she hadn't tingled for what seemed like years . . .

Her reverie was interrupted by the arrival of Adrian Langan and Robbie Porter. Adrian stalked into the room, his skinny figure enveloped in a voluminous sheepskin coat, his thinning red hair slicked back against his skull with gel. He appraised the diners quickly with his small, ice-blue eyes and nodded curtly to each in turn, his gaze lingering slightly longer on Emma, one of the unfamiliar faces. Then, stepping to one side, he held out a hand like a nightclub compère introducing the next act on the bill.

'Robbie Porter,' he said: and the newcomer stepped nervously forward, smiling inanely at the seated people. Jenny experienced a sinking feeling in her gut. She'd been warned to expect young and handsome but she hadn't expected beautiful: and frankly that was the only word that did Robbie Porter justice. He was tall and gangly with a mane of curly jet black hair that wouldn't have disgraced Cher. His hazel eyes were almost too large in that delicately featured face and Jenny was reminded of a young Marc Bolan. His clothes were 70s Oxfam-grunge. A pair of green crushed velvet flares did visual combat with a leopard print velour shirt and a red PVC duffle coat. Jenny found herself thinking that if the kid stayed, the first thing would be to get him into some decent threads. His current outfit made Jonathan Ross look like a snappy dresser.

'Nice to meet you,' mumbled Robbie: and he held out a hand to Jenny, who shook it obligingly. 'I'm a big fan,' he added.

That remark lost him several Brownie points in Jenny's eyes. Just once, she'd like to meet somebody who said, 'Hey, you're really crap.'

'So, you're the guy who thinks he can replace Scott Griffin,' she said. She saw Steve wince and instantly regretted the remark. Given Robbie's situation it was decidedly cruel, but he seemed to take it in his stride.

'It's always been my ambition to play for The Deceivers but I wouldn't have wished it this way in a million years.' He had a soft, lilting voice that was almost girlish, and Jenny could imagine how this beautiful youth had so captivated Adrian Langan, a man who had always listed *Death in Venice* as his all time favourite movie. 'Scott was one of my biggest influences. When I was a kid I used to pose in the mirror with a tennis racket, pretending I was playing one of his solos.' He smiled. 'Eventually, I got bored with posing and bought an old guitar. The first song I ever learned to play was *Looking for Action*.'

Jenny sighed. One of her favourite cuts from the very first Deceivers album, *Night Drive*. It was going to be hard not to like Robbie.

'But you must have been in primary school when that came out,' she observed.

He nodded.

'I had an older brother who was a big fan, so the music was always kicking around in the background, even when I was playing with my Lego set. I was fifteen when *Blood Heat* came out. That was the one that made me want to be a musician.'

Adrian shot an enquiring look at Jenny.

'You've listened to the tape?' he asked her.

She shook her head.

'I'm afraid I didn't get round to it. Neither did Chris.'

'Typical!' Adrian looked more irritated at the news than Steve had, but this was no great surprise. The fastidious keyboard player had never been one to tolerate the failings of less organised individuals. A bit of a martinet, Adrian lived on his nerves and tended to get on everyone else's in the process. Of all the long-time members of The Deceivers, he was the one that Jenny had the most problems with. His usual gripe was about her lack of punctuality, so it gave her irrational pleasure that today, it was actually Adrian who was late. She couldn't resist rubbing it in a little, glancing at her wristwatch and raising an eyebrow.

'We'd about given you up,' she said.

'Ah, yes, the traffic was hellish on the way,' said Adrian defensively. 'And I had to pick up Robbie from his place in Dagenham.'

'Dagenham!' exclaimed Chris. 'I knew a girl lived there once. At least ... I *think* it was Dagenham. Or was it Tottenham?'

Everybody ignored him.

'Why don't you two sit down and eat something?' suggested Lezard. Adrian and Robbie took vacant seats beside each other and Lezard introduced them to Gareth Reed and Emma Savage. Jenny was pleased to see that Adrian was as annoyed about the latter's presence as she had been, but he didn't comment on the fact, preferring to concentrate his attention on trumpeting the virtues of his protégé.

'Robbie had a stab at some of the songs on *Red Tape* last night,' he told Steve. 'Made a bloody good job of it, too.'

'Yeah?' Steve glanced warily at Jenny, unsure about how to react to the news.

'Yes, he had this brilliant idea for *Seventh Heaven*. Tell him, Robbie!'

Robbie was putting together the ingredients of a ham and salad sandwich but he looked up and smiled self-consciously.

'Well, you know how Scott just played the straight chord sequence at the beginning? I tried an overdub, picking out the notes as a riff and using a bottle neck for a kind of Ry Cooder sound. It gives the song a whole different feel ...' He sensed he may have overstepped the mark and he glanced apologetically at Jenny. 'It was just an experiment. I mean, I could play it the same old way if you prefer...'

'Oh no, by all means,' said Jenny coldly. 'Do whatever you think. But remember, it *is* just an audition.'

'Yes, of course. I realise that.' Robbie went meekly back to his ham sandwich.

'Can you sing?' Jenny asked him. 'Scott used to handle the backing vocals.'

Robbie opened his mouth to reply but Adrian got there first.

'Can he sing? Are you kidding? He's got a great voice, haven't you, Robbie? You should hear him doing *Bad to the Bone*. You know, the old George Thoroughgood number?'

'I did lead vocals in my last outfit,' said Robbie quietly.

'Oh yes. What was that song again?' Jenny raised her eyebrows. '*Gob Shite*.'

Robbie's pretty face reddened to a deeper shade.

'Yeah, well, it was no rock classic, that's for sure.'

'Robbie was wasted in that outfit,' said Adrian. 'He's got my vote, anyway. And I know Steve's all in favour of bringing him on board.'

Steve looked vaguely alarmed at this revelation.

'Er... well, now, I... never exactly said...'

'So it's just down to you and Chris. And in the event of a two way split, I suggest that Josh should have the casting vote.'

Jenny reached across the table and stubbed out her cigarette on a used plate, a habit that she knew Adrian couldn't abide.

'Oh, that would be very convenient, wouldn't it,' she said. 'Since Josh has already been converted to the faith. Unfortunately, it doesn't work like that. As the last original member of the band, I have the ultimate say over any personnel changes. If you'd care to cast your mind back, Adrian, you'll remember that it was Scott and me who hired you, all those years ago. And I don't recall Steve and Chris being consulted on the matter.'

'Just as fackin' well,' observed Chris. 'Otherwise Adey would still be playing the Wurlitzer at the Brighton Hippodrome!'

Adrian ignored the remark. He looked at Lezard.

'That right?' he demanded.

'I'm afraid so. You boys are still technically hired hands. Jenny has the right to hire and fire as she pleases.'

There was a brief silence while Adrian considered this information, tapping a carefully manicured fingernail on the table.

'Hardly seems fair,' he said. 'I mean, now Scott's gone, it's surely time we were assigned some say in the running of the band.'

'That's for Jenny to decide,' Lezard told him. 'And don't forget, she still writes the songs.'

'Ah, yes,' purred Adrian. 'Somebody mentioned that you'd come up with some new numbers. Good, are they?'

Jenny felt that every set of eyes around the table had turned expectantly in her direction. She could feel the force of their combined gaze burning into her like hot brands. A wave of anxiety went through her and suddenly she wanted very much to be out of the room, away from their scrutiny. She got to her feet, knocking over a glass of wine as she did so.

'Think I'll go for a walk,' she announced to the table in general. 'I could use some fresh air.'

'I'll come with you,' offered Gareth Reed 'There are some nice walks through the forest, if you—'

'I'd rather be on my own,' she told him, bluntly.

'Yes, of course. But at least let me—'

But Jenny was already heading for the door, leaving an uneasy silence in her wake. She walked along the hallway and let herself out through the front door. She stood for a moment on the step, gazing uncertainly around. A light snow had begun to fall and away to her left, the gardens stretched a hundred yards to a thick wall of forest. At one point this was intersected by a wide avenue which seemed to offer a logical place to enter.

She headed in that direction, strolling past the wreckage of Chris's car, barely thinking about where she was going. She just knew that she needed to put some distance between herself and the other members of the band. Up in the trees the rooks seemed to be staring down at her and, close up, the infernal racket they were making seemed almost deafening.

After a few minutes' brisk walk she was in amongst the trees and following a winding trail that led deep into the forest.

Running away again, she thought glumly, but she didn't slow down. She found herself thinking about a similar location from a couple of years ago, a pine forest in Oslo where the band had found time for a video shoot in the middle of a major European tour. There had been thick snow on the ground and Chris had the bright idea of staging a snowball fight, so they could edit highlights into the video for their Christmas single, *Distant Star*. Scott had been heavily into his speed freak phase at the time and he'd sprinted around the forest like a madman, flinging huge snowballs with deadly accuracy, making Adrian's balding head his chief target.

Adrian had been far from amused but Jenny and Scott had laughed like a pair of lunatics, laughed till the tears ran down their faces. Times like that were rare on the road so it was little wonder that the incident stuck in her mind. And maybe it was the fact that snow was falling and Scott was already in her head, that made her think that she saw him up ahead of her, a distant figure walking away from her along the corridor of trees . . .

She stopped in her tracks with a gasp of surprise and looked again. Her heart leapt into her throat as she realised that this was no figment of her imagination. There really was a figure up there, flitting in and out of the shadows, his slim frame bundled into a thick wool jacket over the collar of which his long blond hair trailed down to his shoulders . . .

'Scott?' she whispered – then realised how ridiculous such a notion was. Scott was dead and the thing from the other night merely a vivid dream, conjured from her fear and insecurity. And yet wasn't there something terribly familiar about that distant figure? She thought about shouting after him but in the silence of the surrounding forest, such an action would have seemed like desecration. She did the only thing she could do.

She followed, quickening her pace in an attempt to shorten the distance between herself and her quarry. And when the figure stepped suddenly off the track and into the gloom of the trees, she did likewise, steeling herself against the moment when the daylight was extinguished. It was dark in there and eerily silent, save for the rhythmic crunching of twigs and dead leaves beneath her feet.

But she had to follow. She had to know if what she was seeing was really Scott Griffin's ghost, and if it was, to find out what it was he wanted from her. She remembered the weird kid back at her mother's house.

I talked to Scott Griffin last night. He isn't happy. He wants to speak to you.

She remembered too, the flip reply she had given.

'Tell Scott to get in touch.'

Maybe that was exactly what he had done.

Hardly daring to breathe, Jenny slipped through the ranks of tightly packed trees, following the distant figure as it moved deeper and deeper into the forest.

Chapter Thirteen

She had been following the man for fifteen minutes when he disappeared – or at least, *seemed* to disappear. His figure had passed behind a thick screen of brambles and when Jenny reached the spot, he was simply nowhere to be seen. She stood for a moment, gazing around in confusion at the closely packed ranks of tree trunks surrounding her, searching for a glimpse of movement, but here in the depths of the forest everything seemed imbued with an unnatural stillness.

She experienced a strange mingling of frustration and relief – the latter because she had been asking herself what she would do if she caught up with the man and it really *was* Scott. She imagined him turning back to look at her with those dead, staring eyes and she shrugged her jacket tighter around herself as a shudder of pure dread went through her. She remembered the dream she'd had, the awful embrace of Scott's cold arms, the way he'd held her immobile as he did things to her that he'd never have done in real life.

Now that the mysterious figure had gone, she had a strange sense of unreality about the whole thing. Had she really seen someone, or was it yet another hallucination, dredged up from her confused senses? Not for the first time she wondered if she was going crazy.

She turned back to face the direction she had just come from

– or at least, the direction she *thought* she had come from, but here too she was confounded. She felt a stab of disquiet as she realised she couldn't even be sure of that. In every direction, the view looked exactly the same, acre upon acre of gnarled, lichen-encrusted tree trunks with not a familiar landmark in sight. In the city it was so easy, you navigated by one pub or church after another. Here there were just trees and trees and more trees and apart from a rudimentary knowledge of the different species, she had no other way of telling them apart. The carpet of rotting leaves on the ground showed no indication of any footprints for her to retrace her steps and glancing upwards to the canopy of bare branches overhead, what little she could see of the afternoon sky appeared to be darkening rapidly. Glancing at her watch she saw that it was already four thirty and the thought of being stranded out here at night was not an agreeable one.

She started walking back in what she hoped was the right direction, telling herself that it would take maybe fifteen minutes to reach the path from which she had strayed – but she walked for twenty-five and seemed to be as deep in cover as ever. Every so often, she saw something that looked vaguely familiar. That outgrowth of slimy grey fungus sprouting from the bole of an ancient oak. She'd passed that earlier, hadn't she? And that fallen birch, the thick roots sticking up from the broken soil like a gorgon's head of fleshy serpents. Hadn't she been obliged to make a detour around that shortly before the blond-haired man had vanished?

Becoming desperate now, she found herself altering course every time she saw something that seemed to strike a chord of recognition, stumbling frantically this way and that. She knew only too well that she could quite easily be heading back into the deep forest. The light was draining out of the day at a terrible speed and it seemed to her fevered imagination that the trees were beginning to crowd in on her, sometimes so tightly packed that low-lying branches snagged at her clothes or she was obliged to change direction in order to get past them.

'I'm going round in fucking circles!' she announced to the forest at large. She had said it quietly but her voice seemed to echo in the silence, unnerving her. She glanced at her watch and saw that an hour had elapsed since she left the house. She could scarcely believe it. 'Oh Jesus,' she whispered. She reached out an arm to pull aside a low hanging branch and something exploded up into the air with an abrupt flapping of wings, almost making her jump out of her skin.

A wood pigeon. She could make out its plump body skimming away in the half-light and Jenny forced an unconvincing laugh: but the incident had scared her badly and her flesh was creeping. She was on the verge of panic and she felt a powerful impulse to weep like a frightened child but she told herself not to be pathetic. She'd been in worse jams than this. If she just kept her head, she'd be fine. All she needed was—

Then she saw it. Up ahead of her, the trees seemed to be thinning out. With a fresh surge of hope, she scrambled forward, telling herself not to run. In the uncertain light she could fall over a root and break her ankle; that would be all she needed. But yes, she hadn't been mistaken, only fifty yards ahead of her the tree line came to a sudden halt with a symmetry that could only be man-made. The track, it must be the track...

But it wasn't. She emerged into a large clearing where the trees had been systematically felled, the roots dug out of the unyielding soil: and within the clearing there was a stone circle, a ring of huge granite monoliths, each one some twelve or fifteen feet in height, regularly spaced. Jenny approached the circle and, passing between two of the stones, she stepped into its perimeter. The silence seemed to deepen – or rather, there appeared to be an entirely different quality to it. It was a silence you could hear.

She thought she discerned a low thrumming as though the stones were imbued with some kind of electrical power. She counted them and saw that there were thirteen. They were vaguely man-shaped, narrower at the base, widening to what would have been the shoulders. At some point in time, chisels had rounded the tops. She approached the nearest and placed the palm of one hand against the rough, lichen-covered surface and she thought that she sensed a low vibration in the granite, the faintest shudder against her fingertips, the feeling you got when you put your hand on a steel rail as a distant train approached.

'Quite a buzz, isn't it?' said a voice directly behind her: and she whipped around with a gasp of terror. Gareth Reed was standing on the other side of the circle, leaning nonchalantly against one of the stones.

'Jesus, you scared the shit out of me!' snapped Jenny. 'What's the idea of creeping up like that?'

He looked dismayed.

'Sorry, I didn't mean to scare you. I was getting a bit worried. Came out to see if you needed any help.' He saw the strained look on her face and stepped nearer, concerned. 'Hey, are you OK?'

'No, I'm not fucking OK!' She gestured over her shoulder into the trees. 'I got lost in there, didn't I? I've been blundering around like an idiot for the last half hour.'

Reed seemed bewildered by this news.

'In *there*? Christ, what were you doing in there? I assumed you'd stick to the track. It's a lot safer when you don't know your way around.'

She frowned. She could hardly tell him her real reason for entering the woods.

'I'm not keen on paths,' she told him dismissively. She took out her cigarettes and extracted a smoke with unsteady fingers. 'Anyway, what made you think you'd find me here?'

He grinned.

'Because this is where the track leads.' He indicated a narrow trail winding back from the circle through the brambles and trees, its surface worn smooth by centuries of passing feet. 'It widens out about a hundred yards up there,' he explained. 'Leads right back to The Grange.'

Jenny lit her cigarette and inhaled deeply.

'Lucky I stumbled across this place,' she said. 'I could have been wandering around in the woods for hours.'

'Luck has nothing to do with it,' he told her. 'The circle is a beacon. It draws people just as surely as a candle flame draws moths.'

Jenny laughed.

'There you go again. The old mumbo jumbo.'

'You know it's not mumbo jumbo, Jenny. What were you doing when I came up just now? You were feeling the power in the stones.'

'I was feeling *something*,' she admitted cautiously. 'Static electricity, I expect. Nothing particularly mind boggling.'

Now it was Reed's turn to laugh.

'Have you always been such a devout unbeliever?' he asked her.

'Always.' She felt better now, much more in control. Looking back at her panic in the woods, it seemed silly, childish. She'd lost it for a moment but now she felt confident enough to enjoy flirting with her would-be producer. As for the figure she had seen in the woods . . . she put the matter out of her mind. For the moment at least, she didn't want to think about it.

'So, tell me about this place,' she said. 'Genuine article is it? Or some Victorian folly?'

'Oh no, it's genuine all right. It's a neolithic site, been here since around 3000 BC. The trees grew around it later and for centuries it was lost. Only a few locals were even aware of its existence. There were various legends about the place…'

'What kind of legends?'

'Oh, it was said that the circle had the power to conjure up the spirits of the recently departed.'

'Naturally.' Jenny's tone was flippant but she couldn't help thinking about the figure she'd just followed through the woods.

'And women who had trouble conceiving would bring their husbands out here for a spot of al fresco rumpy pumpy. People swore blind it worked every time. Then of course, Obediah Wadleigh heard about it.'

'Oh yes, the religious nut you were telling me about? Be right up his street, wouldn't it?'

'Absolutely. His religion was essentially a Druidic revival. They were very popular in the nineteenth century. Probably one of the main reasons why he bought The Grange was because he found out that the circle was located on its land. He had the area cleared of trees and restored those monoliths that had fallen down. Must have cost a fortune but luckily, he was a very wealthy man…'

'Oh yes and don't tell me, they used to hold human sacrifices here, right?'

Reed smiled at her cynicism.

'Well, the Bronze Age priests certainly used to. Wadleigh did some excavations and discovered three cists with the remains of children inside them. He also found some bronze knives and several food vessels. This is where the sacrifices were made.' He led her to the centre of the circle and indicated a low oblong block of granite. At one end, a shallow channel had been inscribed into the stone and led off the side of it. The channel was stained darker than the other stone with centuries of use. 'More usually it would be a goat or a pig that was offered up. The blood would run along this channel into a collecting dish set under the edge of the stone.'

'Charming,' said Jenny, refusing to be shocked. 'And what about old Obediah Wotsit? He go in for this kind of thing, did he? Knock off the odd virgin on a Saturday night?'

'He did, but not in the way you're thinking. Wadleigh and his crew were more interested in sex magic.'

Jenny raised her eyebrows.

'Now that sounds a lot more fun than human sacrifice,' she said.

'Oh, it is,' he assured her. 'They all used to troop out here on a summer's night and have orgies. They believed that indulging in wild sexual acts would harness the circle's pagan forces and give them incredible powers.'

'So that's what you can feel in the stones,' murmured Jenny. 'All those tightly corseted Victorian ladies getting their rocks off.' She smiled mischievously at the unintended pun and glanced around the interior of the circle. 'But if all this happened a hundred years ago, explain something to me.'

'Hmm?'

'How come the grass here is freshly cut?'

'Oh, I'm a great believer in tradition. I send Idris out here with the strimmer every few weeks.' He wagged his eyebrows. 'After all, you never know when you might want to make use of the old place.'

'What, for human sacrifice ... or sex magic?'

'Oh, the latter naturally. For one thing it's less messy. And it does work, you know.'

'Does it really?' Despite her conviction that Reed was trying to wind her up again, Jenny couldn't deny that she was starting to feel distinctly aroused by the conversation. For an instant she had a vision of herself lying naked on the stone altar while Gareth Reed slowly undressed, revealing his hard, slim body ...

She blinked, swallowed, felt her face colour with embarrassment. Reed was smiling at her and she felt as though he knew exactly what she'd been thinking.

'We'd better get back,' she said quickly. 'The others will be wondering what's happened to us.' She dropped her cigarette onto the altar and ground it out beneath her foot.

She thought she saw a trace of disappointment flicker across his face, but he said nothing, simply turned and led the way across the circle and back along the track. The light snow was gradually petering out and it didn't look as though any of it was going to stick. Glancing back, Jenny saw that the last trace of redness on the western horizon was transforming the monoliths into eerie black silhouettes against the sky. They resembled nothing so much as a circle of giant human figures.

She experienced a powerful sense of foreboding: and in a sudden hallucinatory flash, she saw herself running, running as she had in the dream, only now she was running towards the dark outline of the stones as some unspeakable terror followed close on her heels. She gasped, blinked and the image was gone.

'Something wrong?' Reed asked her.

She shook her head.

'Never felt better,' she assured him. But she felt cold and oddly apprehensive, sure now that something bad was going to happen.

She lifted the fur collar of her jacket up around her ears and walked on. The night seemed to settle around her like an enveloping black cloak and she was suddenly aware of her warm breath, clouding in the darkness.

Chapter Fourteen

They must have been walking for something like ten minutes and neither of them had spoken a word. The silence was steadily becoming oppressive. The feeling of presentiment had gradually subsided and Jenny felt obliged to rekindle some kind of conversation. She glanced at Reed but he seemed momentarily lost in his own thoughts. Off in the distance, an owl hooted, a low, mournful sound.

'So,' ventured Jenny. 'You want to produce a Deceivers' album?'

He glanced up in surprise and nodded.

'Yes, I do. Very much.'

'What did you think of the last one?'

He frowned.

'The songs or the production?'

'Whatever.'

'Well, the songs were brilliant, as usual: but John Morse wasn't the man to produce them. Don't misread that, with the right band Morse is an excellent producer. But he's a techno freak, he favours keyboards, and consequently, *Red Tape* is absolutely swamped with them. As for that metallic guitar sound, it just didn't suit the material.'

Jenny didn't say anything but these had been her own thoughts exactly. Part of her suspected that Josh Lezard might have tipped Reed off to her feelings on the subject but she didn't raise the point. If she was going to work with Reed she had to have a little faith in him.

'So how would you have done it?'

'Very simply,' he told her. 'You see over the years, The Deceivers' sound has become increasingly homogenised by technology. We have all this sophisticated equipment in the studio and we just feel obliged to use it. The result is that the most important instrument in the band, your voice, gets swamped in the mix.'

'Well, I wouldn't argue with that, but . . .'

'No, let me finish. Ever heard the Lou Reed album, *New York*? You know the sound he got there? Raw, unsophisticated, but full of energy. He used just a couple of little amps and miked up like he was doing a gig at his local bar. That's how I'd produce The Deceivers. I mean, what are you in essence? Just a good time, kick-ass, bar band. I think you've lost sight of that.'

'Yeah, but musicians always feel they have to progress, so—'

'Forgive me, Jenny, but that isn't progress. That's just window dressing. I hate to sound like a Tory politician but it's time to go back to basics. Bring your voice way up in the mix, use a funkier sound on the rhythm guitar and as for Adrian . . . well, he'll have to be content to keep his contribution to the bare minimum.'

Jenny chuckled.

'Oh, he'll *love* that!' she said.

Reed shrugged.

'Fuck him. It's your band, Jenny. And let me make a wild guess. I bet it was Adrian's idea to bring John Morse on board for *Red Tape*, right?'

Jenny glanced at him sharply.

'It was. But how—'

'Because it's obvious. Adrian knows that Morse is a keyboard freak. The result is that on a great song like *Pearl Diver*, you can barely make out the lyrics.' He shook his head. 'I would love to re-record that track with you. Do it my way and you'd have a number one single, no problem.'

Jenny smiled.

'You always this sure of yourself?' she asked him.

'Pretty much. Anyway...' He made a dismissive gesture with his hand. 'There's plenty of time to think about all that stuff. Right now, the priority is just to get you playing again. It's been a while, Jenny, and it's going to be hard getting back into it.'

'Yeah, tell me about it.'

'You've had a lot of problems to deal with...'

Jenny flashed him a look.

'Has Lezard been shooting his mouth off to you?' she snapped.

Reed shook his head.

'Are you kidding? He worships you, Jenny, he wouldn't dream of speaking out of turn. But it was fairly common knowledge about your uh... breakdown.'

Jenny sighed.

'You can't keep anything secret in this business, can you? Yeah well, I did go kind of out of control after Scott died. Tried drowning my demons in alcohol and had to be hung out to dry for a while.' She looked at him defensively. 'But I'm over that now, OK. I mean, I still drink but now I can stop myself when I've had enough. I've come to terms with my problem.'

'And Scott?'

'That's going to take longer to deal with.'

He nodded.

'When you've had a musical partner all those years, it's... well, it's like a marriage, I guess. You come to depend on one another. When one partner is suddenly snatched away, the other goes through a long period of self doubt and insecurity. I've seen it happen, many times.'

'I can't deny that's exactly how I've been,' said Jenny.

'But it's important not to lose sight of one thing. Scott was a great guitarist and a useful man to have on the team, but at the end of the day, that's *all* he was. When it comes down to it, Jenny, you are the main force behind this band, the person who writes the songs.'

'We wrote together!' protested Jenny.

'Oh sure, Scott had an input into them, but it wasn't fifty per cent, was it? He contributed a middle eight here, a riff there. The lyrics and the concept of the song came from you, right?'

'Well, yes, but...'

'So you only need to deliver another ten, fifteen per cent and you've made up the lost ground. And you are more than capable of that, Jenny, I know you are.'

Jenny sighed. They were emerging from the tree line now and the lights of The Grange were directly ahead of them.

'I wish I could believe that, Gareth, I really do. But you know something? These days I don't feel capable of changing a fucking lightbulb, without help.'

'You'll feel different once you get playing again,' he assured her. 'It's like a kid learning to ride a bike. You put stabilisers on there for a week or so and then one night, when she's asleep, you take the stabilisers off. Next morning, she climbs on that bike and...'

'...falls flat on her face,' finished Jenny, gleefully.

He glanced at her.

'Anybody ever tell you you're a pessimist?' he asked her.

She laughed and, impulsively, she put her arm through his. She was beginning to warm to Gareth Reed, despite all her better judgement. They crossed the lawn and walked under the arch into the courtyard. The other members of the band, together with Cassie and Emma Savage, were standing around Lezard's Shogun.

'Ah, the wanderers return!' exclaimed Chris. He was clearly in the sparky playful mood that he inhabited for several hours before total inebriation set in. 'Just in time. We're heading into the village to check out the little pub Gareth told us about. You coming or what?'

Jenny smiled.

'Just can't resist the lure of the pints, eh Chris?' She shook her head. 'No, I'm bushed. I think I'll have an early night.'

'Yes, me too,' said Reed. 'I have a lot to prepare for tomorrow.'

'Not like Jenny to turn down a drink,' observed Steve, cuttingly.

Emma shot Jenny a sly look, then glanced at Reed.

'Maybe these two have other things on their minds,' she said.

Jenny fixed her with a warning glare.

'Watch it, pal,' she said. 'Or your public will be reading about how I took your knickers down and gave you a good spanking.'

'Christ, I'd pay money to see that,' said Chris: and everybody but Emma laughed.

'Did Mike Watton get here yet?' asked Reed, clearly anxious to steer the conversation into safer waters.

'No,' said Adrian. 'Lezard's giving him a ring before we set off. Myself, I don't see the point in the roadie coming out to something like this. It's not as if we're on tour, is it?'

'Mike always comes to rehearsals,' Steve told him. 'We need him to dispense Chris's medication.'

'Oh, are you ill or something?' asked Cassie innocently and everybody glanced at her.

'Something,' agreed Chris cheerily. 'It's ... an old war wound.'

'You were in the war?'

'He's always in the wars,' said Jenny. 'Pay no attention to him, Cassie, he's just winding you up.'

'Oh ...' The girl looked flustered. She turned back towards the house but Chris reached out and grasped her arm.

'Hey, why don't you come with us, Cassie?' He ignored the filthy look that Emma directed at him. 'It'd do you good to get out of the house for a bit.'

Cassie glanced at him wistfully, but then shook her head.

'Oh, I can't really. Idris will be wanting his dinner when he gets back.'

'Tell the lazy bastard to make his own,' suggested Jenny. 'Or hasn't he heard about women's lib?'

Cassie gave an unconvincing little laugh.

'No, really, I'd better not,' she insisted. 'Maybe another time. Idris will probably be home any minute now.'

'He'd better be,' said Reed quietly, and Jenny noted a distinct edge in his voice. She remembered that the mysterious Idris had been unaccounted for when they first arrived. Cassie excused herself and went up the stairs to the house: she was obliged to step aside as Lezard emerged from the back door and began to descend the steps.

'About bloody time!' yelled Chris. 'Come on, Josh, we're about dying of thirst, here!'

Lezard didn't answer. He was coming slowly down the steps, a grim expression on his face.

'What's up with you?' asked Steve. 'Looks like you found a fiver and lost a tenner. Is Mike coming or what?'

Lezard shook his head.

'No, he won't be coming.' He glanced helplessly around at the others and Jenny saw he had had some kind of bad news. 'I just talked to Mary,' he whispered. 'She … she found Mike dead only a couple of hours ago.'

The sense of shock was palpable. Everybody stood there, gazing up at Lezard in stunned silence. Then Chris broke into a snigger.

'It's a wind-up, right?'

'No, it's bloody not! Do you really think I'd make a joke about something like that?'

Chris shrugged, bowed his head to look at his feet. Lezard sat down heavily on the steps, as though he no longer had the strength to stand.

'What happened?' Jenny asked him.

'Suicide,' he muttered.

'What? No way, not Mike. He's the last person who would do something like that!'

Lezard shrugged.

'What can I tell you? That's exactly what Mary said. Apparently Mike got up early this morning to set off for The Grange. Mary was still in bed, he kissed her goodbye and told her he'd see her in a couple of weeks. She went back to sleep thinking he'd gone. It wasn't till after lunch when she went to the garage to get her own car that she found Mike still sitting in his vehicle with the engine running. The doors were all closed and there was a length of pipe running from the exhaust up through the floor. He'd been dead for hours. Mary had been meaning to phone us but she was still in shock. Some friends are with her.'

'Did he leave a note?' asked Jenny, 'Suicides always leave a note, don't they?'

Lezard sighed.

'Mary didn't say. She—' He shook his head, unable to go on. 'Christ, Mike Watton, I can hardly believe it. If anyone enjoyed life, it was him.'

'We'll have to cancel the session,' said Jenny. Everyone turned to look at her and she stared back at them defensively. 'Well, we *will*!' she protested. 'We can't all be poncing around out here after something like this. We'll have to go back and see Mary, pay our respects.'

'Let's not be too rash,' Lezard warned her. 'The last thing Mary needs right now is the whole crowd of us descending on her like the hordes of Attila.' He thought for a moment. 'Look, I'll drive back to London tomorrow morning, call in and see her. Naturally, we'll offer any financial help she needs.' He glanced quickly around at the others. 'I'm sure nobody has any objections to that?'

Nobody spoke but Jenny noticed that Adrian had a disapproving look on his face, which was typical of him in a situation like this. He had never liked parting with money, whatever the reason.

'Obviously we'll send flowers and we'll take time out to attend the funeral ... but frankly, Jenny, this session is too important and too damned expensive to abort.'

There were nods and grunts of agreement from the others and Jenny stared around in dismay.

'Oh well, that's lovely, isn't it?' she cried. 'Mike slogged his guts out for us for years and now it's just business as usual? You callous bastards!'

'It's not like that, Jenny,' protested Steve. 'Josh is right, Mary won't want us intruding on her grief at the moment. Let's at least wait until Josh has sussed out the situation, OK?'

She shrugged.

'Suit yourselves,' she muttered. 'You usually do.'

There was a long, awkward silence while everyone stood around in the courtyard, looking at each other, each of them locked for a moment in their own private thoughts.

'What happens now?' asked Robbie, uncertainly.

'Well, I don't know about the rest of you,' said Chris, 'but I vote we head on down to the pub, anyway.'

Jenny glared at him.

'You shit!' she said.

'What?' Chris spread his hands in a gesture of helplessness. 'What did I say that was so awful? Let's face it, what are we going to do tonight but sit around and rap about our favourite memories of Mike? So we may as well do it in a nice warm pub and drink to his memory at the same time.'

'Very convenient,' observed Jenny.

'Oh, hey, come on! Mike was as fond of a pint as the next man. I guarantee that if it was me lying dead and him standing here, he'd vote for the pub like a shot.'

'True enough,' admitted Steve.

'The man's got a point,' said Adrian.

'I didn't even know him,' muttered Emma.

'Me neither,' added Robbie.

'Looks pretty decisive to me,' said Chris. He looked expectantly at Lezard. 'If you want, I'll drive us down there.'

'In your state?' Lezard sighed. He got back to his feet and fished his car keys from his pocket. He glanced apologetically at Jenny. 'I guess I'll have to go along,' he said. 'Somebody will have to try and keep them under control.'

'Good luck,' said Jenny, coldly.

'Sure you won't come along?' ventured Chris.

'Oh, just fuck off, will you?' She felt appalled by the band's indifference though their behaviour was hardly a surprise to her. She well remembered the day their old mucker, Freddie, had cashed in his chips, they'd all attended an unofficial send-off at his guitarist's house in Surrey. She and Scott had ended up standing on a table, pissed out of their heads and bellowing a tuneless rendition of *I Want to Break Free*. Not much dignity there: and she knew for a fact that if Scott had been here tonight and he'd announced his intention of going for a drink, she'd almost certainly have gone along with it.

But now she felt alienated from the others, distanced from them in a way that dismayed her: and she knew that wouldn't change until they'd played together as a band once again. She watched sullenly as they piled silently into the spacious interior of the Shogun. Lezard slid into the driver's seat and leaned out of the window to speak to her.

'If you change your mind, Gareth knows where the place is,' he said.

'I won't,' she told him. 'I'm tired, all I want to do is crash out and sleep.'

He nodded.

'Catch you later,' he said. 'And listen, whatever you think, I'm really sorry about Mike. He was one of the good guys.'

'They say the good die young,' murmured Jenny.

Lezard gave her a warm smile and he drove slowly out of the courtyard and through the arch. Jenny watched the Shogun's tail lights moving along the drive and for the first time, she noticed that the snow was coming down again. She felt suddenly very cold and hugged her arms around herself.

'Well, I don't know about you, but I could use a hot bath,' she told Reed: then winced as she realised she'd just issued what sounded like a lewd invitation. 'Uh ... I mean ...'

'I know what you meant,' he assured her. 'I've got stuff to do but maybe I could pop up, later. I've got something that might make a nice nightcap.'

It was in her mind to tell him to back off and leave her alone, but she knew if she did that, it would just be on a point of principle. Actually, the thought of Reed coming up to her room later was far from disagreeable. And maybe, if the mood was right, she'd let him stay.

Now who's the callous bastard? she thought grimly: but she simply smiled at him and said, 'OK, later.' Then she went up the staircase into the house, leaving him standing on the steps gazing thoughtfully after her.

[illegible] and said, "O[illegible]" [illegible] went up the [illegible] on the steps [illegible]

[illegible]

[illegible]

Chapter Fifteen

Jenny went up to her room and filled a bath with near-scalding water, adding copious amounts of the herbal essence she found in the bathroom cabinet. Flinging off her clothes, she lowered herself carefully into the tub and lay back, staring up at the ceiling.

But she couldn't relax.

The more she thought about the suicide of Mike Watton, the more she knew that something was very badly wrong. She had known Mike for nearly ten years and she couldn't imagine a less likely candidate for suicide.

He'd been The Deceivers' road manager for something like six of those ten years, an uncomplicated, straight-talking man in his mid-forties, quietly devoted to his wife, Mary. In all that time Jenny had never seen him depressed. On the contrary, he had been a cheerful, good-natured sort, always ready with a joke when the pressures of touring threatened to prove too much. Loyal, hard working and hard as nails when it was required of him, Mike had also possessed a near legendary ability to handle the awful sleep deprivation that went hand-in-hand with any tour. He had always been the one who could stay awake around the clock, while lesser individuals – even party animals like Chris – succumbed to sleep.

So how was it that Mike had taken his own life, for Christ's sake? Had he been in some kind of trouble he couldn't see his way out of? Maybe he owed money to dangerous people, drug dealers, loan sharks, something like that. Maybe he'd been a secret gambler...

She pictured Mike's smiling face as he pitched her some silly joke he'd heard down his local pub and instantly she rejected the idea. No way. Mike Watton's life had been an open book, she was sure of that. His death on the other hand, was inexplicable and would probably remain so. The thought of it cast a mournful shadow over proceedings at The Grange. She remembered the sense of foreboding she'd had out by the stone circle, the conviction that something bad was coming home to roost. Well, she'd been right about that much at least. But what was she to make of the vision of herself running towards those massive upright stones?

Jenny sighed and, reluctantly, she got out of the bath and towelled herself dry. She unpacked a red silk kimono from her case and slipped it on, then went to lie down on the bed. She noticed a remote control on the bedside cabinet and used it to switch on the television. The picture faded in just in time to catch the tail end of a weather bulletin. On the back-projected map, the whole of Mid Wales was liberally peppered with drifting white asterisks. The weatherman, a curly-haired Max Boyce lookalike was doing his best to make sure everybody got the message.

'...extreme weather conditions over high ground,' he announced gleefully. 'Heavy falls of snow combined with high winds will mean blizzards for large areas of the country, so break out the balaclava and mittens and please don't travel unless it's absolutely necessary!' He didn't stop grinning throughout his report as though the prospect of snowstorms actually filled him with delight.

Jenny frowned, reflecting that she hadn't brought much in

the way of warm clothing: but happily, The Grange was not the draughty old dump she'd envisaged. She could hear the wind gusting outside but lying here in nothing more than a kimono, she felt perfectly snug.

The opening credits for an inane game show came on and she switched off the television with a grunt of disapproval, but not before she'd caught the name of the show's host. She had to smile as she remembered how in the band's early days, that same celebrity had presented an anarchic Saturday TV show for kids. Jenny and the other members of The Deceivers had been persuaded by their management at the time to appear on it. Miming to the latest single had been no great hardship but by the programme's conclusion, they'd found themselves locked in a steel cage and were being pelted with buckets of multi-coloured gunge by gangs of screaming youngsters.

Scott had been furious, she remembered. He'd been wearing a brand new suede jacket, bought with his first real royalties and by the show's conclusion, it had been totally ruined. Closing her eyes, she could picture him slumped in the television dressing room, sadly regarding a pile of sodden hide on the floor.

'Two hundred fucking quid, I paid for that!' he'd moaned and he'd been close to tears about it. In those days, of course, that had seemed like a lot of money and The Deceivers were still poor enough to lament the destruction of something as trivial as an item of clothing. Now, if Jenny wanted a new jacket, she bought it, wore it for a while, then gave it to somebody else. Owning it gave her no pleasure at all. It was just something to wear.

Sometimes she wished more than anything else that she could turn back the clock, go back to those days when she *did* care about clothes. Like every other kid with not much on her plate, she'd yearned for fame and fortune. But she hadn't realised that when it came, it would take the shine off so many of her anticipated pleasures. What did pleasure consist of now? Getting so out of it that she obliterated everything around her. Making herself comfortably numb.

There was a soft rapping at the door and she remembered that there was still one thing she could take fleeting pleasure from – provided she hadn't forgotten how to do it.

'Come in,' she said: and had to exert some effort to keep her voice from rising in pitch. She was excited at the prospect of being alone with Gareth Reed and it was pointless to deny it.

He opened the door and stepped inside. He was carrying a bottle of liquor and a couple of brandy glasses. He looked at Jenny lying there on the bed and then his eyes flicked away, as though he was nervous of jumping to the wrong conclusion. At the same moment, Jenny realised what a sight she must present, stretched out on the bed like Mata Hari on a bad night. She sat up, pulling the kimono tighter around her.

'I don't know what I must look like,' she muttered apologetically.

'Pretty damn good if you want to know the truth,' he said, with his characteristic self-confidence. He closed the door behind him and moved across to the sofa. 'It's not too late, is it?' he asked her, as he uncorked the bottle.

'For what?' she asked him playfully.

'I mean, if you were planning to sleep...'

'Not much chance of that,' she told him, 'after what just happened.' She got up off the bed and went to sit beside him. He poured two generous measures of the clear liquor.

'It must have been quite a shock,' he said and handed her one of the glasses. 'Here, drink this, it'll make you feel better.'

'What is it?' she asked suspiciously, sniffing at the contents of the glass. The liquid gave off a faint citrus aroma.

'My own home brew,' he said mysteriously. 'Best to put it

down in one. *Salud.*' He clinked his glass against hers and they both knocked back the contents.

The spirit had an initial sweet, honeyed taste: but then Jenny experienced a slow blossoming of heat in her chest that made her catch her breath. Her eyes filled with tears and she struggled to hold back a cough: but then she was aware of a delicious, languorous warmth that seemed to spread throughout her body.

'Wow,' she murmured. 'That's got some kick. What's in it?'

'Oh, eye of frog, tongue of newt. That sort of thing. It'll help relax you. I figured you could do with it.' He studied his empty glass for a moment as though consulting a crystal ball. 'Look, I never met Mike Watton, so I can't honestly express any real remorse about his death. But it does seem like a very bad break for the band, coming so close on the heels of Scott.' He refilled the glasses.

'Yeah. An even worse break for Mary. Don't know what she'll do, she absolutely adored Mike. We all did.' She leaned back on her seat and cupped her hands around the bowl of the glass. 'It *is* starting to feel like somebody's got it in for us. Who was that character you were telling me about. The Cosmic Joker?'

Reed smiled, took a sip from his glass.

'You seemed really surprised,' he said. 'When Josh mentioned suicide.'

'Surprised? I was blown away. I just don't believe that Mike would do a stupid thing like that. He valued life too highly.'

'You never know with some people. Still waters run deep.'

'Nah.' Jenny shook her head. 'There was nothing devious about Mike. It's just a complete mystery to me.'

Jenny lifted her glass and drained the contents a second time. She felt the warmth coursing through her body, giving her a delightful melting sensation deep inside. And then quite suddenly, a memory lurched out of the mist like a punch in the stomach.

'Oh shit,' she said.

Reed looked at her warily.

'What is it?'

'I just remembered something.'

She got up from the bed and went to get her jacket from the bathroom. Rooting through the pockets, she finally found what she was looking for. The message from 'Hoochie Coochie Man'. She unfolded the page and studied the contents for a moment, checking that she had remembered it correctly. Then she brought it back to Reed and handed it to him. He set down his glass and read the note. She had expected him to flinch or make an expression of disgust but his face didn't alter. He simply asked, 'Where did you get this?'

'Through the post, the other day.' She indicated the last lines. 'See there? "One down and four to go." Maybe Mike was one of the four.'

Reed allowed himself a grim smile.

'I think you're letting your imagination run away with you, Jenny. This is just a crank letter and every rock star gets them from time to time. Besides, it's almost certain that the "four" he's referring to are the other members of the band. A roadie doesn't have quite the same kudos, does he?'

'Mike was pretty damned close to being a member of The Deceivers,' she said defensively.

'Well, fair enough, but . . . what exactly are you saying? That Mike was murdered?'

Jenny thought about it for a moment, then smiled foolishly.

'No. At least . . . I don't think so.' She shrugged. 'I'm not sure what I'm saying. It's just . . . odd, don't you think? I know it sounds crazy, but . . .'

She lifted a hand to her forehead. A sudden wave of

dizziness had rippled through her and when Reed answered, his voice seemed to have acquired a strange spatial quality.

'I wouldn't mention this to the others. We've got work to do tomorrow and there's no sense in freaking everybody out unnecessarily. We'll wait till Josh has ... hey, are you all right?'

'I ... I feel kind of strange.' She set her glass unsteadily down on the table. 'This stuff must be stronger than I thought. I feel ...'

'How do you feel, Jenny?' He was studying her with a faintly amused expression on his handsome face.

'I feel ...' Her eyes widened in surprise as she realized that what she actually felt was *horny*. There was an ache in her loins and her whole body was tingling with anticipation. She looked stupidly down at her empty glass. 'You bastard, have you slipped me something?'

He laughed easily.

'Of course not! At least, nothing chemical. The drink is made from purely natural products. But some people who try it do remark that it makes them feel less ... inhibited. Relax, Jenny. Enjoy the experience. It isn't going to harm you.'

She glared at him, knowing that she should be furious with him about this. In the early days of The Deceivers, some arsehole had once spiked her drink with acid at a party and she'd ended up having a horrible time, completely out of control. But she didn't feel like that now. She felt relaxed, euphoric, suffused with a delicious, sensual warmth. Reed was watching her intently now with those piercing brown eyes and the fluttering sensation in her stomach deepened to a raw ache of desire. He reached out a tentative hand and placed it on her naked thigh, just below the hem of the kimono. She knew she really ought to brush the hand away and order him out of there, if only to throw that exasperating confidence back in his face:

but somehow she didn't feel she had the strength to do it. She was trembling with anticipation now, like some teenager on a first date.

He grinned, leaned closer and traced the tip of his tongue across her lips.

'Care for a demonstration?' he asked her.

'Well uh . . . my old dad always used to say . . . "Taste and try, before you buy."'

He enfolded her in his arms and she was momentarily surprised by the strength in them: a power that seemed to belie the slimness of his body.

'I don't know,' he murmured in her ear. 'It might not work with a rock legend.'

'Only one way to find out,' she whispered: and she opened her mouth wide to the probing of his tongue, allowing him to push her back on to the sofa.

Whatever he called it, it worked beautifully. Reed was no wham, bam merchant. He took his time, working on her with slow, almost unbearable patience, his skilful fingers probing and caressing her, coaxing forth the most incredible sensations.

Maybe it was the drink he'd given her, but she felt that she kept blissing out to whole sections of what was happening – not to the pleasurable things but the mundane ones. At some point in the proceedings she must have got up from the sofa and walked to the bed, or maybe Reed carried her there: and later, she must have undressed him or watched as he undressed himself, because there they were, naked against each other in the soft, soft bed and he was still working on her and she was ascending to a plateau of sheer pleasure. Somehow, he contrived to keep her there, just on the edge of climax, gasping and moaning with delight as he used his mouth and fingers on her.

And finally his hips were moving against hers in a slow,

controlled rhythm, igniting the sparks that his fingers had kindled. She must have come twice before his thrusts became more urgent and all the time she was dimly aware of his warm breath against her ear and he was whispering ... no *chanting,* something over and over, words she couldn't comprehend because they seemed couched in some ancient tongue she was unable to identify. He kept pushing into her for what seemed a glorious eternity and she realised that he was somehow holding himself back, waiting for her to orgasm again: and just as she was thinking that there was no chance of *that* happening, it welled up in her, spilled through her body like a blaze of sweet, hot fire. She was glad that the others had gone out for the night, because she was screaming now, screaming with delight at such unaccustomed pleasure, her fingernails clawing at his shuddering back as ecstasy claimed them both.

She came gradually back to her senses to find that they were still embracing. Reed was sprawled over her and his regular breathing suggested a deep sleep. The duvet was down around his waist and for the first time, she noticed the little tattoo on his right arm, a picture of a snake with a black zig zag along its back. The snake's body was curved into a perfect circle, its tail gripped in its own mouth.

'What's this?' she murmured sleepily, tracing the circle with the tip of her index finger. 'More mumbo-jumbo?'

But he didn't answer and she realised that his efforts had exhausted him. She eased him gently sideways onto the mattress and he didn't wake. She pulled the duvet up over him, tucking him in like a child.

'You were right,' she whispered. 'It does work.'

She got up and went into the bathroom to relieve herself, then observed her reflection in the mirror. Her face smiled contentedly back at her, the cat that got the cream.

'You horny bitch,' she admonished herself: but somehow,

she couldn't wipe the smile away, even when she reminded herself that Mike Watton was dead and she really ought to be ashamed of herself.

She went back into the bedroom, switched off the light and climbed back into bed beside Reed. She felt more relaxed than she had in years, as though every molecule of her body had been removed, individually massaged and replaced. She was pleasurably sore between the legs and her thighs and calfs ached as though she'd run a marathon.

She didn't care. She was asleep in minutes and lost in a deep, dreamless slumber. When she woke briefly, a couple of hours later, she put out a hand to touch Reed but he'd gone: and she was too tired to resist drifting off again, even when her subconscious mind registered that somewhere in the house, unseen hands were picking out a familiar melody on an acoustic guitar.

Instead of jolting her awake, it served as a lullaby as she settled down once again into the warm welcoming realms of sleep.

Chapter Sixteen

She emerged gradually from darkness, her tranquil slumber increasingly intruded upon by sounds in the big old house: the flushing of lavatories, the sound of a radio down the landing, footsteps on the staircase and the murmur of voices going past her door. She did her best to ignore them, clinging stubbornly to the shirt tails of what had been the best night's sleep she'd had in years – but finally, she had to accept defeat and with a sigh, she pushed the duvet aside and got out of bed.

She went to the curtains and peeped out into the courtyard, which was Christmas card picturesque beneath a fresh fall of crisp, white snow. As she watched, Lezard's Shogun started up with a cough of exhaust, the wipers swatting the windscreen clean of snow. The vehicle rolled smoothly towards the exit, leaving two tyre tracks and an oblong rectangle of grey stone in its wake.

Jenny felt a twinge of disappointment. Part of her had counted on Lezard being around, at least for the first rehearsal: but then she reminded herself about Mike Watton and Lezard's promise to visit Mary. Mike's wife would have bigger trials to face than being called upon to perform a few pop songs. Put in those terms, it made Jenny feel like she was being a real Prima Donna, but it did nothing to quell the sense of apprehension she felt as she washed and dressed herself for the occasion, slipping into a black ribbed T-shirt and blue jeans.

Down in the dining room, she found Cassie clearing up the debris of what had obviously been a hearty breakfast: and she was horrified to learn that the other members of the band had already eaten and were down in the studio, tuning up and setting sound levels. Only Emma Savage was still in bed.

'Maybe I should have set an alarm,' muttered Jenny.

'Oh, I wouldn't worry. They'll probably be hours, yet. All that twiddling and fiddling they do. What can I get you for breakfast?'

'Coffee would be nice.'

Cassie looked disappointed.

'You'll need more than coffee,' she protested. 'How about scrambled eggs, grilled bacon and mushrooms?'

Jenny smiled.

'Are you kidding? I haven't eaten breakfast like that for years.' She took her cigarettes from her breast pocket and set them down on the table. 'I'll just have one of these,' she said. 'Full of flavour and absolutely calorie-free.'

Cassie had to make a major effort to stop her pretty features from arranging themselves into a look of disapproval. She leaned over the table to collect a couple of empty plates and Jenny noticed the silver earrings the girl was wearing. They depicted snakes, their bodies curled into perfect circles, their tails gripped in their mouths. The image was familiar to her but for the moment, she couldn't quite remember from where.

'These are nice,' she said, reaching up the fingers of one hand to touch one of the rings.

'Yes, aren't they? Gareth gave them to me for my last birthday. They're real silver.' There was something about the way she said the last line that put Jenny in mind of a little girl, boasting about some special gift she'd had. What she was actually saying was, 'See, he *does* care about me!' For an instant their eyes met and alarm bells rang in Jenny's head. She had the distinct impression that Cassie knew about last night and that she was far from happy about it. Was something going on between Cassie and Gareth Reed? But then, Jenny thought, why should she worry about that? Cassie was a married woman, when all was said and done. And Reed, presumably, was a free agent...

Then she remembered where she'd seen the circular snake before. The tattoo. She remembered stroking the soft, blue-inked skin of his shoulder...

Thinking of him caused a rush of desire to go through her and involuntarily, she closed her eyes, afraid perhaps that Cassie might read the naked emotion that smouldered within her.

'What, er ... do they signify? The snakes?' Jenny opened her eyes and reached for her cigarettes, attempting to mask her awkwardness with a familiar action.

Cassie shrugged.

'Oh, I don't know. Some kind of pagan image, I guess. Gareth and Idris have got this thing about snakes.' Jenny thought the girl was being evasive but she didn't pursue the point. She lit her cigarette and sat back in her chair. Cassie lifted some plates from the table and started towards the kitchen: then hesitated as she remembered something. 'Oh yeah, I meant to tell you. There's a letter for you.' She indicated a plain white envelope propped against the toast rack. 'Whoever it is, they can't spell properly.'

Jenny picked it up. It had a first class stamp on it and was postmarked Haringey, London. She saw that it was addressed to Jenny *Slayed*, written in the same, familiar black felt-tip pen: and her good humour swiftly evaporated.

'How did this get here?' she asked.

'The postman, of course. They just about got the van up here this morning, but he told me it was touch and go. If it gets any worse, they'll be dropping our post by helicopter!' She noticed the look of apprehension on Jenny's face and expressed concern. 'Hey, are you all right?'

'Uh . . . yes, I'm fine. I was just wondering who knew they could write to me here. I . . . didn't tell many people where I was going.'

Cassie frowned and went into the kitchen to get the coffee. Jenny opened the envelope and withdrew two sheets of plain white paper. Words were printed on the first in bold, black felt tip.

DING DONG DELL
THE ROADIE'S GONE TO HELL.
WHO MADE HIM SCRAM?
THE HOOCHIE COOCHIE MAN.
WHO'LL FOLLOW ON?
COULD BE *ANYONE*
WHAT A CLEVER MOVE I'VE MADE
THE DECEIVERS NEXT . . .
THEN JENNY SLAYED.

Her first feeling was one of profound disgust that anybody could gloat over such a tragedy: and her sense of horror was compounded when she examined the second sheet. This contained some familiar lyrics, printed out in the same black pen. They were familiar because Jenny herself had written them. They were from a song on the *Back to the Beat* album, a song that, uncannily, had actually been written with Mike in mind. At the time she had thought of it as nothing more than a sly dig at the man's unabashed auto-mania. Now the words seemed chillingly prophetic.

You and your automobile
such a perfect love affair.
I don't think you're really happy
any place but there.
And maybe if you're lucky
you'll die at the wheel some day
go speeding on to Paradise
down a four-lane motorway.

She sat there staring at the lyrics in horror. They'd been written so long ago that they simply hadn't sprung to mind when she'd heard about Mike's death – but somebody had remembered them, noted how dreadfully apt they had been and had put the two together. A terrible thought crossed her mind.

Or was it the other way around?

Had Mike's death been orchestrated in such a way that it fitted the lyrics?

Now Jenny thought about the weird kid who'd been hanging around her parents' house, the one who'd quoted *Frightened of the Night*, like he'd memorised it from a textbook. She'd thought at the time he was just another creepy fan, but . . . was it possible that he was behind all this? Was he the Hoochie Coochie Man? But how could it have been him? How could he have traced her to this address . . . and more importantly, how could he have got the letter to her so quickly?

'Oh my God,' she whispered. She had just realised something else. The postmark on the envelope informed her that the letter had been posted the previous day. To have made it here by this morning's post it would surely have to have been despatched some time the previous day: yet according to Lezard, Mary had not even discovered Mike's body until the late afternoon. So there was no way the Hoochie Coochie Man could have acted on an opportunistic impulse, after hearing about the death or reading about it in the papers. He had to have known about it the moment it happened: or possibly even *before* it happened. And the only way he could know that . . .

'Jesus!' Jenny stood up so suddenly that she nearly knocked the cup of coffee out of Cassie's hands as she returned from the kitchen.

'Hey, steady on! What's the matter?'

'Where's Gareth?'

'He's down in the studio with the others. But—'

Jenny turned on her heel, stalked out of the dining room and into the hallway.

'Jenny, what about your coffee?' Cassie called after her.

Jenny ignored her. She approached the soundproofed door under the staircase and pushed it open. It glided back on well-oiled hinges and the sound of rock music swept up the stairs at her, the Deceivers slamming through a perennial warm-up number, their version of an old Booker T instrumental, *Green Onions*. Scott had devised his own sequence of riffs and solos for the song and Jenny felt the hairs on her neck prickle as she realised that whoever was playing down there had got every last lick off to a T.

She went down the carpeted steps, telling herself that maybe the band was actually playing an old rehearsal tape featuring Scott, just to give Robbie an idea of what he might do.

No such luck. When she emerged into the crypt, she saw that The Deceivers were set up on the far side of the glass, and that Robbie Porter really was doing his Scott Griffin impersonation, grinning all over his handsome face and throwing out complex guitar trills and flourishes, as though it was the easiest thing in the world. Jenny could also see that the others were nodding and smiling appreciatively and she realised that to all intents and purposes he had already passed his audition with flying colours.

She waited a moment to let her eyes adjust to the low lighting in the control room, then made her way across to the mixing desk where Reed was hunched over the controls, setting and resetting the various sliders and equalisers to obtain the sound he wanted. He glanced up as Jenny dropped into the seat beside him and she saw a look of disappointment flicker momentarily across his face.

'Thought you were Idris,' he told her. 'Bugger's gone missing again and he knows he's supposed to be engineering for me.' He saw her look of indignation and smiled sheepishly. 'Still, the most important person is here now, so I guess we can begin, huh?' He nodded through the screen at the band who seemed to be cooking up a fair head of steam in there. 'I'm a sucker for this old rhythm and blues stuff,' he told her. 'Wanna listen properly?' He reached for the master volume slider, but Jenny stayed his hand.

'Hold on a minute. We need to talk.' She had the two sheets of paper in her hand, ready to show him, but he threw her completely when he replied as though he'd expected this.

'Absolutely, Jenny, it's about last night, right? What can I say?' He spread his arms in an expressive shrug. 'It was a stupid mistake and I'm really sorry.'

'What?' Now she really was flummoxed. Even if she had intended to speak about last night, she'd have wanted to praise it, not denounce it in such a fashion. 'What d'you mean, it was stupid?'

'Exactly what I say. I'm afraid I let my personal feelings get in the way of my professionalism. I've jeopardised our working relationship. I think it's best if we just pretend that last night never happened. What do you say?'

Jenny glared at him. He was sitting there looking at her as though she was some stranger who'd just wandered in off the street. She couldn't have envisaged a more dramatic change from the ardent seducer who had visited her room the previous night.

'Now just a minute!' she snarled. 'What is this? National Self Denial Week? Or did you just want to fuck a rock star and now you've got another notch on the bed post, it's kiss-off time?'

'It's not like that at all!' He looked wounded by the remark but Jenny was no longer sure she could trust his expressions, convincing though they were. 'What happened was very enjoyable but the point is, I should never have let things progress that far. In my experience, producers who become intimate with their clients lose their sense of objectivity. The music suffers. I want to ensure that I produce your next album to the best of my ability, so I'm simply advocating that we exercise a little self control and—'

'You pompous prick!' Jenny was horrified by his attitude. 'What makes you think *I'm* so keen to carry on? It was a bit of slap and tickle, that's all. Nothing special.'

He smiled knowingly.

'Forgive me, but that's not the impression you gave. I think it was *more* than that.'

'Oh, really? I should have warned you I've had a lifetime of faking orgasms. In fact, I taught Meg Ryan everything she knows!'

She was fuming now and her original intentions were all but forgotten. She crumpled the sheets of paper in her fist and thrust them into the back pocket of her jeans.

'You're angry,' observed Reed, as though she might have been unaware of the fact. 'But when you've had a chance to think about it, you'll realise that I'm right. You're a very attractive woman, Jenny, and last night, I was weak. Now I've got things back under control.'

'Well hooray for you!' sneered Jenny. 'Now if you'll excuse

me, I have some work to do.' She got up from her seat and pushed through the two sets of swing doors into the studio. Seeing her enter, Steve signalled to the others to wind up the tune and he turned to catch Chris's eye. By the time Jenny had strapped on her guitar, plugged into her amp and put on her headphones, the band had brought the tune to a perfectly synchronised conclusion. They exchanged self-congratulatory smiles.

'What did you think?' Adrian asked Jenny.

She glared at him.

'About what?'

'Well, about Robbie of course. I think you'll agree he's got Scott's style down pat.'

Jenny shrugged.

'That's true but I'm more interested in his own style, just at the moment.' She stalked across to the keyboards and asked for an A.

'Er . . . I already took the liberty of tuning your guitar,' said Robbie cautiously: but Jenny ignored him and made Adrian go through a scale while she plinked and retuned all her guitar strings. Her anger must have been evident and there was an uncomfortable atmosphere on the studio floor. When Reed's voice came over the intercom it was like a red rag to a bull.

'Jenny, care to give me a few words for a sound level?' he asked her meekly.

She stepped across to the microphone.

'Wanker, pillock, egotist, shit-head,' she snapped. 'How will that do ya?' She saw Steve and Chris exchange worried looks. 'Fuck, fuck, fuck, fuck, fuck!' she added.

'That's fine, thanks. Er . . . why don't you start with an oldie? *Love's Like a Hunger*?

'No,' said Jenny, turning back to face the band. 'We'll do *Liar*.'

'Christ, that's a blast from the past,' muttered Steve.

'What's up, forgotten how to play it?'

'Er ... no, I was thinking about Robbie.'

'That's OK,' Robbie assured him. 'Just give me the key, I'll follow you.'

'C,' said Jenny. She nodded to Chris. 'Count us in.'

Chris smacked out four beats on the snare and they launched headlong into the song, a fast and furious three-chord rocker. Jenny stepped up to the microphone and spat out the lyrics, directing them at the figure hunched over the console on the other side of the glass.

'Some women get what they deserve,
isn't that what you always said?
Need some man to flatter them senseless
plant pretty lies inside their heads.
And I was no different from the others
the first time I fell for one of your lines
I was too green to know the difference
or recognise the danger signs.

'Should've known you were a liar
you'd tell me black was white.
Nothin' but a dirty liar,
you'd swear that day was night.
And I believed every word you told me
as you led me into the fire ...
I should've known you were a liar!
A low down dirty liar!'

Jenny wasn't happy through the first couple of verses. It was a long time since any of them had played the song and it felt somehow as if everyone was straining in different directions, making the results awkward and unwieldy, like something that was going to fall apart at any moment: but as they hit the second chorus, something meshed, an undetectable squirt of oil onto the various interlocking cogs that held the song together. They swept into the third verse together and Jenny was able to relax a little, using her voice properly instead of snapping out the lyrics like a series of expletives.

She'd written the song about one of her first serious boyfriends, a minor league novelist called Tim, who seemed to be constantly on the point of making it big. She'd trusted him implicitly all through the six months of their relationship and saw herself marrying him, maybe even having kids. Then one day she'd come home unexpectedly and found him in bed with two sixteen-year-old Deceivers' fans, who'd called around in the hope of getting an autograph and had got rather more than they'd bargained for. It was only after she'd thrown him out that she learned he'd been dutifully knocking off everything in a skirt that came within reach, all through their time together. What was even more galling was the fact that all her friends seemed to know about it, but nobody had felt it was their place to tell her.

Now the song seemed a perfectly appropriate choice with which to serenade Gareth Reed. It was also a good baptism of fire for Robbie. Jenny finished belting out the third chorus and nodded to the kid to take the following sixteen-bar guitar solo.

Happily, he didn't try to copy the full tilt, frenetic squalling originated by Scott. Instead, he dropped back to a few spare, staccato notes for the first couple of bars; then gradually he added to them, increasing the speed and complexity as he built towards the crescendo. The effect was like a sports car revving up, then accelerating smoothly up to top speed. Despite herself, Jenny was impressed by the performance. It gave the song a dynamic quality that it hadn't previously possessed. She was so busy listening, she almost missed her cue back in, but she snapped back to the mic just in time to fling the final verse and chorus at the figure seated at the recording desk. Unfortunately, the low lighting robbed her of the pleasure of seeing the expression on his face.

Nor could she see the face of the other man who came gliding down the staircase and went to sit beside Reed in the vacant chair at the sound desk – but as he passed under a small overhead spotlight, she could see that he was tall and thin and that he had shoulder length blond hair tied back with a red bandanna...

The words seemed to hitch in her throat and she abandoned them altogether. She glanced at Steve to see if he'd noticed anything out of the ordinary, but he just seemed puzzled by her sudden silence. He raised his eyebrows in an inquiring look and she nodded through the glass towards the new arrival. Steve followed her line of sight and shrugged, as though he'd seen nothing out of the ordinary. She glanced over at Adrian and Chris but their heads were down over their respective instruments. They probably wouldn't have noticed if Elvis Presley had walked into the studio.

Meanwhile, the blond-haired figure just sat and watched Jenny from his chair. This was enough for her. She stopped playing and gradually the others became aware that something was wrong. The song staggered to an untidy conclusion.

'What's the problem?' complained Chris. 'That was going like fackin' gangbusters.'

'We ... we seem to have a visitor,' said Jenny, nodding meaningfully towards the glass. It had occurred to her that if this really was Scott's ghost, maybe she was the only one who could see the apparition. 'There, beside Gareth ... see?'

'Yeah, so?' muttered Steve.

'No, I uh...' She looked around at the others in dull surprise. 'I ... er ... need a glass of water. Got a frog in my throat.'

'Must stop giving blow jobs to Sacha Distel,' quipped Chris and everybody laughed except Jenny. 'Here, you sure you're all right? You don't look so good.'

But Jenny was already letting herself out of the studio, pushing through into the control room. What the fuck was going on here? Everybody else seemed to be seeing somebody in the other chair, but surely they *couldn't* be seeing what she was seeing...

As she came through, Reed was getting to his feet, a worried expression on his face.

'Something wrong?' he asked her. 'I was just starting to enjoy that.'

'Needed a drink, that's all.' She went over to a small refrigerator at the back of the room and got herself a Diet Coke. She was still aware of the other man watching her silently from the shadows. 'Aren't you ... going to introduce me?' she asked fearfully. She half expected a look of incredulity, Reed peering stupidly around the room as he muttered, 'Introduce you to *who*?' But no, he was smiling apologetically.

'Oh, of course, I forgot you haven't met him yet. He went up to the pub last night to introduce himself to the others, but you ... er ... stayed behind.' Reed stepped aside and the other man leaned forward into a pool of light from an overhead spot. 'Jenny, this is Idris Morgan.'

And Jenny almost laughed with relief. She could see now that the man was much older than Scott Griffin. He had the same build and hair but the face was leaner, more grizzled, the nose long and sharp. The man's small black eyes, deep set beneath blond eyebrows, glittered malevolently.

Jenny smiled back at him.

'I think I've seen you already,' she told him. 'Yesterday, in the woods?

Idris grinned, displaying rows of sharp, misshapen teeth. It was a wolfish face, hard, predatory: and the eyes seemed to settle on her with a terrible intensity, as though considering what her flesh might taste like.

'Is that a fact?' he murmured. He had a coarse, gravelly voice that was little more than a whisper. 'Yeah, I was out there. I don't believe I saw you, though.'

'No, I . . . er . . . was kind of lost. I would have tried following you but you seemed to vanish into thin air.'

He sighed, nodded, but offered no explanation. There was a silence that seemed to go on for ever.

'It's easily done,' he said, at last. 'Those woods can be deadly if you don't know your way around. But still, you're here now, aren't you? And it's a real pleasure to meet you, Jenny. A thrill. You see, the thing is . . . I'm a big fan of yours.'

'That's . . . er . . . nice,' said Jenny lamely. Idris just sat there, grinning at her and it was suddenly very, very quiet in the studio. 'Well, er . . . nice to meet you, at last. I'd better get on with some work I suppose.'

Idris didn't say anything else. He just sat there watching her and smiling. She could feel the intensity of his eyes burning into the back of her head as she returned to the studio.

'OK,' she said to the others. 'We made a cock up of that one. I think we'll try it again, shall we? From the top.' She nodded to Chris and he obligingly smacked out four beats on the snare. They took another stab at the song and, this time, managed to get through it without interruption.

Chapter Seventeen

Back on the studio floor, Jenny ran through some more numbers with the band. They did *Love's Like a Hunger*, *Maneating Woman, Fast and Loose* and a whole bunch of other titles. The songs were all a little unfocused and there were a lot of rough edges but that was only to be expected. Overall, Jenny was encouraged by the way it was going. The band was working well together and she had to admit that Robbie Porter fitted seamlessly into the mix.

She was feeling a lot happier now that she'd realised that the 'apparition' in the woods had simply been Idris Morgan, out for a stroll around his traps. With his long blond hair and lanky frame, it had been an understandable mistake: but the gaunt face that surveyed her through the glass screen was nothing like Scott's. It was a hard-looking face, the pale skin prematurely lined and furrowed, the thin mouth curved in a mocking smile. He had taken over at the desk and his long fingers moved restlessly over its surface, adjusting knobs and sliders to refine the overall sound.

Jenny couldn't help thinking what an unlikely partner he made for a shy, gentle girl like Cassie. She tried to picture the two of them together, but somehow couldn't. They seemed the very antithesis of each other. Maybe that was it, she reasoned, an attraction of opposites. It took all kinds . . .

'Not bad, Jenny, it's coming along nicely. Why don't you try something from *Red Tape* next?

Reed's voice on the studio intercom irritated her with its smugness but she resisted saying anything back to him and, instead, dutifully informed the band that they'd have a stab at *Twist and Turn*, another fast-paced rocker with some tricky time signatures in it. She figured if they could get through this one, they could handle just about anything. The awkward opening sequence caused them a couple of false starts but once they had the song up and running, they settled into their stride and Jenny really began to enjoy herself.

'Some women they have men to burn
Catch 'em at every twist and turn,
Cast the bait and make a wish
Reel 'em in like stranded fish
But no matter what I do,
I can't get my hooks in you.'

Strange song. Jenny wasn't sure where it came from or even who it was about. The elusive male, she supposed. The fabled Mr Right, who she seemed destined never to meet. Last night, just for a while there, she'd begun to wonder if Gareth Reed might not be the man to occupy that coveted post, but this morning, she'd decided, he was just like all the other creeps who'd charmed their way into her bed.

She came out of the third chorus and nodded Robbie to take the final solo. He needed no second bidding, his nimble fingers flying across the frets to produce a maelstrom of shrieking notes. He was grinning all over his pretty face because he was acquitting himself admirably and he knew it.

They all hit the final chord together and suddenly, the mood was lighter, they were laughing, swapping insults, even offering praise to their newest member.

'Fack me, Robbie, that was a bit tasty!' observed Chris.

'Yeah,' agreed Steve. 'Sounded like you'd been playing it for years.'

'Robbie knows all the songs on *Red Tape*,' announced Adrian, sounding for all the world like a proud parent. 'We went over them together, last week.'

'Why don't we break for some coffee?' suggested Reed, over the intercom. 'I taped that one, maybe you'd like to come through and hear it back?'

Everybody downed instruments and trooped through to the control room, where they helped themselves to coffee from the percolator. Reed ran the tape and Jenny had to admit to herself that for all its rough and ready qualities, the song sounded impressive. Her fears that The Deceivers had burned themselves out were evidently ill founded. This sounded like a band that still had plenty to offer and new goals to achieve.

But for all that, Jenny couldn't settle. The thought of the letter she'd received that morning nagged at her repeatedly and she realised that she'd have to talk to somebody about it. Lezard was the obvious choice but he'd be back in London by now, sorting out the details of Mike's funeral. The treatment she'd received from Reed that morning had deterred her from sharing any confidence with him: so she decided to sound out Steve on the subject. There was a no smoking policy in the studio so when he slipped out to an adjoining room for a cigarette, she excused herself and followed him in. Without saying anything else, she handed him the two pages of the letter.

Steve studied them in silence for a moment, a look of disgust on his bearded face.

'Where did you get these?' he asked her.

'They came by post this morning,' she told him. 'Thing is, hardly anyone outside the band knew we were coming here.'

Steve frowned.

'And for this to have arrived this morning...'

'Yeah, that's what I figured. It's almost certainly come from Mike's killer.'

'His *killer*?' Steve looked shocked by the remark. 'Now hold on, Jenny, you can't go jumping to conclusions like that. We don't know that he was murdered.'

'Well, how else do you explain it? For the letter to be posted before Mary discovered the body...'

'I see what you're getting at, but Christ! Who'd want to kill Mike?'

'I don't know. But what worries me, if the guy who wrote that did kill Mike ... well, he knows where to find the rest of us, doesn't he? He obviously has our address. And there's this...' She showed him the first note and pointed out the 'one down and four to go' line. Steve grimaced, reached for his cigarettes.

'Sick fucker,' he muttered. 'But Jenny, poison pen letters are nothing new in this business. We've had our share of them before.'

'This is different. It's just too much of a coincidence, Mike dying the way he did.'

Steve lit his cigarette and inhaled deeply.

'I think you're reading too much into it. It's just some sad no-life fuck trying to throw a scare into you. Next thing, you'll be telling me that Scott's death was no accident, either.'

Jenny lit her own cigarette and studied Steve thoughtfully, as she blew out smoke.

'But we already know it wasn't an accident, don't we? Or do you think somebody "accidentally" cut his heroin with toilet cleaner?'

'Well, of course not. But you know what I mean. It wasn't a deliberate murder, was it?'

There was a long silence during which they just looked at each other.

'Oh, come on, Jenny, this is ridiculous!' said Steve. 'You're starting to sound like a paranoid. I know you had a bad time after Scott died and everything...'

Jenny glared at him.

'I don't see what that has to do with it!' she protested. 'The point is, Mike is dead and we have a letter that appears to claim responsibility. At any rate, I think we should tell the others, see what they think about it.'

'No way.' Steve was shaking his head vigorously. 'Not a good idea, Jenny. How do you think Chris and Adrian would react to a story like that? They'd be running for the hills if they got so much as a sniff of this. It's like Lezard said, this session is too important to just blow it away.'

'Jesus, Steve, what's the big deal? It's only a rehearsal, for God's sake.'

'Maybe just to you!' he snapped. 'It's all right for some of us, isn't it, the ones who have money coming out of our ears. Some of us have more at stake than that!' He was suddenly angry, his eyes glaring in a way that Jenny had never seen before. 'We have to get the band rolling again,' he said. 'We... we just have to. I need the money.'

'What are you talking about?' protested Jenny.

'I'm talking about potential bankruptcy. I'm talking about the bank taking my home off me.' Steve began to pace around the room and Jenny was reminded of a grizzly bear she had once seen, lumbering backwards and forwards around the confines of an inadequate zoo enclosure. 'Moving to the mansion like we did, it ... it stretched us to the limit financially, but I figured we'd be OK, because we had the tour coming up. Then, Scott dying like he did, the tour blown out from under us . . . well, the long and the short of it is, we're in a hole and it seems to get deeper every day. I have to get back on the road, Jenny.'

'Steve, I'm sorry, I had no idea . . .'

'How could you have! You're the one with the publishing deal, you just sit back and the money comes rolling in. The rest of us have to struggle along the best we can.'

'Some struggle,' muttered Jenny. She felt hurt by his obvious resentment of her success. 'A twenty-room mansion. It is a bit over the top, isn't it, Steve? Why couldn't you just live in a normal house, like everybody else?'

He shrugged, sighed.

'Peg had her heart set on the place, didn't she? Wanted to play the lady of the manor. And it's great at Christmas, you can get all your friends and family together . . .'

'Well, OK, so that's one day a year it makes sense. What about the other three hundred and sixty-four of them? Maybe you should sell up and look for somewhere more modest.'

'It's not as simple as that. How many potential buyers do you think there'd be for a place like that? It could take years to sell it and we'd probably have to settle for less than we paid.'

'Yes, but surely . . .'

'We'll be all right,' he interrupted her. 'Once there's a new tour and an album under our belts, I'll be able to salvage the situation. But I can't afford to hang around, you can understand that, surely?' He handed the papers back to her. 'All I'm saying is, cool it with this until we've had a chance to discuss it with Lezard. He'll be back tomorrow and he'll know the best way to handle it. Just don't go freaking everybody out, OK? That's the last thing I can afford.'

Jenny frowned, but then she nodded.

'All right. We'll see what Lezard thinks. But listen, Steve, if you're stuck for money, you could always come to me, you know? I've got more than I know what to do with anyway.'

Steve looked suddenly offended.

'I'd rather pay my own way,' he said curtly.

'Oh come on, don't be like that with me. I'm offering to help, that's all.'

'I don't need your help!' he snapped. He stubbed out his cigarette in a cut-glass ashtray. 'We'd better get back to it,' he said. He went out of the room to join the others.

Jenny was left standing there, dismayed by his attitude. She'd always felt close to Steve Lampton and had assumed that he'd felt the same about her. But his attitude had been cold and resentful. It had almost felt like he hated her.

'Great,' she muttered. 'The wonderful world of show biz.' She sighed, stubbed out her own cigarette and went to join the others back in the studio.

They worked on existing material until twelve thirty when they broke for lunch. Cassie had set out a meal for them in the dining room, a hearty vegetable soup with crusty wholemeal bread and a selection of meats and cheeses. Reed and the band took their seats, but Idris announced that he had things to do, and promptly made himself scarce. Just as they were starting, Emma Savage appeared in the doorway, red-eyed and tousle-haired, looking as though she'd just dragged herself out of bed.

'So glad you could join us,' said Robbie brightly.

'Fuck off,' suggested Emma and everybody around the table oohed in unison. Emma slumped down in a vacant seat, sneered at the food on offer and lit a cigarette instead.

'You *could* wait till we've finished eating,' Adrian chided her. She just gave him a look and went on smoking defiantly.

Through the window, they could see that the snow had started to come down again, large thick flakes whirling out of a sorrowful grey sky. The wind was gusting out there, stirring the snow into whirls and eddies.

'Looks promising,' muttered Jenny. 'There were weather warnings on TV last night.'

'Wouldn't have thought you'd have had time to watch the telly,' said Emma, slyly. She was hunched over the table like a sleepy dormouse, a disagreeable expression on her face.

'Oh, I always watch ten minutes or so, just before I go to sleep,' Jenny informed her. 'Helps me to get off. Of course, if I have really bad insomnia, I read one of your columns instead. Does the trick every time.'

'Love fifteen,' said Chris, and everybody sniggered. Everybody but Emma, that is. She threw a hateful glare around the table.

'This place is the pits,' she complained. 'I don't know why I came here. There's nothing to do and nowhere to go.'

'How about a nice walk in the garden?' suggested Jenny, indicating the thick snow swirling past the window. 'I'm sure Mr Reed will give you directions to the nearest slate quarry.'

'Love thirty,' said Steve, reaching for another slice of bread.

'Oh, very funny,' growled Emma. She elbowed Chris in the ribs. 'Give me some of that acid you were saving, there's a good boy. Maybe if I'm out of my head, this hole won't seem so grim.'

Chris sighed and took a small Victorian pill box from his jeans pocket. Emma opened it and extracted a small yellow tab. She popped it into her mouth and swallowed it down with a gulp of white wine.

'You having one?' she asked Chris.

'I'll wait till we've finished rehearsals,' he said, with uncharacteristic reserve. He took the box from her and returned it to his pocket.

'I think we've been making good progress this morning,'

announced Adrian, disdainfully. He was obviously keen to divert everyone's attention from what he considered to be rather squalid behaviour. 'Maybe it's time we had a look at Jenny's new songs.'

'Yeah, how about it, Jenny?' said Chris. 'Be nice to have some new material to work on.'

Jenny shrugged.

'I don't know,' she said. 'The things I have are just rough ideas. I'm not sure they're ready for the band to play.'

'Hasn't stopped you before,' observed Emma.

'Fifteen thirty,' said Steve.

Jenny fixed Emma with a withering look.

'Emma, *darling*, why don't you just fuck off somewhere and take a nice little overdose?' she growled.

Reed winced.

'Come on now, you two, can't you try and get along with each other?' he pleaded. 'It's very disruptive, all this bitching.'

'Don't worry,' Emma assured him. 'I'm not hanging around much longer, anyway. Reckon I might get a taxi back to London tonight.'

Robbie was amused by this.

'A taxi? Have you any idea how much that will cost?'

Emma shrugged.

'Chris will pay for it, won't you, sweetie?'

Chris stared at her.

'You are joking, I trust! You can get a train back, if you really have to go.'

'A train? I can't get a train! I'm a celebrity!'

'I did warn you, if you came, you'd be here for two weeks,' Chris told her.

'Yes, but you didn't tell me it would be like this. I mean, there's nothing to do here. I'm bored rigid. Couldn't you drive me back to London?'

'I couldn't even get you to the fackin' station,' Chris told her. 'Maybe you forgot, but I wrapped my car around a tree when we arrived here. We ain't goin' anywhere in that.'

'You may be missing an important point,' Reed told them. He nodded at the window and the thick flurries of snow beyond them. 'If that keeps up, *none* of us will be going anywhere.'

Everybody looked at him.

'What are you saying?' asked Adrian.

'I'm just pointing out that if snow settles on the road leading up here, it'll soon be impassable. And it'll be days before the snow ploughs make it out to this neck of the woods.'

'Oh, great,' said Jenny. 'So you're telling us we could get snowed in.'

'If it keeps up like this for the rest of the day, I'd say it's a certainty,' concluded Reed.

There was a pause: then Steve spoke.

'Well, that suits me. We're here to work and there'll be nothing to do but concentrate on the music.' He gave Jenny a meaningful look. 'So, as we were saying,' he reminded her. 'What about these new songs?'

Chapter Eighteen

Back in the studio, Jenny pulled a stool up to the microphone and set her notebook on a music stand. She perused her three sets of new lyrics and wondered which one she should try first. In the end, she decided on the most recent of them, *Live Fast, Die Young*. She turned around to face the others, presenting her back to the people at the mixing desk and she started to strum out the chord sequence on the Gretsch. She was aware of Reed, Idris and a very stoned Emma Savage regarding her from the other side of the glass. Emma had begun to act very strangely indeed, but whereas acid usually blissed people out, she seemed to be even more aggressive than usual. Her voice came over the intercom like a deranged Erich Von Stroheim.

'Come on, let's get this show on the road!' she babbled. 'Lights, camera, action! Hit me with your rhythm stick and play that funky music, white boy!'

Jenny took a deep breath.

'Somebody get that monkey away from the controls, or I'm not playing another note,' she announced to the studio in general.

'Sorry, Jenny.' Reed's voice on the intercom now, meek and apologetic. 'She's been warned.'

'OK.' Jenny looked at her musicians. She began to strum the

chord sequence, talking as she played. 'This is just a straight ahead rock song. It goes C, F, G…'

'How refreshingly original,' muttered Adrian, but Jenny ignored the taunt. She knew only too well that Adrian couldn't have written a pop song to save his life. His few compositions had all been pompous, semi-classical instrumentals, the soundtracks to imaginary movies where everybody wore crinolines and moved around in slow motion. At one time, he'd tried to get one of his pieces included on a Deceivers album, but it had been totally unsuitable and everybody had told him so.

'…then for the chorus, we go A minor, G, E minor, F. Robbie, I need some kind of a riff to go over this, something spiky, ballsy. Adrian, I want you to just hold down a rhythm on the electric piano, nothing too fancy.'

'I dare say I'll manage that,' said Adrian coolly.

'Chris, it's just a four four rhythm and, Steve … yeah, that's fine, just keep doing what you're doing for now. We can pretty it up later.' She listened to them for a moment while Robbie tried various riffs over the rhythm track. Eventually, they settled on one they both liked. 'That's good for me but how about taking it down to a lower key? Chris, lay off the cymbals will you, I can't hear myself think! Just hi-hat and snare … OK, that's better. Now the lyrics.' She took a deep breath and leaned in close to the microphone. *Here goes nothing*, she thought: and began to sing.

'You always knew where you were headed
Let no one stand in your way
Just another kid with a second-hand guitar
Some songs you practised every day.
You always told me that we'd make it

I always knew you'd be a star.
Never dreamed that we'd get so high together
or that you'd take it quite so far.

'And Live Fast, Die Young – you used to tell me
no point in walking when you can fly.
Live Fast, Die Young – oh, my pretty baby
the world looks better when you're high, high, high!
the world looks better when you're high, high, high!'

She had this vague idea of bringing some female backing singers in on a repetition of the 'high, high, high' line, try to imbue it with a kind of gospel feel. Maybe even add a brass section. The trick of writing a good pop song was to be able to imagine how it would sound, once it had been worked on, streamlined, produced.

She ran through the other verses, stumbling over the odd word here and there where the line didn't quite scan. She kept her eyes closed while she sang, not wanting to have to endure looks of disapproval from the others – but when she'd got to the end of it, she saw that Steve and Chris were smiling and nodding their approval. Adrian *always* looked snotty anyway and Robbie was too unsure of himself as yet to comment either way.

'That'll do nicely,' said Steve. 'If we really make something of the chorus, we might have a hit single there.'

Jenny brightened.

'Think so?'

'Yeah, for sure,' agreed Chris. 'It's er ... about Scott, right?'

'How very perceptive,' sneered Adrian.

'Fack off, Richard Clayderman! You just concentrate on getting that piano right, you were all over the shop back there.'

'I was following you,' Adrian assured him.

Steve turned his attention towards the glass.

'What did you think?' he asked.

There was a short pause, then a slurred voice buzzed over the intercom.

'I thought it was bollocks!' cackled Emma. 'Another mawkish tribute to another dead rock star. It was the biggest load of old toss I've ever heard!'

Jenny smiled thinly.

'Now I *know* we've got a top ten hit,' she said.

'Fifteen forty!' announced Robbie, with a grin.

There was a brief struggle on the other side of the glass, then Reed spoke into the intercom.

'Let me just say that I totally disagree with Ms Savage's assessment,' he said. 'Sounded pretty bloody good to me.'

'Thanks,' said Jenny, coldly. She turned back to the others. 'Think you can bear to run through it a few more times?'

This was the way she always worked on a new song, going over and over it, changing the odd detail here, ironing out the occasional hiccup there, until performing it felt like second nature and the song began to take on a life of its own. Sometimes you could do all that and the song still didn't feel as if it was quite there. That was when it was time to junk it and concentrate on something else: but thankfully, there weren't too many of her compositions that she hadn't been able to shape into something worth recording. And the more she played this one, the stronger it felt.

They continued to work on it for the remainder of the afternoon, chipping away at the rough edges. Robbie came up with a ballsier riff and, against her better judgement, Jenny allocated a four-bar synthesizer solo to Adrian.

'Why don't we try one last take on that?' suggested Reed. 'It might be useful to hear it back.'

'OK.' Jenny waited for the red recording light to come on, then cued everybody in. They went through the new song one last time with feeling and it seemed to have acquired a slick, snappy tone that really suited it. Jenny could imagine it with a trio of black female voices belting out the chorus. Maybe Steve was right about it being a potential hit. They reached the last chord together, downed instruments and went through to the control room to hear it back. Reed rewound the tape and punched it in through the big Bose speakers.

But there was a problem. It was Steve's keen ears that caught it first.

'What the fuck is *that*?' he asked the others.

Jenny concentrated. Now she could hear it too. Way, way back in the mix, there seemed to be another guitar playing a totally inappropriate solo: a shrieking, wailing howl of prolonged feedback that was only just loud enough to register as an unpleasant dissonance to the ear.

Reed looked totally bewildered. He tried adjusting various channel faders, attempting to filter the background sound away, but it didn't seem to be working. It was on all of them.

'What is this?' he muttered. 'One of the amps picked up a radio signal or something?' He looked at Idris, but the engineer's face was blank.

'I don't understand it,' he admitted. 'It's definitely not a radio.' He'd put a set of headphones on and was listening intently. 'It seems to be on every channel, as though it was picked up by all the studio mics.'

'Maybe it's some kind of bleed-through,' suggested Adrian. 'Something that was recorded on the tape before.'

'No, the tape's brand new,' Reed assured him. 'I unwrapped it myself.'

'Well, it's coming from somewhere,' muttered Steve. He glanced at Jenny. 'Does it ... does it sound familiar to you?'

It did. Horribly familiar. Listening to it, Jenny was transported back in time to that night in Seattle. She was standing there helpless, watching Scott lying on his back on the stage, his fingers clawing spasmodically at his guitar strings as he fought for his life. And the sounds he was making were very much like the sounds she could discern now. She looked at Steve and saw that he was thinking the same thing.

Oh God, it's Scott. It's the last sounds he ever made.

Steve saw what was on her mind and shook his head.

'It's some kind of gremlin,' he assured her. 'These things happen. Remember when we were doing the second album and from out of nowhere, we picked up a speech by Maggie Thatcher? Jesus, that just about scared the life out of me, I can tell you!'

Jenny looked around at the others. Adrian's face was as impassive as ever, Chris and Emma seemed not to have noticed a thing, Robbie looked simply miffed that his own guitar was being ruined by this unexplained noise. Idris had a strange, thoughtful expression on his face. As for Reed, he looked indignant as he tried in vain to filter out the cacophony of unwanted sound. On the tape, the band hit the final chord and the sound faded along with the weird solo.

'Doesn't make sense,' growled Reed. 'I guess we'll just have to try another take.' He reached out a hand for the 'stop' button but froze as a different sound bubbled from the speakers, emerging from the background of slight tape hiss that followed in the wake of the song.

'Jeeeennnny!'

Jenny flinched as a jolt of absolute terror lanced through her. The voice was a sibilant, drawn-out whisper loaded with reverb, but there was no mistaking it. It was every bit as familiar as the guitar sound that had preceded it. Jenny gave an involuntary gasp of fear and she moved instinctively closer to

Steve. Everybody in the studio was reacting now, staring at the tape deck in pop-eyed astonishment. Apart from Idris. Jenny noticed that he was smiling, as though intrigued by what had happened.

'Jeeeennnny! I'm cold. I'm so cold.'

For a few moments, nobody said anything. Then Chris gave a wild laugh.

'All right, Gareth, very fackin' clever. You owe me a new pair of underpants. But how did you—?'

'Hey, it's not me,' Reed assured him. He spread his hands as though to demonstrate that he wasn't holding any hidden strings. 'I swear I'm as baffled as you are.'

'Ah, bollocks!' said Emma. 'It's just somebody's idea of a joke, that's all.' She looked accusingly at Chris. 'Come on, own up,' she told him wearily.

'Me?' Chris looked wounded. 'Why do you assume it's me? I wouldn't have the first idea how to—'

'Of course it's you,' said Adrian. 'It's *always* you.'

'Not this time, I—'

'Jeeeennnny!' The voice was louder this time, at a volume that made Jenny shudder.

'Turn that fucking thing off!' she snapped and Reed moved to obey her, silencing the eerie whisper at the touch of a button. It was suddenly very quiet in the studio, everyone looking at each other, trying to determine who was responsible for such a cruel prank. Jenny knew that Chris would be viewed as the most likely culprit, but she also knew that he was no mimic: and the voice on the tape had been Scott Griffin.

Reed sat back in his chair and glanced sheepishly around the circle of accusing faces.

'Look, er ... this may be a good time to take a break,' he suggested. 'Idris and I will check over the equipment, see if we can find an explanation for ...'

'The explanation is quite obvious,' announced Idris, with a wry smile. 'We've got ourselves a ghost. What's so unusual about that?' He glanced around at the surrounding crypt. 'Old place like this, there are sure to be ghosts, aren't there? Actually, I think it's pretty interesting.'

His smugness was beginning to irritate Jenny.

'It would need a sound engineer to doctor that tape,' she pointed out. 'And you've been going missing ever since we arrived here.'

Idris laughed, displaying his sharp, white teeth.

'Oh, please, at least be logical. You heard Gareth tell you that it was a brand new tape, didn't you? It would be relatively easy for me to mess around with a recording *after* it was made: but as it's being laid down? I don't think so.'

'So what other explanation is there?' she asked him.

'Face the truth, Miss Slade. Whatever's been added to that tape has been put there by supernatural means. Somebody on the other side is obviously desperate to contact you.' He was still smiling at her in that knowing way. He was giving her the creeps and she felt suddenly that she didn't want to stay down here a moment longer.

'Yeah, well that about does it for me,' she announced. 'I'll come back when you've decided to stop playing silly buggers.' She turned away from the others and made her way up the stairs to the ground floor: but in her mind, her own words kept coming back to her.

Tell Scott to get in touch.

Why was she denying it so vehemently? The voice on the tape had belonged to Scott. No impersonation could have been that accurate. She had to face the possibility that what the weird kid had told her a couple of weeks back was true. Scott was trying to reach her. He was trying to tell her something.

Out of all the confusion, a possible explanation emerged like a light moving slowly out of a blizzard. Could it be . . . could it possibly be, that he was trying to *warn* her about something? The premonition she'd had, that something bad was coming. She'd thought that Mike's death had fulfilled that but maybe it was something worse. Something that affected her more directly.

Maybe she was in danger.

She pushed through the entrance door into the hallway and stood for a moment, unsure of where to go. Then obeying some unidentified instinct, she walked through the dining room and the kitchen and opened the back door, leading to the courtyard.

Taking a deep breath, she stepped out into the storm.

Chapter Nineteen

Jenny stifled a curse as she felt the power of the wind. It flung stinging flurries of snow into her face, but she ducked her head and descended the stairs to the courtyard.

Ahead of her she could see her Aston Martin parked up with the other vehicles, the roof and bonnet already thickly covered with a layer of white powdery snow: and she thought very seriously about getting into the car and driving the fuck away from here before the weather got too bad to allow her any chance of escape.

She trudged across to the vehicle, weighing up the idea as she did so. Her good sense told her that she would at least have to go back into the house to collect her jacket. It was freezing out here and she wouldn't give much for her chances dressed as she was in sweatshirt and jeans. Furthermore, she supposed she'd have to tell somebody what she was doing, or risk having all kinds of recriminations. But she also knew that if she announced her intention of leaving, the others would talk her out of it, give her that whole routine about how important this session was. And after what Steve had said about his finances, it was plain that she couldn't count on him for support.

She was standing there indecisively when she heard a sound from the front drive: the heavy laboured rumble of a car engine coming slowly towards the house. She moved across to the archway and peered into the dazzling white of the falling snow. An eerie yellow glow loomed out of the intervening blizzard and then it formed itself into two bright spheres. The shape of the car became visible as it lurched towards the archway. A Mitsubishi Shogun, the wheels spinning madly on the precarious surface of the drive.

'Lezard!' Jenny lifted her arms to wave them in greeting as the Shogun covered the last few yards and rumbled into the courtyard. She could see him now, hunched over the wheel, looking exhausted. She ran to the vehicle and flung the door open. 'Lezard, thank God you're here!'

He slumped back in his seat with a sigh of relief.

'What a nightmare trip that was,' he muttered. 'I had no idea the weather was so bad. It's absolutely clear in London. For a while back there, I didn't think I was going to make it up the hill. Thank Christ for four-wheel drive.' He looked at her quizzically. 'What the hell are you doing out here with no coat on?'

'Just taking the air.' She felt better now. It seemed that her prayers had been answered. 'But what are you doing back so soon? We weren't expecting you till tomorrow.'

He gave her a strange look, as though he didn't believe what she'd just said.

'Are you kidding? I'm here because you wanted me.'

She laughed at the remark.

'Yeah, but how did you know? Getting psychic in your old age?'

Now he looked weary.

'For Christ's sake, Jenny, this had better not be some kind of practical joke. I nearly killed myself getting back here. I'd only been in the office five minutes when I got your message. Hadn't even had a chance to arrange to see Mary and the . . .'

'Message?' Jenny stared at him. 'What message?'

He sighed, then reached into his coat pocket and pulled out a sheet of fax paper.

'I'm talking about this,' he told her. 'Or had you forgotten you'd sent it?'

Jenny took the sheet of paper and read the brief typed note:

Lezard,
I'm in desperate trouble. Essential that you get back here as soon as possible. Please hurry.
Jenny.

She stood there, open mouthed in bewilderment.

'But ... I didn't send this!' she protested.

'No?' Lezard indicated the I.D. header at the top of the sheet. There it was. The Grange Studio. Today's date. And the time the message had been sent. One twenty-three p.m. 'Somebody did,' he said quietly.

'Yes, but I swear to you, it wasn't me. We ... we broke for lunch around that time, I guess anybody could have got into the office and sent a fax.'

Lezard considered this for a moment.

'If this is one of Chris Spencer's stupid tricks,' he muttered, 'I'll skin the bastard alive. I tried phoning the studio to check on it, but I couldn't get through. Operator told me there was some kind of fault on the line, probably due to the weather conditions.' He sighed, ran a hand through his hair. 'So there's nothing wrong?' he asked her.

'I wouldn't say that. There's some very strange things happening here, Josh. That's why I was so glad to see you. For one thing, I had another of those crank letters. Must have arrived this morning, before you left. It was about Mike. He ... he knew about Mike.'

Lezard made a face.

'Oh, for God's sake, he's traced you *here*?'

She nodded.

'Yes.'

'That's all we need! Letters from some sick fuck, who—'

'It's worse than that, Josh. I figured out the letter must have been sent *before* Mary even found Mike's body.'

Lezard scratched his head.

'But, Jenny, how can that be—?'

'Possible? Oh, I think it's more than possible, Josh. I think Mike was murdered.'

He gave her a wary look.

'Hey, now just a minute,' he said. 'Let's not get carried away...'

'It's the only explanation! And that's not all. We just recorded a track down in the studio and ... I know this sounds crazy, but ... well, when we played it back, Scott's voice was on it.'

Now the expression on his face had gone beyond wary. He was looking at her as though she had flipped.

'Jenny,' he said gently, 'I know you've been through a hard time, but...'

'Don't give me that shit!' she snapped. 'Why is it every time I open my mouth to speak, somebody comes out with that line?'

'I'm sorry, but you must admit, it does sound a little crazy. Scott's voice? How could that happen?'

'I don't know ... but please stop looking at me like that! I'm not a basket case and I'm not imagining things. Ask the others if you don't believe me. We all heard it.'

'You heard *something*,' admitted Lezard. 'But can't you see, Jenny, it's some kind of a trick. Somebody's winding you up. It's most probably Chris, he's always pulling stunts like this...'

'Not this time, Josh, I'm sure of it. I think . . . I really believe that Scott is . . . haunting me. He's trying to get through to me for some reason. Like . . . like maybe there's something he wants to tell me.' She was trembling now, with a mixture of cold and fear. Lezard got out of the Shogun and put an arm around her.

'Let's get back inside,' he said. 'We'll talk this through in the warm, over a glass of brandy.' He slammed the door of the car and turned her around towards the house. He took his mobile phone from his pocket as he walked and punched in a number. 'Better just phone the office, let them know I arrived safely.' He listened for a moment, then cursed. 'Now *this* isn't working!' he snapped. He tried again a couple of times with no better luck.

'It'll be the weather,' said a voice and glancing up, they saw Reed, standing at the top of the steps. 'The phones in the office are down too. Must have gone off some time this afternoon.'

'Yeah? Well the lines were evidently working at one twenty-three p.m.,' snapped Lezard.

Reed looked puzzled by the remark.

'What do you mean?'

'Somebody sent me a fax.' Lezard pulled it from his pocket and thrust it at Reed. He glanced at it non-committally.

'Yeah, well obviously *Jenny* sent it. It has her name on it.'

'She says not. Actually, my money's on Chris Spencer.' Lezard tried dialling the office number again, without success. 'Goddamn!' he snapped. 'This thing's supposed to be state-of-the-art and it's making noises like the Twilight Zone.'

'It's the snow,' said Reed, gesturing out into the courtyard. 'I'm amazed you managed to get through, Josh. What was it like coming up the hill?'

'Desperate. We're going to have to get that problem sorted

out in the spring. We can't be having this trouble every time there's a fall of...'

He broke off, but not before Jenny had caught the inference in what he was saying.

'We?' she echoed. 'What do you mean, *we*?'

'Er ... nothing, it was just a figure of speech.'

But glancing up at Reed, Jenny saw an expression of pure guilt on his face. He was looking off across the courtyard, as though he'd suddenly become very interested in the vehicles parked across the way.

'It's more than a figure of speech,' persisted Jenny. 'What's going on, Josh? Is there something I should know?'

Lezard sighed.

'I ... was going to tell you about it, anyway. Sooner or later.'

'Tell me what?'

'That Gareth and I are business partners in this place.'

Jenny felt a jolt of dismay go through her.

'You ... you're partners? Since when?'

Lezard looked shamefaced, now, like a child caught doing something he shouldn't.

'From the beginning. Gareth found the property but he needed somebody to come in with him. So—'

'You two-faced bastard!' she cried. 'You never mentioned it to me when you asked me to come up here.'

'I ... didn't think it was important.' He shrugged. 'I mean, I don't see what difference it makes.'

'Are you kidding? Do you think I'm stupid or something?' She slipped into a sarcastic approximation of Lezard's American accent. 'A friend of mine has just opened this new studio in Wales. It's the most extraordinary place. Get out in those mountains and forests and you'll soon feel inspired!' She laughed bitterly. 'No mention of the fact that you had a financial stake in The Grange. Or how good it would be for the studio's credibility if The Deceivers recorded here.'

'Oh, now, Jenny, that was the last thing on my . . .'

'But do you know what really hurts, Josh? The fact that you couldn't bring yourself to tell me that the place was half yours. Did you think I'd go off the idea if I knew? That I'd assume you were trying to exploit the band?'

Lezard was staring down at his snow-encrusted shoes now.

'It wasn't like that,' he protested. 'I was going to tell you when the time felt right.'

'Oh yeah? And when would that be? When the new album was climbing the fucking charts? You shit! Of all the people here, at least I thought I could trust you.' Another thought hit her. 'And I suppose getting Mr Sexual Healing here to coax me into bed was all part of the deal, was it?'

Lezard seemed stunned by this news. He glared up at Reed, who stood there looking decidedly uncomfortable.

'Gareth?' he growled.

'Hey.' Reed spread his hands in a shrug. 'It just happened, Josh. It's not like the two of you are married or anything, is it?'

'I told you she was out of bounds. Can't you keep your cock in your pocket, just once?'

Jenny had heard enough. She ran up the steps and pushed past Reed, into the house. Behind her she could hear the two men launching into a loud argument. She was almost numb with cold and swamped by a terrible sense of betrayal. Was there nobody in this place she could trust?

She went straight to the dining room and opened the drinks cabinet. Pulling out a bottle of tequila, she poured a stiff shot into a glass and gulped it down in one. She gasped and her eyes filled with tears but it wasn't because of the drink.

'Lying bastards,' she snarled. 'Every last one of them!' And with shaking hands, she refilled her glass to the brim.

Chapter Twenty

That night the weather worsened dramatically. The wind increased in ferocity, until it was whipping the falling snow into frantic blizzards and distributing large drifts around the courtyard. At the same time the temperature dropped to several degrees below zero, eliminating any chance of a thaw. It quickly became apparent that this was going to be more than just a brief disruption. They might be marooned out here for quite some time.

With any prospect of adjourning to the village pub well and truly out of the question, Jenny and the other members of the band took refuge in the large front sitting room, where a blazing log fire did its level best to imbue the place with a cheerful atmosphere – but the effect was marred somewhat by the huge portrait of Obediah Wadleigh, which scowled down upon the motley collection of musicians in silent disapproval. They were soon joined by Reed and Lezard, the latter distinctly sheepish after his skirmish with Jenny. Cassie and Idris had retired to their own quarters at the top of the house.

The mood in the room was listless, edgy. Jenny was in a bad humour and this had communicated itself to the others. She was silently cursing the fact that she had not taken the opportunity to leave while she had the chance. Instead, she had steadily drunk her way through a bottle of tequila during the afternoon and had now lapsed into a moody silence. She sat curled up in an armchair, staring pensively into the fire, resisting all attempts at conversation.

Most of these came from Reed and Lezard, who like the dodgy double act they had always been (at least in Jenny's estimation), were making steadfast attempts to jolly everyone up. It had to be said that they weren't having much success. The problem was that musicians generally have low boredom thresholds. After just a couple of hours of enforced incarceration, The Deceivers were acting as if they'd contracted a major bout of cabin fever and seemed ready to climb the walls with frustration.

As usual it was Chris Spencer who was the most voluble person present. He and Emma had been imbibing a fearsome quantity of pills throughout the evening and in Chris's case, much of it must have been amphetamine-based. He'd left his pill box open on the mantelpiece so that anyone who felt like joining in could do so. Now, he and his erstwhile fiancée had staked out their territory on one of the large sofas and Chris, much to everyone else's irritation, was holding forth about one irrelevant subject after another. His current topic was a depressingly familiar one to the other members of The Deceivers. They'd heard it propounded at various times in various parts of the world, usually in a dressing room in the bowels of some anonymous football stadium as the band prepared to go on stage. But tonight, Chris had Robbie, Reed and Lezard to bounce his ideas off, three people who'd never heard any of this rubbish before.

'It's like, Gareth, right, who was the first, you know? You ever wonder about that? Who was the very first?'

Sitting cross-legged on a bean bag on the other side of the room, and dressed in loose-fitting linen casuals, Reed resembled some third world guru who had just been asked to explain the meaning of life.

'Who was the first *what*?' asked Reed innocently, eliciting a chorus of groans from the other members of the band, who knew the folly of rising to Chris's bait.

'It's like a loaf of bread, right? Everybody eats bread, we all know what it is and how it's made. You put yeast and water into flour and you knead it all up. Then you let it prove and when you put it in an oven, it rises, and you've got bread.'

'Er ... yes, but I don't see ...'

'Well, what I'm saying is, who was the first person to realise you could do all that, eh? I mean, for thousands of years, man was crawling around in caves and eating chunks of raw brontosaurus for his dinner. Then, *suddenly*, one of 'em thinks, "Hey, supposing I get a bit of yeast and sprinkle it in this water and add this flour? I wonder what would happen?" Know what I mean? Somebody must have been the first, right?'

'Er...' Reed looked uncomfortable. 'Well, Chris, surely that kind of development is very gradual and it happens pretty much all at the same time, in evolutionary terms.'

Chris stared at him for a few moments and blinked a few times while he tried to absorb this information.

'Uh ... yeah, but ... but somebody must have been *first*, mustn't they? Even if it was only by a few minutes. Mr Arthur Ugg must have beaten Mrs Elsie Ogg, even if it was by seconds! If it happened now, they'd probably build a statue to Arthur Ugg, or stick a plaque on the wall of the cave where he lived. "On this spot, twelve thousand years ago, Mr Arthur Ugg accidentally created the world's first loaf of bread." I mean, they'd organise fackin' coach trips, wouldn't they? But of course, that was long ago before they'd even thought about merchandising so we'll never know. And that's tragic, man, that really is.'

'I'll tell you what's tragic,' muttered Adrian, who had been hopelessly attempting to read a Gabriel Garcia Marquez novel for the past twenty minutes. 'A man who scrambles what few brains he has with a skipload of drugs and talks utter drivel for the rest of his life. They should put up a plaque about that.'

Chris's answer to the putdown was to go off at a tangent.

'Of course, the Red Indians used drugs to foretell the future, didn't they? Visions and that. And I saw this documentary about this South American tribe, right, and they was taking this hallucinogenic stuff and blasting it up each other's nostrils with a blowpipe.'

'Now you know where to go for your next holiday,' observed Steve, gleefully. He was sitting on the floor, leaning against the corner of Jenny's chair, picking out a melody on an acoustic guitar.

'I've already been there,' Chris assured him. 'Not on holiday, I sat in on that "Save The Rainforest" tour a couple of years back. We did a photoshoot in the Amazon with this bunch of guys with big lips and bones through their noses. I got to try the blowpipe gig too. Saw some pretty weird things before I came to, I can tell you. I thought I was this bird, right, flying high over the jungle. He was like my spirit guide. And later there was this dam and a storm came and washed it all away...'

'Hang on,' said Robbie. 'That sounds like a film I saw. *The Emerald Forest*?'

Chris frowned, scratched his head.

'Does it?' He shrugged, not in the least bit fazed by this revelation. 'Yeah, maybe. I get mixed up sometimes.' He made a valiant attempt to return to his original theory. 'But what I'm saying, Gareth, there are stranger things, Horatius, than what are dreamed of in your er ... philanthropy.'

'That's *Horatio*,' Emma corrected him. She appeared to be hanging on very tightly to the arm of the sofa, as though afraid of slipping off it. 'Horatio's *Philosophy*.'

'Yeah, yeah, I know that. And it's like, you take what happened today in the studio. Now that was fackin' weird, man, I don't care what you say. That had to be a genuine supernatural phenomenon.'

Lezard pricked up his ears at this. He was sitting on the other armchair directly across from Jenny: and he glanced at her sheepishly as he spoke.

'I'm not so sure,' he said. 'Gareth has played me the tapes and I have to admit that the music and the voice *are* there and they do sound kind of like Scott. But whether I accept a supernatural explanation is another matter. It's my opinion that the tapes have been doctored in some way.'

'But I've already explained,' said Reed irritably. 'There's no way the tapes could have been tampered with. We were all there, I unwrapped the tapes myself. Nobody would have had the opportunity to do anything to them. I'm afraid I have to agree with Chris on this one. It was an occult occurrence.'

'Occult, my arse,' sneered Adrian. 'That's the result of an elaborate practical joke. Besides, Gareth, we've only got your word for it that you unwrapped brand new tapes. I certainly didn't see you do that. Did you, Robbie?'

The young guitarist looked uncomfortable.

'Well, no, but I'm sure Gareth wouldn't have ...'

'See?' said Adrian, brushing aside his protégé's reservations. 'It's a wind-up. Nicely done, I'll grant you, but a wind-up, just the same.'

Reed looked wounded.

'I hope you're not suggesting that I—?'

'You or that spaced-out assistant of yours, I'd lay even money on it. At first I suspected Chris, but then I realised he hasn't got the brains to set up something like that.'

'Thanks very much,' muttered Chris.

Now Reed looked horrified.

'But what earthly reason would we have for doing something like that?'

Adrian shrugged.

'Sometimes people do a thing just because they *can*.'

'That's ridiculous.' Reed looked across the room at Jenny. 'What do you think?' he asked her.

There was a brief silence, during which they could hear the mournful wail of the wind outside as it rose and fell.

Jenny frowned, stared into the fire a while longer, then sighed. It was pointless to try and deny what she felt any longer.

'It was Scott,' she told him. 'His voice, his music. I don't believe anyone here could have faked it so perfectly. And I can't see that anyone would have a reason to.'

'You mentioned somebody you met back in Manchester,' Lezard reminded her. 'Some guy who told you that Scott was anxious to contact you. Do you think he could have been right?'

Jenny glanced at Lezard. She hadn't quite decided whether she was talking to him or not.

'You remember? You mentioned him when I came up to meet you that time.' Lezard's expression had a pleading quality to it. He couldn't stand it when she had a sulk on with him.

'Yeah,' she said at last. 'Just some creep who was hanging round my mother's house. Claimed to be a medium or something. At the time, I laughed at him. I said ... that he should tell Scott to get in touch with me.' She glanced around the room, smiled sadly. 'I'll admit it seemed funnier at the time.'

'Yeah, well, supposing it really is Scott?' muttered Chris, who seemed intent on spooking himself out. 'What d'you suppose he wants to tell you?'

'Ask him for the lottery numbers,' said Steve, grimly and a couple of people laughed.

'Maybe he wants to write music from beyond the grave!' suggested Adrian, mockingly. 'You know, like that sad fuck who claims that Beethoven dictates new symphonies to her.'

'Yeah, or maybe he wants vengeance on the scumbag who sold him bad drugs!' cackled Emma. 'You know, like in *The Crow* or whatever it's called. Gonna come creepin' back in the dead of night and tear the dealer limb from limb.'

'I'm glad you all find this so amusing,' snapped Jenny. 'I'm afraid I don't find it remotely funny.'

There was another silence, then Reed spoke.

'Why don't we find out what he *really* wants?' he said.

'What are you suggesting?' asked Steve.

Reed smiled and looked slowly around at the others.

'A séance,' he said, at last.

'Yeah, far out!' said Chris: and there was a general shout of agreement from most of the others. Only Jenny and Adrian seemed opposed to the idea. Jenny had read somewhere that occult experiments could be dangerous. They opened up the minds of suggestible people to bad influences. Adrian, on the other hand, evidently believed that such goings on were beneath him.

'Oh, for God's sake. It's just a silly parlour game!' he protested.

'Maybe, but it's better than sitting here being bored,' Robbie argued.

'Sure, come on, where's the harm?' asked Emma. 'It could be a real hoot!'

Lezard glanced warily at Jenny.

'You don't have to do this if you don't want to,' he assured her. 'Nobody will think less of you if you stay out of it.'

'Yes we will!' chuckled Chris. 'We'll think she's a yellow-bellied 'fraidy cat with no balls!'

'Chris, Jenny doesn't need this right now, OK? She and Scott were close and she may not want to have his memory cheapened by something like this.'

Jenny decided that Lezard was simply trying to worm his way back into her affections and the thought irritated her, made her want to throw his creepy words straight back in his face.

'Fuck it, let's do it,' she said. 'Like Robbie says, it beats sitting around waiting for the snow to stop falling.' She flung a challenging glance at Reed. 'I suppose you do know what you're doing?'

'Sure. I've done dozens of séances.' Reed got to his feet. 'Give me a few minutes,' he told them. 'I'll see if Cassie and Idris want to join us. They're very receptive to this kind of thing. Then we'll get everything set up in the dining room.'

'Give you a chance to rig up some sound effects,' said Adrian sneeringly.

Reed fixed him with a look of intense dislike.

'Now what would be the point of that?' he asked.

Adrian didn't reply so Reed turned and went out of the room.

'What's up with you, Ade?' muttered Chris. 'Why do you think everybody's trying to rip you off?'

'Because they usually are,' replied Adrian gloomily. Jenny noticed that he cast a sideways glance at Robbie as he said this. The young guitarist reddened and looked away. 'People only believe in this bullshit because they *want* to. It's easier than accepting that the world is just as we see it. No mysteries, no conspiracies, no *magic*.'

Jenny sighed. 'I used to think like that,' she announced to nobody in particular. Now that she had agreed to the séance, she felt distinctly apprehensive. She'd heard countless stories about people who fooled around and unwittingly unleashed supernatural forces that drove them mad. In the stories, the perpetrators of the deed – or at least, the few who survived – were generally found white-haired and gibbering the following morning. Often they were splattered with the blood of their friends who, at some point during the night, they'd torn limb from limb. Of course, she didn't believe that anything so extreme was going to happen here. But she did realise that she was in a dangerously suggestive state and anything she saw or heard during the séance was liable to have a profound effect on her.

But it would have been a major loss of face to back down now, something that the guys in the band would rib her about for months afterwards. She knew only too well that for a woman to be accepted into an otherwise all-male band, it was necessary to match them in most things that they did. She'd been doing it successfully for fifteen years and she didn't intend to stop now. So she kept her peace and waited for the session to begin.

Twenty minutes later, Reed reappeared and made an announcement.

'Ladies and gentleman,' he said, making a theatrical bow, 'I'm pleased to announce that everything is now prepared. If you would care to accompany me to the dining room, tonight's entertainment is about to begin.'

Chapter Twenty-One

Reed had taken considerable trouble to set the scene. The main lights had been switched off and dozens of tall black candles had been placed strategically around the room, giving the place an atmospheric feel. The curtains of the french window that looked into the courtyard were open and the naked candle flames burning in the centre of the big table were reflected in them as orbs of glowing light.

Cassie and Idris were on hand and seemed to have dressed for the occasion in simple, full-length robes of black cloth. Jenny thought that they looked like a couple of escapees from a Dominican monastery and she had to fight down an urge to giggle. From their calm, matter-of-fact manner, she got the impression that such an event was nothing unusual for them. She noted that Cassie was wearing the circular snake earrings again and, more disturbingly, that she had a large bruise under her left eye, as though somebody had recently punched her. Jenny glanced at Idris and saw that he was looking defiantly back at her, his little eyes glinting malevolently in the candlelight, that habitual smile on his lips. She had no doubt whatsoever that the punch had been administered by him, but for what reason, she could only guess.

Reed quickly took charge of proceedings. He went and sat at the head of the rectangular table and told Idris to take a seat at the other end. Then he directed everybody to their places, four people on each side, seeming to take great care in placing them. Jenny found herself sitting between Idris and Lezard. Then came Steve and Cassie. Directly across the table from her, making silly faces, sat Chris. Next to him was Emma, then Robbie and Adrian. Once everybody was seated Reed took a few moments to allow everybody to settle.

'Clear your minds,' he said, when they were all silent.

'Shouldn't be difficult,' said Adrian, and a few people sniggered; but Jenny couldn't make a joke of this. She felt horribly apprehensive now, anxious to get the whole thing over with.

'Try to make your minds a total blank,' continued Reed, ignoring Adrian. 'Make room to allow another's thoughts into your head.' There was a long silence then, while Reed waited until he felt the atmosphere was right. 'Now,' he said, 'let's all join hands and experience the silence.'

Jenny reached out her right hand and Lezard took it in his firm, capable grip. Then Idris took hold of her left hand and she nearly gasped in surprise. His flesh felt as cold as ice, as though he'd just come in from a walk in the snow. She glanced at him, but he was staring straight down the table at Reed.

A deep silence fell, in which they could hear the restless rush of the wind outside the french window. A flurry of snow crystals pattered against the glass. Through in the kitchen, a clock was ticking.

'I am speaking to Scott Griffin,' said Reed calmly. 'We believe that you have a message for somebody in this room. If you are here with us, please make your presence known.'

Another silence, while they sat there feeling vaguely ridiculous.

'Scott Griffin. If you are with us, please make your presence known. We are waiting to speak with you.'

'Knock once for yes, twice for no,' sniggered Chris.

'Shut up!' hissed Steve, giving him a threatening look.

'I thought that was what you were supposed to say!' protested Chris.

'Please!' said Reed. He glared daggers at Chris. 'Be silent. I think . . . I think there's something . . .' His voice trailed off and the silence returned, the mournful rise and fall of the wind and . . . something else. Jenny became aware of it only gradually and at first, she thought it was the product of her overworked imagination. But no, there it was, rising and falling with the sound of the wind and distant, very distant. The sound of an electric guitar, wrenching out a cacophony of sound, distorted, fuzzed, teetering on the edge of feedback. Jenny knew that sound. The same she had heard on the tape.

'Oh my God,' she whispered. She had an impulse to push away from the table but the hands on either side of her held her in a vice-like grip.

'Clever,' muttered Adrian. 'How'd you rig that one up?'

Reed didn't take his eyes off the candle flames burning in the centre of the table.

'Scott, we can hear you,' he said. 'But you're very distant. Come into the room and speak to us if you can.'

'Oh, please,' said Adrian. 'Spare us the theatrics.'

'Shut up and listen,' snapped Robbie, with unexpected vehemence. Adrian glanced at him in dismay. Then he turned back to face the table.

Jenny sat there shivering. She realised that she was shivering, not with fear, but because the warmth was being drained out of the room, as though somebody had just opened the french window to the elements. Her breath clouded suddenly in front of her face and, gazing horrified across the table, she saw the others reacting in amazement as the same thing happened to them. The candle flames in front of them guttered as though hit by a breeze and then seemed to burn with a clear blue light.

Adrian's superior grin had slipped right off his face.

'Still think it's a trick?' asked Reed, calmly.

'I . . .' Adrian shook his head. He had nothing to say.

'Scott,' murmured Reed. 'We sense your presence. Can you speak to us?'

The music was louder now, still an undertow but more defined, rising above the sound of the wind. Then, shockingly close at hand, they heard the sound of laboured breathing. It came from no particular direction but seemed to be all around them. Jenny stared across the table at the faces in front of her. They had all turned white and were almost masked now by the clouds of white vapour that spilled from their mouths.

'Scott, can you . . . ?'

'Cold!'

The one word, little more than a grunt, seemed to have been spoken directly into Jenny's left ear. She snapped her head to one side to look at Idris, but he was still staring straight ahead, his eyes blank, his mouth hanging open. He appeared to be in some kind of trance and as she stared at him, the vapour clouding from his mouth seemed to be shaping itself into something imbued with life. She would have moved away from him but his cold grip was as tenacious as ever and she was horribly reminded of her dream, the night that Scott came to her room and climbed into her bed.

'Jen . . . ny!' Another word, emitted as a hoarse whisper that sent jolts of terror down her spine. 'Be . . . ware. He wants you. He . . . wants . . . you!'

Now all eyes at the table were turned on her and she would have run away if she could: but she was held immobile and she could only stare at the shifting, wraith-like cloud that was still spilling from Idris's mouth, the cloud that even as she watched was changing into what looked like a writhing snake.

'Who wants me?' she gasped. 'Scott, who?'

'Pain! Can . . . not rest. He . . . sees you. He . . . tastes you. Be . . . ware. He is coming!'

'Who? For God's sake, give me a name. Give me some kind of . . .'

An abrupt movement outside the french window caught her attention. A bluish-white face seemed to swoop towards her out of the falling snow and press itself up against the glass – a manic, screaming face with bulging eyes and a gaping, slobbering mouth. Jenny screamed involuntarily and the surprise of it made Lezard release his hold on her hand. She got to her feet, aware that Idris had slumped forward over the table as though exhausted, but she couldn't think of that now, because a pair of fists was beating against the glass of the window and the face's open mouth was yelling incoherently: and everybody was getting up from the table, turning to stare at the stranger who had come raving out of the night.

'What the fuck?' yelled Chris.

'It's a ghost!' shrieked Emma.

But Jenny was shaking her head. After the unexpected shock of its first appearance, the face was only too familiar. She had last seen it sneering at her outside a Manchester club only a couple of weeks ago, when she'd had the pleasure of slamming a fist into it.

'It's Des McGuire,' she said, and hurried across the room to switch on the lights.

Chapter Twenty-Two

They unlatched the french window and helped McGuire inside.

'Cold!' he whispered. 'I'm so c... cold.'

This much was evident. His skin was an unpleasant shade of blue and his thin body was trembling helplessly beneath the black leather duffle coat he wore. He seemed just about ready to drop in his tracks. Jenny, Steve and Lezard helped him through to the front room and sat him down in front of the log fire. Then Cassie came through with a large glass of brandy and the others, including a rather dazed-looking Idris, followed and stood around in the doorway, mystified. Most of them had never met him before.

McGuire's hands were shaking so badly, he was in danger of spilling the brandy. Lezard steadied it for him and helped him to guide the glass to his mouth.

'What the hell were you doing out there in this weather?' he wanted to know.

McGuire's reply was a barely understandable stammer.

'My car ... c ... conked out ... back on the hill. C ... couldn't go either way. Figured I b ... better start walking. Didn't realise it was s ... so far. I thought I was g ... gonna die out there.' He gulped down the last of the brandy, then proffered the glass hopefully to Cassie. 'Please. I'm so c ... c ... cold.'

His words sent a chill through Jenny's bloodstream, reminding her of what Scott had repeatedly said in the dream. She tried to assure herself that it was just a coincidence.

Cassie hurried back to the dining room for a refill. McGuire was leaning so close to the fire his coat was steaming, but at least a little colour was creeping back in to his face.

'Fuck,' he whispered. 'That was c... close. I really didn't think I was g... gonna make it. I even started praying. C... can you imagine that, Jenny? Me praying!'

'Excuse me if this seems an inappropriate time,' interjected Adrian. 'Am I to take it you know this man, Jenny?'

'Of course she knows him,' said Steve. 'It's Des McGuire, the band's first drummer. Don't you remember? He turned up backstage when we played the Manchester Apollo, a few years back.' Steve narrowed his eyes. 'Borrowed ten quid off me for the taxi fare home.'

'Oh yeah.' Chris smiled dopily. 'Yeah, I remember now. You had some really good blow with you, that night. Thai stick, I think it was. You was telling me how you had an audition coming up for Rod Stewart's band. How did it go?'

Jenny glanced at Des in disbelief and saw that he wasn't even slightly fazed by the question. He was grinning as confidently as ever.

'Oh yeah, that's right. D... didn't work out though. Well, I didn't want to be p... playing all that commercial shit, night after night, did I? Once you've played with The Deceivers, nothing else is ever going to be as good, right?'

'Yeah?' Chris seemed happy enough with this explanation. 'Well, if you've come to ask for a gig, it's customary to wait till the current drummer has left or died, know what I mean?'

McGuire forced a laugh.

'Quit kidding,' he said. 'You k... know why I'm here. You c... could have warned me about the weather conditions, though.' He gazed around him at the circle of puzzled expressions. 'Oh, d... don't say this is some kind of hoax!' he said. 'I nearly killed myself back there!'

Cassie came in with the second glass, filled almost to the brim. McGuire took it from her with a grateful smile and gulped eagerly at the contents.

'That's better,' he said. 'Feel it warming me, now.' He gazed at Jenny for a moment. 'You g ... going to own up or what?'

'Des, we haven't got the faintest idea what you're on about,' Jenny assured him.

'Well, you *invited* me, didn't you? Here, look, this c... came in the post yesterday.' He fished an envelope out of his pocket and handed it to her. She experienced a sinking feeling when she noted McGuire's name and address printed in large black letters. She glanced at Lezard and he raised his eyebrows in recognition. Jenny opened the envelope and withdrew two sheets of white paper. She scanned the first page.

'What does it say?' asked Adrian, impatiently.

'It's in the form of a poem,' she told them.

'Read it out,' suggested Lezard.

She did as he suggested, realising as she did so that she would have to go on to explain to the rest of the band about the other letters: and about her fears and suspicions over the death of Mike Watton. In a way, she was glad it had finally come to this. It would take the matter out of her hands.

'To former drummer, Des McGuire
I send this invitation
the band are gathered at The Grange
and owe you reparation.

> Fame and fortune passed you by,
> as you have often stated
> come January twenty-fifth
> and you'll be compensated.'

The second sheet contained a detailed map and directions on how to get to The Grange.

After she had finished reading, there were a lot of puzzled looks from the others.

'What's this about compensation?' asked Adrian, tetchily. 'Nobody said anything to me about compensating this guy.'

'It's not from anybody in the band,' Jenny told him. Then added: 'At least, I don't *think* it is. It's from somebody calls himself the Hoochie Coochie Man. There've been other letters.'

'Jenny,' muttered Steve. 'I don't know if...'

'Shut up, Steve. They have a right to know about this. I only wish I'd said something earlier.'

Chris gave Steve a quizzical look.

'What's going down here? You *knew* about this?'

'Aww, it's just some stupid poison pen letters. Nothing to get worked up about.'

'I think they should be the judge of that,' said Jenny.

McGuire sat there scratching his head.

'I don't get it,' he said. 'If you guys didn't send me the invitation ... then who did?'

Jenny looked at him. It was a bloody good question and one she didn't have the first hope of answering. Not yet, anyway.

'Look,' she said. 'Everybody sit down and make yourselves comfortable. This could take some time.'

'I guess this doesn't include us,' announced Cassie. 'Idris and I had better go and prepare another room ... that is, I assume Mr McGuire will be staying?'

Reed nodded.

'We can hardly throw him out in this storm,' he admitted. 'Put him in the small spare room up on the top floor.'

Cassie nodded and she and Idris went out.

'OK,' said Jenny. 'But I'd like the rest of you to stay. I'll tell you what I know, which isn't much. Then we'll see if anybody has any ideas about it.' She walked over to stand with her back to the fire, beneath the scowling portrait of Obediah Wadleigh. She fished the crumpled sheets of paper from her back pocket and opened them out for inspection.

Then she took a deep breath and began to speak.

She told them everything that was worrying her. She showed them the letters she'd received and she pointed out how the latest one had been addressed to her here at The Grange. She explained her fears about Mike Watton, her belief that whoever had written the letters must have been responsible for his death: and finally she asked them why the same unknown writer should have taken the trouble to invite Des McGuire out here to the middle of nowhere.

She waited for their reactions – but if she had hoped for any sympathy from them, she was to be sorely disappointed. It was Adrian who spoke first, the familiar condescending smile on his lips as he pronounced judgement on her evidence.

'Oh, come on, Jenny, it's a bit unlikely, isn't it?' He looked around at the others. 'I mean, we all get wacko letters from time to time. I remember getting a whole bunch of them myself. Some nutcase who was convinced he was receiving strange signals from my keyboard patterns. Said it was linked to the Chinese horoscope or some such bollocks!'

'Yes,' said Jenny, 'I remember that, but...'

'And what about that guy used to dance around at our gigs

with Bacofoil on his head?' Chris reminded her. 'Turned out he reckoned radio signals from Mars were bombarding his skull and that was supposed to deflect 'em.' He crossed his eyes and drilled an index finger into the side of his head. 'It's fackin' Looney Tunes out there, Jenny. You should know that better than anyone.'

'What's that supposed to mean?' snapped Jenny.

'Nothin' . . . I just mean that you've had more of those letters than the rest of us put together. What about that head-the-ball who stalked you all through the last American tour? When the cops caught up with him, he had fackin' photographs of you all over his house. Not to mention knives, axes and automatic weapons.'

'Yes, I know all that!' protested Jenny. 'But you're missing the point. How is this guy able to trace us here? It wasn't exactly open information, was it?'

Reed shrugged his shoulders.

'The ingenuity of hardline fans never ceases to amaze me,' he said. 'They can find their way to all kinds of restricted information, particularly since the advent of the Internet. You're probably aware that there's a Deceivers fan club that operates on the Net? I browsed though it the other day and I was amazed by what was on offer. I was able to get in touch with people who could tell me every tiny detail about this band, right down to the colour of Chris's underpants.'

'Yeah, so what colour's that?' sneered Chris.

'Red.'

Chris thought about it for a moment. Then he reached down, pulled open the waistband of his trousers and took a peek.

'Fack me,' he said. 'Even I didn't know that.'

There was general laughter and Jenny realised that she was in danger of losing their attention.

'So what you're saying is, I'm talking complete bollocks.'

'Don't over-react,' Steve warned her. 'I'm sure the letters are genuine enough, but I just don't believe that there's some psychopath planning to kill us all. It's just ... too unlikely.'

'How is it unlikely?' cried Jenny. 'Crazier things than that happen every day. You're just scared of admitting the possibility of it. It's easier for you to write me off as a hysterical fool than accept that there just might be something in what I'm saying.'

'Nobody's saying you're hysterical,' soothed Lezard. 'But face it, Jenny, if this was happening a year ago, you'd be laughing it off with the rest of us. It's only one of hundreds of wind-ups we've had.'

'This one is different! There's something about this guy's letters that ... I don't know, there seems to be method in it.'

'Let's not be sexist,' Emma warned her. 'There's nothing to say it has to be a man. This may come as a surprise to you, but there's a lot of women out there who'd take the greatest pleasure in winding you up.' She caught the look that Jenny directed at her and held up her hands in a gesture of innocence. 'Oh, not me, sweetie, I can assure you. Not my style.'

'On the contrary, I'd say poison pen letters were right up your street. It's what you do for a living, isn't it?'

Emma chuckled.

'But not in *verse*, dearie. That is a bit vulgar, don't you think? Actually, it's more like what *you* do for a living.' She waggled her eyebrows, meaningfully.

'What are you getting at? I hope you're not suggesting that I've been sending letters to myself!'

Emma shrugged.

'It's amazing what some people will do for attention, and it would be relatively easy to arrange. You'd just need an accomplice to send them to you at regular intervals.'

'Oh for God's sake, don't be stupid!' Jenny glowered around the room at the others. 'Anybody else subscribe to this half-arsed theory?' If anybody did, they weren't about to admit to it. She caught Des McGuire's eye. Now that he had recovered from his ordeal, he was sitting there on the sofa, grinning at Jenny and looking as though he was enjoying the proceedings immensely.

'What are you looking so pleased about?' she asked him. 'Let me point out that if I was sending out invitations, you'd be the last name on the list.'

'Well, thanks for that,' he told her. 'I half killed myself making it here and all I get is insults.'

'Why exactly did you come?' asked Robbie.

McGuire shrugged.

'I was invited, wasn't I? And it's rude to snub an invitation. Besides, the letter made it sound like there might be something in it for me. I was ... intrigued. And I thought it would be an excellent opportunity to combine business with pleasure.' He slipped a hand into his inside coat pocket and pulled out a small jiffy bag. 'Bit of extra insulation,' he said. 'Didn't know how you people would be fixed for recreation, so...'

Chris and Emma immediately perked up. So did Robbie, Jenny noticed.

'What you carrying?' asked Emma.

'Some great quality Colombian snort, best I've ever had. Didn't know if you folks had a connection out here, but I thought, what the hell, carry a little weight with me and see how it goes...'

'Great,' murmured Jenny, realising that for at least three people present, the impromptu meeting was as good as over. 'Just what we needed. I ought to throw you back out into the snow to take your chances.'

'Hey, leave the boy alone!' Chris told her. She could see that he'd already decided that he and McGuire would be great friends, drummers both and sharing similar interests. Jenny looked at Lezard.

'You're not going to allow this, are you?'

Lezard sighed.

'I'm afraid they're all adults, Jenny. They can do as they see fit.' He got up from his seat. 'Anyway, I wouldn't mind another listen to the tape you made today. Gareth?'

'Sure. Anyone else interested?'

'Yeah, I'll come with you,' said Adrian. He openly disapproved of drugs of any description. 'Robbie?'

The young guitarist made no move to get up from his seat.

'You go ahead,' he said. 'I believe I'll stick around for a while.'

Adrian looked dismayed.

'We . . . have a full day's recording tomorrow,' he reminded him.

Robbie looked up at him defiantly.

'So?' he said.

Adrian scowled and seemed to be about to pursue the point. But then he became aware of people's eyes on him. He turned on his heels and followed Reed and Lezard out of the room. Steve excused himself, saying that he was going to have another try at phoning home. Peg and the kids would be worried about him. He went out and that left the five of them, Jenny still standing in front of the fire, the others perched around the smirking figure of Des McGuire who in a very short space of time, Jenny reflected, had gone from a shivering, helpless wreck to the guy everyone wanted to be best mates with. Some transition. She watched as he opened the Jiffy bag and slid out the plastic container of cocaine. He snapped his fingers at Robbie.

'Hey, kid, bring over that coffee table, will ya?'

Robbie moved to obey him, then resumed his seat and watched as McGuire tipped a mound of white powder onto the glass-topped table and began to chop it up with a credit card. He glanced at Jenny.

'How about a couple of toots?' he asked her. 'Just for old times' sake.'

'Fuck you,' she told him.

'Hey, come on, Jenny, that's not very nice,' Chris chided her. 'It's not his fault he's here, the least we can do...'

'Chris, you don't know anything about him, so just shut up, OK? You don't imagine for one moment that he's giving you that stuff out of the goodness of his heart, do you?' She turned her attention back to McGuire. 'First snort's free and then they pay. That's how it's usually done, right, Des? Give 'em the good stuff first time, then introduce the shit that's been stepped on, they won't notice when they're still buzzing from the first hit.'

McGuire sneered.

'Oh yeah, I was forgetting you were the expert junkie. Well let me tell you, my produce is pure, and that's why it's expensive. Anybody doesn't want to pay the price, that's fine by me.' He glanced around at the others but got no reaction. 'They seem happy with the arrangement, Jenny. The only one kicking up a fuss is you. And you know what I really can't stand? Ex-users who preach. Because they couldn't handle it they assume that everybody else is just like them. Now if you feel so badly about this, why don't you split and let the others enjoy it in peace?'

'What are you *doing* here, Des?' Jenny asked him. 'What's your angle?'

'No angles. It's like I said, I was invited and now I'm just trying to make the best of it. So why don't you chill out and stop giving me a hard time?' He began to arrange the mound of powder into white lines. 'Sure you won't change your mind? Might help cure that paranoia of yours.'

'As I remember,' she told him, 'the effect is just the opposite. Do me a favour, Des. We can hardly throw you out but while you're here, just keep out of my face, OK?'

He didn't say anything to that, just grinned his mocking grin. Jenny headed for the door, then paused and glanced back, meaning to bid the others good night: but their heads were down over the table, snuffling like pigs after truffles and she felt a sense of revulsion go through her. Five years ago, she thought, she'd have been in the thick of it, snorting and grunting with the rest of them.

She went out into the hallway and up the stairs to her room.

Chapter Twenty-Three

Jenny couldn't sleep. She lay in her bed in the darkened room and listened to the sounds of the storm beyond her curtained window, the various other sounds in the big, old house. Her overworked imagination seemed to detect ominous portents in every creak of a floorboard, every ticking of a pipe, and when she dared to let her eyes wander around the room, she was horrified to note that every item of furniture seemed to resemble some nameless horror waiting to pounce on her.

It had been overlooked after the unexpected arrival of Des McGuire but now she found her thoughts going back to what had been happening just before his white face had appeared at the french windows – the voice, the music, both of them unmistakably belonging to Scott Griffin. What was she to make of all that now? Already the events had acquired a weird misty patina, but at the time she'd been absolutely terrified, and she was pretty sure that everyone else had been too.

Or had one of them been acting? The person who'd set the whole thing up? And if that was the case, who was the most likely culprit? Chris, with his background of elaborate practical jokes? Idris and Reed with their technical know-how?

From downstairs she heard the muffled sound of manic laughter. Chris and the others having their idea of fun with Dr McGuire's travelling medicine show. The ex-drummer's presence in the house seemed to Jenny to be one of the most sinister occurrences of all. What was he doing here? Who had sent him his invitation? Maybe, she thought, he had written it to himself and simply used it as his excuse for being here, staying out in the snow just long enough to make it look convincing without doing himself any real harm. He'd always been a devious bastard, she certainly wouldn't put it past him. But all that, just to score some money from Chris and the others? No, it had to go deeper than that. What had the invite said? Something about compensation...

The questions whizzed and whirled like fireworks in her skull and the idea of sleep moved further and further beyond her reach. She was almost relieved when she heard the sound of knuckles rapping on her door. She sat up and switched on the bedside light.

'Who is it?' she called out.

'It's Josh. Can we talk?'

She considered for a moment, then sighed.

'Yeah, I suppose so. You'd better come in.'

He tried the handle of the door to no avail.

'It's locked,' he said.

'Just a minute.' She climbed out of bed and slipped into her kimono. She didn't remember locking the door. It was unlike her to do such a thing and was an indication of how worried she was. She turned the key in the lock and strolled back to the bed as Lezard came sheepishly into the room, closing the door behind him.

'I'm sorry,' he muttered. 'I know it's kind of late.'

'No problem, I wasn't asleep. Christ, who can sleep with all this row going on, anyway?'

He grinned ruefully and perched himself on the edge of the bed. He looked, she thought, decidedly uncomfortable.

'You referring to the storm or to our resident lotus eaters downstairs?'

'A combination,' she said. 'What's on your mind, Josh?'

'I suppose I felt I needed to square things with you,' he said. 'I guess you're still mad with me, huh? That business about my half share in The Grange...'

'Well, maybe I've come to terms with that. A little more support in the meeting just now, that would have made me feel better disposed to you.'

He shrugged.

'Jenny, I said what I thought. That's all I've ever done where this band is concerned. And if I'm guilty of not telling you everything that's going down, I hope you know that it's generally done with your best interests at heart.'

'Maybe. But I'm getting very tired of being treated like I'm made of porcelain. Like you're trying to protect me from things.'

'Yes, but with respect, Jenny, I saw the state you were in when I checked you into that clinic. And that all happened because you couldn't handle the truth of Scott's death. I have no wish to see you in that condition ever again.'

Jenny reached for her cigarettes from the bedside cabinet and lit one up.

'That may be so,' she said, blowing out a cloud of grey smoke. 'But there comes a point where such protection becomes downright invasive. I'm thinking particularly of that line you came out with to Gareth Reed. Something about me being "out of bounds"? Bit extreme, wasn't it?'

Lezard frowned.

'Just healthy caution. Mr Reed has a certain reputation with the ladies ... but then, you must already know that, mustn't you?'

'*Mr Reed*? Bit formal. Anyone would think you weren't friends with him.'

'He's a business partner, Jenny. And a damned good producer. As a human being, I'm afraid I'm not quite so enamoured of him. I've discovered since we formed our partnership that he's uh ... how can I put this ... ?'

'Dick happy?' suggested Jenny brightly.

'That's pretty much it, yes. He's a good-looking man and opportunities tend to come his way. I've never known him pass one of them up. Neither have I seen him commit himself for more than a few days at most. Unless of course, you include ... er ...'

'Cassie?'

Lezard looked surprised by this.

'He's *told* you about that?'

'No, but I got the feeling there was something going on. Must be difficult for them with Idris around all the time.'

Lezard gave a dismissive laugh.

'As far as I can ascertain, Idris knows all about it. Indeed, he encourages it.'

Jenny arched her eyebrows.

'That kind of arrangement, huh? Well, it takes all kinds I guess. And she is a very pretty girl. Anyway, Josh, all this fatherly advice is sadly a little too late to help me make an informed choice. The horse has, as they say, bolted. Time was when you would have told me all this *before* I fucked him.'

'I know. I regret that.' He eyed her warily. 'Was it much of a blow when he ducked out?'

She laughed at his reticence.

'A pain in the arse is what it was. It pissed me off but I can't say I'm going to lose much sleep over it. At the end of the day, for all his New Age posturing, he turned out to be just another typical male.' She thought for a moment. 'I have to say that it's definitely an odd couple set up, this partnership. I mean, he's so cosmic and you're so ... normal.'

Lezard grinned.

'Yes, I know what you mean. But it's like I said, he's a first rate producer with impeccable references. I saw the set-up here as an ideal business opportunity and I jumped at it. It was only later that I discovered his other interests. The sex magic stuff.'

'You think there's anything in it?'

Lezard laughed uncomfortably.

'Please! As far as I'm concerned it's malarkey. Basically I have no problem with it so long as nobody gets harmed.'

'Yeah, but what about the thing he pulled off tonight? The séance. I mean, if Des McGuire hadn't showed up when he did, who knows where it would have finished up?' She glanced up at him sharply. 'Or are you going to tell me that I was imagining that happened?

Lezard shook his head.

'Oh no, we all heard it. And I'd like to think that Reed didn't set it up as some kind of a hoax...'

'But?'

'Well...' Lezard sighed, fiddled with a gold signet ring on the index finger of his left hand. 'If anybody could set it up, he and Idris would be just the people. They're both techno-wizards, they could have equipment hidden all over the house to make noises, project images. Be a piece of cake for people with their skills.'

'But why would they? What's in it for them?'

'I'm not saying that they are. Only that they *could*. If they wanted to. Maybe it's easier for me to think that than to believe that we really did hear Scott's voice. I don't know.' He made an effort to change the subject. 'Anyway, I think we should try and forget about all this stuff and press on with some real work. Reed played me the tape of the new song. Aside from the ghostly guitar and creepy stage whispers, I think it sounds pretty damned good. So I vote we work on it tomorrow, lay down some other new material, if we can. The weather report says we can expect this to go on for a couple more days, so . . .'

'You'd think it would have blown itself out by now,' murmured Jenny. 'You managed to phone London yet?'

'Uh uh. The phone lines are still dead and we can't seem to get a single mobile to work. But on the plus side, we've got electricity, oil for the radiators, several tons of solid fuel and enough food to last us till the spring, if necessary. We also have one of the world's best singer/songwriters in residence.'

'Yeah? You'll have to introduce me some time.'

He smiled at her fondly, then impulsively he reached forward and pecked her on the cheek.

'You're a tonic, Jenny, you know that? Christ, it didn't change you, did it?'

'What didn't?'

'The money. The success. I see some of them, you know, kids who haven't got an ounce of your talent and overnight, they're little monsters with egos the size of Trump Towers. Won't cross the road without an entourage. Need a limo to take 'em to the off licence. Then I see Jenny Slade, travelling in on the number 15 bus. Same old blue jeans, same old scuffed leather jacket. I come down to your home town and where do I meet you? In the local ale house. Couple of hours later, you're decking some dope dealer outside a club.' He shook his head. 'Incredible,' he said.

Jenny laughed uneasily. She didn't feel comfortable with Lezard talking about her in those terms. Like she was some kind of working class heroine.

'Christ, Josh, I haven't been on a bus in years,' she protested.

'Ah, you know what I'm saying, Jenny, you've no airs and graces. You're *real*. That's something to be proud of in this business. And . . . if you really want to know the truth, I'm sick that Gareth Reed knows you in a way that I never have.'

Jenny looked at him dismayed.

'Hey, come on, Josh, we've been through this before, remember? I already told you I don't like the idea of sleeping with my manager.'

'But sleeping with your record producer is allowed?'

'He isn't my record producer, not yet. And frankly, the more I find out about him, the less likely a proposition it becomes. Besides, the whole thing was a mistake. A one-off.'

'That doesn't make me feel any better,' said Lezard strangely. He reached out a hand and placed it on hers. 'Tell me something. If I stopped being your manager . . . if I retired and handed the responsibility on to someone else. Would you consider me then?'

'Oh, come on, get real, will you? What are you babbling about?'

'I was merely asking . . .'

'Yes, I know what you were asking! But for goodness sake, what's brought all this on? Give up on being the band's manager? Why would you want to do a dumb thing like that?'

'Because . . .' He sighed, picked at a loose thread trailing from the edge of the bedspread. 'Because sometimes I ask myself, "Is this it?" Y'know, making deals, jetting around the world, never taking a holiday. I was just thinking before, this is the first time I've spent a day sitting about in years. And why? Because I'm snowed in and the phone and fax machines are out of order! Maybe there's more to life, Jenny. Maybe I should get out of the business while I'm still young enough to enjoy it. Maybe we both should.'

She caught the inference in his voice but chose to ignore it.

'Are you kidding? After two days we'd be climbing the walls with boredom. The Deceivers has been my life since I was eighteen and I'm not ready to give up on it yet. I don't believe for one minute that you are, either.'

Lezard frowned.

'You could be right,' he admitted. 'Perhaps I'm just sounding off because I'm jealous of what happened between you and Gareth.'

'Then you're jealous of not very much,' she assured him. 'An above-average fuck, that's all it amounted to.' She reached over and stubbed out her cigarette. 'It's late, Josh. We should try and get some sleep.'

He nodded, got obediently to his feet.

'Yeah, well, at least you're talking to me again,' he observed. 'It's a start.'

She pecked him fondly on the cheek.

'No more nasty surprises, OK?'

'OK. Sleep well.' He walked across to the door then hesitated and glanced back at her. 'Jenny,' he added, 'at least think about what I said, will you?'

'Sure. I'll think about it.'

He went out of the room, closing the door behind him. A few moments later, she heard the door of the room next to hers open and close. She smiled, shook her head, then caught herself getting out of bed with the intention of locking her door.

Quit that, will you !

She had never been prey to irrational fears in her life and she didn't intend to start now. She threw off her kimono, switched off the light and lay down again.

She closed her eyes and was fast asleep in minutes.

Chapter Twenty-Four

She was running for her life.

She was outside in the front garden of The Grange, dressed only in her nightgown. There was thick snow on the ground and her bare feet kicked up shimmering concussions of icy crystals as she ran. She was heading for the break in the tree line, the start of the long winding track that led ultimately to the stone circle.

Something was following her, something unseen and brutishly malevolent. She could hear the coarse panting of its breath, the frantic thudding of its feet as it came after her, close upon her heels . . .

She slipped and almost fell, had to fling out her arms like a tightrope walker in a desperate attempt to stay upright. Then she was in among the trees, the skeletal black outlines of them rearing up on either side to block out the light of the full moon.

Run, Jenny ! The voice was a hoarse whisper in her ear, an urgent command that seemed to envelop her in a cloud of chill vapour. *Run to the circle. It's your only hope* !

She had to snatch back a gasp of terror, because she recognised the voice and knew that the man who was speaking to her was long dead: but his presence here was nothing compared to what followed her, to what would happen if she allowed herself to be caught . . .

The trail was narrowing now and she was scrambling past flanks of thick forest. Low hanging branches clawed at her face, snagged in her hair. Her breath was exploding like a furnace in her chest, but up ahead of her, she caught a glimpse of brooding grey stone.

The circle, Jenny! Go to the circle !

She began to slow her pace, exhausted now, but then a crashing in the undergrowth behind her galvanised her to fresh efforts. She plunged through a screen of brambles and ran for the circle. The tall stones stood like a ring of silent cloaked figures in the moonlight.

Something snatched at the sleeve of her nightdress and she pulled away with a gasp of terror, ripping the fabric. She lengthened her stride across the thick snow, aiming for a narrow opening between two of the biggest stones. She ran into the circle, hoping that its ancient powers would protect her from the evil that followed. She slowed her pace as she moved to the very centre of the circle and...

The ground beneath her feet was softening, dissolving and...

She realised that it was nothing but a thin shell of crumbling ice, that her feet were breaking through it and...

She fell into darkness, only a short distance, because...

She had landed face down on a soft, yielding surface and she lay still for a moment, winded and confused, trying to get her breath back and at first she was only dimly aware that the surface she had fallen on to was moving and...

She felt something smooth and supple brush against her cheek with a loud hiss and she arched up in surprise and terror because...

Snakes. She was lying on a bed of snakes.

And she couldn't hold back the scream that came bubbling up her throat like acid and she thrashed herself upright, horribly aware of the coiled, writhing bodies beneath her hands, her bare knees and...

She got to her feet somehow and stood there, rigid with terror as hundreds of vividly patterned bodies swarmed around her, ankle-deep. Glancing up she saw that she was in a circular pit, set some twenty feet beneath the surface. High above her she could see the black circle of the night sky, peppered with rhinestones and...

As she looked a face appeared over the edge of the pit, smiling down at her gleefully.

'Gareth!' she gasped. 'Help me!'

But he just laughed.

'Relax, Jenny. They're just trying to be friendly,' he assured her. 'Snakes are good. If you don't believe me, ask Cassie.' And he pointed down into the coils beside her. Jenny looked down and saw a face rising slowly up from the sea of snakes like a round, pink island. It was Cassie's face and her mouth was open, she was moaning softly, and her expression was one of ecstasy. As her body rose up, Jenny saw that she was naked, and that her flesh was covered with tiny pinpricks of sweat. Then as the girl's body shuddered convulsively, Jenny saw the thick probing coils of a huge vermilion snake, pulsing and twitching between her open legs. Another smaller snake darted into Cassie's open mouth, muffling her moans of pleasure.

'Now do you understand?' asked Reed.

'Gareth, please, just get me out of here!'

The snakes were coiling around her shins now, their flickering tongues exploring her bare flesh and...

Other faces were appearing at the edge of the pit. Idris. Lezard. Emma Savage. And now one by one, the other members of the band, all of them watching her intently as the lithe, sinewy serpents moved over her, their thick heavy coils sliding now beneath the folds of her nightdress, girdling her waist, encircling her arms, the increasing weight of them pulling her inexorably down to the floor beside Cassie, where more of them waited to entangle her in their fleshy embrace...

Something had wakened her, a fact for which she was extremely grateful. She reached out and flicked on the bedside lamp, then lay there for a few moments, letting her breathing get back to normal. Her body was coated with a thick sweat of sheer terror and she could feel trickles of perspiration moving over her bare skin...

Or at least, she thought it was perspiration...

So why ... why did it feel so *heavy*?

She reached out a trembling hand and took hold of the duvet that covered the lower half of her body. She took a deep breath and snatched the covers away.

They were in the bed with her: dozens of them, their vividly patterned bodies coiled around her legs and waist, moving beneath the flimsy material of her nightdress. She opened her mouth to scream and...

This time she really was awake. At least she *thought* she was. Warily, she put out her hand and switched on the bedside lamp ... then was taken with a sense of terror so powerful, she thought she would have to scream out loud. Something was moving against her bare flesh. She looked down at the duvet that covered her body and then took the corner of it gingerly in one hand and eased it slowly aside, steeling herself to leap out of the bed. But there were no unwanted occupants this time. The tickle against her flesh had only been beads of sweat, trickling down to soak into the mattress.

'Jesus,' she whispered. She reached instinctively for her cigarettes and her clumsy hands managed to get one of them alight. Then she heard a muffled voice and realised that this was probably what had woken her. It seemed to be coming from the room next door, not on Lezard's side, but the other. She made an effort to remember who'd been billeted there. Robbie Porter, she thought. But the voice she heard next belonged to Adrian, slurred and aggressive, as though he'd been drinking. Adrian had never been able to handle his drink.

'... disgusting exhibition! Never had you taped as a fucking junkie!'

'Don't be stupid!' Robbie's voice, now, sounding just as angry as his partner. 'Recreational use, that's all. Nothing to get worked up about. Anyway, you're a fine one to talk. Look at you, you can hardly stand!'

'What do you expect? I was worried about you. Can't you see, I don't want anything bad to happen to you...'

A long pause. Jenny lay there, telling herself that she shouldn't really be listening to this, but short of putting her hands over her ears, there was no way she was going to avoid hearing it.

Now Robbie spoke again, louder, more dismissive.

'I said *no*! I'm not in the mood.'

'Oh, come on, what's the matter with... ?'

'I told you. I just want to be alone.'

'Yeah, who are you all of a sudden? Greta fucking Garbo? Listen, kid, you owe me.'

'Fuck off, it doesn't work like that. I owe you nothing!'

'Oh, I get it. Made your connection with the band, didn't we? Now it's fanx, tara!'

'Don't be ridiculous. It's not like that!'

'Sure it is. You little shit, you took me for a sucker, didn't you? Just wanted me to introduce you to Jenny and the others. I can't believe I was so...'

'Look, get off my back! You're getting it all wrong. I'm just not in the mood tonight, OK?'

'Not tonight, dearie, I've got a headache! Well fuck you, pal, that won't be all you've got when I've finished with you.'

'What's that supposed to mean?'

'You're not in The Deceivers yet, my friend . . . though come to think of it, with a name like ours, it should suit you down to the ground.'

'For Christ's sake, will you simmer down? You'll wake everyone in the house!'

'Think I care? Let them all know what a conniving little mother you really are! Well, don't worry, kid, you haven't heard the last of this. Nobody plays me for a sucker. Nobody. I'll get you back, you just see if I don't!'

'Adrian, listen to me . . .'

'No! You just fuck right off!'

A door opened and slammed with such force that Jenny winced. Then she heard Adrian stumbling along the corridor and up the next flight of stairs to his room on the second floor.

She sighed. She supposed she should have been grateful for having been woken from that awful dream, but this had been one conversation she'd have preferred not to have overheard. She lay there smoking her cigarette and staring up at the ceiling. Sleep now seemed very far away and after her recent experience she was far from anxious to succumb to it. So she lay there through the long hours, smoking one cigarette after another and listening to the eerie howl of the restless wind outside.

Somewhere in the small hours of the morning, sleep did steal over her again: but thankfully, this time there were no dreams waiting for her.

Chapter Twenty-Five

She finally woke around nine o'clock to be greeted by the sound of the wind still blustering aggressively outside her window. She dragged herself out of bed and, pulling back the curtains, peered blearily down into the courtyard. She was momentarily shocked to see that the parked vehicles were all but buried beneath snowdrifts. She could make out the roof of Lezard's Shogun, but her beloved DB5 was no more than a snow-covered hump. What's more, the snow was still falling, perhaps not as heavily as before but enough to worsen the situation.

'Great,' she muttered. 'If this keeps up we'll be here till the fucking spring.' She stumbled to the bathroom and went through the routine of showering herself awake, aware of the sounds of movement and laughter from downstairs. *Late again*, she thought but told herself that the band could take the opportunity to do a warm-up before she got there.

She dried herself, dressed in jeans and sweatshirt and went downstairs to the dining room, where she found herself in a virtual replay of the previous morning. There was Cassie, clearing away the remains of what looked like a hearty breakfast.

'I'm going to have to invest in an alarm clock,' said Jenny, as she slid into a vacant chair.

Cassie turned to smile at her, wiping her hands on a tea towel. 'I wouldn't worry,' she said. 'The others have only just gone down to the studio. Actually, you're not the last one up this morning. Emma and Mr McGuire still haven't put in an appearance. And there's been no sign of Mr Langan.'

Jenny grimaced.

'I'm not surprised. I gather he was a little the worse for drink last night.'

'You heard it too?' Cassie lowered her voice. 'That was an unpleasant scene, wasn't it? Took me ages to get back to sleep afterwards. Some people just shouldn't touch alcohol. It's like poison to them.'

'Amen to that,' murmured Jenny. She presumed that Cassie knew nothing about her own history of alcohol abuse.

'Anyway, perhaps you'll let me make you a proper breakfast this morning.'

'Uh uh. A proper cup of coffee will do nicely, thanks.' Jenny picked up her cigarettes and saw that she was down to her last four. This knowledge filled her with dread. It wasn't as if she would be able to pop out to the nearest shop for more. She watched as Cassie brought the flask of coffee from the kitchen and leaned across the table to fill Jenny's cup. She was wearing the snake earrings again and they served as an unpleasant reminder of last night's dream. Jenny made an effort to put her mind on to something else.

'That was quite a show you put on, last night,' she observed.

'Show?' Cassie looked puzzled. 'Oh, you mean the séance? Yeah, it was getting scary, wasn't it? Tell you the truth, I was kind of glad Mr McGuire turned up when he did. I was about to freak.'

'Me too.' Jenny lit her cigarette and blew out a long stream of smoke. 'How long have you been doing stuff like that?'

'Oh, that's Idris, it's really nothing to do with me. He has the gift, he's had it since he was a boy. He comes from a little village in the sticks and his mother was a white witch, used to heal people in the village with herbs and stuff. He must have got it from her, I guess.' She thought for a moment. 'I think Gareth has it too. Maybe not as much as Idris, but when they get together, oh boy!' She blew air out from between pursed lips. 'Watch out!'

'It's not faked then?' Jenny asked her. 'Hidden tape machines and stuff like that?'

Cassie looked offended.

'God, no,' she said. 'What would be the point of that? The two of them have something going between them. Maybe we don't really understand it, but that doesn't mean it has to be phoney. They share something precious, you know?'

'Including you, by all accounts.'

Cassie looked embarrassed.

'Who told you about that?' she whispered.

'Lezard. He said that Idris approves of the situation. Is that true?'

'We're not doing anything wrong!' said Cassie, defensively. 'I mean, it's not like we're breaking laws.'

'No, I guess not. You're free-thinking people and it's nobody's business but yours, right?'

'Absolutely.' Cassie was glaring at Jenny now, as though defying her to push it any further. But this morning, Jenny was in the mood to push.

'That's quite a bruise you've got,' she observed. 'I noticed it last night.'

'Uh . . . yes.' Cassie glanced away. 'I walked into a cupboard door.'

'Oh yeah? And there was me thinking you'd walked into somebody's fist.'

'I have things to attend to,' said Cassie dismissively. She

turned away then seemed to remember something. 'Oh, yes, and there's another letter for you.' She indicated a white envelope lying on the table.

'Christ, I'm amazed the post managed to get through the snow,' muttered Jenny.

'Oh, it didn't. There's no stamp on it. I found it on the table when I got up this morning. It's another one from whoever it is that needs spelling lessons.'

This revelation hit Jenny like a clenched fist in the solar plexus. She opened her mouth to ask another question, but Cassie had already moved through into the kitchen. Jenny just sat there, staring at the envelope. As Cassie had said, there was no stamp or address on it. Printed in black felt-tip pen were two words: JENNY SLAYED.

'Sweet Jesus,' she whispered.

Because this meant ... could *only* mean, that whoever had been sending the letters was here at The Grange. The Hoochie Coochie Man was somebody she already knew.

With trembling hands she opened the flap of the envelope. Inside, there was one sheet of white paper. She unfolded it to read the printed message.

> THE DECEIVERS' NEW GUITARIST
> JUST WANTS TO BE A ROCKER
> HE'D BETTER PLAY IT CAREFULLY
> OR HE'S IN FOR A SHOCKER!

At first, Jenny didn't quite take it in. New guitarist. That of course, was Robbie Porter ... who at this moment was down in the studio with some of the other members of the band, doubtless warming up with a song or two. Play it carefully ... a shocker? Christ, surely it didn't mean ... ?

Suddenly she was up on her feet, pushing back from the

table so violently, that the chair fell over with a clatter. She began to walk towards the hall door, then broke into a run.

'Jenny?' She heard Cassie call inquiringly after her but there was no time to stop and explain what had happened. She ran to the studio door and pushed it open. Just like yesterday, music drifted up to her, the band slamming through an old George Thoroughgood number, *Bad to the Bone*, sounding spiky and abrasive without the keyboards. Robbie was singing the chorus as she pounded down the stairs and she remembered that Adrian had mentioned that this was the kid's party piece.

The lyrics were interspersed with a tasty guitar riff. Maybe her interpretation of the Hoochie Coochie Man's latest message had been wrong. Robbie was down there using his guitar with no apparent problems: and yet she couldn't get that last line out of her head.

She pounded down the staircase and into the control room, yelling as she did so. Surprised heads turned to stare at her in dull surprise. She saw Reed and Idris sitting side by side behind the mixing desk, Lezard relaxing on a small leather sofa behind them. The three men were looking at her as if she'd lost her mind. Perhaps she had. She gestured frantically at the illuminated musicians on the other side of the glass.

'Stop them!' she yelled. 'Get them out of there!'

Reed glared at her.

'What's the matter with you?' he protested.

She ignored him and ran to the glass partition, her fist raised to hammer on it. She could see Robbie directly ahead of her, his eyes closed, his skinny body moving to the beat as he spat the lyrics into the microphone. He was wearing earphones and he didn't even hear the sound of Jenny's fist striking repeatedly against the acoustic glass partition.

Steve was staring at her now, a puzzled expression on his face, but his fingers still moved across the strings of his

Rickenbacker. Jenny realised how it must look. The lead singer throwing a wobbly because some upstart had had the nerve to get up and sing a song.

'Reed!' she yelled. 'Get on the intercom for God's sake. Cut them off! Tell them they've got to—'

And then it happened. Robbie struck a major chord and lifted a hand to hold the microphone stand. There was an intense flash of light from the fretboard of Robbie's guitar, an overload so powerful that all the lights in the control room dimmed. Robbie's skinny frame jerked as though he'd been hit by a sledgehammer and he began to shudder uncontrollably, his left hand still clutched tight around the metal stand. His head snapped back and for an instant, it would have been easy to mistake his expression for one of rapture. But his long hair was bristling like the spines of a hedgehog, plumes of smoke were trailing from under his fingernails and when he opened his mouth to scream, Jenny saw sparks dancing from the fillings in his teeth.

Jenny screamed something, she didn't know what and anyway it was lost in the ululating shriek of Robbie's guitar as his body pitched backwards like a demented marionette and lay, kicking and convulsing on the studio floor, while Steve and Chris looked on in mute horror. He was still clutching the stand, his hand seemingly locked to it.

'Switch off the fucking power!' screamed Jenny – and at last Idris moved to obey her, stumbling sluggishly over to the fusebox on the far wall, moving like a man who had just awakened from a dream to find himself in a nightmare. The main lights went out to be replaced by the dull red glow of the battery-powered safety lamps. Robbie's supine body stopped kicking and lay still. Jenny wrenched open the studio door and ran inside, to be greeted by a scene of chaos.

Robbie was lying in a foetal position, plumes of grey smoke

rising from his hair and clothing, the guitar and microphone stand still clutched in his charred hands. Chris was trying to get to him but Steve was holding him back, fearful no doubt that the guitar might still be live: in the panic he hadn't realised that the safety lights had come on. Jenny pushed past them and went down on her knees beside Robbie. This felt like a hideous replay of Scott's death in Seattle but at least that time, there had been professionals on hand to try and save him. This time, there was only Jenny and her rudimentary knowledge of first aid.

'Don't touch him, Jenny!' yelled Steve. 'The guitar it might be . . .'

'Power's off!' she told him. 'Give me a hand here.' She was feeling at Robbie's throat, trying to locate a pulse but she was having no success. His chest displayed no sign of movement either. Grimly, she wrenched the guitar away from him, yelping as her fingers brushed the steel strings which felt red hot to the touch. She threw the instrument aside then attempted to prise his other hand away from the stand, having to exert considerable effort to manipulate his charred fingers. Then she did her best to administer the kiss of life, tilting Robbie's head back to create an airway: but when she clamped her lips over his, her mouth filled with foul-tasting smoke and she had to force herself to go through the routine, breathing into his lungs, pushing down on his chest and counting the intervals: and she kept right on doing it, long after she knew in her heart that she was wasting her time. His young life had been snuffed out by a massive electrical shock and nothing she could achieve with her bare hands was ever going to change that.

Finally, she stopped kidding herself. As she numbly got to her feet, she saw three pale faces staring at her through the glass partition and she fought down an impulse to scream at them. She walked back into the control room. Her body was trembling now but not so much with fear as with anger. She still had the latest note crumpled into a ball in the palm of her hand. She unfolded it as she walked to Lezard. Then she thrust it into his hands.

'Maybe now you'll believe me!' she hissed.

He took it from her, stared at it uncomprehendingly for a moment.

'But . . . how . . ?'

'Delivered by hand, this morning,' she told him. Then, when his eyes widened in realisation, she nodded. 'Yes, that's right. He's here, Josh. The Hoochie Coochie Man is right here and he must be one of us.'

Lezard looked slowly around him. He looked like he was about to be sick. 'And Robbie?' he ventured.

'Dead,' she assured him. 'As a doornail.' She glanced back as Steve and Chris came shuffling fearfully out of the studio. 'Now tell me I'm being paranoid!' she snarled. 'Don't you see, he means to keep his threat? One down, four to go! He's going to kill us all.' The sense of shock was palpable. There was a long silence while everyone stood there staring at each other.

'I don't understand.' It was Gareth Reed speaking, his voice hoarse as though he'd been crying. 'This can't happen. The studio is designed to be safe, there . . . there are trip fuses on all the mains leads, we absolutely insist on it.' He snapped an accusing glance at Idris. 'You're supposed to run a safety check,' he said.

'I did, yesterday. Everything was fine then and as far as I'm aware, nothing's been touched since.' He pointed at the contorted figure on the other side of the glass. 'Besides, look at the way he's all burned up. That was no ordinary shock, somebody must have been in during the night and sabotaged the equipment.'

'Of course they have,' agreed Jenny. She indicated the note that Lezard was still holding. 'See here? "He'd better play it carefully." It's like whoever wrote this was giving us a sporting chance. Christ, if I'd only been up half an hour earlier! I'd have read the note while you guys were still having breakfast…'

'It's not the only warning we had,' Steve told her. He held out another sheet of paper. 'We found this pinned to Robbie's amp when we came down here. We couldn't figure out why you'd left it there, Jenny.'

'Why *I* left it? What are you talking about? Why would I leave anything? I haven't *been* down here!'

'Well…' Steve shrugged. He couldn't seem to look her in the eyes. 'I guess I just assumed it was you. They are your lyrics, after all. And they do seem horribly … appropriate.'

Jenny snatched the sheet of paper from him. Same sheet of white cartridge, same printed black handwriting, but this time they had reproduced some of the lyrics from *Live Wire*, a song from The Deceivers' first album, *Night Drive*.

YOU TRIPPED THE LIGHT FANTASTIC
YOU PLAYED A DEADLY GAME.
PLUGGED INTO THE CIRCUIT,
YOU BURNED UP LIKE A FLAME.

'Robbie even joked about it,' said Chris, quietly. 'Said you must have it in for him or something, leaving cryptic messages around the place. But we never thought for one minute…'

'Oh come on, what are you talking about?' Jenny stared at them, horrified by what they could be … *must* be thinking about her. 'You think I did this? I can't even wire a thirteen amp plug. This would take an expert.' She glanced at Idris. 'Somebody like him.' She jabbed a finger at Reed. 'Or him.'

'Hey, now just a minute,' protested Reed. 'I hope you're not trying to suggest that we…'

'Well who else here could have done it?' she reasoned. 'I

think we'll all agree that it would take specialist skills to set up a lethal booby trap like that.' She glared at Idris. 'Well? Am I wrong?'

He shrugged.

'It would take somebody with a sound working knowledge of electrical procedure,' he admitted. 'But most people in bands have a good idea of how it works.'

'Well not me,' she assured him. 'I wouldn't have the first idea how to go about it.'

'Yes, but you would say that, wouldn't you?' sneered Idris.

She glanced desperately at Chris and Steve.

'Come on, you guys, think about it for a moment.' She waved the piece of paper at them. 'This is … this is just somebody trying to make me look bad, that's all. Jesus, why do you think I came down here like a lunatic, trying to get you to stop?'

Steve frowned.

'Maybe you had second thoughts,' he said.

'Oh, come on, come on, this is nuts! How can you even think I'd be capable of such a thing? Josh, what do you say? Tell me you don't believe I had anything to do with this.'

'Of course not,' he muttered: but he didn't sound convinced.

'What about Adrian?' muttered Chris: and everybody turned to look at him. 'Well, he knows all that technical stuff, doesn't he? He builds his own keyboards. And he's fixed the amps plenty of times when Mike wasn't available.'

Jenny thought about it.

'That's it!' she said. 'Steve, what was Adrian's job before he became a musician?'

Steve's eyes widened slightly as he remembered.

'He was an electrician,' he said quietly.

'And where exactly *is* Adrian?' she asked.

'Still asleep, as far as I know,' said Steve. 'I knocked on his door this morning but there was no answer. Tried the handle but it was locked. Figured he was just sleeping off a hangover.'

Jenny nodded.

'He and Robbie argued last night,' she said.

'Yeah, I heard them too,' said Lezard. 'Sounded pretty nasty. Come to think of it, I'm sure I heard Adrian making threats. Something about how he was going to get Robbie back...'

'Let's not jump to conclusions,' warned Steve. 'At least not till we've heard Adrian's side of it.' He glanced through the glass at the slumped figure on the floor. 'Jesus, one of us is going to have to tell him about this.'

'If he doesn't already know about it,' said Chris, grimly.

Steve frowned.

'Can't we get his body covered up or something? I can't bear to see it lying there like that.'

'I'll get a sheet,' said Idris. He turned and made his way up the stairs.

'We'd better go and have a quiet word with Adrian,' Lezard told Jenny. 'Steve, Chris, you can break the news to the others. And try not to get everyone too stirred up. Just tell them there's been an accident...'

'What's the point in lying about it?' protested Jenny. 'This was no accident, it was murder.'

'I appreciate that, Jenny. But just think about it. We're all stuck inside these four walls for the foreseeable future. We can't get out because of the weather conditions and we can't even phone for help.'

'Can't we try your mobile again?'

Lezard looked uncomfortable.

'We could, if I could find it.'

'What do you mean?'

'I left it in the office, last night. When I looked for it this morning, it was gone. I thought maybe one of the guys had borrowed it, but when I asked around this morning, nobody seemed to know anything about it.'

Jenny stared at him.

'Oh, Jesus,' she whispered. 'Can't you see what's happening here? Somebody took it deliberately. Whoever wrote the letters is making damned sure we can't call for help.'

Lezard placed a hand on Jenny's shoulders.

'We don't know that for sure. Look, Jenny, the last thing we need on our hands is a panic. We go round shouting about murder and that's exactly what we'll have.'

'He's right,' agreed Steve. 'There's no point in scaring everybody.'

'They should be fucking scared,' she snapped. 'I know I am. And what about *warning* them? Don't you think they've got a right to know?'

Lezard frowned.

'We'll talk about it later. But we'll do it properly, we'll call a meeting and give everyone the facts. But first, I really think we should have that word with Adrian. Maybe he can shed some light on what's been happening here.'

Jenny sighed, nodded.

'OK,' she said.

Lezard started for the stairs and Jenny followed him. She was still holding the pieces of paper. Glancing back, she saw that Steve and Chris were gazing after her with open suspicion in their eyes. She could imagine what they were thinking. About her nervous breakdown. About the crazy raving creature that had been admitted to a drying-out clinic, convinced that she was covered with cats and rats and spiders. They were asking themselves if she was really cured. But at the moment, this was the least of her worries. She couldn't stop thinking that somebody in this house was a murderer. They'd killed Robbie, almost certainly murdered Mike Watton ... and maybe even Scott Griffin all those months back. Who was to say that his heroin hadn't been deliberately spiked with toilet cleaner?

If she was right about this, then the Hoochie Coochie Man wasn't going to stop at three victims. He would go on until he was discovered ... or until they were all dead. Every last one of them.

The thought settled around her shoulders like a heavy black cloak as she followed Lezard up the staircase to the second floor.

Chapter Twenty-Six

The door to Adrian's room was still closed. Lezard knocked, gently at first, then louder, then louder still. When this failed to bring anyone to the door, he tried calling out the keyboard player's name, with similar results. Finally, he resorted to trying to turn the handle, but the door was locked. He frowned, kneeled and peered into the keyhole.

'He has to be in there,' he concluded. 'I can see the key, it's obviously been locked from the inside.'

'Then why doesn't he answer?' asked Jenny, grimly. 'He can't be that badly hung over.'

Lezard frowned. He thought for a moment, then stepped decisively back from the door, lifted a leg and slammed his foot against the lock. The ancient door shook in its frame but it was solid and after a half dozen attempts, Lezard was prompted to look for something to assist him. At the end of the hall, there was a fire extinguisher and a glass case containing a heavy fire axe. Lezard walked along to it and after a moment's hesitation, he broke out the glass panel with his elbow and removed the axe. He hefted it in his hands and turned back to face the door but Jenny held up a hand to stop him.

'Jesus, there's no need for that. Just give me a couple of minutes.' She went down to her room and found a newspaper and a steel comb with a long pointed handle. She hurried back up to the top floor, opened the newspaper and slid it beneath Adrian's door. Then using the long handle of the comb, she pushed it into the keyhole and poked out the key. It fell with a thud on to the paper and Jenny was able to ease the key back under the door.

'Amazing,' said Lezard, putting down the axe. 'I had no idea you sidelined as a cat burglar.'

'Just a sign of a misspent youth,' she assured him. 'A lot of nights spent out at the disco, before Mother would let me have a key of my own.' She picked up the key and handed it to him. 'After you,' she said uneasily.

'Thanks,' he muttered. He slotted the key into the lock and turned it. He glanced at Jenny and gave her a look, a raised-eyebrows expression that seemed to say, 'Well, here goes nothing!' Then he reached out a hand to open the door. He grunted in surprise. 'Jesus, they built these things solid,' he observed. It required considerable effort to push it fully open.

Jenny peered apprehensively into the room, which appeared to be empty and very cold. The reason for the latter was quickly evident. The window was wide open and wind and snow were gusting into the room. Jenny and Lezard entered, looking around. The room was tidy, the double bed looked as though it hadn't been slept in – but there was a strange smell in there that even the rushing wind could not entirely dispel, a raw, gamey stink mingled with an unmistakable odour of defecation. Beyond the bed, the open doorway of the en suite bathroom beckoned.

'Maybe he's in there,' said Jenny quietly.

'I'll go look,' offered Lezard.

He started walking towards the bathroom. Jenny remained where she was, not wanting to go in there, afraid of what she might find. She watched Lezard walking towards the open doorway, moving slowly with visible reluctance. He was holding his body in a stiff, unnatural posture as though steeling himself for a shock.

Behind her, Jenny was vaguely aware of a creaking sound as the open door swung slowly back on itself and closed with a thud.

The noise made Lezard start and he glanced back over his shoulder in surprise.

'Relax,' Jenny told him. 'It's just the door.'

But his reaction sent a chill of fright through her. His body jolted as if it had been hit with a cattle prod and his eyes widened in shock and surprise. He was staring at Jenny in horrified fascination...

No, not *at* Jenny. At something *behind* her.

She span around in dread and couldn't hold back the scream that came involuntarily out of her lungs. She clamped a hand over her own mouth to stem the noise of her terror.

Adrian was hanging on the door. Jenny vaguely registered that this was why it had seemed so heavy, but she couldn't think about that now because...

There was a short length of rope around his neck, pulled so tight that it had cut deep into the flesh of his throat. The rope had been secured to a cast-iron coat hook that protruded from the top of the door. Adrian's feet were suspended a few scant inches from the floor. His tongue, which poked from between his teeth, was black and bloated and his face would have been dark grey, were it not for the garish makeup he was wearing: powder, blusher and bright red lipstick, inexpertly applied. Even more shocking was the fact that Adrian was wearing women's lingerie – a black lace bra, panties, suspender belt and stockings – and that the backs of his legs were streaked with faeces, which accounted for the awful smell in the room. As a last indignity, somebody had affixed a small slip of paper to his forehead with a drawing pin.

All of this Jenny saw in an instant. Then she was backing away from the door, shaking her head in disbelief. She bumped into Lezard, who flung his arms around her, steadying her.

'Easy,' he whispered.

But she was shaking violently, overcome by the horror of it, by the tortured expression on Adrian's painted face that suggested he had still been alive when the rope had tightened around his neck. His eyes were staring blankly at Jenny and it seemed to her in that instant that he could see her standing there, that he was somehow relishing her reaction.

'Jesus,' she heard Lezard whisper. 'What an awful fucking way to kill yourself.'

'Who says it was suicide?' she replied. Her voice was little more than a hoarse whisper.

'Got to be,' he reasoned. 'Door was locked from the inside. If somebody had strung him up, they'd still be here.'

'But what about that?' She gestured at the note pinned to Adrian's skull. 'He was hardly in a position to do that to himself while he was hanging there, was he?'

Lezard shrugged.

'I . . . guess not . . .'

'And what did he stand on? There's nothing near to the door, no stool or chair within reach. Somebody must have lifted him up there, murdered him, Josh, just like somebody killed the others!' Her voice was rising to a shriek now and Lezard hugged her close, trying to calm her.

'OK, OK, try not to panic. We've got to keep it together, Jenny, whatever happens.'

She nodded, buried her face against his shoulder.

'The note,' she whispered. 'What does it say?'

'Say?' He swallowed with an effort.

'There are words on the paper . . .'

He nodded, detached himself from Jenny and moved slowly

back to the door. He made a sudden retching sound and had to grab a handkerchief from his pocket, holding it tightly over his mouth and nose. His face had drained of colour. He managed to get close enough to read the note and he studied it in silence for a moment.

'Well?' she prompted him.

'Lyrics,' he said, from behind his handkerchief. 'One of your old songs. I...' He shook his head and turned away in disgust. Jenny was obliged to move closer herself. There were the words printed in what was becoming a very familiar hand.

> SOME STAY IN THE CLOSET
> SOME STAY UNDERGROUND
> AND SOME LIVE IN A LANDSCAPE
> WHERE BEAUTY CAN'T BE FOUND.
> SOME GIVE UP ON LIVING,
> SOME GIVE UP ON HOPE
> AND SOME FIND THEIR SALVATION
> SWINGING FROM A ROPE.

She recognised the lyrics easily enough. They were from *Casualties of War*, a song from the third Deceivers album. Once again, somebody had selected an apt obituary from her extensive back catalogue.

She glanced at Josh and saw that he was watching her with apparent suspicion in his eyes.

'Christ,' she whispered. 'Not you, Josh, please! Steve and Chris already have their doubts about me, if you start to think the same way, I—'

'I don't think anything,' he said dismissively: but the look was still there in his eyes, and she knew he was wondering about her, about the breakdown she'd had, how much it might have affected her...

'I . . .' She struggled to find words, aware of a dull sensation of nausea rising in her throat. The smell in the room now seemed overpowering. 'That's it,' she said. 'I've had enough of this shit, I'm getting out of here, now.' She reached out to the door and edged it open, even though the action made her skin crawl. Adrian's head jerked forward and back, bumping against the wood with a hollow thud. She squeezed through the gap and hurried along the landing to the staircase.

'Wait, Jenny! Where are you going?' Lezard's voice shouted after her but she paid it no heed. She hurried down the steps and along the landing to her own room, where she threw on her jacket, a scarf and a pair of gloves. Then she went downstairs. She could hear voices talking in the lounge but luckily the door was closed. She turned back and hurried through the dining room to the back door. She opened it and stepped out into the blizzard. She stood hunched in the porch for a moment, shocked by the sheer power of the wind as it hammered at her, snatching her breath away and whipping icy flakes of snow into her eyes. Somebody had left a snow shovel propped against the wall and she grabbed it, then descended the precarious ice-covered steps to the courtyard. Out in the open, the wind nearly blew her off her feet.

She shrugged deeper into her jacket and moved across to the snow-covered mound that was her car. By the time she reached it, her hands and feet felt frozen. She brought the shovel into play and began to channel the snow away from the driver's door of the car, then she flinched at the sound of a voice behind her.

'Jenny, what the hell do you think you're doing?'

It was Lezard. He must have grabbed his coat and come straight after her. He had to shout at the top of his voice to make himself heard. 'You *can't* leave. The weather—'

'Fuck the weather!' she shouted back. 'If it's a choice of

being murdered or risking hypothermia, I know which one I'd rather take.' She went on shovelling grimly.

'But there's no reason to suppose...'

'There's every fucking reason! First Mike, then Robbie, now Adrian. Two suicides and a fatal accident, all within a couple of days? I mean, don't you think that's a little bit more than coincidence?'

'Of course, but maybe it's all over with now!'

'What are you talking about?' She turned back to look at him, throwing up an arm to shield her eyes from the stinging onslaught of snow. 'How is it over with?'

'Well, don't you see? Maybe Adrian was the Hoochie Coochie Man. Maybe he was sending you the letters. He killed Mike for whatever reason and then after he and Robbie argued, he booby-trapped the guitar. When he realised what he'd done, he went crazy with guilt and took his own life.'

Jenny laughed bitterly.

'All nice and neat, huh? Well, I don't buy that for a minute, it sounds like a serious case of wish fulfilment to me. Someone else is responsible for Adrian's death and I don't believe it's going to end here.'

'OK, maybe you're right, but head out into this storm and you could be in just as much danger as you are here.'

'I'll take the chance,' she said. She had got the car door free of snow now. She wrenched it open and slid into the seat, fumbling the keys from her pocket with her gloved hands.

'So that's it,' yelled Lezard. 'You're just going to drive off and leave the rest of us to it?'

She glared at him.

'No, of course not. I'm going to fetch help. Bring back a helicopter load of pigs, let them sort it all out. Christ, Josh, you don't think I'd just desert you, do you?'

'It had crossed my mind,' he admitted.

She got the key into the ignition and twisted it but the engine didn't even turn over. She tried again, a couple of times, with the same result.

'Oh, great,' she muttered. 'Battery must be flat.'

Lezard fumbled in his pocket for his keys.

'Never mind. Take the Shogun. At least with four-wheel drive, you'll have some chance of getting through the drifts. Here, give me the shovel.'

She got out of the car and followed him to the next bump in the snow. She huddled against the side of the Shogun and watched as Lezard began to channel snow away from the driver's door. Jenny's feet and hands were now virtually numb. She wondered how long Des McGuire had been out in the snow, before he'd got to the house. He'd said that his car broke down on the hill, a good half mile from here. Could anyone really have got that far on foot, in weather like this? True, it hadn't been quite as cold then and the snow hadn't got such a good grip, but even so . . .

'It would be better if you prepared for this a little,' Lezard shouted over his shoulder. 'You could do with taking some hot coffee or soup, in a flask. There's no telling how long you'll be stuck behind the wheel. And maybe . . .'

'No,' she told him. 'I don't want to think about it too much. I just want to go. And I don't want to say anything to the others.'

He looked surprised by this.

'Why not?' he asked her. 'One of them might want to ride along with you.'

She looked at him.

'That's what I'd be worried about,' she said.

He stared at her for a moment.

'Jesus. You really think one of them is a killer, don't you?'

'Josh, I don't see how one of them *can't* be.'

'But who? Surely there must be somebody you could trust?

I mean, for God's sake, what about Steve, or Chris? You've worked with them for years. I'd have thought you could trust them.'

She frowned, shook her head.

'I ought to be able to,' she admitted. 'But when it comes right down to it . . . I wouldn't like to stake my life on it.'

He stopped digging for a moment and looked at her warily.

'And what about me, Jenny? Supposing I offered to go along?'

She shrugged, looked away.

'I'd rather you didn't ask me to make that decision.'

He turned away in disgust and continued digging with renewed ferocity.

'Oh, that's nice. That's really cute. Jesus, for all I know it could be *you*. I could be aiding and abetting the escape of a killer!'

'You don't believe that,' she told him.

'Jenny, I don't know what to believe any more.'

He had the door cleared of snow now. He got his key into the lock and wrenched the door open, then climbed into the driver's seat. He slid the key into the ignition and twisted it.

Nothing. The engine didn't even cough.

Lezard punched his gloved fist against the steering wheel.

'I don't believe this!' he snapped. He tried again, several times, with the same results. 'That's a brand new battery,' he protested. 'Something doesn't add up here.' He reached down and pulled the bonnet catch: then getting back out of the car, he walked around to the front and lifted the snow-covered bonnet. He stood there for several moments, staring at the engine. Even over the howl of the wind, Jenny heard his exclamation of disbelief.

'What is it?' she demanded, moving closer.

He shook his head, began to walk away.

'Tell me!' she shrieked. 'What is it?'

'The spark plugs!' he yelled in her ear. 'Somebody's taken the fucking spark plugs! The jeep isn't going anywhere until we find them.'

He stood there, looking at her, his arms spread in a gesture of helplessness.

'*My* car then,' she pleaded. 'We'll ... we'll get jump leads and . . .'

'Don't be stupid, Jenny. They've obviously fixed that too. It wasn't a flat battery. It's hopeless.'

'No!' She shook her head stubbornly. 'I'll walk! I'm not going back into that house!'

'That's crazy. You won't get a hundred yards on foot.'

'I've got to try. Don't you see, if I don't, I'm going to end up like the others. The Hoochie Coochie Man. He ... he's not going to stop till he's killed us all.'

'Jenny, listen to me!' He took her by the shoulders and shook her hard, then pulled her close and wrapped his arms around her shivering body. 'I'm not going to let anything happen to you, you hear me? Not a chance. I'm still your manager and you're still my first concern.' He pulled away a little and looked her in the eyes. 'And I sure as hell am not going to let you freeze to death out here,' he concluded.

She was sobbing now, helpless with her own escalating fear.

'What's happening, Josh?' she cried. 'This is crazy. What's happening to us? I'm so afraid . . .'

'That makes two of us,' he assured her. 'But don't worry, we're going to be OK, you hear? As long as I'm alive, my first priority will be to protect you. That's a promise. Now come on, before we fall down dead where we stand.'

He took her hand and pulled her back towards the front door. She resisted at first and he had to coax her, cajole her, easing her along a step at a time.

'It's going to be all right, Jenny, I promise you. I won't let anything bad happen. You're too precious to me.'

Step by step, they crossed the courtyard and climbed the stairs back up to the house. Lezard reached into his pocket and found the keys. He unlocked the door and they stepped back into the warmth of the hallway.

Chapter Twenty-Seven

Jenny trudged dejectedly back up the staircase to her room. She felt dazed and sick with worry and her priority now was to take a hot shower and chase the chill out of her bones. Lezard had announced his intention of calling a meeting in half an hour's time, an opportunity, he said, for everyone to 'talk things through'. Jenny was glad that he was taking her suspicions seriously, at last, but she wished his attention could have been obtained in a less dramatic way.

She could not rid her mind of one inescapable fact. Somebody in the house was a murderer – and the removal of the spark plugs from Lezard's car suggested that whoever it was, he had no intention of letting anyone escape his retribution.

But who was it? The dream of the previous night kept coming back to her, all those mocking faces leering down as she cowered in the snake pit. For some reason, Gareth Reed's face seemed most prominent amongst them. Could it be him? Had she ... my God, had she slept with the killer? Or what about the sly, sinister Idris? There was a man with secrets, if ever there was one. And there was Des McGuire to consider. Robbie and Adrian had died the day after he appeared on the scene and he had made no secret of the fact that he bore a powerful grudge against the band...

She hesitated outside her room. The door was slightly ajar and she could see through the resulting gap, that the lights were on: and yet, she was sure, she'd switched them off when she went out to her car. She reached out a tentative hand and pushed open the door, steeling herself ready to make a run for the stairs at the first sign of trouble.

Cassie was standing beside Jenny's bed, her back to the door. She appeared to be placing something on the pillow, but Jenny was unable to see what it was. She stepped decisively into the room.

'What are you doing?' she snapped.

Cassie span around in surprise, a guilty expression on her pretty face.

'Oh, Jenny, I didn't hear you!'

'Evidently not. What's that?' Jenny could now see what lay on her pillow. It was an old book, bound in mottled brown leather.

Cassie waved a hand ineffectually.

'It's ... just something I thought might interest you. I knocked but there was no answer, so I decided to leave it for you. It ... might help explain things ...'

'Explain?' Jenny moved forward and picked up the book. The title was etched into the ancient leather binding. *The Grange: A History* by Professor L. G. Wallace. Jenny looked at Cassie quizzically. 'You really think I'd be in the mood for reading after what's happened?' she asked. 'I take it you've heard about Robbie and Adrian?'

Cassie nodded.

'It's terrible,' she said. 'I can't believe it. It's like ... some kind of judgement.' She seemed to be about to say more, but she thought for a moment, then shook her head. 'I'd better get back downstairs,' she said.

'No, wait.' Jenny reached out a hand and grabbed the

girl's arm. 'You know something, don't you?'

'Know something? About what?' Cassie affected an air of wide-eyed innocence, but it didn't quite come off.

'About what's happening here.'

Cassie shook her head.

'I don't know anything,' she said. 'I'm a complete ignoramus.' But she seemed unable to meet Jenny's eyes.

'No you're not. And you *do* know something. Or at least you have an idea.'

Cassie frowned.

'Well . . . I will say this,' she murmured. 'It's kind of strange, the way things are slotting together. Do you . . . do you believe in history repeating itself?'

'How do you mean?'

'I mean, like, I've read about this, right? Certain places, they have bad things happen in them. And they're supposed to be like, you know, big video recorders. It's like the walls just soak up the events and some time later, maybe a hundred years later, the whole thing kicks into replay mode and the same events start to happen again.'

'Not unless somebody *makes* them happen,' Jenny told her. 'But you're referring to the guy that used to live here, right? Obediah . . . ?'

'Wadleigh. That's right. There's a lot of stuff about him in that book.'

Jenny nodded. She sat down on the bed and ushered Cassie to do the same.

'Gareth is pretty big on Wadleigh, isn't he?' she ventured 'And Idris too, I shouldn't wonder.'

Cassie nodded.

'Gareth says he was a great man. A misunderstood genius.'

'Hmm. And this thing that you have going between the three of you, that's all tied up with Wadleigh's teachings, right?' She reached out a finger to touch one of Cassie's earrings. 'And these have something to do with it too. Gareth has a tattoo exactly the same.'

Cassie seemed to become suddenly nervous.

'I really should go,' she said. 'Idris will be wondering where I've got to.' She started to get up off the bed but Jenny put a hand on her shoulder and pulled her back down again.

'Hold on, lady, you're going nowhere till we've had this out. This isn't some game we're playing. Two people are dead. And I've just discovered that somebody's stolen the spark plugs out of Lezard's car.'

Cassie stared at her.

'What are you talking about? Why would anybody do a thing like that?'

'I thought maybe you could tell me.'

'Well, it's nothing to do with us, if that's what you're thinking. I mean, I know that some people would find what we do strange, but we'd never harm anybody.'

'And what exactly *do* you do, Cassie? As far as I can figure it, the three of you are having what the French call a *ménage à trois* . . .'

'It's more than that!' said Cassie indignantly. 'How typical to assume that it's something sordid. Actually it's . . . it's like . . . well, the way Gareth explains it, it's a harnessing of power. It makes us strong, gives us the ability to change things for the better. To heal, to give comfort, to prosper . . .'

Jenny gave a dismissive laugh.

'And you and Idris fell for that, did you? Where I come from, that's known as "having your cake and eating it"!'

'It's not like that! You're trying to put it down because you don't understand. You've never attended one of our ceremonies. When we go out to the stone circle and make love, you can actually *feel* the power being generated. You can hear it. You can hear the voices of the dead coming out of the stones. And it's better than any drug you could name, believe me.' She stared at Jenny for a moment, then seemed to become angry at the sceptical expression on her face. 'It *works*! For goodness sake, how do you think a young guy like Gareth got so successful in such a short space of time? He's only produced three albums and every one of them a platinum seller!'

'Could be he's talented,' reasoned Jenny. 'Some people have an ear for the right noise, you know. And others just get lucky...'

'No, no, don't you see? He's harnessed the power of nature. He's tapped into the life force. His success is just the outward show of that.' Cassie frowned, examined her hands for a moment. 'But then, I shouldn't have to tell you about Gareth,' she said quietly. 'You've been with him. You know what he's capable of.'

She looked so worshipful as she said this that Jenny had to laugh.

'Oh come on, Cassie, let's not get carried away! He was good, I'll grant you. But he wasn't *that* good. In fact, as I remember, it was all down to some special drink he gave me. He had me half stoned before he laid a finger on me, anything would have seemed above average.' She thought for a moment. 'I'll bet you all drink that stuff before you go out for one of your ceremonies, right?'

Cassie gave Jenny a disparaging look.

'It's pointless trying to put him down. I know Gareth and I know his true value. If you didn't discover it then there's something lacking in *you*. You have to learn to open yourself up to the experience. It takes time.'

'And *practise*, presumably.'

This was a sly dig and the look of disgust on Cassie's face demonstrated that the barb had found a target.

'I'm wasting my time talking to you,' she hissed.

'No, look, Cassie, I've got nothing against sexual experimentation between consenting adults, that's fine. But when it comes dressed up as some kind of religion, that's when I draw the line. It seems to me that this cult you're involved with, this religion, whatever you want to call it, it's similar to what Wadleigh and his crew practised.'

'It's more than *similar*,' said Cassie scornfully. 'It's the same religion. The Order of the Snake. I thought you knew that. It's why I brought you the book, so you could learn more about us, so you'd realise that we couldn't be responsible for—'

'The Order of the—?' Jenny broke off. Things were falling into place for her now. She remembered the story that Reed had pitched her the first time she'd met him. 'Oh yes, that's right. Reed told me there were thirteen of them, Wadleigh and his twelve disciples. They believed in something called The ... Cosmic Joker, right? And they all committed suicide ...'

Cassie shook her head.

'No! It wasn't suicide. You should read the book, it will explain everything to you. It was a necessary sacrifice. Wadleigh knew what was coming. He knew what the fate of the world would be if he didn't act quickly. He had to make the ultimate sacrifice but he didn't hesitate to—'

'Cassandra!' Cassie broke off with a gasp of fear. Idris was standing in the open doorway. He was looking in at his wife with cold, venomous eyes. Instinctively, Jenny leaned back and with a surreptitious movement, she slid the book beneath her pillows, out of sight. She wasn't sure why, but she was convinced that Idris would be far from happy to see that Cassie had given it to her.

'We were just chatting,' said Jenny, defensively.

'So I gathered.' Idris didn't take his gaze off his wife. 'I've been looking all over for you,' he said. 'I need your help downstairs.'

'Yes, Idris.' Cassie got obediently to her feet and moved towards the door. She looked scared, Jenny thought, and probably had every reason to. Idris placed a hand on her shoulder and the girl winced involuntarily.

'I'm instructed to tell everybody that there will be a meeting in fifteen minutes time, in the lounge,' said Idris. 'Mr Lezard has requested that everybody should attend.'

'Yes, I already know about the meeting,' Jenny told him. 'You planning on being there?'

'Of course.'

'Well, don't forget to bring back the spark plugs, OK?'

Idris's brow furrowed. His look of puzzlement seemed genuine enough, Jenny thought, but it could have been an act.

'Spark plugs?' he muttered. 'I haven't the faintest idea what you mean.'

'It's just that they've gone missing from Lezard's car. I thought maybe you might know something about it: you or that dodgy employer of yours.'

'Gareth? I can't imagine that he'd know anything about it, either.'

'No, I guess not. After all, Mr Reed is a regular St Francis of Assisi, by all accounts. Harnessed to the powers of nature and all that. So good of him to share his gifts with ordinary folk like you two.'

Idris looked blankly at his wife and then back at Jenny.

'What are you getting at?' he asked her.

'I'm merely suggesting that Gareth Reed might not be as squeaky clean as he makes out. That maybe he's got something to hide.'

Cassie laughed dismissively and she and Idris exchanged glances.

'She's jealous,' said Cassie, knowingly.

'What?' Jenny found herself infuriated by the younger woman's smugness. 'And what could I possibly be jealous of?'

'That Gareth came to you and you were found wanting!' said Cassie, gloatingly. 'You see, he only goes back to those who have the potential to share his power!'

'Oh, do me a favour! You may have fallen for that bullshit, but some of us have got a bit more sense than that. You can pretty it up as much as you like, Cassie, but I suspect that the only "magic" he sees in you is the chance to avail himself of a delectable piece of ass, night after night.'

'That's enough!' snapped Idris. 'Cassandra, downstairs, now!'

Cassie scuttled out of the room, but Idris stood his ground, glaring at Jenny, his muscular arms crossed over his chest. He was doing his best to keep his cool but a twitching jaw muscle betrayed his inner rage.

'What's wrong, Idris?' Jenny asked him. 'Not quite as convinced by Gareth's omnipotence as your wife is? Could it be that deep down, you suspect the pair of them are just using this religious shit as an excuse to cheat on you?'

Idris sneered at her.

'What do you know about it?' he said. 'You're just a rock singer. You haven't seen what we've seen. You haven't heard what we've heard. It's strange though that you're so sceptical. I should have thought after the little demonstration we laid on the other night, you'd at least be receptive to the ideas behind our faith.'

'What demonstration? The séance? All that table-rapping and ghostly whispers? You're trying to tell me that wasn't faked?'

'Of course it wasn't faked! What would be the point? No, that was a genuine message from your departed friend. And you know something? It was nothing! The tip of the iceberg. Gareth has shown us wonders that you couldn't even begin to credit. And he's taught me how to realise the full potential of my own gifts.'

'Oh yeah, I bet he's a regular David Copperfield.'

'How dare you compare him to a mere conjurer! Gareth's powers are genuine.'

Jenny shrugged.

'Maybe they are, at that. But you're a red-blooded male under that don't-give-a-fuck exterior. You must get jealous. It's only human.'

Idris made a dismissive gesture.

'I really do think I've had enough of this conversation,' he said. He glanced at his watch. 'The meeting is in ten minutes. I'm sure you'll have every opportunity to air your views then.' He went out of the room, closing the door behind him.

'Asshole,' muttered Jenny. She pulled the book out from under her pillow and traced the shape of its title with her index finger. Then she felt a shiver run through her. She still hadn't warmed up properly. She pushed the book back out of sight, threw off her jacket and went to the bathroom to take her shower. The floods of hot water warmed her body but there was still a cold sliver of ice lodged deep inside her chest that no amount of heat was going to dispel.

And then she got the distinct impression that somebody was watching her. She knew it was impossible and yet the conviction clung to her, making her skin crawl with dread. She got out of the shower, dried herself and dressed in fresh clothes.

She went downstairs to the meeting.

Chapter Twenty-Eight

When Jenny entered the lounge, she found that the others were already assembled, seated in a roughly circular arrangement around the room. Lezard stood with his back to the fire. He had the air of a harassed schoolteacher waiting to take assembly. Jenny gave him an apologetic shrug and slipped into a vacant seat on one of the sofas, beside Steve Lampton. She scanned the circle of faces. Everybody looked understandably apprehensive.

Reed and the Morgans sat off to one side on wooden chairs and Jenny noticed that Idris had Robbie's amplifier laid out on a coffee table in front of him, the backplate removed to expose the electrics. Chris and Emma sat huddled together on the other sofa, both of them chainsmoking nervously, while Des McGuire occupied an armchair near to Lezard. For once, his smug air of superiority seemed to have deserted him and he looked pale and drawn.

'All right,' said Lezard, calling the meeting to order. 'Thanks for coming, everybody. I thought that with everything that's happened here today, we should all get together and talk it through.' He paused for a moment and looked slowly around the circle before continuing. 'As you all know by now, Robbie Porter died during rehearsal this morning after receiving a massive electric shock. Idris has shown me evidence that convinces me there's no way this could have been accidental. Furthermore, shortly afterwards, Jenny and I discovered Adrian's body hanging from the door up in his room. Now, I know some of you haven't actually been to look at the ... the crime scenes, so I'll just mention that in both cases, lyrics from one of Jenny's songs were found near to or on the body...'

Jenny was aware of everyone's eyes on her and felt like clawing a hole in the floor and climbing into it.

'Idris, perhaps you'd like to say something about Robbie's death,' continued Lezard.

Idris lifted the amplifier in his powerful arms and panned it slowly around the room so that everybody could see into the charred recess at the back.

'Somebody did a pretty radical rewiring job on this,' he said. 'You can just about see that the earth has been taken out from its usual contact and connected to the live. Also, the same person bypassed the circuit breaker on the lead. The guitar must have been live the minute Robbie switched it on, and when he earthed himself by touching the microphone stand, the power took the quickest route to earth, straight through the kid's body.'

'Don't you think you should have left that alone?' Steve asked him. 'It's evidence. The police may want to examine that.'

'Police?' Idris looked faintly amused by the remark. 'And how are they supposed to get here? On a magic carpet?'

Steve shrugged.

'OK, but they'll be here eventually, won't they?' he reasoned. 'I mean, the snow can't last forever, the phones are going to come back on line eventually. At which point you're going to have some explaining to do. Anyway, how do we know you didn't rig up the accident in the first place?

Examining it will give you a perfect excuse for having your fingerprints all over it!'

'What are you getting at?' snarled Idris. 'If you're saying—'

'All right, all right, hold on a minute,' interrupted Lezard. 'Let's just cover some other points, shall we, before we all start making accusations at each other. You'll also recall that Jenny has been receiving letters from somebody calling himself the Hoochie Coochie Man, and that the last of them managed to arrive here without the benefit of a stamp. So whoever this person is, it has to be somebody who was already in the house.'

'Well, Adrian, obviously,' said Chris.

Lezard frowned.

'I'll admit, that was my first thought: that he'd sent the letters, engineered Robbie's death, then killed himself in a fit of remorse . . .'

'Still sounds the most likely explanation to me,' said Steve. 'Adey was a technical whizz and we all heard him and Robbie arguing the other night.'

'Yes, and somebody said that Adrian's door was locked from the inside,' added McGuire. 'A killer could hardly have strung him up and left the room, could he? Not unless he was thin enough to slip under the door.'

'Well, I thought the same,' agreed Lezard. 'But Jenny disagrees.'

'Oh?' Des looked at Jenny. 'Why's that then?'

'Three things,' said Jenny. 'One, the note was pinned to his forehead with a drawing pin. I don't accept for one moment that anyone, no matter how deranged, would calmly do that before stringing themselves up. Besides, there was no blood on his face, and if I remember my detective stories correctly, that indicates that the wound was made *after* the heart had stopped beating.' She paused for a moment and glanced around to see how her theory was going down. 'Two, there was nothing by the door he could have stood on. Admittedly, his feet were only just off the floor but he'd have needed something to get him high enough to reach that hook. So either he floated up there or the killer lifted him. And three ... well, it's the way he was dressed, the makeup and underwear. Adrian was obsessed with the way he looked, he couldn't bear to be made to look ridiculous.'

'He *was* a closet TV though,' Chris reminded her. 'I was at his place once and there was loads of women's gear hanging in a wardrobe. He told me that they belonged to some chick who'd been staying there but I didn't believe him for a minute.'

'Maybe so, Chris. But doing it in private, that's one thing. Letting the whole world see, even after you're dead, that's another. And I just don't buy it. I think somebody dressed him up like that in order to humiliate him.'

'But you heard what they said,' argued Emma. 'The door was locked from the *inside*.'

'That's true,' said Reed. 'But you're forgetting something. The window was open.'

Lezard looked at him sharply.

'Yes, that's right. But how do you know, Gareth?'

'Because I went and had a look, naturally. While you and Jenny were *otherwise occupied*.' He raised his eyebrows meaningfully. 'The window was open and there's a cast-iron drainpipe only a few feet to the left of it. It wouldn't take a world class athlete to shin down the pipe and there's plenty of snow to break somebody's fall. And getting back inside would be no problem: you were all issued with a front door key when you arrived.'

'Apart from me,' said McGuire quickly.

Reed ignored the remark.

'Actually, I'm glad I did look out of the window,' he continued. 'That's when I saw Jenny and Mr Lezard trying to make their escape.'

There was a gasp of surprise from several people. Lezard could only shake his head.

'Now hold on a minute, let's not jump to conclusions,' he said. 'I was going to get around to this point.'

'Oh yes, I'm sure you were,' muttered Des McGuire.

'No, really. Jenny suggested that one of us should try to get away in the Shogun...

'Yeah, I bet,' sneered Emma. 'No prizes for guessing which one of you. The one whose bloody lyrics are all over the two crime scenes.'

'Er ... actually, we hadn't decided on that,' said Lezard, gallantly. 'At any rate, one of us was going to make an attempt to go and get some help.'

'Oh, silly us,' said Emma sarcastically. 'And there we were thinking that the two of you were planning to scarper and leave us in the lurch.'

'There was never any thought of doing that,' protested Lezard. 'I figured, with four-wheel drive and all, there might be just a slim chance of making it through the snow. But someone got there before us...'

'What do you mean?' asked Cassie.

'I mean that somebody has removed the spark plugs. From the Shogun, from Jenny's car. Probably from all of them.'

The silence that followed these remarks was oppressive. Everybody sat there, peering sullenly at each other, each of them wondering about the person who was sitting opposite them. It was a horrible feeling, Jenny thought, to realise that there wasn't one of them she felt she could trust one hundred per cent.

'It ... it could have been Adrian,' reasoned Steve. Everybody looked at him. 'Maybe after he'd set up the guitar for Robbie, he wanted to make sure that nobody went for the police ... and ... he took the spark plugs ... then committed suicide.'

'I thought we'd already established that it *wasn't* suicide,' said Lezard. 'If we accept that Adrian was murdered, then whoever killed him must have taken the spark plugs.'

'That's right,' said Reed. He was staring pointedly at Jenny now and she felt compelled to challenge him.

'Well, it's hardly likely to be me, is it!' she protested. 'I was the one who suggested driving out of here.'

Reed nodded.

'Thus establishing an alibi courtesy of Josh. All you had to do was act surprised when he lifted the bonnet and naturally, he'd assume it couldn't be you.'

'What utter bollocks!' cried Jenny. 'What possible reason could I have for doing any of this?'

Reed smiled grimly.

'Well, let me see. You made no secret of the fact that you resented Robbie being brought in without being consulted: and I distinctly remember you telling me that you and Adrian didn't get along. You also said that he'd ruined the *Red Tape* album by swamping your voice behind layers of keyboards ...'

'No, Gareth, I seem to remember that *you* suggested that last bit.'

'All right. But you didn't disagree, did you?'

'Well ... no, but that's hardly motive enough to want to kill them, is it?'

'Look, let's all calm down a little,' Lezard urged them. 'Jenny, I'm sure Gareth isn't accusing you of anything.'

'That's not the impression I get. Look, I know my lyrics have been left at the scene of both murders ... but you have to ask yourself something. If I was the murderer, is it likely I'd implicate myself like that? Obviously, someone else is leaving those lyrics in order to make me look bad.'

'Oh, *obviously*,' said Emma, rolling her eyes. 'I mean, it couldn't possibly be a double bluff, could it?'

Jenny glared at her.

'A what?'

Emma inhaled on her cigarette and Jenny noticed that the girl's hand was trembling slightly. For all her studied coolness, she was frightened.

'You leave the lyrics to implicate yourself, so we'll think it can't possibly be you.'

'Oh right. And what about a few awkward little details. Like the fact that I wouldn't know how to rewire a guitar ... or what a fucking spark plug looked like if it jumped out and bit me!'

'So *you* say! But then you'd hardly admit to it, would you?'

'Well, how about you, Emma? Would you know how to rewire a guitar?'

'Of course not!' Emma looked positively disgusted at the idea. 'But if I *wanted* to know, I'd buy a manual and I'd learn how to do it, like anybody else. So don't come the helpless female routine with me.' She glared around the room. 'And remember,' she said, '*I'm* not the one who recently had a nervous breakdown. I'm not the one who spent time in an *institution*.'

Jenny had to exercise considerable restraint in order not to throw herself at Emma and punch her in the face. She realised too, that in the current situation, it wouldn't help to argue her case.

'Oh yeah,' she said, 'I wondered when somebody would have the bad taste to bring that up. And predictably, it had to be you, didn't it? Well, for your information, Emma, it was a drying-out clinic, not a fruit farm. I didn't experience any psychotic episodes and I had no urges to rip up the staff with a carving knife!'

'But you *were* subject to hallucinations,' said Emma, gleefully. 'You were suffering from chronic *delirium tremens*!'

Jenny couldn't conceal her shock at this news.

'How did you—?' She noticed that Chris was suddenly doing his level best to merge with the fabric of the sofa and that Lezard had a distinctly sheepish expression on his face. As far as Jenny had been aware, only Lezard knew the full story of her problems with alcohol – and he had promised her that he wouldn't tell anybody else.

'Josh?' she whispered.

He held his hands out to her in a pleading gesture.

'I . . . I told the guys in the band, Jenny. I *had* to tell them something, they were worried about their future. But I made them promise it would go no further.' He glared at Chris. 'I should have known it was a bad idea to confide in Mr Mouth Almighty here. Chris, for once, couldn't you be trusted to keep it zipped?'

Chris made an apologetic gesture.

'It just kind of slipped out,' he said. 'I was talking to Em one night and I'd had a lot of hash, right, and it always makes me talkative. But don't worry, I told her it wasn't for publication.'

'Oh well, that's all right then,' said Jenny, rolling her eyes. 'You arsehole, it'll be in her column the minute she gets out of here.'

'Yeah? What makes you think you're so newsworthy?' sneered Emma. 'A washed-up rock star with a few screws missing . . .'

'This is getting us nowhere,' observed Reed.

'Where d'you expect it to get us, man?' asked Chris. 'The thing is we're stuck here and if we're to believe Jenny, one of us is a psychotic nutter. We can't get out without freezing to death, all the phones are either out of order or missing and no facker is going to own up to being the killer anyway. So what's the point of this meeting? Eh? You tell me that! What's the fackin' point?'

Lezard looked deflated by the question.

'Well, I suppose I thought we could at least examine the evidence,' he explained.

'The evidence!' Steve laughed scornfully, his big shoulders moving up and down. 'What evidence? All I know is that two people are dead...'

'*Four* people,' Jenny corrected him. 'Don't forget about Mike and Scott.'

Steve stared at her.

'But Mike died before he even got here. And Scott's death was an accident...'

'Was it hell an accident! The inquest said that the drugs he took were cut with toilet cleaner. Somebody deliberately did that. Up till now, we've assumed it was just some scummy dealer trying to extend his profit margin. But what if it was the same person who killed Robbie and Adrian? And we've all said that Mike wouldn't have killed himself. Maybe somebody was waiting for him in his garage.'

Reed gave a derisive laugh.

'How would they make it look like suicide?'

'I don't know. Hit him with some chloroform, maybe. They could have had the car all rigged up to go. Just sit him in the seat and turn on the engine. He'd be dead before he woke up, right? I don't know, I'm guessing.'

'Sounds pretty damned convincing to me,' said Idris.

Lezard frowned.

'You're suggesting that somebody has been ... stalking members of the band? Maybe for a long time?'

'Why not? Maybe the Hoochie Coochie Man has had his eye on us for years. Maybe it's an old grudge.'

'That probably makes me a prime suspect,' said Emma, drily. 'I've hated all your records since I was two years old.'

Chris looked at her irritably.

'Give it a rest, will you?' he snapped. 'This isn't the time for cracking jokes, OK?'

'Who's joking?' sneered Emma. 'I was being deadly serious.'

'And I'm warning you,' snapped Jenny. 'Shut it or there'll be another murder around here!'

The uncomfortable silence that followed told her that she could have phrased that a little better, but she was past caring.

'So what do we do now?' asked Chris. 'Take a fackin' vote on who we think done it? Get out the "Cluedo" board? I think it was Des McGuire, in the cellar, with 40,000 watts of electricity.'

Nobody laughed.

'I guess there's not much else we can do,' said Lezard at last. 'Just take sensible precautions. I suggest that we devise a rota, so that three of us stay awake through the night and keep watch. Tomorrow night another three can perform the duty. Anybody got any problem with that?'

There was a general shaking of heads.

'Me and Em will stay up tonight,' offered Chris. 'Ain't much chance of getting any kip with all this going on, anyway.'

'Thanks. Any other volunteers?'

McGuire raised his hand.

'Oh great,' muttered Jenny. 'All the resident junkies. Now we can sleep safe in our beds.'

Lezard ignored the remark.

'As for the rest of us, we'll just have to lock our doors and windows, and pray that the weather improves.' He sighed. 'Tomorrow, if the wind drops, one of us may have to try walking out of here.'

Reed shook his head.

'Big mistake,' he said. 'Even without the wind, it would be fifteen degrees below zero out there, with deep snow drifts. You probably wouldn't get more than half a mile before you dropped.'

Lezard looked at him.

'Even so, I might have to try,' he said. He looked around at the others. Nobody said anything much after that. They just sat around, staring into the fire and nursing their own private thoughts and suspicions, while they listened to the sound of the wind roaring fitfully past the windows.

The door opens and a nurse comes into the room, a heavy-set black woman with a warm smile. She is pushing a stainless steel drugs trolley before her.

Detective Sergeant Gill feels an irrational urge to tell her to get out. She has broken his train of thought. He glances at his watch and realises now that it is getting late, he hasn't even noticed the passing of time. He has immersed himself in Jenny's story, and is now hooked on it. He's been sitting here for hours, no longer making notes, just listening to her slow, meticulous voice relating the facts of this incredible tale and though he is eager to know how it ends, yet he is reluctant to urge her to cut to the conclusion. A story like this one must be told in its own time. It cannot be hurried.

'Time for your medication,' says the nurse. 'Something to help you sleep.'

Gill feels a jolt of disappointment go through him. If she sleeps now he will have to wait till tomorrow to know the ending.

'Is that strictly necessary?' he asks. 'This lady is giving me some valuable information.'

The nurse regards him for a moment and makes a sucking noise at the corner of her mouth.

'You still here?' she asks. It's a patently obvious question and he doesn't bother answering it. He watches as the nurse checks the information on Jenny's wristband, then pops open an orange blister pack containing a small white pill.

'I'll take it later,' Jenny tells her, but the nurse shakes her head.

'I'm supposed to wait,' she says. She drops the pill into a plastic cup and hands this to Jenny, together with a beaker of water. Jenny sighs. She opens her mouth and tosses the pill inside, then washes it down with a slurp of water.

'Good girl,' says the nurse approvingly. Gill gives a grunt of irritation and the nurse shoots him a sideways look of disapproval. 'I think maybe you should be running along now,' she tells him.

'Can't I just stay until she's asleep?' asks Gill hopefully.

The nurse sighs.

'I suppose so.' She turns and pushes the trolley back towards the door, then pauses and adds, 'Then you're gone.' She opens the door and goes out into the corridor beyond. The door swings silently shut.

'That's a pity,' says Gill. 'I guess we'll have to finish this another time.

'I doubt it.' Jenny opens her hand to reveal the pill still nestled in her palm. 'Oldest trick in the book,' she tells him. 'A friend taught me that.' She glances sideways and grins at nothing. 'You remember the time you pretended to swallow Chris's entire stash that way? He thought you were dead for sure!' She laughs at the memory, tilting back her head and closing her eyes.

Gill frowns. He wishes she'd quit with the spook routine.

'So,' he says, lifting the notebook. 'There you all were. You knew one of them was the killer...'

'I *believed* one of them was,' Jenny corrects him. 'And then ... then the next bad thing happened and...' Her fingers move unconsciously across the guitar strings, picking out a delicate melody and her eyes lose their focus as she stares off into the middle distance, remembering what she has seen, what she has survived...

PART THREE

The man that hath no music in himself
Nor is not moved by concord of sweet sounds,
Is fit for treasons, stratagems and spoils:
The motions of his spirit are dull as night,
and his affections dark as Erebus:
Let no such man be trusted.

William Shakespeare
The Merchant Of Venice

Chapter Twenty-Nine

That night, Jenny *did* lock her bedroom door. She'd have felt too vulnerable undressed and lying between the sheets, so she kept all her clothes on and covered herself with a blanket she found folded up on the top shelf of the wardrobe. Sleep was about the last thing on her mind, so she reached under her pillow and fished out the old book that Cassie had given her.

She traced a fingertip around the curves of the ornately scripted title and then opened the book. She noticed that a slip of paper had been inserted in it to mark the start of Chapter Four, so it was here that she began to read.

> Of all the various happenings that occurred in the house, one infamous episode will always stand above all others for notoriety: I refer of course to the terrible incidents that took place over the days leading up to 27 January 1896...

Jenny felt a jolt of fear go through her. It had just occurred to her that today's date was 26 January 1996. Tomorrow would be the 100th anniversary of these 'terrible incidents'. With everything that was going on, it was impossible to write this off as just another coincidence. She read on with mounting apprehension.

But first it is necessary to investigate what little we know of the main protagonist in this lurid melodrama. His name was Obediah Wadleigh and of his origins, we have only the sketchiest details. The earliest record that we have of him is a report in the (now defunct) Hereford *Argus* of 2 February 1890. The piece detailed the outrage of local society when it was discovered that Wadleigh, newly arrived in the city (and nobody seems to know where he had dwelled previously) had purchased a house in the town centre and had set up home with several female 'followers', self-avowed disciples of a cult rather grandly named 'The Order of the Snake'.

The origins of this cult – one hesitates to use the word 'religion' – are rather obscure. It appears to be Druidic in flavour (Druidic revivals were popular during this period) but with elements of Aztec symbolism thrown in for good measure. In an interview granted to a little-known publication called *Awakenings*, two years later, Wadleigh spoke of a trip he once made to Mexico, where he had visited the ruined temples at Tenochtitlan and where he had first been granted a 'vision' of the 'great serpent'. Given his predilection for using mind-altering drugs, it seems likely that he may have indulged in a local hallucinogen called peyote: and that the so-called vision would almost certainly have been inspired by carvings and paintings of the ancient Aztec deity, Quetzalcoatl, the feathered serpent. In his vision, Wadleigh had seen the serpent come coiling out of the blackness of space. As he watched it swelled to a gigantic size and literally swallowed the world whole. In due course, he came to believe that this was an event that would quite literally come to pass on the 'day of Armageddon'. He also hinted in the interview that such a day would not be long in coming.

Later, he incorporated a long held belief in the existence of The Cosmic Joker – a cruel and twisted god that delighted in playing pranks on mankind. One can only wonder at the arbitary way in which this 'religion' developed: but in this author's opinion, Wadleigh was a seriously deranged human being, and madmen make their own rules. However fanciful his beliefs, he was unquestionably a man of great personal charisma, and perhaps this accounts for the fact that he managed to attract so many disciples, most of them respectable (and often wealthy) individuals.

At any rate, having outstayed his welcome in Hereford, Wadleigh announced his intention of purchasing The Grange in the spring of 1892, and shortly afterwards did exactly that, paying the then prodigious sum of £50,000 for it. The fact that he was able to pay cash for the property will give some indication of the wealth he had managed to accrue, most of it gifts from his wealthier followers.

The Grange must have suited his purposes well. It was spacious, remote and included in its grounds a megalithic stone circle, long abandoned and overgrown, which Wadleigh immediately set about restoring to pristine condition. It is interesting to note that he only allowed twelve chosen acolytes to live with him at The Grange, despite the fact that 'The Order of the Snake' had, by this time, over forty members. Other followers were allowed to visit and to bring 'offerings' of food and money, but never to pass so much as one night under the roof. After the move Wadleigh referred to his little gathering as 'The Thirteen'. (Another interesting fact is that the megalithic circle in the grounds of The Grange is composed of thirteen stones – a coincidence? Or was this what made him decide to thus limit the numbers?) In retrospect, it is easy to see what Wadleigh was doing. He had received another of his visions, this one telling him of the date when Armageddon was due. Though his followers could not have guessed it, he was preparing them for the event . . .

Jenny started at the unexpected sound of knuckles rapping gently at her bedroom door. She lay there, skin crawling, holding her breath while she listened intently.

Perhaps she had imagined it, she told herself. Perhaps it was just the sound of the old timbers creaking . . .

Then the knock came again, a little louder than before. Jenny remembered to breathe.

'Who is it?' she called out.

'It's Gareth. Can I come in?'

Jenny swallowed hard.

'Uh . . . no, not right now. I'm . . . trying to sleep.'

The door handle turned and there was a creak as he put his weight against it.

'Come on, Jenny, unlock the door. We need to talk.'

His voice sounded slurred, she thought, as though he'd been drinking.

'I'm sorry,' she told him. 'It'll have to wait till tomorrow.'

'Oh, don't be daft! I'm not going to harm you, am I? There's something I want to discuss with you, that's all. I . . . I've got a bottle of something good with me. Thought we might have a nightcap. It'll help you to sleep . . .'

'Listen, Gareth, I'm sorry but I'm not letting you in. Go and knock on Cassie's door, I'm sure she'll be glad to oblige.'

There was a sigh and then a drunken snigger.

'Cassie told me she'd spoken to you about our . . . arrangement. But I don't want you getting the wrong idea about us.

We're not cranks, you know. Look, just let me in a moment and I'll explain everything...'

'You can knock all night,' Jenny assured him. 'But you don't get in.'

Another laugh.

'For your information, Jenny dearest, I can come in there any old time I like. I have master keys to all the rooms.'

Jenny thought about this for a moment but refused to be brow-beaten.

'You just try it, sunshine,' she growled. 'You'll be walking with a limp for a month.'

She heard him mutter something beneath his breath. Then his footsteps moved away along the landing towards the staircase. Jenny waited a few minutes to assure herself that he was gone. Then she went back to her reading.

Over the week leading up to 27 January a terrible storm ravaged the area. The temperature dropped to below freezing and thick snow blanketed the landscape. It was not until the 29th, when the storm had abated, that one Agnes Farrow, a follower of the cult, who lived on a farm some five miles from the house, resolved to make the long and arduous journey across the fields to The Grange to ensure that 'The Thirteen' were safe and well. Receiving no answer to her knock at the front door, she made her way around to the back courtyard and found the kitchen unlocked. She entered the house, where a scene of absolute carnage greeted her. Wadleigh and his twelve followers were found lying dead in various places around the great house.

Overcome with horror, Mrs Farrow fled the scene and summoned the police. Shortly thereafter, an Inspector Reece, together with several officers from the Brecon

Constabulary, attended the scene. The details of the killings were considered too distressing to be made public knowledge at the time and thus were not reported in detail, but luckily, many years after the event, Inspector Reece wrote his memoirs which were published by A. A. Gillis, a small press based in Hereford who very kindly loaned me a copy from their archives.

Dealing with the events of 27 January, Inspector Reece expresses his revulsion and confusion at what was clearly the most baffling case of his career. He had first assumed that he was attending the scene of a mass suicide, but closer investigation led him to the conclusion that only one of the deaths – that of Wadleigh himself – was self administered. The other bodies all bore the hallmarks of bloody and brutal murder. Reece concluded that Wadleigh had, over a period of several days, murdered all his followers. Unable to leave the house, due to the ferocity of the storm, they had succumbed, one by one, to death and dismemberment.

One element that Reece found particularly baffling was the presence by each body of a small note inscribed with a jocular (but horribly apt) couplet of poetry . . .

Jenny couldn't suppress a gasp of surprise when she read this, and she remembered what Cassie had said about 'history repeating itself'. Almost breathless with amazement, she read on.

Inspector Reece was soon able to identify the source of the poetry. The couplets came from the collected works of Lady Helen Forster, one of 'The Thirteen' and an accomplished and widely published poet. Wadleigh had made no secret of the fact that he regarded Lady Helen as his most valued convert, and yet he had slain her as readily as the others and in a manner so barbaric that it beggars belief. (Though even in his memoirs, Reece declined to give a detailed account of the killing, he infers that various parts of the unfortunate Lady Helen's body were discovered in different locations all over the house, and the discovery of a blood-stained axe in the crypt suggests that this had been the instrument of her slaughter.)

Reece concludes his account of The Grange's most infamous hour by noting that all the bodies were removed and due to their strange religious beliefs were buried in unconsecrated ground, adjacent to the chapel graveyard in Brecon. The Grange lay empty for several years before it was occupied once again but as we shall see in later chapters, all subsequent attempts to occupy the premises seemed doomed to failure. It was as though the terrible events of 1896 had cast a dark pall over the future of the house – and all who were reckless enough to enter it.

Jenny set down the book and lay there staring up at the ceiling. She understood now, what Cassie had been telling her. The events of a hundred years ago – *exactly* one hundred years ago – seemed to eerily foreshadow what was happening now. 'The Thirteen' had all perished in the midst of a storm.

It suddenly occurred to her to do a head count of all who were present in the house, including the dead bodies of Robbie and Adrian. She made it eleven people in all. Then she remembered Mike Watton who had also been expected here. That made it twelve. And then she thought, if she included Scott Griffin, as the presence that was undeniably haunting the place, that made it thirteen. If every person in the house died by tomorrow, that would be thirteen deaths and history would indeed have repeated itself.

She was taken by a sensation of terror so real, so palpable, that for a moment she was unable to move a muscle. She lay there, rigid with fright, aware of the prickling of her skin as beads of sweat broke out all over her body.

A terrifying thought sprang into her mind.

We're all going to die!

She didn't know what to do. She thought maybe she'd like to run through the house, screaming at the top of her lungs ... or maybe she should run out into the blizzard to die a quick, clean death from hypothermia. But she did none of these things. She just lay on the bed as the hours slipped slowly by until eventually, against all the odds, she found refuge in sleep.

And when she opened her eyes again, Scott was sitting on the end of her bed. She supposed she should have been frightened, but after what had happened lately, it was simply good to see his face, pale and expressionless though it was. His thin fingers picked out a fragmented melody on an acoustic guitar and his blank eyes stared at Jenny and through her.

'What should I do?' she asked him.

'Do nothing,' he told her, and his voice was little more than a whisper, rising and falling with the restless rush of the wind.

'But I don't want to die.'

'Nobody wants to die,' he told her. 'But it's not so bad when you get here.'

'Who did it?' Jenny asked him fearfully. 'Who killed you?'

'The Cosmic Joker.' Scott attempted a grin, but his teeth seemed too large in his mouth and all he achieved was a horrible grimace.

Jenny shook her head.

'Can't you help me?' she asked him.

He seemed to consider for a moment.

'I'll try,' he said at last. He stopped playing and set the guitar down on the floor. He stood up and moved closer to her. 'I'm still cold,' he told her. 'Will you keep me warm?' A tingle of panic buzzed at the back of her mind, but it seemed to her that it wasn't like last time. There was no threat in his manner, he just seemed sad and so very alone.

'Of course,' she said. She reached out and took his hand. It was like holding a snowball. 'Come here to me,' she murmured and pulled him closer. He lay down beside her and wrapped his arms around her, buried his face against her shoulder. The chill of his body enveloped her but she thought to herself that if she just lay still and held him close, she could warm him. She lifted a hand to stroke his hair and that too felt cold.

'Sing to me,' he whispered.

So she sang the song she'd written for him, slowing it right down and doing it as a soulful ballad and it seemed to work just fine like that. When she'd finished singing, it occurred to her to ask him another question.

'Scott? Who *is* The Cosmic Joker?'

But he was asleep, his chest rising and falling in a slow, steady rhythm: and she thought that the coldness was receding now, that gradually the warmth of her body was seeping into him.

She closed her eyes and she slept, too.

[illegible]

[illegible]

[illegible]

[illegible]

[illegible]

[illegible]

Chapter Thirty

She woke alone and lay still for several minutes, letting her senses come gradually back to her, vaguely aware that something was different. After a little while, she was able to identify what it was. The sound of the wind had died away during the night.

She sat up in bed and glanced at her watch. A little after seven a.m. She yawned, stretched, reached out her hand for her cigarettes, then remembered that she had smoked her last one just before falling asleep. The thought of being without cigarettes filled her with a vague sense of panic, but she supposed that she'd be able to scrounge a smoke off Chris or Steve.

She swung her legs over the side of the bed and the heel of one foot connected with something that was lying on the floor, something that made a soft, gonging sound. She stared down in disbelief. An acoustic guitar lay beside the bed, exactly where Scott had placed it in her dream. Or at least, what she supposed had been a dream. She was no longer sure where the reality ended and the world of dreams began.

Sidestepping the guitar, she walked to the window and pulled aside the curtains. Sure enough, the wind had died away and the snow had stopped falling, but the courtyard was still covered with a thick mantle of snow and she guessed that it was still very cold out there.

She turned back and looked at the open book, lying on the bed where it had fallen. The revelations of the previous night came rushing back at her and she decided to sound out Lezard with her new evidence. She went to the bathroom, washed her face and brushed her teeth, then, scooping up the book, she unlocked her door and stepped cautiously out on to the landing. She stood for a moment, listening for the usual sounds of morning, but the house seemed still and silent. Perhaps nobody else was up yet. She shrugged and walked along to the next door in line. She rapped loudly on the ancient wood.

'Josh?' she shouted. 'You up yet?'

There was no answer. She tried the door handle, expecting to find it locked, but it opened easily and swung back on well-oiled hinges. Lezard was still in bed, a humped outline beneath the red patterned duvet.

'Come on,' she told him, advancing into the room. 'It's time you were up. And what's the idea of keeping your door unlocked?'

She hesitated, looking down at the bed and then she smiled, realising now that Lezard couldn't be under the covers, because the shape didn't conform to the outline of a human figure at all. No, it was just that he hadn't bothered to make the bed, he'd simply left his covers in a heap and had gone down to breakfast.

She was about to turn away when it occurred to her that the duvet didn't match the rest of the room at all. The crimson on white, Jackson Pollock splash design seemed all out of kilter with the soft, plain tones of the other furnishings. She turned back slowly and stepped closer to the bed, noticing for the first time the scrap of paper pinned to the wooden headboard.

'Oh no,' she whispered.

The lyrics were from a more recent song entitled *Man Eating Woman.*

> SHE SEEMED LIKE SUCH A PUSSY CAT
> HE WANTED HER TO STAY.
> SHE RIPPED THE GUTS RIGHT OUT OF HIM
> AND THREW THE REST AWAY.

She felt the sickness rising in her throat but just the same, she felt compelled to reach out and take a firm grip on the duvet, dimly registering how the pop art pattern felt sticky against her fingers. She snatched in a deep breath and pulled the covers back...

Red. Her horrified gaze registered that colour first. Then purple and pale green and orange. Then the colours seemed to rearrange themselves into shapes, hideous glistening loops and whirls and bulges. She realised she was looking at the insides of a man. Somebody had expertly removed them from their more usual resting place and had strewn them in the bed, liberally splattering thc duvet and undersheet with gore.

Jenny took what she thought was a step backwards but it must have been more than that, because her back slammed against the wall behind her with a force that drove the air out of her body, silencing the scream that was rising within her. She slid down the wall on to her haunches, gasping for breath, her eyes blurring with tears, her shoulders hunching convulsively. Finally, she found her voice and throwing back her head, she howled her fear and rage at the ceiling, at a volume that soon brought people running.

Steve was first into the room. He ran in, saw what was in the bed and span away with an oath. He clapped a hand over his mouth and came around the room with his back pressed to the wall, like a man traversing a narrow ledge.

'Jesus,' Jenny heard him whisper. Then he was kneeling beside her, his arms around her but she couldn't fall into his embrace because she kept thinking *Steve could have done this*: and now other people were pressing into the room. She saw Chris register the bed then turn away with a groan, a spray of vomit gushing from his mouth on to the carpet. And she saw Gareth Reed standing there, his face registering only a mild revulsion, handling it so much better than the others. Then he glanced sideways at Idris as if sharing some secret knowledge with him: and Jenny thought about what he'd said the other night, about how he had a master key for every room.

Now he came around the bed and crouched down in front of her, an expression of concern on his face.

'Jenny, are you all right?' he asked her.

And that was when she went crazy. She lunged at him, her claws extended to tear at his face, and her head seemed to fill with a red, roaring heat and she wanted to kill him, because Lezard was gone and with him, it seemed, her last hope of getting out of here alive.

'You bastard!' she screamed. 'He was going to look after me! He promised.'

Her claws raked against flesh and she heard a bellow of pain. Then hands were grabbing her, restraining her, holding her down as she kicked and struggled and cursed. A fist thumped into the side of her head and she fell back, her shoulders thudding against carpet. She lay there staring up at the clean white of the ceiling. A pool of blackness seemed to open up inside her skull, spreading like a stain until it covered her eyes with a dark impenetrable veil and she slipped into a place where, for the moment at least, the Hoochie Coochie Man could not reach her...

Chapter Thirty-One

She came slowly back to her senses, clawing her way up through layers of red noise. When she finally surfaced, she found that she was lying on one of the sofas in the lounge. It was only when she tried to move that she realised her hands and feet were tied with lengths of rope. She lay for a moment in outraged disbelief. Then she struggled to get herself around into a sitting position.

She was not alone in the room. Chris and Emma were slumped into their habitual places on the sofa opposite and Steve occupied one of the armchairs. They were all regarding her sheepishly as though embarrassed by her current predicament.

'Would somebody mind telling me what the fuck is going on here,' she growled.

'It's for your own good,' Steve told her evasively. 'You went crazy, back there. I thought you were going to kill Gareth.'

She stared at him.

'Of course I went crazy,' she protested. 'I'd just found what was left of Josh. Now untie these fucking ropes.'

Steve shook his head.

'We can't do that, I'm afraid.'

'You can't—' Jenny broke off in exasperation. 'Look,

what's going on? OK, so I freaked for a moment, but I'm all right now.'

'Gareth's orders,' said Chris awkwardly. He was hunched in his seat, a cigarette jutting from his lips. He looked very scared, Jenny thought, and she knew that in any bad situation, Chris had a tendency to avoid any kind of responsibility.

'Look, for Christ's sake, this is stupid,' she protested. 'I mean, what do you suppose I'm going to do?'

'We've already seen plenty of evidence of what you can do,' said Emma tartly. 'So I think we'll all feel a lot happier if you stay as you are.'

It was like a punch in the stomach. It actually made Jenny gasp for breath.

'You . . . you think I did that to Josh? Are you mad?'

'*I'm* perfectly sane, thanks,' said Emma. 'But then I'm not the one going around offing people and leaving samples of my lyrics all over the shop, am I?'

Jenny laughed at that. She had to, it just seemed so ridiculous. She looked at Chris.

'You believe this?' she asked him.

He took a deep drag on his cigarette and kept his eyes fixed on his snakeskin shoes.

'I dunno,' he said. 'All I know is I'm fackin' scared shitless and I want to get out of here alive. Gareth says he reckons you killed the others, so—'

'Gareth says? Jesus, I bet he does! Gareth who was roaming around last night, trying to get into my room? Gareth who told me he had master keys to every room in the place?'

Steve and Chris exchanged doubtful glances at this information.

'It's true!' Jenny told them. 'But there's plenty of things he hasn't told you, I'll bet. I don't suppose he's mentioned anything about the wacky religion he's involved with, has he?'

'What religion?' muttered Steve.

'A little thing called The Order of the Snake. A religion founded by that dodgy-looking geezer over the fireplace.' She nodded her head at the scowling portrait of Obediah Wadleigh. 'And I don't suppose he mentioned the fact that exactly one hundred years ago, that guy murdered twelve people in this house in order to keep the world from being devoured by a giant snake . . .'

She saw the incredulous looks on their faces and realised that she'd blown it. Who could be expected to believe such an outrageous story, even though it was true.

'Flip city,' muttered Emma. 'It's a wonder they ever let you out of that nut-house.'

Jenny ignored the taunt. If she lost her temper now it would simply make her look unstable.

'The book,' she told them. 'It's all in the book that Cassie lent me. She and Idris are part of it, too. I . . . I had it with me when I went into Lezard's room, I guess I must have dropped it. If one of you would like to go and get it . . . ?'

'You *are* joking, I trust!' said Chris. 'I wouldn't go back in there if you paid me.'

'Then untie me and let me go and get it. I'll prove to you that I'm not making this up.'

'Do we look stupid or something?' asked Emma, scornfully. 'You just stay right where you are, sister, and keep it buttoned.'

Everybody glanced up as the others came into the room. Cassie entered first, keeping her gaze straight ahead, unable, Jenny thought, to look her in the eyes: then Des McGuire, who couldn't resist directing a gloating grin at her. Last came Reed and Idris deep in conversation. Jenny saw to her dismay that Reed had several nasty-looking scratches on his face, which she could only assume she'd inflicted. More worryingly, both he and Idris were carrying shotguns.

'Who the fuck let them have guns?' protested Jenny.

Reed broke off his conversation and gave her a cold glare.

'Oh, so you're a bit more rational now, are you?' he sneered.

'Yes, even if everybody else seems to have taken leave of their senses.' She held her tied arms out in front of her. 'You really believe this is necessary?'

Reed lifted a hand to trace his fingertips over the scars on his cheek.

'After your little episode upstairs, I'd say it's in everybody's interest,' he told her.

'Oh, and I suppose it's also in their interest for you and Idris to walk around with dangerous weapons, is it?'

'Absolutely. It's clear from what's happening that we can't just sit here and let things happen. We have to fight back.'

Jenny sneered.

'Oh, well I'm sure we'll all feel a lot safer for that,' she said. 'Actually, you came in at an interesting point. I was just telling the others here about your old pal, Obediah. How he murdered twelve people in this house, one hundred years ago.'

'Is there any truth in it, Gareth?' asked Steve.

Reed looked at him and smiled.

'Absolutely not,' he said. 'I've never heard such nonsense in my life.'

Jenny stared at him in disbelief.

'You ... you lying bastard! You *know* it's true. You told me about it the first day I was here. It ... it was in the book Cassie lent me.' She turned her attention to Cassie. 'Tell them,' she pleaded. 'Please Cassie, tell them it's true.'

Cassie shrugged and gave a puzzled smile.

'I haven't the faintest idea what you're on about,' she said.

'The book, Cassie! The one you bought to my room. The history of this place ... for God's sake, just tell them!'

'Book?' Cassie shook her head. 'I'm sorry, Jenny. What book?'

Jenny groaned and sank back on to the sofa. She didn't know why they were lying, but they'd effectively painted her as a raving maniac and the others were not going to trust a single word she said from now on. She lapsed into a miserable silence.

'OK, listen up, folks,' said Reed, suddenly all brusque and businesslike. 'Idris and I have been out to check the other vehicles. They've all been sabotaged, every last one of them.' He glanced at Jenny. 'I don't suppose you'd care to tell us where you've hidden the spark plugs?' he ventured. She ignored him, so he continued. 'Now, Idris and I have been talking and he reckons he's got a fair chance of getting out of here on foot and fetching some help.'

'I don't know about that,' said McGuire. 'It's a long trip. I only just made it here from the hill where I broke down. It must be another six miles on from there to the nearest village.'

Idris shook his head.

'If I went that way,' he agreed. 'My plan is to cut through the woods and head out to Cadfan Morris's garage. Hopefully, the snow won't be as deep under the trees and the way I'd go, it cuts the distance to about three miles. If Cadfan's phone is down, he's got an old CB radio we can use to scare up some help. I figure if I move fast and put on plenty of layers, I'll have maybe an hour to do it. If I take any longer, I'm deep frozen pizza. But it's got to be better than sitting around here waiting to die.'

McGuire frowned, then nodded.

'Well, amen to that,' he said. 'I'll come with you.'

'No way. You'll only slow me down.'

'Don't worry about me, I can take care of myself.' He gave

Idris a sly look. 'Besides, if we let you go on your own, we'll only have your word for it that you're really going for help.'

'Where else would I be going?' growled Idris.

'Who knows?' McGuire spread his hands in an expressive gesture. 'Off to a quiet part of the house to plan another murder?'

Idris laughed derisively.

'You're crazy,' he said. 'Far as I'm concerned, we've got the killer tied up, right there.' He jerked a thumb in Jenny's direction.

'You're dead wrong,' Jenny told him. 'I should think carefully if I were you, Idris. Des could be pulling a double bluff. Maybe he's the killer and he wants to get you out there on your own.'

Idris thought about it for a moment, then smiled mirthlessly. He hefted the shotgun.

'If he tries anything on me, he'll be more than sorry.' He gave McGuire a meaningful look, then shrugged. 'OK, what the hell, we'll both go. But I warn you, if you fall behind, that's your problem. We'd better dig out some protective clothing for the two of us. I've some spare stuff that should fit you.' He glanced around at the others. 'The rest of you will just have to sit tight until help arrives.'

Jenny laughed bitterly.

'Some of us don't have any choice,' she observed.

Idris turned back to Reed.

'On no account let her persuade you to untie her,' he said.

'No sweat,' Reed assured him.

Idris nodded. He turned to look at his wife.

'Cassie, we'll need some things putting into a rucksack. A flask of hot coffee and some brandy would be useful. Des, we'll go and get our stuff together.' The two men left the room and Cassie went to the kitchen to prepare their supplies.

'I'm sure the two of them will be very happy together,' said Jenny brightly.

'Nobody asked you,' muttered Reed. He moved past her and dropped into a vacant chair. 'The rest of us will stay together,' he said. 'It was a big mistake going up to our rooms last night. My suggestion is that we stay right here till help arrives.'

'That's the idea, Gareth,' murmured Jenny. 'Don't let any of them out of your sight.' She nodded at the gun. 'Or should I say, "out of your *sights*"?' She glanced at Steve. 'You really think it's a wise move allowing him to sit there with a gun in his hands?'

Steve eyed her nervously. 'Why not?' he asked her. 'I ... suppose I trust him.'

'I wouldn't if I were you. He's just lied to you.'

'Why don't you shut up?' Reed warned her. 'Nobody's going to believe anything you say.'

'Can you wonder after the hatchet job you and Cassie just did on me? Why lie about it, Gareth? Was it because you realised how dodgy the truth would make you look? Like some kind of religious maniac?'

Reed glared at her.

'I told you to shut up,' he said.

'I know you did. But what are you going to do, Gareth, shoot me in front of all these witnesses? Oh, but there's four of us here and you couldn't get all of us without reloading, could you?'

'You're raving,' he told her. 'I've got no intention of shooting anyone, unless they try to harm me.'

'Well, who's going to do that? If you're so sure that I'm the killer, why do you need the gun anyway?'

'That's a bloody good question,' said Chris. 'Actually, Gareth, I'd feel a lot happier if you'd put the gun down. It's making me nervous.'

'You've got every right to be nervous,' Jenny told him. 'Gareth, here, is the man who claims to have the master keys to all our rooms. When I went to Josh's room this morning, his door wasn't locked, despite his warnings to everyone to do exactly that last night. Now how do you suppose I'd have got into his room to perform that . . . that butchery on him?'

'Easy,' said Emma. 'You just knocked on the door and asked to come in. We all know Lezard had the hots for you, God knows *why*.'

Jenny scowled.

'Do me a favour, Gareth,' she said. 'When you start killing them, shoot her first, will you? I'd kind of like to watch.'

Reed smirked, but said nothing.

'You still haven't put the gun down,' Chris reminded him. 'And Jenny has a point, you know, if you're so sure it's *her* . . .'

Reed scowled.

'OK, maybe I'm not one hundred per cent certain,' he admitted. 'But you have to admit that most of the evidence points to her.'

'Is it true about you having master keys?' Steve asked him.

'Well, yes . . . of course. We have them in case of fire and so forth. But that doesn't mean that I've ever used them.'

Jenny flashed her eyes mockingly.

'Hey, well that's a relief, eh, gang?'

Reed looked at her irritably.

'Will you *please* shut up,' he said.

'Gareth,' said Chris meekly. 'You still haven't . . .'

'Yes, yes, *all right*!' Reed laid the shotgun down alongside the chair. 'Happy now?' he asked the room at large.

Nobody answered the question. They sat in nervous silence for several minutes. Chris and Emma stubbed out their cigarettes and lit up fresh ones, chainsmoking frantically. Jenny gazed at them enviously for a moment.

'Any chance of a fag?' she asked Chris. 'I'm gasping.'

'Sure.' Chris began to get to his feet, reaching into his pocket, but Reed waved him into his seat again.

'Leave it,' he said. 'Could be a trick.'

'Oh, for Christ's sake,' complained Jenny. 'What do you suppose I'm going to do. I'm *tied*.'

'Just the same, forget about it. Besides, I'm doing you a favour. Smoking's bad for you.'

'Fuck you!' she told him.

Idris and McGuire reappeared, dressed in several layers of hiking gear. They both sported gloves, scarves and balaclavas.

'Fack me,' said Chris. 'Looks like a remake of *Scott of the Antarctic*.' Nobody laughed, but it was a pretty unreceptive audience. Cassie came in with a small rucksack and handed it to Idris. He slung it over his shoulder and nodded to Reed.

'We'll get going,' he announced. Jenny noticed that he was still carrying the shotgun.

'Let me see if I can guess how this works,' she said. 'These two walk off out of earshot and Idris blasts Des with the shotgun. Then he reloads and comes back here. Once he's back inside, you have two shots each. Cassie already knows that she has to die so there's no problem with her. And I'm hogtied, so you can finish me off at your leisure. That leaves you four shots to finish off three people and at close range, you can hardly miss, can you?'

'For fack's sake,' protested Chris. 'Will you stop it, Jenny? You're scaring the shit out of me!'

'I hope so,' she told him. 'Because you've got every reason to be scared.'

'I've heard enough of this crap,' muttered Idris. He punched McGuire on the shoulder. 'Come on, let's go.'

'Yes, hurry along, Des,' Jenny mocked him. 'Like a good little lamb to the slaughter.'

She could only see McGuire's eyes framed in the circle of his balaclava, but as she watched, they narrowed suspiciously.

'Maybe I ought to take the other gun,' he suggested.

'No way,' said Reed.

'But why, when you've got her all tied up?' protested McGuire.

'That's a good question,' said Chris.

'I'm not staying here without protection,' Reed told him. 'Besides, it's *my* gun and I'm hanging on to it.' He sounded like a little boy playing cowboys and Indians, Jenny thought.

'Enough,' growled Idris. 'I'm going,' he told McGuire. 'You can come or stay, it doesn't make any difference to me.' He headed for the door and after a long silent moment of indecision, McGuire followed him. Cassie trailed them to the front door and everybody heard it open and close. After a few minutes, the two men were visible through one of the windows, flailing across the grounds towards the forest, their legs sinking knee deep into the snow at every step.

Cassie came back into the room and settled herself into a vacant chair. Jenny studied her in disgust.

'You know,' she said, 'I can accept Reed lying the way he did. I wouldn't have expected anything more from him. But after all that shit you gave me about The Order of the Snake . . . about how wonderful it all was . . . and then to turn round and deny all knowledge of it. You must have expected a cock to crow three times, mustn't you?'

Cassie studied her hands, which were folded in her lap.

'I don't know what you're on about,' she said, tonelessly.

'Oh, I understand what's happened, of course. The great god Gareth has issued instructions, no doubt. He wants to keep us here, all nice and quiet. It doesn't help if people realise that there's three religious nutters practically drooling all over the furniture . . .'

'We're *not* religious nutters!' snapped Cassie, irritably, and Reed directed a warning look at her.

'What's the matter, Gareth? Afraid she'll blow your cover?'

Reed laughed dismissively but the effect wasn't too convincing.

'You're pathetic,' he said.

'And you've changed your tune. When I first arrived here you were so far up my arse, you could see nothing but the soles of your shoes.'

'Yeah, well that was before I knew what you were capable of.' Reed traced his fingertips over the deep scratches on his left cheek. 'You need help, Jenny, and I'm going to make sure that you get it.'

'That's big of you. This "help" wouldn't entail being sacrificed to The Cosmic Joker, would it?'

'Will you lot please stop bickering!' shrieked Emma. Everybody turned to look at her. It was clear that the girl's habitual act of studied cool was coming apart at the seams. She looked terrified. She got up from the sofa and moved across to the fireplace, where Chris's pill box stood in its habitual spot on the mantelpiece.

'I'm losing it,' she told Chris. 'What have you got left?'

'Not much. A few barbs I bought off Des. Actually, that's not a bad idea. Might help calm us down a bit. Bring 'em over.' He fished a half-empty bottle of vodka out from behind the sofa. Emma brought the pill box to him and they took a tab each, swigging them down with a mouthful of vodka.

'Oh yeah, that's really bright, isn't it?' said Steve. 'We're sinking into the shit and you decide to get stoned. Very helpful.'

'It helps *me*, man,' Chris told him. 'I can't handle a situation like this straight.' He took another gulp from the bottle and wiped his mouth on his sleeve. 'Coke would be better,' he said, regretfully. 'I wonder if Des had any of it left?'

'Des probably has his own worries right now,' Jenny told him.

'Don't be ridiculous,' Reed told her. 'By now he and Idris will be into the trees and making their way through the forest. Once they alert the rescue services, it'll only be a matter of minutes before help gets here. Then you're going to have some explaining to do.'

'Yeah, that's right, Gareth. Keep spinning them the fairy stories. That way nobody is going to—'

She broke off at the distant sound of two muffled shots. Everybody jerked upright in their seats, including Reed and Cassie.

'What the fuck was that?' whispered Reed.

'Oh, very convincing,' said Jenny. 'I thought Idris would at least have waited until he was out of earshot.'

Reed stared at her.

'I don't know what you're talking about,' he said. He grabbed the shotgun and got up from his chair. 'Stay here,' he told the others. 'I'll go to the front door and have a look.' He strode out of the room, leaving Jenny sitting there with four terrified-looking individuals. Even Cassie seemed convincingly scared and Jenny began to wonder if she was in on this part of the plan.

'All right,' she said quietly, hunching forward on the sofa. 'There isn't much time. If you want to get out of here, one of you is going to have to untie me, right now.'

Steve licked his lips nervously. He looked as though he might be considering the idea.

'Don't listen to her,' Cassie warned him. 'She's making everything up. You've got nothing to fear from Gareth, I swear to you. He's as much in the dark as any of us.'

'Yes, but you heard those shots,' reasoned Steve. 'What was that all about?'

'I don't know,' Cassie told him. 'But I swear to you on my life, there's no plan like *she* mentioned.' Cassie flung a scornful look at Jenny. 'She's just trying to sow seeds of discord amongst you. You shouldn't listen to anything she says.'

There was a long silence and then, unexpectedly, Emma spoke, her face contorting into a mask of pain.

'Oh ... Jesus ... my stomach!'

Everyone looked at her in surprise. She was doubled over, her teeth clenched, her hands clawing at her stomach. Jenny noticed that she had gone pale and that she seemed to be sweating profusely.

'Em?' muttered Chris. 'What's the matter?'

'I don't know. I've just got this ... pain. It's like ... oh!' She doubled over again with a gasp.

'Emma?' Chris leaned over to her to put an arm around her. 'Don't worry, darlin', it's probably just nerves. We'll be all right, you'll see. Idris and Des will fetch help and—' Now he broke off, his eyes widening in an expression of surprise. 'Fackin' hell,' he grunted. 'I ... I got it too!' He put a hand to his stomach, then doubled over with a gasp of pain. His shades fell to the floor.

'Chris?' whispered Jenny. 'What is it?'

'Oh Jesus! Pain in me ... gut. Like a knife...' His expression creased into a mask of agony.

Suddenly, Jenny knew exactly what was wrong with him.

'Oh God, Chris, the *pills*!'

'What?' He stared at her stupidly for a moment. Emma gave a low moan and slid from the sofa on to her knees.

'Ah God, Jesus,' she hissed. 'Help me!'

Chris grabbed the pill box from his pocket with shaking

hands. He opened it and the other pills scattered on to the floor as his body gave a convulsive jerk. He stared into the box as though it held some incredible secret.

'There's ... something in here,' he croaked. He reached in and plucked out a folded sheet of paper pressed into the bottom of the box. He dropped the box and unfolded the paper. He too was sweating profusely now. He gave a hysterical little giggle.

'Lyrics,' he whispered. 'Jenny ... more lyrics ...' He made a low groan and fell to his knees beside Emma, dropping the slip of paper. Steve went down beside him and retrieved it. He read the lyrics aloud. Jenny remembered them well. The song was called *Victims* and it was written about a kid she'd known a couple of years back, a junkie like Chris, but without the drummer's iron constitution. The kid was long dead now.

WHY DO YOU DO IT? GO DOWN THAT LONELY ROAD
INTO YOUR DOMINION OF SENSORY OVERLOAD.
WHAT ABOUT YOUR FUTURE?
WHAT ABOUT YOUR PRIDE?
CORRUPTED BY THE POISON
THAT FESTERS DEEP INSIDE.

Chris's eyes widened as he registered the insinuation.

'Oh no,' he whimpered. 'No, Jenny, it can't be. You didn't ...'

And then Emma screamed, a long howling scream of pure agony. She flipped over on to her side and began to thrash and flail like a wounded animal ...

And Jenny was screaming with her, unable to move to help her because of her bonds. All she could do was yell instructions at the others.

'Steve, try to make her sick! Get your fingers down her

throat! Cassie, do the same with Chris. Quickly, don't just sit there looking at them!'

But Emma's whole body was shuddering now and a gout of dark blood burst from her mouth and nose as Steve moved clumsily towards her. He tried to cradle her in his arms but she flailed and clawed at him, like some wild animal and he shrank back as . . .

Reed burst back into the room, alerted by the noise. He had the shotgun held in front of him as though expecting some kind of an attack and he stood there, staring at a scene of complete madness.

Emma's body gave a last convulsive lurch. She curled into a foetal shape on the carpet and . . .

Chris flopped down on to his back and began to thrash his arms and legs in a wild frenzy of unspeakable pain. He was making low guttural grunts deep in his throat, his skinny chest pumping up and down, up and down, as he fought to control his failing breathing.

Cassie tried desperately to get her fingers down his throat, then wailed in agony as Chris's teeth clamped convulsively shut, biting through the flesh and . . .

A thick gob of blood burst from Chris's throat, spattering Cassie with drops of crimson.

She reeled back from him, sobbing helplessly.

A puddle of urine spread out beneath Chris, soaking into the carpet, and his hands gesticulated on the empty air, his horrified gaze locked into Jenny's staring eyes.

She knew he thought that she was responsible, that she had done this to him. Her eyes filled with hot tears as . . .

Chris's legs kicked a couple of times, feeble little kicks, and he gave a last, bloody cough. Then he stopped breathing and lay still. A silence fell, so deep, so impenetrable that it seemed to swallow everything in the big old house.

Jenny sat there, tied into position, staring down at the two dead bodies on the carpet.

It was a long, long time before anybody spoke after that.

Chapter Thirty-Two

Now there were four of them and they sat in numbed silence as the clock ticked away the hours inexorably. For what seemed a very long time, nobody said anything, they were all of them locked into their own private thoughts. They just sat in dumb misery and tried not to look at the two humped shapes on the floor, covered with a length of curtain material that Cassie had insisted on dragging down from one of the windows. She had been too scared to venture upstairs in search of blankets or sheets.

Jenny had never felt more frightened or more helpless in her entire life. She kept expecting Idris to reappear, brandishing his shotgun, but there'd been no sign of either of the two men since the sound of gunshots, several hours ago.

Reed sat in his armchair opposite her, the shotgun cradled in his arms again, and now nobody dared object to him holding it. He had a look of intense concentration on his face, as though he was trying to puzzle something out, and every so often he would get to his feet and go to the window, to scan the snow-covered landscape for signs of life.

Steve sat upright in his chair, his big hands gripping the arms as though nervous of falling out of it. He kept his gaze on the dwindling log fire. They had put on the last of the fuel some time ago and nobody was anxious to volunteer to go out to the wood store to replenish their supplies.

Cassie looked simply terrified. She sat in her chair with her legs drawn up under her, her arms around herself, as though she felt cold. Her pretty eyes seemed large and vulnerable in her pale face, which was still spattered with drops of Chris Spencer's blood.

Jenny felt like screaming at the top of her lungs. Here they all sat like idiots, afraid to leave the room for food or drink or even to use the toilet – and Chris and Emma's awful deaths served as a hideous reminder that even in here, none of them were safe. For Jenny, the most frightening aspect of the situation was that she still remained tied. If the killer came after her, she would be unable even to run away.

'Maybe Idris and Des got through,' said Steve, suddenly. The remark seemed to be addressed to nobody in particular and Jenny thought, under the circumstances, was hopelessly optimistic.

'You heard the shots,' she reminded him.

'Yes, but . . . that doesn't mean they're *dead*,' argued Cassie. 'Maybe they just . . . just . . .'

'Stopped for some target practice?' ventured Jenny scornfully. She glanced at Reed. 'Thing is, what's taking Idris so long? Shouldn't he have made it back here by now?'

Reed shook his head.

'Whatever you think, Idris and I had no hidden agenda. He told me he was going for help and I had every reason to believe him.' He thought for a moment. 'In retrospect, maybe it was a mistake to allow McGuire to go along with him.'

'What do you mean?' asked Cassie fearfully.

'Only that we know very little about him. But I've been thinking.' He paused for a moment and glanced around at the others, as if to ensure that he had their full attention. 'Just before he took the pills, Chris said that he'd bought them from McGuire. Maybe McGuire's the Hoochie Coochie Man.'

'That pill box was there all night,' Steve reminded him. 'Any one of us could have got to it. Besides, it was Idris who had the shotgun, not McGuire.'

'Maybe. But out there in all that snow, if McGuire jumped him ... well, anything could have happened.' He glanced warily at Cassie. 'I'm sorry, I'm not trying to frighten you,' he added. 'It's equally possible that McGuire tried something and Idris let him have both barrels.'

'But if that had happened, wouldn't he have come back here?' ventured Cassie.

'Not necessarily. If they'd already covered quite a distance, he might have chosen to press on for the garage. He might be nearly there by now...'

'Christ, what is this?' muttered Jenny. '*Listen with Mother*? We don't have the first idea about what might have happened out there, just as we can't be sure that Idris or McGuire is the killer. One thing I do know.' She held up her bound wrists for them to look at. 'If somebody comes after me like this, I won't have a snowball in hell's chance of getting away. Now, how about undoing the ropes? Or do you suppose I'm also an expert in the use of poisons?'

The others looked at her doubtfully for a moment. Then Steve sighed and got up from his chair. As he did so, Reed snapped the shotgun around to point it at him.

'What do you think you're doing?' he said.

'I'm going to untie her.'

'No way. You sit down and let her be.'

'But why? For God's sake, man, you surely still don't think—?'

'I don't know *what* to think. I'd just feel a lot happier having one less person to worry about.'

There was a long uncomfortable silence while the two men appraised each other.

'I don't see what the problem is,' said Steve, at last. 'After all, you're the only one with a gun. If Jenny tries anything, you've got the edge on her. And anyway, how *can* she be the killer? What about the shots we heard?'

'That could have been anything,' protested Reed. He was beginning to lose his authority and he knew it. 'Maybe . . . maybe the gun just went off by accident.'

Steve considered this for a moment, then shook his head.

'I don't think so,' he said.

He took another step towards Jenny and then froze in his tracks as Reed cocked the hammers of the shotgun.

'I'm warning you,' he said quietly.

Steve glared at him.

'Come on, man, you're not thinking straight!' He glanced sideways at Cassie. 'What do you say? You reckon Jenny is a threat to us?'

'I . . . I don't know. I guess not.' Cassie gestured helplessly.

'You think she should be given the same chance as you and me? A chance to run if somebody comes after her?'

Cassie frowned.

'Well . . . I suppose so.'

Steve took a deep breath and looked back at Reed.

'Tell you what I'm going to do,' he said. 'I'm going to reach in my pocket here and take out my Swiss army knife. Then I'm going to cut through Jenny's ropes. You got a problem with that, you're just going to have to take whatever action you think is appropriate. Way I look at it, you'd probably be doing me a favour. The insurance would pay off the mortgage and Peg and the kids would never have to worry about money again.'

He slid a hand into his pocket and eased out the knife, doing it slowly to avoid throwing Reed into a panic. Then he moved across to Jenny. Reed tracked him with the shotgun but made no attempt to fire. Steve went down on his knees and used his finger and thumb to open the blade. Jenny stared over his shoulder and flinched as she found herself looking down the twin barrels of the shotgun. If Reed was the killer, he'd never get a better shot than this, two of them for the price of one...

Steve reached out to take hold of the ropes.

'I'm warning you,' said Reed. 'Don't do it.'

But Steve ignored him and began to saw methodically at Jenny's bonds. After a few moments, he had sliced through them. He gave Jenny a sly wink, then bent down to release her ankles.

'Thanks,' she said. She felt like crying with relief as blood rushed back into her wrists and ankles, making the flesh tingle.

'That's OK,' he told her. 'Anything else you need?'

'A cigarette would be nice.'

'You got it.' Steve reached slowly into his pocket and brought out a packet of Bensons and a lighter. He handed them to Jenny, then got slowly back to his feet, folding the knife as he did so. Never taking his eyes off Reed, he returned to his seat.

Reed was scowling with displeasure but he said nothing. He swung the gun back around and laid it across his lap. Then he threw a warning look at Jenny.

'Just stay quiet,' he advised her. 'If there's any repetition of what happened upstairs, I won't hesitate to shoot you.'

She nodded, swallowed hard. She lit a cigarette and inhaled thankfully. She didn't know what to think now. If Reed really was the Hoochie Coochie Man, she told herself, then surely he would have blasted the rest of them by now. Or was it simply that he was working to some pre-ordained ritual in order to satisfy The Cosmic Joker? Was he staying his hand merely because he had something more appropriate lined up for them?

That really didn't bear thinking about. She massaged her wrists and ankles until the pins and needles were gone and tried desperately to formulate some kind of plan of action.

'What happens now?' Steve asked the room at large.

'We wait,' Reed told him. 'If we're lucky, Idris will have made it through to the garage and help will be on its way.'

'And if he hasn't?' Jenny asked him. 'I don't know if it's such a good idea waiting around for something to happen. Maybe we should be thinking about getting out of here while there's still a few hours of daylight left.'

'Out there?' Reed shook his head. 'We wouldn't have a hope in hell. Idris had a chance because he knows the woods like the back of his hand. We'd wander around in circles until we dropped dead of hypothermia and believe me, it wouldn't take long.'

Cassie was on the verge of tears now. She could hardly control her voice as she spoke.

'But we ... can't spend another night ... in this place,' she pleaded. 'We just can't!'

'Cool it,' Reed urged her. 'Maybe Idris got through, huh? Maybe help's on the way.'

'Yeah, and maybe John Wayne and the Seventh Cavalry are doing manoeuvres just over the next ridge,' said Jenny scornfully. 'Listen, we need to come up with a plan of action. We can't just sit here hoping for salvation. Besides, there are certain practical considerations ...'

'Oh,' said Reed. 'Such as?'

'Well, I'm sure I'm not the only one who's busting for a pee.'

Reed shrugged, glanced around the room, then indicated the empty log scuttle standing on the hearth.

'Use that,' he said unhelpfully.

'That's easy for you to say. A man can do that standing up and still walk away with a little dignity. But . . .'

'But nothing! Look, we've already discovered the folly of doing things separately, when we went up to our rooms last night. Clearly, we have to stick together now, whatever happens. You want to take the scuttle and rig up some kind of screen to preserve your modesty, that's fine – but there's no way I'm going to allow you to wander off upstairs to the loo. That wouldn't be in your interest or mine.'

'Oh, you're all heart, aren't you,' observed Jenny. 'Tell me something, what puts you in charge of everyone's welfare?'

Reed waved the shotgun.

'This does,' he said. 'Look, wise up, Jenny. The name of the game now is survival. This killer works by separating us, getting us when we're on our own. There's safety in numbers.'

'That didn't help Chris and Emma much,' said Steve grimly. 'But if that's the company policy . . .' He got to his feet again and Reed snapped the gun around into the firing position.

'Relax,' Steve told him. 'I'm just organising the toilet facilities.' He picked up the log scuttle and carried it up to the other end of the room. Then he lifted a couple of large oil paintings down from the wall and stood them around it in an 'L' shape. 'Rudimentary but serviceable,' he announced. 'And just to get the ball rolling . . .' He went behind the paintings and a moment later, they heard the sound of him urinating into the scuttle.

'All the comforts of home,' muttered Jenny.

'That's not all,' said Reed. 'Check in the top drawer of the unit there and you'll find some board games. Might help us to while away the time.'

Jenny got up and went to the unit. She pulled open the

drawer and looked into it. The first box that caught her eye seemed horribly apt.

'Anybody for Snakes and Ladders?' she asked. Unsurprisingly, there were no takers. Instead, she picked out an ordinary pack of playing cards. She found a folding baize table tucked into the corner of the unit and she brought it over to the middle of the room.

And so they settled down to wait, listlessly playing hand after hand of poker, though nobody had any thought of winning or losing. The hours creaked slowly by and the fire gradually dwindled to a last few glowing embers. The sun began to decline on the western horizon and they were obliged to switch on the lights, but still there was no indication of anybody coming to their aid. And as the winter afternoon lengthened into evening, Jenny felt a hopeless sense of dread settling around her like a chilly shroud.

She was beginning to think that their cause was hopeless – that they were all destined to die here in this ancient house, just as Wadleigh's twelve disciples had perished before them, one hundred years ago.

And then, just when their collective spirit had sunk to its lowest ebb, just when they were ready to roll over and accept whatever awful fate had been reserved for them, something incredible happened. Something magical, though in different circumstances it would have seemed the most ordinary thing in the world.

Out in the hallway, the phone began to ring.

Chapter Thirty-Three

The first reaction was one of incredulity. Everybody sat there staring at each other: then they were all up on their feet, yelling delightedly.

'The phone!' cried Jenny, clapping her hands together like an excited child. 'Somebody must have repaired the line.' It was a patently obvious remark but after several days without it, the restoration of the phone line seemed little short of a miracle. She started towards the door, then hesitated, looking at Reed, who was still holding the shotgun. 'I take it it's OK if I go and answer that?'

'We'll *all* go,' he told her. 'Lead the way.'

Jenny opened the door and looked cautiously out into the hallway. The nearest phone stood on the hall table, just past the entrance to the recording studio. Out here, the shrill tone of it seemed almost deafening. As far as she could tell the hall itself was completely empty.

'OK,' she told the others. She stepped out from the doorway and started to walk briskly towards the phone. The others followed. Reed brought up the rear, the shotgun held ready for use. As they passed the staircase, he paused to look up to the next floor as though suspecting some kind of trick.

Jenny approached the table and reached out to lift the handset: but seconds before her fingers connected with it, the phone stopped ringing. She swore under her breath but told herself that it didn't really matter. If the phone could receive calls it could transmit them, and that meant they'd be able to summon help.

She raised the handset and held it to her ear. The line was dead. She had a split second to register this before all the lights went out.

She heard Cassie give a gasp of terror and right behind her Steve's gruff voice snapped out a curse. Then for a few seconds there was a silence as deep and total as the pitch darkness that surrounded them.

Jenny tried to replace the handset but misjudged it. It fell with a clatter that made everybody start. Jenny stood there trying hard to control her breathing. She was teetering on the very edge of panic.

'What do we do now?' she whispered.

'I know where there's a torch,' said Reed's voice, and that too seemed unnaturally loud in the silence of their surroundings. 'It's in a cupboard in the kitchen. Just let me get by . . .'

'No, wait!' said Cassie. She sounded terrified. 'We're supposed to stay together, remember?'

'I know that, but there's no sense in all of us blundering around in the dark, is there? Jenny, any chance of you dialling the emergency services in the dark?'

'The phone's dead,' she told him. 'Not even a dial tone.'

'How is that possible?' muttered Steve. 'We all heard it ring.'

'Maybe . . . maybe somebody *made* it ring,' whispered Cassie. 'To get us all out here.'

'I'll get that torch,' concluded Reed. Jenny felt a push against her shoulder as Reed attempted to get by her. Then something cold and hard brushed against her ear and she realised with a thrill of terror that it must be the barrel of the shotgun.

'For God's sake, be careful with that thing,' she hissed.

There was a loud clatter off to their left which almost made her jump out of her skin.

'What the hell was that?' she asked the darkness.

'A framed gold disc, I think,' muttered Reed irritably. 'Everybody just stay put. I won't be long.' Jenny heard his footsteps moving uncertainly towards the dining room and the kitchen beyond it, his passage punctuated by a series of crashes, thumps and curses.

Jenny stood absolutely still, her skin crawling with apprehension. It seemed to her highly unlikely that the power supply, having weathered the worst excesses of the storm, would choose that particular moment in time to go down: and she knew the others must be thinking the same thing.

'You OK, Cassie?' she asked.

'I'm scared. I don't like the dark.'

'Nobody likes the dark. Here.' Jenny reached out a hand and groped around until she encountered the girl's arm. She moved downwards until she was able to enclose Cassie's hand in her own. The hand felt very cold.

'How about you, Steve?'

'Hanging in there. Wish I had my lighter on me but I gave it to you, didn't I?'

'Yes. I left it on the arm of the sofa.'

'Think I should go get it?'

'No, we'd better stay right here and wait for Reed.'

'You think it was wise to let laughing boy go off by himself?'

'I don't see that we had much choice. We can't do anything without a light and—'

She broke off in alarm as she became aware of a gust of

cooler air playing against the right side of her face. It seemed to her that somebody had just pushed open the swing door of the studio.

'Did you feel that?' she asked Steve.

'Feel what?' he muttered.

'I thought somebody just opened a door.'

'Can't say that I – uh!'

'Steve?' The last sentence had terminated in a long exhalation of air. 'Steve? You all right?'

There was no answer. Jenny thought she sensed movement on her right side and she reached out her free hand in an attempt to locate it. Mystifyingly, her fingers brushed against what felt like the heel of a boot and she recoiled in surprise.

'What is it?' whispered Cassie.

'I don't know.' Jenny put a protective arm around the girl and drew her back down the hall a short distance. Then she edged backwards until her shoulders rested against the wooden panelling of the staircase. Instinctively, she dropped to her haunches, pulling Cassie down with her.

'Steve?' she said again. 'Are you still there? Speak to me!'

Now there was a dull thud, followed by a low drone of machinery.

'What the fuck is that?' gasped Jenny.

'Sounds like the service lift,' said Cassie. 'Steve must be going down to the studio.' Cassie was fighting a losing battle with her own mounting terror and her voice was a tremulous whisper, pushing at the very edge of tears. 'Why didn't he answer you?' she gasped. 'Jenny, what's happening? I'm scared!'

'I know, Cassie. Just sit tight, Gareth should be back in a moment. Maybe ... maybe Steve decided to go after him, see what's taking him so long, huh?'

The girl's answer was puzzling. It was a brief hiss of exhaled air. Her cold hand tightened around Jenny's fingers with a pressure that threatened to break them. Jenny told herself that the best thing she could do for the girl was to keep talking to her, and the first thing that popped into her mind was a recollection from childhood.

'You know, Cassie, when I was very small, I used to be really frightened of the dark...'

Jenny heard a sound like the soft rustling of paper, but she did her level best to ignore it and went on with what she was saying.

'I remember, I went to this boy's birthday party when I was maybe six or seven years old. After we'd had the jelly and ice cream, somebody suggested we play hide and seek...'

Now there was the soft thump of the studio door closing again. Cassie's body was trembling as though she had totally succumbed to her own terror.

'It was a big old house,' continued Jenny, desperately. 'We ... we all ran off to find places to hide. I ran into a bedroom and there was one of those walk-in closets in there. I pulled back the door and I pressed inside among all the coats and dresses and I pulled the door shut behind me...'

Cassie gave a long, shuddering gasp of fear and Jenny tightened her grip around the girl's shoulders.

'Well, I crouched there in the darkness, waiting for somebody to come looking for me but nobody did for quite a while and then I got this idea into my head, and it really scared me. I started to think that there was somebody else in the closet with me...'

Cassie's body stopped trembling and she seemed to calm herself a little. Maybe the story was working.

'I kept telling myself that I must be imagining things. But then, out of the blue, somebody sneezed right beside me and I freaked out! Damn near screamed the house down. Anyhow, people came rushing in, turned all the lights on, and what do you think...?'

As if to illustrate the point, a beam of light issued from the open door of the dining room. Reed was coming back with the torch.

'Another kid had climbed in there just before I did and he hadn't said anything in case I was somebody who was looking for him. Everybody seemed to think it was pretty funny apart from me. For weeks afterwards I insisted on sleeping with the light on...'

Reed emerged from the dining room. He still carried the shotgun in one hand and, in the other, a powerful torch. He stood looking around for a moment, puzzled that the others were not where he had left them. Then he saw Jenny and Cassie crouched in the shadow of the staircase. He moved closer.

'Where's Steve?' he asked.

'I don't know. We heard noises. One minute he was there, the next he was missing. I think he must have gone down to the studio in the service lift.'

'The studio? Why would he...?' Reed broke off in mid sentence. He was shining the beam of the torch at Cassie. 'My God,' he whispered.

Jenny turned her head to follow his gaze. Then she flinched away from the girl with a gasp of terror, scrambling to her feet.

Cassie's throat was hanging open like a second mouth and the front of her dress had been soaked by a cascade of blood, which had also spread out in a shimmering pool at her feet. Her eyes were wide open, staring straight ahead in an expression of intense concentration. In one hand, she was holding a small slip of paper.

Jenny turned away with a groan and pushed her face against the reassuring hardness of the wood-panelled staircase.

'I thought she was just frightened,' she sobbed. 'I was talking to her ... telling her a story, trying to get her to relax...'

'And that's when you killed her?'

Jenny flinched as she heard him cock the hammers of the shotgun. She span back to face him.

'No, I swear to you, it wasn't me!'

He sneered, then swept the beam of the torch across the floor.

'Well I don't see any other suspects, do you? What did you do with the knife, Jenny? Have you still got it on you?'

'Gareth, listen, you've got to believe me. It ... it was pitch dark out here, I couldn't have done this even if I'd wanted to.'

'Well *somebody* managed it, didn't they?'

'It's like I said. Somebody came in through the studio door.'

'Somebody who could see in the dark, no doubt?'

'I ... suppose so. I mean, I don't understand it any better than you do. I ... felt a breeze as the studio door opened. Then Steve wasn't talking to me any more. Then ... then there was the sound of the lift...'

'You're saying Steve did it?'

'No! At least, I don't think so. If he went down to the studio, I don't think he had any choice in the matter.'

Reed frowned. He handed Jenny the torch and indicated that she should hold it on Cassie's body. Then, going down on one knee and taking care not to get any blood on his clothes, he reached gingerly out and plucked the slip of paper from her dead fingers. He scanned the lyrics and then handed them to Jenny.

'Another of your charming little ditties,' he observed.

Jenny saw that this time, they had come from a recording called *Thicker Than Water*.

SHE WAS JUST SOMEBODY'S DAUGHTER
SHE WAS JUST SOMEBODY'S WIFE
BUT YOU DROVE HER TO THE SLAUGHTER
AND YOU ROBBED HER OF HER LIFE
BLOOD'S ALWAYS THICKER THAN WATER
WHEN YOU TEST IT WITH A KNIFE.

Jenny sighed. She crumpled the note and threw it aside. Reed was still looking at her, his mouth twisted into an expression of distaste.

'I swear to God, Gareth,' she told him. 'I had nothing to do with any of these killings. I—'

She broke off in surprise as she heard the muted sound of music, pumping up from the studio below. It must have been playing at an awesome volume to get past the ample soundproofing that surrounded it. She recognised it instantly as the version of *Live Fast, Die Young* that the band had recorded just the other day. She glanced at Reed and saw the look of bewilderment on his face.

'And I suppose I organised that too, while you were looking for a torch!' she said.

He shook his head.

'Maybe it's Steve,' he murmured.

'But how? The power's off, isn't it?'

He shrugged.

'Fuse boxes are all down there. Maybe he just took out the fuses for the lighting circuits on these floors. We'll see,' he added grimly. He took the shotgun in two hands and gestured at her with the twin barrels. 'We're going down to the studio to investigate.'

She shook her head.

'I'm not going down there,' she protested.

'Oh yes, you are,' he told her calmly. 'Now get moving.'

Reluctantly, she moved across to the studio door and pushed it open. The music leapt up the stairs at her at a volume that made her wince, and she saw that the lights were on down there, too. She switched off the torch and placed a foot tentatively on the first step. A stab of naked fear lanced into her and she hesitated, terrified of what might be waiting for her below. Reed prodded her in the back with the shotgun.

'Down you go,' he said.

She swallowed hard. Then, taking a deep breath, she began to descend.

Chapter Thirty-Four

Down in the control room, the volume was ear splitting, the music pumping out of the huge, wall-mounted speakers, the bass so loud it seemed to kick like a trip hammer in Jenny's chest. She made it to the bottom of the stairs and looked warily around. Ahead of her, in a pool of light, two figures were sitting in the swivel chairs at the mixing desk. The backs of the chairs hid most of their bodies but the balding head that stuck up above the rim of the producer's chair was undoubtedly that of Steve Lampton. And the head of blond hair that occupied the engineer's seat could only have belonged to Idris Morgan.

Jenny opened her mouth to shout to them but realised that she had no chance of making herself heard over the grinding roar of the music.

The lights were on in the studio itself, but it seemed empty. Jenny's attention was drawn to one of those familiar scraps of paper affixed to the glass door. With a sinking feeling inside her, she went across to retrieve it. Reed, meanwhile, made a beeline for the desk, where he punched the off button on the tape deck. In the silence that ensued, they both heard the sound of the service lift rising back to the ground floor.

Reed and Jenny exchanged puzzled glances. Then Jenny reached up to remove the note. The lyrics were from *Mr Universe*, one of the band's singles, a top twenty hit in 1982.

GETTING BETTER ISN'T EASY,
IT'S LIKE CHARLES ATLAS SAID,
'TAKE CARE OF YOUR BODY
IF YOU WANT TO GET AHEAD.'

She turned to shout a warning to Reed but it was already too late. He had reached out to turn Steve's chair around to face him and the action caused Steve's head to tip sideways off his neck and fall with a loud thud on to the mixing desk. Reed jumped back retching violently, giving Jenny a clear view of what had happened. Looking at Idris side on, she could see that his body had been prepared in the same way. His head had been neatly severed then balanced carefully back on the stump of the neck to give the impression that the two parts were still joined together. The torsos of both men were saturated with their own blood and pools of it had collected amidst the knobs and sliders of the mixing desk.

Reed turned away with a groan and he glared at Jenny, his face a white mask of anger.

'McGuire!' he hissed. 'It has to be McGuire! There's nobody else it *could* be. That must have been him we heard, going back up in the service lift!'

Jenny nodded. She turned back to the studio door and pressed her forehead against the cold glass. A wave of faintness rippled through her and for a moment, she thought how easy it would be, how comforting to just let herself fall into unconsciousness and be far away from this charnel house in which she was trapped. But then some deeper resolve asserted itself. She thought of Des McGuire's gloating face, the way he had talked about Scott when she'd met him in Manchester only a couple of weeks ago. She wasn't going to admit defeat to scum like that. She steeled herself, opened her eyes and found herself looking in at the two shrouded bodies on the studio floor...

'I'm going to see if I can find the missing fuses,' Reed announced. 'Then we're going to hunt down that evil sonofabitch and take care of him, once and for all.' He moved away to the top end of the room where the fusebox was located, but...

Jenny was staring through the studio glass now. *Two* bodies? She knew that Robbie Porter's corpse had been left down here after the electrocution but... who was the other one? As far as she was aware all the other victims had been left where they dropped...

She glanced up to the top end of the room where Reed was fiddling with the fusebox, muttering to himself. Numbly, she reached out a hand and pushed open the studio door. She stepped inside and moved to the nearer of the bodies, went down on her knees beside it. She took hold of a corner of the first sheet, noting how it was splattered with blood and wondering at that, because Robbie had been electrocuted, and as far as she remembered, there hadn't been a single drop of blood on his body...

Glancing back, she saw that Reed was still preoccupied with the fuse box so...

She pulled back the sheet and sure enough, it was Robbie Porter, his waxy grey features still frozen in the death-grimace she remembered so vividly; but as more of the sheet lifted, she saw that some awful butchery had been carried out on his body. The chest was hacked open leaving a dark empty opening and...

She couldn't bear to see any more. She let the sheet drop back again and shifted her position slightly to reach for the second sheet. She almost jumped out of her skin when a voice crackled over the intercom.

'Jenny, it's no good, I can't fix it, somebody's buggered up the fuses permanently!' Turning her head she saw that Reed had moved across to the mixing desk and was talking into the studio microphone. 'We'll need your torch. What are you doing in there, anyway? We should get after McGuire.'

Jenny steeled herself and pulled back the second sheet to reveal a face, half of which had been horrifically mangled by a shotgun blast, the lead pellets laying open the cheek and jaw so that Jenny could see the back teeth. But the other half of the face was still recognisable...

'Jenny, are you listening to me? We need to get after him. He's probably hiding in the house somewhere, planning his next move!'

She was looking at Des McGuire.

'You were almost right,' Reed told her, 'when you said that Idris was planning something out in the snow. Only it must have been the other way round. McGuire must have jumped Idris, got the gun off him somehow. He blasted him, then dragged his body back into the house. He could have got back in through the hatch in the fuel store without us hearing anything. There's a connecting door to the studio. He must have known that none of us was likely to disturb him down here, with Robbie's body lying around.'

Jenny let the sheet fall back on the ruined mask of McGuire's face and she stood up unsteadily, reeled back against the wall, aware that the door behind her was opening, that Reed was coming into the studio. She tightened her grip on the handle of the heavy torch as Reed came to a halt beside her.

'Come on,' he said. 'We have to get moving. I'm sorry about being so suspicious before, but you understand, don't you, that I couldn't take any chances? At least now we know who the enemy is.'

And Jenny, thinking: *It's you, you bastard. It has to be you, there's nobody else left, you've butchered all of them, every last one.*

And Reed, reaching out a hand to place it on her shoulder, saying, 'Don't worry, Jenny, it'll be all right. I'll take good care of you.'

Jenny whipped around and hit him in the face with the heavy torch, putting all her strength behind the blow. He reeled aside with an oath and there was a deafening roar as the shotgun discharged both barrels into the ceiling, raining down plaster dust and chunks of polystyrene. Jenny didn't wait around to see if Reed was going to get up again. She turned, raced through the open studio door and headed for the stairs.

Behind her she heard Reed bellow something and then he was scrambling up after her. She raced up the stairs, taking them two at a time, until she emerged into the darkness of the ground floor. She hesitated a moment, fumbling with the torch. She managed to switch it on, then took an exploratory step and slipped in the puddle of blood that had spread out from Cassie's corpse. She went down in an ungainly sprawl, horribly aware of the palm of her hand making contact with something warm and sticky; but she got to her feet in an instant, veered left and made for the staircase up to the first floor. The beam of the torch stabbed into the darkness ahead of her and she started up the stairs, just as Reed came blundering out of the studio entrance.

'Jenny, wait, why are you doing this? McGuire might be waiting for you up there!'

She paid him no heed, only ran on in silent terror, not even aware of where she was going, only that she wanted to put as much distance as possible between Reed and herself. She was horribly aware of his footsteps pounding up the stairs in pursuit and it occurred to her that she was simply delaying the inevitable. There was nowhere to run to, no escape in this direction. Her only hope was to find some kind of weapon and fight back.

She gained the first floor landing and blundered along it, following the wildly see-sawing beam of the torch.

'Jenny, wait a minute! You've got it all wrong, I promise you! It's McGuire. It has to be McGuire!'

Jenny didn't waste time answering. She had just remembered something from the previous day. Lezard and herself, trying to gain admittance to Adrian's room. There had been a fire axe, hadn't there? She'd managed to dissuade Lezard from using it, but as far as she recalled he'd left it propped against a wall, up on the second floor...

She stumbled over something unseen in the shadows of the balcony and fell forward, striking the carpeted floor with an impact that drove the breath out of her body. The torch went rolling out of her grasp, slipped between a gap in the banisters and fell into the stairwell. She heard the glass shatter on the stone flags below. She cursed her own clumsiness and as she tried to struggle upright, Reed came blundering along the landing and fell on top of her.

She gave a howl of terror and drove back hard with her elbow, felt the yielding crunch of what could only have been his nose. He gave a squeal of mingled pain and indignation, fell backwards and something metallic went clattering into the stairwell after the torch. The shotgun? Jenny scrambled back to her feet and went blindly up the next flight of stairs.

Breathless with panic, she made it to the top landing and saw to her relief that a little moonlight was coming in through an arched window at the far end of it, casting a pale glow along its length. And there, leaning against the wall, was the two-handed fire axe that she had been praying for.

With a yell of triumph, Jenny ran to it, swept it up in both hands and span around to face the stairs. For a long, terrible moment, there was nothing. Then Reed's face moved slowly into view, his handsome features marred by the blood that was pulsing from his broken nose. He was staring at her in silent malevolence as he came slowly up the stairs. She was relieved to see that he no longer had the shotgun with him. He reached the landing and kept right on coming, so Jenny retreated slowly until she was standing in front of the window. Then it occurred to her that he wasn't going to stop until she did. She set her feet apart and took up a more openly defensive stance, raising the axe above her head.

'That's far enough,' she told him.

He shook his head, mopped at his nose with the sleeve of his shirt.

'You've got it all wrong,' he told her again. 'I've already told you, it's McGuire. It *has* to be him. Instead of chasing each other around like this, we should be teaming up to take care of McGuire.'

'You lying bastard,' she told him. 'I *know* it's you.'

He laughed derisively.

'You've flipped,' he told her. 'You've totally lost it. Now look, put down the axe and let's talk this through like rational people.'

He took a step closer as he said this and she hefted the axe threateningly.

'I'm warning you,' she said. 'You come one step closer and I'll split your lying head like a melon.'

Reed giggled, made a mock gesture of feeling cold, wrapping his arms around himself.

'Ooh, Jenny, *frosty*! You're quite something when you're angry, you know that?' He traced his fingertips across his nose and looked ruefully at the blood. 'You've broken my fucking nose, you realise that? Now come on, stop fooling around and put down the axe. It's McGuire you have to worry about, not me.'

'Oh yeah? Is that why I just found McGuire's body down in the studio?'

The grin faded abruptly from his face.

'That's not funny,' he said. He took another step closer.

'It's not meant to be funny: and I'm warning you for the last time.'

Reed spread his hands in a gesture of bafflement.

'Look,' he said. 'I don't understand it either. But I know one thing. The killer isn't me. Yeah, I know I'm bound to say that, but it happens to be the truth, and you'd be well advised to believe me. I'll tell you something else, Jenny. You aren't the killer either and you wouldn't have the guts to put an axe into somebody. So I'm just going to take it away from you and we're going to sit down together and work this out.'

'One more step, Reed. Just one more step and I swear, I'll use this thing.'

He studied her for a moment in silence. Then he smiled. He lifted a leg to take another step and in that instant, his whole body seemed to jolt as though he'd been struck by a powerful impact. His eyes widened in surprise and he opened his mouth to say something: but all that emerged was a long, slow exhalation of tortured breath. He took the step he had intended to take but his legs seemed to have turned to putty. The outflung foot came down on its side and he lost his balance, pitched forward onto his face.

In the moonlight, Jenny could see, quite clearly, the crossbow bolt jutting up from between his shoulder blades. She could see too, the scrap of paper attached to the top of it like a tiny flag. Reed gave a low groan and tried to lift himself on his arms. But his strength seemed to give out suddenly and he flopped down onto his face and lay still.

Jenny stood there staring down at him in bewilderment. Then she lowered the axe and knelt beside him. She began to reach for the note, almost against her will: but she snatched her hand back in terror as Reed gave a long shuddering gasp. She scrambled back from him on her hands and knees and cowered beneath the window, her whole body shaking with fright.

'What's the matter, Jenny? Too frightened to read?' The voice was familiar and it came to her from out of the darkness beyond the staircase. 'It's one of your best numbers. And very appropriate. *Look Out For Number One*. Shall I sing it to you?'

Jenny crouched there, shaking her head. This wasn't happening. It couldn't be happening, because . . .

But the voice came out of the dark at her, singing in a clear, resonant baritone.

> 'Always watch your ass, kid.
> Be ready for attack.
> There's people queuing up to shaft you
> To stab you in the back.'

And now Jenny heard the creak of a footstep on the staircase as another figure mounted to the landing. She could see the man's tall outline, the crossbow slung nonchalantly across his shoulder. As he moved into the moonlight, she noted the way his white shirt was liberally splashed with blood, the leather harness of tools and knives he wore around his waist. He was wearing some kind of hi-tech helmet incorporating adjustable goggles, which, she presumed, were infra red, allowing him to see in the dark. But as he moved into the moonlight, he reached up and removed the helmet and now she could see his face, his familiar smile, the piercing blue eyes that had always been his best feature. For someone who was dead, he looked to be in surprisingly good shape.

'Hello, Jenny,' he said.

She shook her head, bewildered. Maybe she finally had gone mad, she decided. That had to be it. Otherwise, how was this possible?'

'You seem puzzled,' he observed.

She laughed at that, a shrill manic laugh that was dangerously close to complete hysteria.

'You could say that,' she murmured. 'Oh yeah, you most definitely could.'

He nodded.

'Well, then let me explain it to you, if I can. After everything you've been through, Jenny, I think the very least I owe you is some kind of explanation.'

Chapter Thirty-Five

They stood there in the moonlight like two lovers enjoying a secret liaison. Lezard had set down the crossbow now and he was smiling at Jenny, explaining everything in his familiar calm, reassuring way, just as he had always explained things to her. He seemed in no great hurry to tell it, because he knew that she had no place to go, and the fire axe, which lay beside Reed's sprawled body, was an equal distance between them.

'First, the little matter of my death, reports of which, to paraphrase a famous quote, were greatly exaggerated.'

'But... I saw...'

'No, Jenny, what you saw were some vital organs, kindly donated by young Robbie Porter. He made no complaint about me helping myself to them, since he was lying dead in the studio at the time.' He gave a mischievous smile. 'I'm tempted to say that the kid had guts, but that would be in very poor taste, don't you think?' He crossed his arms over his blood-stained chest and sighed. 'So yes, Jenny, I'm the Hoochie Coochie Man. It was me right from the start. I killed Scott first, just to test the water. I engineered Mike's "suicide". You were pretty much on the nail with that, by the way, except I didn't use chloroform. I hit him with a syringe full of insulin. They say it's very hard to detect.' He smiled, spread his hands in a gesture of culpability. 'And every bad thing that's happened here, I've orchestrated. Now, I guess I could give you a blow by blow account of how I killed them all but I dare say you're not so much concerned with "how" as—'

'*Why*?' she prompted him. She glanced down at Reed's prone body. 'I thought it was him and Idris. I thought it was to do with that crazy religion they were involved with . . .'

'Oh, it *was*,' he assured her. 'And not so much of the crazy, if you don't mind! Here, allow me to show you something.' Lezard was unbuttoning his shirt. He held it open to display the small tattoo of a snake on his right shoulder. Jenny stared at it in disbelief.

'You . . . you're a member too?'

'Yes, but *they* didn't know it. It was a secret I kept from everyone, including them.'

'But, I don't understand. If they had the same beliefs as you . . .'

Lezard made a dismissive gesture.

'They were dabblers! Amateurs! They'd only just started on the path to fulfilment. The first level of attainment concerns itself with simple sex magic and fertility rites. It takes a lifetime's work to become a true adept and as you progress your way through the higher levels, you find access to deeper, darker secrets.' He took a step forward and prodded Reed's body with his foot, eliciting no response. 'I very much doubt that our friend here would have progressed much further. I think he found everything he wanted in the first level.' Lezard took another decisive step forward before Jenny could react and he put a foot down on the handle of the axe. She shrank back against the arched window, but Lezard continued to talk as though nothing much had happened.

'To fully understand, you'd have to go back to the days of our glorious leader, Obediah Wadleigh. Now, I don't know how familiar you are with him . . .'

'I know more than you might think. Cassie lent me a book about the house. It had a chapter all about him.'

Lezard looked vaguely amused by this information.

'Good, that makes it somewhat easier to explain. Well, Wadleigh was a man of many talents and one of them was a talent for fathering illegitimate children. My great grandfather was one of them. His mother, Agnes McLennon, was not the only woman who bore Wadleigh a child, though she seems to have been his favourite. At any rate, a couple of months before the great sacrifice, Wadleigh sent Agnes and her son away to America, where she eventually married into the Lezard family. Agnes and her son were spared for a reason and only on a certain understanding.'

Lezard dropped to one knee and picked up the axe. He ran a thumb experimentally across the blade and smiled in satisfaction. Jenny could only wait in helpless silence as he went on with his story.

'Wadleigh had realised one important fact. The sacrifice he was making would protect the world from the Great Serpent, but it would only be effective for a period of one hundred years. When that time had elapsed, one of his descendants would be required to perform the ritual once again. The rules were brutal and quite straightforward. Whoever inherited the responsibility would be required, one day, to execute the twelve people that made up his closest disciples, and they would have to be killed in a way that proved pleasing to our Lord, The Cosmic Joker. When Wadleigh performed the original ritual, he devised a clever concept utilising the poems of his most esteemed follower . . .'

'Lady Helen Forster. Yes, I know about that.'

Lezard seemed impressed and, Jenny thought, rather pleased by this revelation.

'Then you'll already understand why I've done the things

I've done! It was nothing personal. Just a series of rituals that I have been destined to carry out since before either of us were born. My grandfather, my father, each of them knew that when the time came, whichever eldest male descendant was alive at that time would have the honour of performing the task.'

'The *honour*?' Jenny was horrified. 'You can't dignify such butchery by that name!'

'Oh, but I can. Since I was old enough to understand the basic premise of our faith, it's been impressed upon me that this was to be my glorious destiny.'

Jenny shook her head in disbelief.

'And you're telling me that because of this crackpot religion, you've murdered eleven people?'

'Not with any pleasure,' he assured her. 'That's the point, Jenny. The chosen one is required to make the ultimate sacrifice. And believe me, killing you is going to be the hardest, most heartbreaking task of all. I can only console myself with the thought that after it's done, I'll follow close on your heels. We'll dwell in paradise together.'

'That's really not much of a consolation,' she told him bluntly. 'Josh, I can't believe you. All this for some stupid fairy tale about a giant snake?'

'Not a fairy tale,' Josh told her with what sounded like genuine regret. 'Fairy tales invariably have a happy ending. This one, I fear, ends in tragedy.' He hefted the axe, testing it for balance. 'But you have to weigh up the consequences of the ritual *not* being performed. What are the lives of thirteen people worth when weighed against the fate of the whole world?' He took a step forward and Jenny made a desperate attempt to play for time.

'So how . . . how did you come to find your way back here?' she asked him.

'It was always my long-term plan. But there was no reason

why I shouldn't have a career in the time that I had left. So, as things moved on, and I became a major player in the music business, I ensured that the bands I worked with were always based in England. One reason why I was so keen to work with The Deceivers. And meanwhile, I kept an eye on The Grange, biding my time, looking for an opening. It's funny how fate always seems to step in and offer an opportunity. When I found out about Gareth Reed and his interest in setting up a studio here, it was too good to miss. I met up with him and offered to become his partner, an offer he accepted when he found out how much money I was prepared to put into the business. I almost bankrupted myself in the process, but what the hell? I won't be needing it where I'm going.'

'And... you introduced Gareth and Idris to the ... Order of the Snake, did you?'

'No. The interest was already there. As it grew, I watched with some amusement. But I knew they lacked the strength of character to become true adepts.'

'So... why did you fake all that stuff about Scott? The séance, the tape. What was the point of that?'

Lezard smiled.

'That's something I can't take any credit for,' he told her. 'That was just something that happened. I was as amazed by it as you were. And for your information, I don't think Reed or Idris engineered it either. I'm afraid that bit was genuine.'

'Genuine? You mean Scott really is...'

'Haunting you? A loaded word, Jenny, but I can't think of a better one. Anyhow, you'll be seeing him soon enough. We both will.'

'No, wait, there's something else...'

'Jenny, I understand exactly what you're trying to do, but the more we put this off, the harder it's going to be. So let's just get the show on the road, shall we?'

He took another step forward, raising the axe above his head, and Jenny pressed back against the window.

'Josh,' she whispered. 'Please, don't do this.'

'It's no use, Jenny. It has to be done. But don't worry, I'll make it quick. You won't suffer.'

'Josh, listen to me—'

'Actually, I've already picked out your epitaph. It's from *The Queen of Rock n' Roll*. Remember that one? "Listen well, my momma said, The Queen of Rock n' Roll is dead. The mourners dance, begin to sing, the Queen is dead, long live the King."'

He swung the axe back and Jenny cringed, her body anticipating the impact of the first blow...

And then Gareth Reed's right arm shot out and grabbed Lezard's ankle, jerking him over to one side. He gave an exclamation of surprise, lost his balance and fell with an impact that shook the floor, dropping the axe in the process. Reed scrambled over and launched himself at Lezard's throat and the two men began to grapple on the landing. Unable to get by them, Jenny could only crouch there, looking for an opening, a chance to grab the axe, but for the moment it was hidden under the two men's sprawled bodies. Now Lezard threw up a hand and, grabbing at the wooden shaft that still protruded from Reed's back, he began to twist it around in the flesh.

Reed screamed and rolled towards the banisters, where he began to claw himself upright. Lezard scrambled into a crouching position and Jenny, seeing the handle of the axe for the first time, made a grab for it, but she encountered Lezard's fist instead. He struck her hard in the face and she reeled backwards. Her elbow hit the window behind her, breaking the glass. She was only dimly aware of it shattering because she was yelling a warning to Reed as Lezard came upright in a lithe bound. He swung the axe at Reed, who was just turning back to face his adversary.

The blade caught Reed across the throat, gashing him so deeply that his head hinged backwards at an impossible angle, blood spraying from the rupture in a crimson fountain. Reed's body reeled back against the balustrade, the arms outstretched, the hands gesticulating wildly, trying to come to terms with a world that had turned abruptly upside down.

Lezard lifted a foot and slammed it into Reed's chest. His body lost its balance and tipped over backwards into the stairwell. It fell in a sprawl of flailing limbs and landed with a thud on the stone flags two floors below.

Lezard reeled to the banisters and peered over into the darkness. He was panting, trying to get his breath back. He turned back to face Jenny.

And that was when she went out of the window, smashing her way through the remaining glass, oblivious to the sharp edges that tore at her clothing. She dropped a short distance to a snow-covered sloping roof and she began to slide downwards, clawing desperately at the icy covering beneath her in a vain attempt to slow her rate of descent.

The heel of her boot made contact with slate, spinning her around, and now she was looking up at Lezard's furious face as he glared at her from the broken window. She was still sliding downwards, moving much too fast. She felt her toes clunk briefly against metal but it failed to slow her down and her legs pushed out into empty air.

She glimpsed dull metal gleaming in the moonlight and made a grab at what must have been a length of cast-iron guttering. Her fingers caught a precarious hold and for an instant, she was jolted up sharp; but then there was a rending noise and one end of the guttering detached itself and tipped her down again. She lost her grip completely and fell, her legs pedalling wildly, her hands clawing for support that wasn't there.

She seemed to fall for a long, terrible eternity. She tasted her own death like an acrid bile in her throat.

Then she hit the ground and blackness closed around her.

Chapter Thirty-Six

So this is what death feels like, thought Jenny. She lay suspended in blackness and an all-pervading chill pressed around her on every side, but in a strange way, it felt comforting. She was away from the fear and the horror of the house now, and how sweet it would be just to float here for eternity, remote and detached from the terrors of the past few days.

And then she heard a familiar voice whispering in her ear.

Jenny, get up! He's coming after you !

The sound of the voice galvanised her into movement. She thrashed into a sitting position and her head broke through into the chill moonlight air. She glanced around in dull surprise. She had been lying in a deep bank of snow that had drifted up against the front wall of the house. Peering up, she could see, high above her, the window from which she had jumped, the wide track mark that her body had created as she slid down the angle of the roof. The impact of landing had knocked the wind out of her but so far as she could tell, she had sustained no serious injury.

Jenny, get on your feet, quickly !

Again the voice, an insistent buzz against her ear drum. Obediently, Jenny floundered upright. An instant later, the front door of the house burst open and Lezard stood framed in the doorway, the fire axe still clutched in his hands.

Run, Jenny! Run !

She needed no second bidding. She turned and ran, lurching and staggering through the deep snow. Behind her, she heard Lezard give a bellow of anger and she knew, without looking back, that he was coming after her.

The circle, Jenny. Run to the circle.

She wasn't even sure in which direction that lay but she had no reason to disobey the voice, since she had no better plan. She just kept running, making tortuous progress over the treacherous surface of the frozen snow, her feet sinking deep at every step, and it occurred to her, that she was reliving her recent dream, the dream of being pursued by some unseen evil: only now, the evil was all too tangible, it had a name and a face she recognised. Glancing back over her shoulder, she saw that Lezard was gaining on her.

He was racing across the snow like some malevolent lifeforce, his head down, his breath clouding around him like a devil's halo, his long legs propelling him forward at a speed she couldn't hope to match.

But she redoubled her efforts just the same, her feet kicking showers of ice crystals as she ran, the muscles in her legs aching with the effort. Now she was aware of the cold, settling around her like an icy fist, seeping into flesh and bone, but she couldn't even think about that now because he was gaining on her...

She was approaching the opening in the trees now, the dark, skeletal outlines rearing up on either side of her. She remembered that the track that lay directly ahead of her would lead, eventually, to the stone circle – but Lezard would be on her before she even got halfway along it. Her lungs were almost bursting.

Into the trees. To the left !

The voice – Scott's voice – seemed to know what it wanted, and she had no better option but to obey its instructions She veered left, clambered up a deep bank of snow and pressed into the enveloping shadows of the trees. The light of the moon was suddenly extinguished and only occasional shafts of it managed to pierce the interlaced canopy of branches overhead: but the snow wasn't deep here and she was able to discern a narrow track leading into the heart of the forest.

She lifted an arm to shield her face from low-hanging branches and she ran on, horribly aware that Lezard was clambering up the snow bank now.

'It's pointless to run, Jenny!' he yelled after her: and his voice seemed to echo in the black spaces between the trees. 'You know I'll get you sooner or later. It's time you surrendered to your destiny.'

'Fuck you!' she screamed back, and immediately regretted wasting her breath. There was a terrible heat in her chest and an electric flicker of pain running in a stitch down the right side of her body. She willed herself not to slow down, aware now that Lezard was very close to her, only a few short steps behind...

Turn right! Duck under there !

She didn't question the instruction until she had followed it and found that she was looking at a narrow opening beneath a thick screen of brambles, a passage made by a fox perhaps. She envisaged herself being stuck half in, half out of it, where Lezard could butcher her at his leisure, but this was her only chance and she had to take it. She threw herself down on to her hands and knees and pushed into the opening. Thorns raked the back of her sweatshirt and snagged in her hair, but she crawled forward, scrambling along the tunnel. A hand grabbed at her ankle and she yelled, kicked back hard, then crawled onwards, deeper into the thicket. Behind her, there was a thrashing in the undergrowth and a string of muffled curses, but nobody followed. Lezard's broad shoulders must have proved too wide for the opening.

Jenny crawled through darkness, her heart thumping, her nostrils filled with the rich odour of soil and vegetation. Despite the awful cold, she was sweating profusely. She saw light ahead of her and pulled herself through into a clearing on the other side of the thicket. Scrambling to her feet, she glanced quickly around but for the moment at least, there was no sign of Lezard.

She started to move but Scott's voice whispered a warning.

No, not that way! Go left along the track!

She located the narrow trail cutting through deep vegetation and began to move along it at a more cautious pace, while she tried to steady her breathing. She was aware now of a stinging sensation on her cheek, just below the eye and when she lifted her fingers to investigate, they came away streaked with blood. She realised a thorn must have cut her and was thankful that it hadn't been an inch higher. Maybe somebody really was looking out for her...

Around to the right. It's not far now...

She pushed aside a low-hanging screen of branches and found another track, angling away from the one she was on. She took several steps along it, then froze as she heard a rustle of vegetation somewhere close at hand. She stopped and set her back against the trunk of an ancient oak tree. She held her breath and listened intently, but now everything seemed eerily silent. She gazed slowly around but in the uncertain light it was hard to be sure of anything.

Jenny, watch out!

Lezard came out of the cover of some bushes right behind

her, bellowing like a mad bull. She snapped around to face him and saw the wicked glint of the axe, swinging towards her in a deadly arc. She ducked her head and the heavy blade thudded into the tree trunk an inch above her skull. She screamed her defiance and aimed an instinctive kick at her adversary, driving the toe of her boot upwards at his testicles: but his reactions were too quick. He twisted aside and the foot caught him instead on the outer thigh. The yell of pain he made told Jenny that she had, at least, hurt the bastard. Caught off balance, his leg buckled under him and he dropped to one knee.

Jenny ran for it, pounding onwards along the track, racing through the surrounding trees in determined silence.

Close now. Nearly there. Just keep going . . .

But what happened when she got there? What possible refuge could an ancient stone circle provide? She remembered what had happened in the dream, the ground opening up to plunge her into a pit of writhing serpents. The memory of it jittered like alarm bells in her head as she burst out from the cover of the trees, descended a deep snow bank and saw the circle in a clearing directly ahead of her. She paused to look at it uncertainly. The thirteen stones stood like eerie sentinels in the moonlight. They seemed to be waiting.

In that same instant, Lezard came hurtling down the snow bank behind her, his chest slamming her between the shoulder blades and knocking her headlong to the ground.

She tried to struggle up, floundering in the snow, but he bore down on her, wrestling an arm up behind her back. She howled with pain, twisted free of his grip and, rolling over, she tried to claw at his face. He grabbed her wrists in a powerful grip and forced her back again. As her head thudded into the snow, she was aware of the axe lying only a few inches away, where he had dropped it. She flung out an arm but her fingers stopped several inches short of the handle. Lezard was breathing hard from the run but he was grinning triumphantly. His eyes blazed with feral glee.

'That was quite a dance you led me,' he observed. 'Just where the hell did you think you were running to?'

She twisted aside to stare at the stone circle. He followed her gaze and then he laughed, delightedly.

'The circle? You were running to the circle? But that's *perfect*!' He got to his feet and pulled her up with him. Jenny tried to make another grab for the axe, but Lezard hit her across the face with his open hand, snapping her head back and making coloured lights dance before her eyes. He grabbed a hank of her hair with his left hand and stooped to retrieve the axe with his right. Then he began to drag her towards the circle.

'What could be more appropriate?' he asked her. 'We'll conclude the ceremony in Wadleigh's holiest of places. We'll consecrate the altar with fresh blood. Why, I couldn't have asked for a more perfect ending.'

Jenny struggled against him, fighting against the awful burning agony in her scalp, but Lezard was merciless, jerking her along in his wake like some dumb animal.

'But what's the matter, Jenny? I thought you wanted to get to the circle? Did you think perhaps it would protect you?'

'You crazy fuck! Let go of me!'

'Don't worry, Jenny. It won't take a moment. There'll be no pain . . .'

They stepped into the circle.

'Josh, please, for the love of God, don't do this.'

'For the love of *who*?' He chuckled. They had reached the very centre of the circle now. Lezard located the snow-covered mound that was the altar stone and swept it free of snow with the edge of the axe. Then he twisted Jenny around to face him and flung her down onto it. She tried to scramble up again but he lifted a leg and stamped down hard on her chest, driving all the breath out of her body and pinning her securely in place. He raised the axe above his head...

'Great serpent,' he whispered. 'Accept this, the penultimate sacrifice and my most treasured possession...'

He broke off as he became aware of sounds – an eerie, jumbled ululation of voices and music that seemed to swell up all around them, quiet at first but rapidly getting louder and louder. Jenny lay there, transfixed, listening in disbelief, remembering how Idris and Cassie had told her of this phenomenon. Sure enough, the sound seemed to be coming out of the stones. Lezard stared around for a moment, then glanced down at Jenny.

'You hear them?' he asked her. 'The voices of the dead are sending you their welcome!'

Jenny could only lie there on the rock, her arms and legs spread in abject submission. She was too exhausted to fight back any more and now that she had stopped running, she was aware of the cold, the bitter, icy cold, seeping into her body. She concentrated her attention on Lezard's wild-eyed face and the upraised axe which hung poised in the air above her. It occurred to her that she could see everything very clearly now. The scene seemed to be lit by an unearthly glow, which even as she watched, was rapidly growing brighter.

Now Lezard was aware of it too. He lowered the axe and stared around in bewilderment. Jenny allowed herself to look too. She saw that the top part of each stone was beginning to glow with an intense, blue-white light. Over the roaring of the voices, she became aware of a new sound – a rising crackle of static.

'What the fuck?' Lezard's mouth shaped the words but Jenny could no longer hear them. Lezard looked worried now. This was clearly beyond his experience. The light was growing more intense by the second, brighter than any natural light ever could be. Lezard was obliged to throw up one arm to shield his eyes . . .

. . . and among the jumble of sounds erupting all around her, Jenny made out what sounded like an electric guitar playing a frenzied solo.

Lezard seemed to sense that something was wrong: that whatever power was manifesting itself in the circle, it was definitely not on his side.

'Time to finish this, Jenny,' he said – and he swung the axe above his head again.

Then he froze, his eyes bulging in surprise. His face adopted an expression of discomfort.

'No!' he said. 'It . . . can't be . . .' He attempted to use the axe again, but the sound of the guitar swelled in volume and hit a series of power chords. The sound was still oddly muted. Jenny realised that the music was coming from inside Lezard's head. It must have been like wearing the loudest Walkman in all creation.

Lezard gritted his teeth and threw up his hands to clamp them over his ears. He dropped the axe and Jenny just had the strength to twist aside as the blade came swinging down at her. It glanced off stone a few inches from her shoulder and spun uselessly away. She lay there looking at Lezard. His head was tilted back now, his eyes squeezed shut, his face set in a grimace of agony. The corded sinews of his neck stood out like ropes as he bellowed at the sky.

'Turn if off!' he yelled. 'Turn it off!'

But the music was growing steadily louder. Lezard's body began to jerk and convulse. He took his hands from his head a moment and Jenny could see that blood was pulsing out of his ears. His screams were becoming shrill, almost inhuman.

'Please,' he sobbed. He looked at Jenny imploringly. 'Tell him to stop! Tell him . . .'

The music swelled again and now it seemed loud, even to Jenny. Lezard's mouth opened wide, revealing harp strings of saliva at the back of his throat. He began to run across the circle, blindly seeking escape from the volume that was bursting the blood vessels in his brain. He kept screaming, a series of long, howls and he almost made it out of there. But a last shattering power chord spun him back around to face Jenny and he stood for a moment, on the very edge of the circle, framed by two standing stones, his body shuddering violently, his hands gesticulating in helpless supplication.

And then, quite suddenly, his head exploded, blowing apart in a gout of blood, brains and bone fragments. His headless body stood there for a few moments, the hands still reaching out, the fingers clenching and unclenching. Then it sank slowly backwards into the deep snow between the stones.

The light died abruptly. Jenny tried to get up from the altar but the cold had sapped her strength and she fell back with a groan, aware of unconsciousness creeping up on her and also, dimly aware of another light, a searching, probing light that seemed to be coming from the sky above her. As the noise from the stones faded, she heard a different sound – a chugging, whirring sound. It was coming from above her and was moving rapidly closer. Now she saw a black silhouette hanging in the air. As she lay there, fascinated, a man descended from the sky, a weird alien-looking creature in a khaki uniform and a round helmet.

His hands were moving over her but her body was numb and she could scarcely feel them. She wanted so badly to sleep, so she closed her eyes and did that, for what seemed a second, no more. But when she opened her eyes again, she was rising upwards, she was flying, just as she'd flown in dreams when she was a child and...

She closed her eyes again, only for an instant, but when she opened them this time, an unfamiliar face was peering down at her, an alien, she decided: only if that was so, why was he talking in a broad Welsh accent?

'Christ, you were lucky, girl! We just happened to be flying over, see, and we saw this bright light. Anyhow, we came down to investigate and there you were. Incredible light, it was. How the hell did you set it up?'

Jenny smiled dreamily up at him.

'I had some help,' she whispered.

She closed her eyes again and this time, she felt no obligation to open them.

Epilogue

Detective Inspector Gill closes his notebook. It's very late now and it's quiet in the hospital ward. He sits there looking at Jenny and he doesn't know what to say to her. The story she has told him has stretched his credulity to breaking point, but the earnest, matter-of-fact manner in which she has told it has convinced him that she is telling the truth – or at least, what she *believes* to be the truth. Now all he has to do is explain it to his superiors and hope that they don't think that *he's* lost his marbles.

Jenny seems to have momentarily forgotten his presence. She has turned her attention to the scrawled notes scattered on the bed around her and she's talking again, speaking to the imaginary third person in the room.

'I don't know,' she mutters. 'Maybe we should put in a third verse before we go to the middle eight. And maybe you could come up with a more melodic solo, you know, something mellow...?'

Gill coughs and she glances up at him in surprise.

'What er ... what are you working on?' he asks her, self-consciously.

'A song, what else? A ballad. At least, I think it's a ballad, *he* sees it as more of an uptempo thing.' She smiles. 'He always did prefer the rockers. Tell you what, why don't we do it for you? You could tell us what you think.'

'Oh, well, I'm not much of a judge, I'm afraid.'

'Sure you are. Here, I'll just give you one verse, the one I'm most happy with. It's called *Out of the Darkness*.'

She picks out a brief introduction on Gill's battered old acoustic, tilts back her head and begins to sing. Gill feels an involuntary shiver go down his spine. She still has an extraordinary voice.

'Out of the darkness you called me
You shouted out my name.
You led me to the circle
To touch your healing flame.
And all the fears and torments
That followed me that night
Were banished when you called me
And led me to the light.'

She stops singing and looks at him inquiringly. 'Well, what do you say? Ballad or rocker?'

'A ballad,' he says. 'Most definitely.'

Jenny grins and glances sideways.

'See,' she says. 'I told you.'

Gill sighs. He slips his notebook into his pocket and gets up from his chair.

'It's late,' he says. 'I'd better get weaving. Thanks for the talk.'

'And thanks for the loan of this.' She holds the guitar out for him to take, but he makes a dismissive gesture.

'You hang on to it,' he tells her. 'I never could play the damned thing anyway.'

'Thanks,' she says. 'I'll take real good care of it.'

'I'm sure you will. Take care of yourself, that's more important.'

'Oh, I'll be all right,' she assures him. She glances sideways. 'I've got my guardian angel to look after me.'

He nods, walks across to the door, opens it and peers outside. There's just the uniformed policeman, asleep in his seat, his paperback book cradled in his lap. Gill steps into the corridor and closes the door behind him. From within, he can hear the sound of her guitar as it begins to play again, the slow, swaying rhythm of the new song. Gill smiles. He starts to walk away but then freezes in shocked surprise.

Because now there are *two* guitars playing in there, he's sure of it. He moves back to the door and listens intently. Yes, he can differentiate the sound of the battered acoustic strumming the rhythm and a second, electric guitar, picking out the haunting melody. There is no mistaking the unique style and distinctive tone of the lead guitarist.

Gill feels a jolt of pure terror go through him. It's like somebody has plunged a shard of ice into his heart. He thinks briefly about going back into the room but he dismisses the idea, knowing only too well that if he does that, he will see only Jenny sitting in the bed, smiling her crazy smile, asking him if maybe he's forgotten something. Besides, if he went in there now, he would feel somehow that he was intruding. After all, it's been quite a while since those two played together.

So he does the only thing a sane man can do in such extraordinary circumstances. He tells himself that his ears are playing tricks on him, he buttons up his coat and walks quickly down the corridor towards the exit.

When he steps outside into the chill January night, he sees that the snow has started falling again.

More Thrilling Fiction from Headline Feature

PHILIP CAVENEY

Speak No Evil

THE LATE-NIGHT WHISPER FROM HELL . . .

Radio presenter Tom Prince hosts the graveyard slot: the after-midnight phone-in programme for Manchester's *Metrosound*. Despite a broken marriage, he now finds personal happiness with a caring girlfriend and his seven-year-old son Danny. Otherwise Tom is stuck in a rut . . . and about to be hurtled out of it with terrifying momentum.

It begins with just another late-night call, from a man who talks in a strange whisper. But this one claims he has committed a murder, and is standing over his victim's corpse.

Thus begins a chilling nightly dialogue between Tom and 'the Whisperer'. Badgered by police intent on tracing the killer, Tom reluctantly keeps the line open, while the gruesome deaths continue. And as his audience constantly grows, he suddenly finds himself a celebrity.

Though Tom himself is the focus of this terrifying bloodlust, his child and his girlfriend are soon exposed to extreme danger – never knowing from which dark shadows the next surprise blow will fall.

And as he begins to understand the full horror of the Whisperer's psychosis, Tom realises that his success may cost them all too high a price.

FICTION / THRILLER 0 7472 4045 0